Prais

"Lauren's independence and reliance on herself is relatable. The pacing is steady throughout, making it easy to stay engaged."
—*RT Book Reviews* on *Trusting the Cowboy*

"Carolyne Aarsen writes with tender empathy and a true understanding of the struggles her characters endure in *A Family-Style Christmas*."
—*RT Book Reviews*

"An emotional story with a heroine who is in danger of making bad decisions out of love and a hero who discovers God's plans are always best."
—*RT Book Reviews* on *The Baby Promise*

Praise for Mindy Obenhaus and her novels

"This is a quick, solid read about trust, forgiveness and childlike faith."
—*RT Book Reviews* on *The Doctor's Family Reunion*

"A relaxed pace and the characters' strength make this an enjoyable tale."
—*RT Book Reviews* on *Rescuing the Texan's Heart*

"In this quick, brisk read, Celeste illustrates the difficulties associated with trying to follow the plans of others versus what we believe God wants for us."
—*RT Book Reviews* on *A Father's Second Chance*

Carolyne Aarsen and her husband, Richard, live on a small ranch in northern Alberta, where they have raised four children and numerous foster children and are still raising cattle. Carolyne crafts her stories in an office with a large west-facing window, through which she can watch the changing seasons while struggling to make her words obey. Visit her website at carolyneaarsen.com.

It took **Mindy Obenhaus** forty years to figure out what she wanted to do when she grew up. But once God called her to write, she never looked back. She's passionate about touching readers with biblical truths in an entertaining, and sometimes adventurous, manner. Mindy lives in Texas with her husband and kids. When she's not writing, she enjoys cooking and spending time with her grandchildren. Find more at mindyobenhaus.com.

The Rancher's Claim

Carolyne Aarsen

&

Mindy Obenhaus

Previously published as
Trusting the Cowboy and *Their Ranch Reunion*

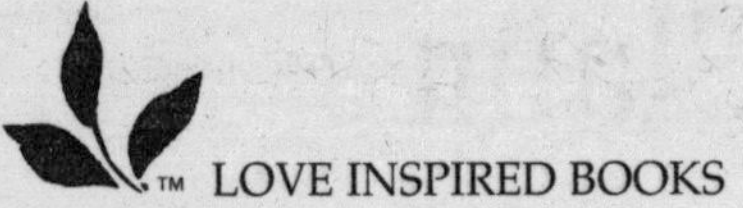

Recycling programs for this product may not exist in your area.

ISBN-13: 978-1-335-46854-3

The Rancher's Claim

First published as Trusting the Cowboy by Harlequin Books in 2016 and Their Ranch Reunion by Harlequin Books in 2017.

This edition published by arrangement with Love Inspired Books.

www.Harlequin.com

Printed in U.S.A.

CONTENTS

TRUSTING THE COWBOY

Carolyne Aarsen

To my husband, Richard,
who has shown me the meaning of trust.

Trust in the Lord with all your heart
and lean not on your own understanding;
in all your ways submit to him,
and he will make your paths straight
—*Proverbs* 3:5–6 (NIV)

Chapter One

She wasn't supposed to be here yet. Her sister Jodie had told him she was arriving in a couple of weeks.

But there she sat, perched in one of Drake's worn chairs, as out of place in the shabby lawyer's office as a purebred filly in a petting zoo.

Lauren McCauley appeared to be every inch the businesswoman Vic knew her to be. Tall. Slim. Blond hair twisted up in some fancy bun, a few wisps falling around her delicate features. She wore a brown blazer over a fitted dress tucked under her legs. Her high heels made her look as if she might topple to the ground if she stood.

A silver laptop rested on her knees and she frowned at the screen.

When she was a teenager, coming to Montana to visit her dad during the summer, she'd had a look that promised great beauty. But she always managed to seem cool and unapproachable. And she had never been his type.

Vic leaned more toward girls who rode horses and weren't afraid to get their hands dirty mucking out horse stalls, running a tractor or feeding cows.

In spite of that, Vic couldn't help a faint flutter of attraction when he peeked over at her again. She'd always been pretty. Now she looked stunning.

Lauren McCauley glanced up from the laptop she was typing on with her manicured fingers. She gave him a polite smile, her lips glistening a pale peach color, and she turned back to the computer.

Dissed and dismissed, he thought, glancing down at his cleanest blue jeans with the faded knees and the twill shirt he'd figured would be good enough. Now it seemed scruffy with its worn cuffs and grease stain on the arm. He felt exactly like the cowboy he was.

He pulled his hat off his head and walked over to where Jane Forsythe, Drake's secretary, pounded on her keyboard, glowering through her cat's-eye glasses at the computer screen. The overhead light burnished the copper of her hair, making it look even brassier than the fake color everyone knew it to be.

"Hey, Vic, you handsome cowboy, you." Jane tugged off her reading glasses and tossed them on a pile of papers that threatened to topple. "Drake will be right with you." She angled her head to look past him to where Lauren sat, then leaned forward, her hand cupping her mouth. "He has to see *her* first." Jane put emphasis on the *her* as if Lauren were some strange species of woman.

"That's fine. I'm early," Vic said. "But let him know I'm here." He took a chair along the other wall. There were two empty ones on either side of Lauren, but he felt more comfortable giving himself some distance.

Besides, he had a better view of Lauren from this angle.

"Always so responsible," Jane said approvingly, slipping her glasses on. "How's your mother?"

"She has her days. It's been hard."

"Losing a parent can be difficult," Jane said. She looked past him again at Lauren. Vic guessed from the way the secretary scrunched up her face in sympathy, she was getting ready to take a stab at distracting Lauren from her work. "And how are you doing, Miss McCauley? It's only been a few months since your own father died. Vic here lost his father, too, about four months ago. You two could compare notes."

Vic forced himself not to roll his eyes. Jane had a good heart and meant well, but for the secretary of a lawyer she was completely unaware of personal privacy and space.

Lauren's gaze rested on Jane, then shifted to Vic, her eyes a soft gray blue fringed with thick lashes.

"You're Vic Moore, aren't you?"

"Yes, I am," he said. "I rent your father's ranch."

"I thought Rusty Granger did."

"Not for the past three years."

Vic wasn't surprised Lauren didn't know that. After her parents' divorce, when Lauren was about nine, she and her sisters had lived for ten months of the year with their grandmother in Knoxville. Two years later, after their mother died, they came to the ranch for the summer to visit their father. But when Lauren turned eighteen, she and her twin sister, Erin, stopped coming. The last time he remembered seeing Lauren here was maybe four years ago, and then only for a few days.

Their younger sister, Jodie, ducked out of her last visit when she was seventeen and never came back at all. She had returned a couple of months ago, to fulfill the terms of their father's will, and was now living here permanently.

Everything he knew about Lauren, Vic had learned over time while working with Keith McCauley on his ranch as well as the occasional coffee-shop chitchat at the Grill and Chill, Saddlebank's local restaurant. Though chitchat was the wrong thing to call the steady litany of complaints Keith leveled at anyone who would listen about life, the government, the lax sheriff's department and his wayward daughters.

The rest he'd learned recently from Lauren's sister Jodie, now engaged to Vic's good friend Finn Hicks. He knew Lauren worked as an accountant. That she was single and dedicated to her career.

Still not his type.

"I shouldn't be surprised Rusty isn't renting it anymore," Lauren said, giving him a polite smile and closing her laptop. Either she had finished whatever it was she was working on or she had given up. "My father never particularly cared for him."

Vic held his tongue. Keith hadn't cared for too many people, so Vic had handled the man carefully. Vic and Keith had had a lease-to-own agreement for Vic to buy Keith's ranch.

Vic wanted to ask Lauren more about her plans. He knew that she was here to satisfy the terms of her father's will, as well. Her sister Jodie, who was coming to the end of her obligation, had told him all about the conditions their father had put on the girls inheriting the ranch.

Two of the three girls had to stay at the ranch for two months each before all three of them could make a final decision.

He'd spoken to Jodie about his deal with her father. But all she could tell him was that she'd have to defer to Lauren's wishes, and all she knew was that Lauren was agreeable to selling.

But he wasn't about to bring that up now. He still had a couple of months.

"I heard you'll be staying at your father's place while you're here," he said. "Jodie was excited to see you."

"Yes. Jodie said she got my old room ready. I'm headed there next."

"Is Erin coming back?"

Lauren shook her head. "If I stay the two months, she won't have to, and Jodie and I will make the final decision on what to do with the ranch."

She didn't seem to know anything about the deal he'd made with her father, either.

Her cell phone rang and she pulled it out of her purse. She turned away from him, speaking in a low voice, and he tried not to listen. However, in the small room, it was hard not to. The man on the other end had a loud voice and Vic heard snatches of conversation.

"I'm at the lawyer's office… I can't make a final decision until I speak to him… Of course I'm leaving after my time is done. I've no intention of sticking around." She pressed her lips together and fingered a strand of hair away from her face. "Your offer is fantastic, but I need to talk to my sisters first, but yes, I think you'll get it."

A chill slid through his veins.

Was she talking about the ranch?

He swallowed down a knot as she spoke again.

"Come down in a week or so and I can show you the ranch. That's all I can say for now…fine…see you then." She ended the call, a frown creasing the perfection of her forehead. Then she dropped the phone in her purse.

The room felt short of air as the reality of what she was talking about sank in.

"Was that a buyer for the ranch?" he blurted out before he could stop himself.

Her look of surprise clearly showed him what she thought of what he had just done. But it didn't matter. It was out there now.

"Actually, yes. It was."

"But I had a purchase deal with your father," he said, trying to keep the frustration out of his voice. "That's why I was renting it."

She lifted her chin, her hands folded primly on her laptop. "Jodie mentioned your situation to me, but we could find no paperwork substantiating your claim."

"Your father told me he'd taken care of it." Vic remembered discussing this with Keith after his cancer diagnosis, knowing that they needed to get something in writing to protect their agreement. Keith had promised him he was putting his affairs in order. That he'd written something out for him and signed it.

"As I said, we didn't find anything. But if you're interested in purchasing the ranch, you'll have an opportunity to counteroffer."

Vic stared at her, doubts dogging him. Keith had given him a deal on the price and Vic knew it. He doubted Lauren would do the same for the future buyer or for him.

Fury at Keith's failure to keep his promise surged through him.

The intercom beeped. Jane answered it, then she looked at Lauren.

"Drake will see you now," she said, her eyes darting from Lauren to Vic and back again.

Vic pressed his lips together as Lauren slipped her laptop in her leather briefcase, picked it up and stood all in one smooth motion.

But as she took a step, her purse strap caught on the chair. She stumbled and Vic jumped up to help her, catching her by the elbow, which made her totter. Her briefcase fell. She jerked her arm away. "I'm okay. I don't need your help."

He didn't say anything but bent down to pick up her briefcase. But she moved too quickly and snatched it off the floor.

She spared him a glance as she straightened. Then she strode across the carpet in her towering heels, shoulders straight, head high.

And as the door closed behind her, Vic slumped back in his chair, dragging his hand over his face, feeling stupid and scared.

He'd just about made a fool of himself in front of this woman.

Lauren had a buyer for the ranch.

And there was no paper from her father.

He had promised his younger brother, Dean, that they were getting the ranch. Guaranteed it. Now they might lose it.

If that happened, how was he supposed to help his brother?

"Lauren, how lovely to see you," Drake Neubauer said, getting up from behind his desk.

Outwardly Lauren was smiling but her insides still shook and her hands still trembled.

Mr. Vic Moore had looked so angry when she told him about the buyer for the ranch.

You did nothing wrong, she told herself, taking a deep breath as Drake walked toward her outstretched hand. *He has no claim.*

You could have let him help you.

She dismissed that voice as quickly as it slid into her brain. She'd been doing fine until he'd interfered and almost made her fall.

And wouldn't that have come across all dignified?

"So glad you could make it here," Drake said as he shook her hand, his other hand covering it, squeezing lightly. "Goodness, girl, your hands are like ice."

"I'm just cold-blooded," she joked as she returned his warm handshake.

Harvey had always accused her of that. At least that was the excuse he gave her when he dumped her a few days before their wedding.

"It's good to be back," she said, relegating those shameful memories to where they belonged. The past.

"I'm sure you missed all this," Drake said, waving one hand at the window behind them.

Drake's offices were situated above the hardware store, and through the window Lauren saw the valley the Saddlebank River snaked through. Her eyes shifted to the mountains, snow frosted and craggy, cradling the basin, and her mind slowed. Though she and her sisters had resented coming here every summer, when they were back home in Knoxville she'd found herself missing these very mountains.

"It was a part of my life," she said, her voice quiet.

"Does it feel good to be back?" Drake asked.

Lauren gave him a brief smile as she lowered herself to the chair, setting her briefcase on the floor and tucking her skirt under her legs. "Yes, it does." Though the restless part of her wasn't sure how she would stay busy on the ranch, the weary part longed for a reprieve from the stress and tension of the last year and a half.

And a break from the pitying stares of friends each time they met. Harvey hadn't only taken a wedding away from her, he'd also robbed her of her money, her dignity and her self-esteem. She had been scrambling to show to the world that he hadn't won.

"And how are you doing since your father's passing? Ironic that it wasn't the cancer that killed him but a truck accident." Drake sat down, opened the file lying on his desk and flipped through it.

She wasn't sure how to respond, so she said nothing.

Though losing her father had bothered her more than she'd thought it would, the true reality was neither Lauren nor her sisters had ever been close with Keith McCauley.

"Has the accident been cleared with the insurance company yet?" Lauren asked as Drake made a few notes on a piece of paper in the file. "Jodie had said there were some difficulties?"

"They're still dealing with it, but last I heard, it should be finalized in the next few weeks."

"Where is the truck?"

"At Vic Moore's. The accident happened as your father was going down his driveway."

"Any liability at play?"

"No. That much has been determined already. The truck was in perfect working order."

"And Vic's driveway?"

"Your father hit a deer, then lost control and rolled the vehicle. Neither Vic nor the Rocking M were at fault."

"I wasn't thinking of filing a lawsuit, if that's what

you were worried about," Lauren said, her mind ticking back to the tall man still sitting in the waiting room. With his dark eyebrows, firm chin and square jaw, he commanded attention. When he had stridden into the office, she had been unable to look away.

But all it took was a glance at her bare ring finger and her father's will to remind her of the hard lessons life had taught her about men. Men were selfish and undependable. Between her father, Harvey and her now-former boss, she should be crystal clear on that point.

In Christ alone...

The words of a song she had been singing lately slipped into her mind, and she latched on to them. Men might not be able to give anything up for loved ones, but Christ had.

Which only reminded her again that she needed to be self-sufficient and self-reliant.

"No. Of course not." But Drake's hasty answer, and the way he fluttered one hand in a defensive gesture, told her that he had, indeed, thought exactly that.

She tried not to feel overly sensitive, reminding herself that Drake knew nothing about her other than what her father had told him.

"So I'm guessing you're here to officially check in," Drake said, settling into his chair behind his desk.

"Or clock in," Lauren returned. "I wasn't sure of the protocol, and I did end up coming a couple of weeks earlier than anticipated." Getting laid off was a stark motivator.

"No. It's fine." Drake gave her an apologetic smile. "I know your father had his reasons for doing this, and just for the record, I tried to talk him out of it. Tried to explain to him that it could come across as being manipulative."

Lauren shrugged. "Let's be honest here. Like Jodie said after the funeral, it seemed he never gave us anything without strings attached."

Her words came out more bitter than she'd intended. Though she and her father hadn't had the adversarial relationship he and Jodie had, they hadn't been close, either.

"I'm sorry, but at least not all three of you had to stay here. You can decide what to do after your two months are up."

Lauren heard the unspoken question in his voice and decided to address it directly.

"Erin said she would go along with whatever decision I make, but you may as well know that we will be selling the ranch."

"To Vic?"

Lauren shook her head. "No. I have a buyer lined up. A client from the firm I worked…used to work for. He has various real estate holdings and has been looking for another investment opportunity. When I told him about the ranch, he was interested."

"But Vic has rented your father's land for the past three years. I thought they had an agreement."

"Is that going to be a problem?" Lauren straightened, leaning forward, her heart racing at the thought that he might jeopardize the sale. She would receive one-third of the proceeds, and she would need every penny of that for her new business venture. A venture that she was in a rush to put together after losing her current job. "Does he have a legal right to the property?"

"As far as I know, your father never gave me anything

in writing, if that's what you're concerned about. I believe it was a handshake deal. Not uncommon around here."

"So I have no legal obligation to sell it to Mr. Moore?"

"None whatsoever. But I do have to warn you, your father was thinking of drawing up something legal for Vic. If that is the case, and this paper does show up, it will need to be dealt with."

"Had he mentioned a price?"

Drake gave her a number.

It wasn't close to what her potential buyer was offering. "And if such documentation isn't found?"

"Then he has no claim."

Relief flooded her. "That's good to know. I don't want anything preventing the sale." Or forcing her to sell it to Vic at a significantly reduced price.

As far as she knew, Jodie hadn't found any paperwork, so it seemed they were in the clear.

"A word of advice, if I may, Lauren," Drake continued. "You might want to give him a chance to counteroffer or at least match what your buyer is willing to pay."

"Of course. I could do that."

"I know he was hoping to get the ranch for his younger brother, Dean."

Lauren dredged her memory and came up with a picture of a young man who partied hard and spent the rest of the time riding rodeo. And trying to date her twin sister, Erin. "Dean is ranching now?"

"Not at the moment. He was injured in a rodeo accident a while back. Vic leased your father's ranch with an eye to adding it to his holdings and making room for Dean."

"Tell Vic to talk to me if he wants to make an offer. He's waiting to see you next."

"Why don't you tell him yourself?"

Lauren thought back to the anger he'd revealed when she told him she had a buyer, then shook her head. "No. Better if it comes from a third party."

"Okay. I'll tell him to come up with some numbers." Drake tapped his pen on the open file in front of him. "Is there anything else I can help you with?"

"Not right now. Like I said, I wanted to check in."

Drake leaned back in his chair, looking as if he had a few more things he wanted to discuss, then he shook his head and stood up. "Okay. You know how to get in touch with me if you have any further questions."

She got up and Drake came around the desk to escort her to the door. But before he opened it, his eyes caught hers, his expression serious. "Again, I'm so sorry about your father. I wish you girls had had a chance to get some closure in your relationship before he died."

"Jodie mentioned some letters that Dad wrote to each of us before he died. Maybe that will help."

"He was a sad and lonely man," Drake said.

Lauren forced back her initial response and the guilt that always nipped at her. "I know we should have come to visit more often," she agreed. And that was all she was going to say. The burden of guilt shouldn't lie so heavy on her shoulders. Her father could have initiated some contact, as well.

She thanked Drake again and walked through the door.

Vic still sat there, but as she came out, he stood, his hat in his hand, his eyes on her. The gesture seemed so courtly, and for some reason it touched her.

"I need to talk to you" was all he said, his words clipped.

Lauren did not want to deal with this right now.

"I'm going to presume it has to do with your agreement with my father," she said, weariness tingeing her voice, dragging at her limbs. She felt as if she'd been fighting this exhaustion for the past year. The stress of losing her job and trying to start a new business, and now needing to fulfill the terms of her father's will, had made every decision seem momentous. Impossible.

"Can we talk now? Can I buy you a coffee at the Grill and Chill?"

"Not really. I just want to get to the ranch."

"Meeting at the ranch would work better. We could do this right away."

This was certainly not the homecoming she had expected, but in spite of her fatigue she sensed he wouldn't let go. "May as well get this over and done with," she said.

"I'll meet you there in an hour."

Lauren nodded, then walked to the door, disconcerted when he pulled it open for her, standing aside to let her through.

"Thank you," she murmured, thankful she had worn her heels to see Drake Neubauer.

Though she doubted they'd made an impression on the lawyer, as she glanced up at Vic she appreciated the advantage they gave her.

The grim set of Vic's jaw and his snapping brown eyes below dark, slashing brows sent a shiver down her spine that told her he would be trouble.

Chapter Two

Vic parked his truck beside Lauren's car and gave himself a moment to catch his breath, center himself. He rested his hands on the steering wheel and looked out over the Rocking M. The house stood on a rise of land overlooking the corrals below. The corrals and pasture eased toward the Saddlebank River on one side and the rolling hills leading to the mountains on the other. So often he had driven this yard, imagining his brother living here

It was the promise he'd held out to Dean and himself that got him through the past ten months.

A way to assuage his own guilt over the fact that he had been too late to get Dean off that rank bronc at the rodeo. As a pickup man, it was Vic's job to get the riders safely off the horse as soon as he saw they were in trouble.

But Vic had had other things on his mind that day. Other things that drew his attention.

It had only been a few seconds, the smallest moment when Vic made eye contact with Dean's ex-girlfriend Tiffany sitting in the arena a few feet away. Smiling at her. Thinking about how they could be together again. She had told him that she'd broken up with Dean. She had called out to him just before Dean's ride and blown him a kiss.

Then Vic had turned his head in time to catch the sight branded into his brain forever.

The bronc Dean was riding spinning away from where he and his horse were, ready. The horse making another turn, crushing Dean's leg against the temporary panels set up in the arena. Dean's leg getting caught in the crossbars as the horse pulled away.

Vic still heard his brother's cries of agony, saw him writhing on the ground in the arena.

The girlfriend walked away from both of them a week later. Dean started walking four months later.

His brother still struggled with resentment and anger over what had happened.

And Vic wrestled with a guilt that gnawed at him each time he saw his brother grimace in pain. Each time he listened to Dean talk about how Tiffany had broken his heart.

Buying Keith McCauley's ranch was supposed to fix all that.

And now?

Please, Lord, let that piece of paper be somewhere in the house. I need this place for Dean.

The prayer surged upward as he eased out of the truck, heading up the walk, the futility of it clawing at him. He and Jodie had discussed it only briefly, but she hadn't found any evidence of this agreement.

Maybe she hadn't searched hard enough, he thought as he trudged up the stairs to the house. Maybe his presence would coax it out of its hiding place.

Keith hadn't left anything about the lease agreement at Drake's and he hadn't given anything to Vic, so the only other place it could be was here. In Keith's office in the ranch house.

As he sent up another prayer, he knocked on the door.

He heard laughter from within, and he eased out a wry smile. His own house was a somber, sad place. His father's death a few months ago had only added to the heavy atmosphere looming over the house since Dean came home from the hospital three months before that, disabled and bitter. There'd been no laughter in the Moore household for a long time.

No one came to the door, so he rang the doorbell. Cheerful chimes pealed through the house, then he heard footsteps coming.

He wasn't surprised to see Jodie answer, her head tipped to one side, her dark hair caught back in a loose ponytail, her bangs skimming eyes so blue they looked unnatural.

They were a different blue than Lauren's, which were more gray. Cooler.

He shook that thought off. Lauren was attractive, yes, but he had to keep a level head. Too much was at stake to be distracted by a good-looking woman.

"Hey, Vic. Lauren said you were coming," Jodie said, stepping aside to let him in. "I thought you'd be here sooner."

"I had to stop at the dealership to get some parts for my horse trailer." Nestor, who owned the place, had been particularly chatty. Then John Argall stopped in and asked him how Dean was doing and if Vic was coming back to Bible study. Vic had felt bad at the disappointment John had displayed. The past month he had taken on extra work. Work Dean would have done.

He didn't blame his brother. Dean wasn't as sure as Vic was that Keith had made proper arrangements to protect their handshake agreement so he went back to work for Jan Peter, a local carpenter. Vic hadn't signed anything, but Keith had assured him that he had written something up.

He just needed to find it. Then Dean could stop working for Jan and they could start ranching together.

"Come in," Jodie was saying. "Lauren and I were catching up. She's trying to talk me out of purple bridesmaid dresses."

"You're not looking for my opinion, I hope?"

"I thought you could weigh in. When Lauren has an idea, she's immovable."

That didn't bode well for any negotiations, Vic thought.

"Can't say I have a lot of expertise in that area. I'm only standing up for Finn, and he told me to wear clean blue jeans."

"Listen, mister, when it comes to wedding attire, you check with me before you check with my future husband." But she spoke in a cheerful tone, adding a wink.

He returned Jodie's smile, wide and open and happy, a much different woman than the one who'd come to Saddlebank with a chip on her shoulder and a cocky attitude. Now, engaged to Vic's good friend Finn Hicks, she looked relaxed. Happy.

Vic wondered what Jodie thought of the potential buyer of the ranch and if she liked the idea. He was thinking of asking her but quashed that thought as he toed off his boots. He had to figure this out on his own. Bringing Jodie in would only create complications.

He set his scuffed and cracked cowboy boots beside Lauren's high heels, the contrast making him laugh.

"We're sitting in the dining room. Do you want some coffee?"

"Sure. Sounds good." He followed Jodie through the kitchen. His steps slowed as he passed Keith's office, which was opposite the eating bar of the kitchen, and he glanced inside the open door.

Papers covered the desk that ran along one wall. The filing cabinet's top drawer was open.

"We've been going through Dad's stuff," Jodie said, catching the direction of his gaze. "I meant to do it when I first came but thought I would wait till Lauren was here. She's the organized one."

He suppressed the question that nagged at him. He had time yet. Lauren might have a buyer all lined up, but she still had to stay at the ranch for two months before she could make a decision.

He followed Jodie to the end of the house. Vaulted ceilings soaring two stories high arched over the living and dining room. Light from the upper windows slanted down into the space. A fireplace made of river rock bisected the far wall, framed by large bay windows overlooking the pasture and the mountains.

To his left a set of stairs led to the loft and a couple of bedrooms above, and the basement with its bedrooms downstairs. He knew the layout of the house because he had spent time here before.

Though all those stairs might not be best for Dean at the moment, his leg would get better. Vic had to believe that. And when he did, it would be a perfect place for his brother to live. A real home.

"Sit down. Ignore the mess," Jodie said as she padded barefoot to the kitchen. She wore blue jeans, frayed at the cuffs, and a gauzy purple and pink shirt that had tiny bells sewn to the hem. The bells created a happy tinkling sound as she took a mug out of the cupboard and poured him some coffee.

Lauren, in her stark dress and hair still pulled back in a bun, was a complete contrast to her sister. She glanced up from papers strewn over the table. Her dark-framed glasses gave her an austere air. She held his eyes for a moment, then looked away.

Dismissed once again, he thought, remembering their earlier encounter too well.

"Finn told me you're working the rodeo coming up?" Jodie said, setting the mug of coffee on the table.

"Yeah. Walden was short a pickup man, so I thought I'd help out." Vic settled in the chair across from Lauren, taking the cup with a smile of thanks.

"You always were a pickup artist," Jodie joked as she sat as well and shuffled through the papers in front of her.

"Oldest joke in the book," Vic groaned.

"I feel like I should know what a pickup man is," Lauren said, slipping her glasses off her face and setting them on the table.

"See that, Vic?" Jodie said, her voice holding a note of admiration. "That's why I should wear glasses. People think you're all smart and important. And when you take them off, it looks like you're getting ready to do business. People take glasses-wearing people seriously."

Vic chuckled as Lauren shot her sister a wry look. "You should take that show on the road," Lauren said.

"It's my only joke," Jodie said with a grin. "Wouldn't take me far."

"Oh, I'm sure you have more you could add to your repertoire," Lauren said, smiling back at her sister.

"You'd have to come with me as my straight man, though. A role you play to perfection."

Lauren laughed again and Vic couldn't look away. She was a beautiful woman in her own right. But now, relaxed, smiling, a glint of humor in her eyes as she teased her sister, the light from the window behind her lighting her hair, she was luminous.

He groaned inwardly as he took a sip of his coffee, frustrated with his response to this woman. He was here to talk business and he was coming up with mental compliments?

"Getting back to my original question, what is a pickup man?" Lauren asked.

Vic waited for Jodie to answer, but she was frowning at a piece of paper, seemingly unaware of her sister's question. So Vic replied.

"We ride along the outskirts of the arena during the rough stock events—bareback, saddle bronc, bull and steer riding. We help the guys off the horses if we can, make sure the bulls and horses get out of the arena safely. That kind of thing."

"I see," said Lauren, the vague tone of her voice conveying her lack of interest.

"I know Walden is glad you'll be there," Jodie said. "He told me you guys work well together."

"Who's Walden?" Lauren asked.

"The other pickup man," Vic said. "We always work in pairs."

"You'll have to come to the rodeo, Lauren. See Vic in action," Jodie said. "And that horse that Finn trained. Adelaide, one of his clients, will be riding it in the barrel riding competition."

"We'll see how that works out." Lauren's polite smile seemed to dismiss that line of conversation. She slipped her glasses on her face and it was back to business. "We've been looking through our father's papers and so far haven't found anything referring to your deal."

Vic glanced down at the folders lying on the table between them, resisting the impulse to riffle through them himself. "Your father and I agreed on a lease-to-buy agreement," Vic said, struggling to keep his tone even. Pragmatic. "Are you sure he didn't say anything about that to you or make a note of it anywhere?"

Lauren shook her head, picking up another file and opening it. "We haven't seen everything yet, mind you, but it doesn't look good."

"Are there any files left? Did he have anything on the computer?"

Lauren frowned as she held his gaze. "Dad didn't do much on the computer," she said, dismissing that possibility. "Besides, we couldn't figure out the password on it. I don't suppose you would know?"

"Not a clue. Did you try the horses' names?"

"Yeah. And his birth date, our birth dates—though I doubt he remembered them anyway—and in a pinch his and Mom's anniversary. The name of the ranch. Nothing."

"I can't help you there." He didn't know Keith that well.

"Even if we could log on, I doubt there's anything there, and even there was documentation, if it wasn't signed..." Her voice trailed off.

Annoyance snaked through him. It was so easy for her to dismiss his claim. She didn't know what was at stake.

"Would you mind if I looked through the papers myself?"

Her lips tightened and he wondered if she was afraid he might find something that would help his case. He held her eyes, as if challenging her, then she looked at Jodie.

"What do you think?" she asked her sister.

"I don't care," Jodie said with a shrug. "If Vic has a claim, maybe we need to see if we can find evidence for it. He might know better what he's looking for."

Lauren nodded and turned back to Vic, taking her glasses off again, ignoring Jodie's chuckle at her action. "I doubt you'd find what you want. But if we don't discover anything, I'm willing to sell the ranch to you, provided you can match the buyer's price."

"What price is that?"

When she named it, Vic's mouth fell open as blood surged to his throat and chest, threatening to choke off his breathing.

There was no way he could meet that amount, but there was also no way he was telling her that. He swallowed hard and tried to claim some remnants of composure.

"I'll have to talk my banker," he said, attempting to inject some confidence into his voice. "But before I do that, I'd like to make sure that there is absolutely no evidence of the agreement. And I'd like to look for myself."

Lauren gave him a tight nod. "I guess that's fair,

though, like I said, we didn't find anything. You'd have to come here, though. To look at the papers. And one of us will have to be here."

"You don't trust me?" The words burst out of him before he could stop them.

Way to create a good impression.

Jodie patted him on the shoulder. "We trust you, Vic." She turned to Lauren. "I trust him. He's Finn's friend and a good guy."

"Don't take it personally," Lauren said, her mouth twisting in a cool smile. "I don't trust any man." Then she turned to Jodie. "But as far as his agreement with our father is concerned, there are other factors at play. If he finds something that corroborates his claim, it's best that it happens here with us watching. That way no one can challenge it."

He. His. She spoke of him as if he suddenly wasn't there.

Vic took another sip of his coffee, reminding himself that he just had to get through this.

And, more than ever, he had to find some evidence of the deal he and Keith had drawn up.

There was no other choice.

"Confess. You think he's cute." Jodie plinked out a few more bars of her new composition on the piano in the corner of the living room and turned to her sister, grinning that smirk of hers that Lauren knew was trouble.

Lauren sent her sister a warning look over her laptop. "I'd be lying if I said I didn't think he was attractive, but it's irrelevant." She turned her attention back to the purchase agreement the lawyers had drafted, sent to her by her future partner, Amy.

Part of her mind balked at the price tag, but it was an investment in building clients and staff. All of which would cost more to gather if they started from scratch.

"How is it irrelevant?" Jodie got up from the piano and fell onto the couch across from her. She dropped her feet on the coffee table, looking as if she was settling in for one of the heart-to-heart chats she loved.

"Don't put your feet on the table," Lauren chided.

"Don't be Dad," Jodie shot back, but her smile showed Lauren she hadn't taken her seriously.

Lauren sighed and closed her laptop. Clearly she wasn't getting anything done tonight.

"I think you should sell the ranch to Vic," Jodie said. "He's put a bunch of work into it and I'm sure he wants to buy it for Dean."

"I'm not averse to selling the ranch to him," Lauren said, slipping her reading glasses into their case. "If he can even match Alex Rossiter's offer, he can have it. But I doubt he can. When I told him what Alex was paying, I thought he would keel over."

Jodie twisted a strand of hair around her finger. Though her frown was partially hidden by her long bangs, it wasn't hard to read her dissatisfaction.

"I can tell you don't like the idea," Lauren continued. "I'm not alone in this, you know. The ranch is one-third yours."

"I know. Trouble is, I think you're right in saying that Vic can't match what Alex would pay you." Jodie took her feet off the table and set them on the couch, lounging sideways. "What does that Alex guy want with the ranch?"

"He owns property in the Caribbean and now he wants a ranch."

"A hobby ranch. To add to his collection." Jodie's voice held a faint sneer that Lauren chose to ignore. She wasn't wild about the idea, either. She would prefer to see it sold as a working ranch to someone personally invested in the property.

Someone like Vic.

"I think he sees the ranch as more of an investment," Lauren said. "But the stark reality is I need every penny of my third to buy into this new business. It's a huge opportunity I can't afford to let go. And if Vic needs the land base, he could lease it from Alex and run his cows."

"It's not the same. Alex would have all the control."

Lauren understood Jodie's concern. Wasn't that the very reason she was buying this business—so she could have control over her own life instead of depending on the whims of employers?

And worthless fiancés?

"I can't believe you would want to buy an accounting firm." Jodie shifted her position, curling her legs under her. She could never sit still long. "Why don't you just start your own accounting business? Just you. Why buy in to this one?"

"Because I need clients and I can't take any of the accounts I brought into Jernowicz Brothers or the last firm I worked at with me to a new business without being sued, and it would take too long to build up a new customer base. Even one-third of the amount Alex is willing to pay, after taxes, is barely enough for my buy-in. But I can't pass this up. It would mean a substantial income down the road, which means independence in many ways."

"And that's important to you." Jodie's words were more comment than condemnation.

It was important, Lauren thought, but not in the way that Jodie was implying. Not because money was the end-all and be-all for her.

After being dumped at the altar only to discover that she'd been lied to and milked dry by her ex-fiancé, then, in the past couple of months, fired by her most recent boss, Lauren needed some control in her life. Though Jodie knew about the canceled wedding, she knew little about the amounts of money Lauren had set aside to get the business she and Harvey had hoped to start on their own. She'd worked at Jernowicz Brothers, disliking every minute of the high-pressure job, while Harvey got things together for their eventual departure from the firm.

When he'd left her at the altar, he'd not only broken her heart, he had broken their bank account. The money they had set aside for the start of their new business had disappeared with him.

But she was too ashamed to tell Jodie that. She had always been the good example of what hard work could do. She wasn't about to share how badly Harvey had duped her.

With anyone.

"It's important to me to establish my independence," Lauren said instead. "I've lived enough of my life for other people—" She stopped there, not wanting Jodie to think that she resented the time she'd spent taking care of her. Taking care of their grandmother.

"You've done enough of that," Jodie agreed. "And I can understand that you'd want that, but I know enough of Vic that he wouldn't make this claim lightly. And if we find something to prove Vic's claim—" Jodie pressed, clearly unwilling to let this go.

"We haven't yet, and I doubt Dad would have hidden a paper like that away."

"He didn't exactly make the letters he wrote to us easy to find."

"They weren't hard to find, either," Lauren said, stifling a yawn. It had been a long, tiring day. Her head ached from thinking and phoning and planning and from reading her father's letters.

After his cancer diagnosis, their father had written each of the girls a letter apologizing for his behavior to them. It had been emotionally draining reading his words.

Though regret dogged her with every sentence her father had penned, she couldn't forget the tension that had held them all in a complicated grip each time they came to visit. He alternated between domineering and absent, angry and complacent. Though Lauren was sad he was gone, his loss didn't create the aching grief losing her mother and grandmother had.

But knowing that he did care, that he had felt bad about their relationship, had eased some of the residual bitterness from their time together.

"So what did you think about what Dad wrote?" Jodie asked. "Do you feel better about him now?"

Lauren reached over to the coffee table and picked up the handwritten letter Jodie had given her shortly after she'd arrived.

"I never had the issues with Dad that you did," Lauren said. "We never fought like you guys did, so I don't think I had as much to forgive him for. Knowing that he had sent money to Mom after their divorce helps. Mom always made it sound like he didn't support her and us at all. I don't want to get all psychoanalytical, but I think his absence in our lives, and how he treated us when we were here, had repercussions for all of us."

"Probably. Even Erin, who has always toed every line in her life, followed every rule without questioning, has had her relationship issues." Jodie shifted herself on the couch again. "I thought for sure she and that doctor guy she was dating would get married, but they broke up over half a year ago."

"She say anything to you about why they broke up?"

"Not a word. I know she's secretive, but she's been freaking me out with the radio silence she's been maintaining." Jodie sighed.

"I know, but at least she's staying in touch."

"If you want to call the occasional two-word text with emoticons staying in touch."

"It's better than nothing." Lauren had her own concerns about Erin, but she also knew her twin sister. Erin was a quiet and private person, something their ebullient younger sister didn't always understand. When she wanted to talk, she would. "You have Finn now, and it looks to me like you've found a place to settle after all the wandering you've been doing."

"I have. I've learned many things about myself over the years, and Finn has helped me through a lot. He makes me feel…complete. Loved. Treasured."

"I'm happy for you," Lauren said, trying hard to keep the note of envy out of her voice. She knew how unworthy Jodie had felt for much of her life. Lauren could identify all too well and was thankful her sister had found someone. Was thankful Jodie dared trust someone again.

She wasn't sure the same could happen to her.

"Oh, Lauren. I'm sorry," Jodie said, sitting up, instantly contrite. "I shouldn't be…all…happy and stuff."

"Of course you should," Lauren hastened to assure her. "I am happy for you. So happy. You had so many disappointments in your life. You deserve this."

"Don't know if *deserve* is the right word, but I am grateful," Jodie murmured. She gave Lauren a reassuring smile. "There's someone for you. I just know it."

"There might well be," Lauren said, crossing her arms over her chest. "But I don't want or need another relationship."

Jodie nodded, but Lauren saw her glance at the diamond ring on her finger. Her satisfied and peaceful smile created a nasty twist of jealousy.

At one time Lauren had worn a ring, too. At one time she had been making wedding plans.

She wasn't ready to go there again. Between her father's neglect and anger, and Harvey's lies, and her past bosses' treatment, she'd had enough.

But your father apologized.

She held that voice a moment, realizing that the apology had gone a long way to helping her settle the past.

However, he still had placed conditions on them. And as she fought a touch of resentment over that, a picture of Vic sitting across from her, holding her gaze, slipped into her mind. She knew Vic wasn't letting go of his claim on the ranch until he knew, without a doubt, that her father hadn't written anything up.

Which meant he would be around more than she liked. Not that she was attracted to him. She was never going down that road again.

Vic drove the tractor into the yard and pulled in front of Keith McCauley's shop, frustrated that he hadn't checked the amount of twine he had left in the baler before he started out this morning. He should have taken more with him, but he had been rushing all morning ever since he overslept.

Too much thinking last night, he told himself as he climbed out of the tractor. Too much on his mind. Dean. His widowed mother.

The missing deal with Keith. If he didn't find the papers, Lauren was ready to sell the ranch. At a price he couldn't afford.

He'd prayed about it and struggled to release it all into God's hands, but he kept pulling back.

Stay focused. You'll find the agreement.

He just wasn't sure when that was supposed to happen.

He stepped into the shop, the light from the open door slanting into the dark of the cool building. He blinked, letting his eyes adjust to the indoors from the bright sunlight outside.

But as he walked across the uneven concrete floor, he heard rustling and clanging coming from inside. He walked closer, listening. He reached for the door just as it opened under his hand.

Lauren stepped out carrying a shovel.

She wore blue jeans today and a dark T-shirt. Her hair hung in a loose braid over one shoulder, and as she looked up at him, the shovel fell to the floor with a clatter, her hand on her chest as she stumbled backward.

She would have fallen, but Vic caught her by one arm, pulling her upright. They stood that way a moment and he caught a whiff of her perfume.

She stared up at him, her eyes wide, a soft gray in the low light. There was a smudge of dirt on her cheek, some grass stuck in her hair.

"Oh. It's you," she said, breathless as she pulled away from him.

The speed with which she did it almost unbalanced her again, but this time she grabbed the door handle, looking hastily away.

"Yeah. I just needed some more twine for the baler." He poked his thumb over his shoulder. "Sorry I bothered you."

"No. No. That's fine. I just was startled. That's all." She pushed her hair back with the palm of her hand, creating another smudge of dirt. "I thought you were Jodie. She went to town and said she would be back soon."

With her blue jeans and casual shirt, dirty face and messy hair, she looked even more appealing than she normally did.

And he was, suddenly, not in any rush to find another roll of baler twine.

"You've got some dirt on your face," he said, pointing.

Lauren hastily scrubbed at her cheeks but only managed to make it worse.

Vic pulled out a hankie from his pocket and handed it to her. "Here. Use this."

She frowned as she looked down at the red polka-dotted square.

"I haven't used it yet," he assured her.

"Thanks, but that's not what I was worried about. I don't meet many men who actually use the hankies they carry." She hurriedly wiped her face, as if embarrassed he had caught her looking less than her best. "Though they're not called hankies, technically they're pocket squares and they're usually white, artfully folded and peeking out of a suit pocket." Then she released a short laugh. "Sorry. Babbling." She looked up at him, her expression questioning. "Did I get it all?"

"Still some on your left cheek," he said, pointing with his right hand. She wiped her right cheek. "No. The other left cheek," he said with a grin.

She wiped furiously at her left cheek but still missed the spot.

"A little more to the left," he said. A deep frown creased her forehead as she moved to the right, scrubbing again as if it was important she remove this dirt.

He finally took the hankie from her, caught her chin in his hand and wiped off the dirt himself. It was still smudged, but the worst was off.

He was disconcerted to see her looking up at him, her face holding a curious expression. "Sorry," he said, lowering his hands. "I thought…you…you'd…"

"No. Thanks. It's okay. I hate being dirty. Just a thing. Thanks."

"Well, if that's a problem, you've also got some grass in your hair." But this time, instead of explaining, he plucked it out himself.

"I guess I'm ready to face the world," she said with a nervous laugh, pulling away as he tugged at another piece.

As she did, his hand accidentally brushed her cheek, and she jumped as if he had struck her.

"Sorry," she said, sounding breathless as she leaned over to pick up the shovel. "Still jumpy. I wasn't expecting to see you."

"That was my fault. I didn't think anyone was in here, either. What are you doing with the shovel?"

"I'm cleaning out the flower beds. They're horribly overgrown. I used to take care of them every summer when we came to visit. Dad must have let them get out of hand."

"Your dad wasn't much for gardening," Vic said.

Lauren smiled at him and something dangerous shifted deep in his soul. He knew those first few whispers of attraction. Had felt them many times before. The last time was with Tiffany. Dean's ex-girlfriend.

The memory was like a slap and he knew he should leave. Yet, against his better judgment, he lingered.

"The lawn is crazy, as well," she continued as he mentally made his retreat from her. "I'm going to have to do three passes with the lawnmower before it's acceptable. And I'd like to go into town tomorrow to pick up some flowers. I think the greenhouse is still selling them."

"Why are you even bothering?" he asked, curiosity keeping him from stepping away. Curiosity and a deep loneliness that had been haunting him the past few months. He hadn't dated since Tiffany had told him she loved him. That she wanted to break up with Dean and get back together with him. They had dated previously, but she had broken up with him to date his brother. Then realized her mistake and wanted to get back together with Vic. He'd told her she had to do the right thing and tell his brother.

Her timing was atrocious. His inattention and Dean's anger had contributed to Dean's accident. Vic felt he was still paying for that mistake.

But now Lauren stood in front of him, attractive, appealing and, truth to tell, probably just as off-limits as Tiffany had been.

"Why bother?" she repeated with a gentle smile that didn't help his resolve. "It's something to do and, well, I'd like to make it nice for the future buyer."

Her words created a clench deep and low, bringing reality into their cozy little conversation.

"Of course. Good idea." He straightened his shoulders as if readying himself for whatever lay ahead. "I'll be done baling this field in a couple of hours. Would it be okay if I come inside and look through your father's papers afterward?"

"I'm meeting Keira Fortier for supper at the Grill and Chill tonight, so I don't think so."

"Another time, then?"

"Sure. When it works."

Vic fought down his frustration at her nonchalant attitude. This was as important to her as it was to him.

But she had choices.

He didn't.

Chapter Three

Vic lay on his back on the hay field, straining at the wrench. Grass slithered down his back as he wrestled with the bolt on the broken U joint connecting the PTO drive to the baler. Another day, another breakdown.

Yesterday he'd managed to get most of the one field baled. Today he wasn't sure he would get as much done.

Sweat streamed down his forehead into his eyes. It was hot and he was only half-done baling when the power take-off connecting the tractor to the baler rammed up.

He blinked and tugged again, pushing even harder. Finally the wrench moved. But his damp hands slid along the handle of the wrench banging into the shaft of the PTO, scraping the skin off his knuckles.

He sucked in a breath, allowed himself a flash of self-pity, then picked up the wrench and got the bolt off, blood mingling with sweat on his hands.

He pulled the shaft of the PTO loose, ignoring the throbbing ache in his hands he finished the job.

He pulled out the broken U joint and got to his feet.

As he brushed dried grass off his shirt and pants, he

stared at the clear blue sky that seemed to mock him. Hard to believe that rain would be pouring down tomorrow as the forecast on his phone showed. But he'd been fooled by that cloudless blue sky before, so he had to get to town as soon as possible, get the U joint welded, get back, fix it and get going until either evening dew or impending rain forced him to quit.

He shifted the U joint in his hands and trudged across the stubble of the hay field, thankful that the breakdown had happened so close to the yard. He saw his truck, parked now beside Lauren's car.

And beyond that, he saw Lauren working on the flower beds by the house.

Her car had been gone when he got here early this morning. Last night he hadn't had the opportunity to look for the agreement. So he had come early. But she hadn't been in the house this morning, either. Instead he'd gone directly to the tractor, hooked up the baler and gotten to work. She had returned about an hour ago. Now she was outside, working.

He climbed over the fence and headed toward his truck, wondering if he should stop and say hi.

Trouble was, he could still feel a flush of embarrassment at that little moment they had shared in the garage yesterday. He still wasn't sure what made him do it. He'd thought he was just being helpful, but when his hand brushed her cheek, a tiny shock had shot through him. Like electricity.

Like the feeling of a growing attraction he couldn't allow himself to indulge in.

He dropped the U joint into his jockey box at the back of the truck and was about to get in when he heard Lauren call his name, then saw her jog toward him.

As she came closer, he was unable to stop his heart lifting at the sight of her. Sandals and blue jeans again today, white tank top, hair tied back, tiny curls framing her flushed face.

She ran the back of her hand over her damp forehead as she stopped in front of him, breathless.

"Sorry to bother you. I was hoping to go into town again this afternoon, but my car has a flat tire. Do you know whom I can call to get it fixed? Jodie is in Bozeman and not answering my calls. And Aunt Laura has been gone the past few days."

"I can change the tire for you."

"No. You've got your own work to do," Lauren said, turning down his offer with a flutter of her hands, her bright red nail polish flashing in the sun. "I don't want to be any trouble."

"If you've got a decent spare, it's no trouble."

"I should know how to do it myself, but living in the city..." She shrugged her shoulder. "I'd just call roadside assistance."

"Well, even if you called the tow truck, it could take a couple of hours before Dwayne got here." Vic gave her a crooked smile. "So, that leaves me, I guess. Unless you want to wait."

"I feel bad asking you."

Vic didn't even answer, just headed over to her car. The rim of the front driver's side tire was resting on the ground, the tire a puddle of rubber underneath it.

"Doesn't get much flatter," he said. "Where's your spare and jack?"

"All I know is that it's in the back. Sorry."

"No worries. I'll figure it out."

He opened the trunk and a few minutes later managed to finagle the full-size spare tire out of its compartment. When he dropped it on the ground, instead of a little bounce, it landed like a rock on its rim, as flat as the tire he was supposed to replace.

"Oh, no. I forgot that I'd already had a flat tire a couple of weeks ago," Lauren said with a note of disgust. "Stupid of me."

"I'm going into town now," Vic said. "I'll bring the tires in and get them fixed."

Lauren nodded, but Vic saw that she looked disappointed. Then he remembered. "You said you needed to go into town yourself. I can bring you where you want to go."

She hesitated, then gave him a sheepish smile. "That'd be great. I feel silly about that, too, because I was in town this morning and when I came home I realized I forgot some groceries."

"Get in. I'll drop you off and get your tire fixed."

"I just need to change, if that's okay."

"No problem," he said, though he wondered why. He thought she looked fine.

Of course he wasn't one to judge what was suitable, he thought, glancing down at his grease-stained blue jeans and dirty shirt.

He manhandled the tires into the back of the truck, getting even more dirt on his shirt. He called the machine shop to see if he could get the part in, and thankfully they could repair it while he waited.

He brushed some hay off his shirt, beat his dusty cowboy hat against his leg and ran his fingers through his tangled hair. That was about as changed as he was getting.

A few moments later Lauren came down the walk and

Vic felt even shabbier. She wore a blue-striped button-down shirt, narrow black skirt and white canvas shoes. Her hair was pulled back again into a ponytail and she had even put on some makeup.

In a mere ten minutes she had transformed from a country girl to a city slicker.

"We'll bring your tires in first, then I'll need to drop my part off at the machine shop, if that's okay," Vic said as they got into the truck.

"You're doing me a huge favor. I can hardly dictate the terms of the arrangement," Lauren said, setting her purse on her lap.

Vic acknowledged that with a nod, then headed down the driveway toward the gravel road and town.

"I noticed you were haying. How many acres of the ranch are in hay?" Lauren asked.

"About two hundred and fifty." He wondered why she asked.

"Is that a lot?"

"It's enough to keep my cows in feed. My dad and I turned our own hay fields on the ranch into pasture, because the land here is more fertile and gets me better yields."

"But there is some pasture here?"

"Oh, yeah. I run some cows here, too. Mostly up in the high pasture behind the ranch and across the road."

"I see." Lauren folded her hands on her purse and gave him a quick glance. "Sounds kind of silly that I know so little about the ranch. I never paid much attention to it. Erin was the one who liked to help. She'd spend hours wandering the back fields and occasionally working with our father."

"I remember Erin. She was a sweet girl."

"Very sweet. Hard to believe we were twins. She always made me try to be a better person. Somehow, she was the only one of us girls who got along with our father when we came back here. She never resented leaving Knoxville like Jodie and I did."

He kept his eyes on the road, but half of his attention was on Lauren.

"So you didn't like it here?" he asked. "Coming every summer?"

"I missed my friends back home and I always felt bad leaving Gramma behind, but there were parts I liked."

"I remember seeing you girls in church on Sunday." Jodie had usually worn some goofy outfit that Vic was sure Keith had vetoed, Erin a ruffly dress and Lauren the same simple clothes she favored now.

"Part of the deal," Lauren said, but a faint smile teased one corner of her mouth. "And I didn't mind that part, either. I liked hearing Aunt Laura play, and the message was always good, once I started really listening. I can't remember who the pastor was at that time, but much of what he said resonated with me."

"Jodie and Erin would attend some of the youth events, didn't they?"

"Erin more than any of us. Like I said, she was the good girl."

"I remember my brother, Dean, talking about her," Vic said, surprised to see her looking at him. "I think he had a secret crush on her."

"He was impetuous, wasn't he?"

"That's being kind. He was out of control for a while. But he's settled now."

Vic thought of the journey Dean had made to get to

where he was. Which brought up the same pressing problem that had brought him early to the ranch.

His deal with Keith.

"So, I hate to be a broken record," he continued, "But it's supposed to rain tomorrow. I was wondering if I could come by the house then? To go through your father's papers?"

Lauren's sigh was eloquent as was the way her hands clasped each other tightly.

Vic tamped down his immediate apology. He had nothing to feel bad about. He was just doing what he'd promised himself he'd do after Dean's accident. Looking out for his brother's interests.

"Yes. Of course. Though—" She stopped herself there. "Sorry. You probably know better what you're looking for."

Vic shot her a glance across the cab of the truck. "I'm not trying to be ornery or selfish or jeopardize your deal. When I first leased the ranch from your father, it was so that my brother could have his own place. And I'm hoping to protect that promise I made him. Especially now. After his accident."

Lauren's features relaxed enough that he assumed he was getting through to her.

"I'm sorry. I understand," she said, her smile apologetic. "I know what it's like to protect siblings. I did plenty of that in my life."

"Are you the oldest?"

"Erin and I are twins, but I'm older by twenty minutes. And you?"

"The same. So yeah, I hear you on the protecting the younger ones."

Lauren smiled back at him. And as their eyes held,

he felt it again. An unexpected and surprising rush of attraction. When her eyes grew ever so slightly wider and her head lowered just a fraction, he wondered if she felt it, too.

He dragged his attention back to the road and fought down the emotions.

You're no judge of your feelings, he reminded himself, his hands tightening on the steering wheel as if reining in his attraction to this enigmatic woman.

He'd made mistakes in the past, falling for the wrong person. He couldn't do it again. He couldn't afford to.

Especially not with Lauren.

"You can still plant these this year, but you won't see them flower fully until next season."

The young girl wearing a green apron, a huge smile and a smudge of dirt on her neck held up the pot holding the spiky-leafed lily. She turned it as if checking it from all angles. "It's a stargazer and they tend to bloom a little later in the season than the Asiatic does."

The warm afternoon sun filtered through the greenhouse, creating a tropical warmth. Plants in full bloom filled most of the wooden benches with swaths of pink and yellow petunias, the delicate blue, lavender and white of the lobelia, the hard red, salmon, white and pink of geraniums. People filled the aisles, talking, comparing, and laughing. A few people had greeted Lauren, some she recognized, but she couldn't pull their names out of her memory.

The atmosphere in this place was one of quiet and peace. As she drew in a deep breath of the peaty scent, a sense of expectation thrummed through her. Though it was getting close to the end of the planting season, the shop still had a lot of stock.

"Which color is this lily?"

"This is the deep pink one. The flowers are edged with white and the spots on them are a darker shade of pink. They smell heavenly, though some people find it strong."

The young girl, Nadine, had been a veritable font of information. Lauren found herself wandering deeper and deeper into the greenhouse and buying far more plants than she had anticipated.

She had quickly gotten her groceries, and instead of waiting, had come into the greenhouse, which was right beside the grocery store.

And then she met Nadine, and here she was, eight pots and seven twelve-packs of flowers later. Helping her aunt in her flower shop had given Lauren some knowledge. Though she knew little about bedding out plants and perennials, she was learning.

She shot a quick glance at her watch. Vic had said he would meet her in front of the store at two. It was only one forty-five.

"They come in white, as well," Nadine said. "Just think how nice they could look together. A cluster of white in the middle of a bunch of pink. You'd have to buy more than one white, though."

"You're bad for my wallet, girl," Lauren chided as she picked up the tag attached to the plant Nadine had pointed out. It showed a large white six-petaled flower with ruffled edges. She was imagining them in the rock garden that edged the deck. Neither she nor her sisters had met their father's mother who, apparently, was an avid gardener when she lived on the ranch.

Lauren's mother had never been interested in gardening, and when Lauren and her sisters had visited the ranch, they'd been too young to care.

"Did you get your grocery shopping done?"

The deep voice behind her made her jump and Lauren spun around to see Vic standing there, thumbs hanging above the large buckle of his belt. He had rolled up the sleeves of his stained twill shirt, the hat pulled over his head now tipped to one side.

His mouth curved in a laconic smile, but she easily saw the warmth of his eyes.

She swallowed, frustrated again at the effect this man had on her.

"Yes. I put the bags close to the entrance," she said. "One of the cashiers said she would watch them for me."

"They're in the truck already," he said, shifting his weight to his other leg. "Sonja told me you were in here and that you'd left her in charge of your food."

She had felt strange enough leaving her groceries with the chatty woman at the front desk who assured her she wouldn't eat her food. But then to have Vic simply load them in the truck?

"Everyone knows everyone in Saddlebank and even worse, everyone's business," he said, his grin deepening. "Am I right, Nadine?" he asked the greenhouse clerk, winking at her.

The girl blushed, looking down at the pot she still held, turning it over. "Yeah. Well. That's Saddlebank." She gave Vic another shy glance, her flush growing.

Nice to know she wasn't the only one he had this effect on, Lauren thought, reminding herself to stay on task. To keep her focus.

You have your own plans. He's just a hindrance and a distraction.

A good-looking distraction, she conceded, but a distraction nonetheless.

"So what do you all have here?" he asked, pointing to the plants.

"Gerberas, lilies, petunias, some marigolds. Lobelia, geraniums and million bells—"

"Gotcha," he said, holding his hands up as if to stop her, looking somewhat overwhelmed. "Do you need help packing these up?"

Lauren glanced from the wagon holding the flowers she had chosen to the rest of the greenhouse. She could spend another hour wandering, planning and dreaming, but she had taken up enough of Vic's time and she knew he was anxious to get back to work.

"I have to pay for them first," she said. She turned the cart around and walked down the wooden aisles to the checkout counter.

But her feet slowed as she passed a preplanted pot of pink and purple million bells, white lobelia, trailing sweet potato vine and yellow aspermums. She pinched off a dead flower, her hand arranging the one vine.

"That's pretty," Vic said, his voice holding a note of approval.

"I love the colors they've used. It would look lovely on a deck." Then she pulled her hand back, knowing that she had already spent more than she should, and marched on, resisting the temptation.

She got to the cashier, unloaded her plants on the old wooden counter, pulled her debit card out of her wallet and slapped it on the counter as if afraid her more practical self would convince her it was a waste of money.

"You've got some lovely plants." Sonja bustled about as she rang them up on the old-fashioned cash register, her gray curls bouncing. She was an older woman, with a rough voice and a broad smile. Her T-shirt proclaimed Life's a Garden. Dig It. "If you need any help or advice, you just call. We can answer all your questions. 'Course, you have your aunt to help you out. I know you used to help her at the flower shop from time to time," she said.

"I'm sorry, I feel like I should remember you," Lauren said.

"I used to deliver perennial pots to your aunt's shop," Sonja said. "Used to see you and your sisters there once in a while."

Then Lauren did remember. Sonja was always laughing and joking, her personality filling the store, making it a fun and happy place to be.

But before Lauren could say anything, Sonja was finished with her and already on to the next customer. Lauren looked around for Vic, doing a double take as she realized he was purchasing the pot she had just admired.

"Figured if you liked it, so would my mom," he said as he pulled his wallet out of his back pocket.

"Your mother will love them." Sonja rang up his purchase, smiling her approval. "Very considerate of you."

"I'm angling for son of the year," Vic said.

"And he'll get it, don't you think, Lauren?"

"I guess" was all Lauren could muster. She was still wrapping her head around a guy buying a potted plant for his mother.

"Our Vic is an amazing young man," Sonja said, her voice heavy with meaning. She gave Lauren a knowing look that she didn't have to interpret. "A girl would be lucky to have him."

"I think it's time to load up what we got and get out of here," Vic cut in with a sheepish smile as he set the pot he'd just bought on the two-layered cart holding Lauren's plants.

"You know I'm right," Sonja teased, looking from Vic to Lauren as if connecting the two. "You won't find better in all of Saddlebank."

"Now it's really time to go," Vic said, ushering Lauren out of the store. His truck was right out the door and he opened the back door of the double cab. "If it's okay with you, I thought we could set them here," he said as he started unloading them.

"But you'll get the floor of your truck dirty," Lauren protested. The carpet was immaculately clean and the seats even more so.

"It's honest dirt," he said, tossing her a grin as he took the pots from her and set them on the carpet. "Sorry about Sonja, by the way. She's the local busybody."

"I remember her coming into my aunt's flower shop," Lauren said. Sonja's comment had made her even more aware of Vic than she liked. "She was like this ball of energy."

"That about sums her up." He got into the truck. "Do you need to do anything else?"

"I think I've taken enough of your time and spent enough of my money. I know you want to get back to your hay baling."

"Yeah. I do. Thanks."

A few minutes later they were back on the highway, headed toward the ranch. Lauren's groceries were stashed on the floor of the truck by her feet.

"By the way, I can't thank you enough for taking

care of the tires," Lauren said. "But shouldn't we have stopped to pay for them?"

"You can next time you're in town. I talked to Alan, who runs the place. He said it was okay."

Lauren shook her head. "Small towns," she said. "I can't imagine getting away with running a business like that in Boston or Fresno."

"You lived in both those places?"

"And Chicago, and New York for a month. I live in Charlotte, North Carolina, now."

"That's a lot of moving."

"Harvey, my fiancé was a real go-getter. Always looking for a better job."

"And you followed him around?"

"Sort of. His opportunities were good for me, as well." She was surprised at how his comment made her feel.

"Your dad said you worked as an accountant."

Lauren chuckled at the grimace on his face. "It's good work."

Vic shuddered. "Numbers are not my friends. I can't imagine working with them all day."

"To each his own," she said. "I like how predictable and orderly they make life. There's no surprises or guesswork. One plus one will always equal two."

"Do you enjoy it? Is it your passion?"

Lauren opened her mouth to say yes but hesitated. To say it was her passion wasn't correct. "I'm good at it and it pays well."

Vic laughed and she shot him a puzzled glance. "Is it the money? That why you do it? You don't seem like that kind of person."

Lauren's back stiffened. "No. Of course not. I do it

because I'm competent. I'm trained for it and because… because…well… I've got this opportunity now to start my own business and…" For a few long moments she couldn't latch on to any solid reason why. No one had ever asked her. Harvey had always assumed this was what she should do.

She turned away from Vic and his probing questions and curious expression. The uncertainty his comments raised frustrated her. Then came a chilling realization.

It's because that's all you've ever done.

"I'm sorry if I've upset you," Vic said. "I was just making conversation."

She suddenly felt as if the ground that she had always thought of as solid and unmoving had shifted.

You don't seem like that kind of person.

How did he know what she was like?

"It's all right," she said, giving him a careful smile. "For some reason your comment caught me unawares."

"Never a good place to be caught," Vic said. "I'm sorry."

"No. Please don't apologize. If I'm honest, money is part of it, that's true enough. There never was enough when I was growing up. I remember reading the beatitudes and Jesus saying, 'Blessed are the poor,' and I thought he was wrong. There was no blessing in being broke. There was no honor in buying clothes from a thrift store and getting teased about them. Jodie managed to find her own style. But I used to be ashamed that my clothes were secondhand, and Gramma chastised me many times for that. She often made me feel guilty that I wanted more. Even Dad would tell me not to be so proud."

"Keith was a frugal man."

"That's a kind way of saying he was stingy."

Vic gave her another one of his killer smiles that touched her soul.

"So what was your passion when you were younger?" he pressed. "What did you always want to do? Where were you the happiest?"

Lauren considered his questions. "You know, my favorite times were when I was in my aunt's flower shop. My dad would send us there once in a while when he didn't know what else to do with us. I loved working with the flowers. I loved watching my aunt arrange them and combine colors and textures and create interesting displays. When I was older, she let me try my hand at it." She released a light laugh. "I think the true appeal of my aunt's shop was the calm I felt there. The happiness. It was like a little sanctuary for me and my sisters."

"Sounds like it was a good place for you."

A memory floated upward and she caught it. "When I was eighteen, my last summer here, I remember my aunt suggesting that I stay in Saddlebank and help her in the flower shop."

"So why didn't you?"

"My grandmother became ill and she needed me back in Knoxville."

"And being the responsible person you are, you went and you took care of her."

"I owed her a lot. Erin had just been accepted at college, and I wasn't sure what I wanted to do and hadn't applied anywhere, so I figured it was best if I stay. Jodie was only sixteen and still in high school. Someone needed to help Gramma."

Vic looked at her with a fleeting sadness. "That's

quite a sacrifice for such a young girl. And quite amazing."

She heard warmth, approval and sympathy in his voice, and for some reason, it made her feel emotional.

"She'd given us a home. It was the least I could do."

"And now, this business you're buying?"

His question lingered as if he wasn't sure what he wanted to ask about it. She knew her decision was the reason she was selling the ranch and that it had a huge impact on him, but she had to stay the course.

"It's an opportunity. A good one. The woman I'm partnering with is energetic and hardworking, and I think this is a good chance for me to strike out on my own."

"Working with numbers every day."

"You don't need to make it sound like a death sentence," she added with a light laugh. "I'm good at it and this business I'm buying in to is a… I think this is a good opportunity. A chance to take care of myself."

"But I understand you'll be doing that with a partner."

"Yes, but she's someone I can trust."

You thought you could trust Harvey. You thought you could trust your boss.

The words slammed into her and she had to clench her fists to control the anger that rose within her.

Even as she spoke she found herself reaching. As if she had to convince herself as much as him.

"And what about you," she countered, tired of analyzing her own life. "What's your passion?"

"Ranching. Always ranching," he said, his voice strong with a conviction that she envied. "That's never changed. My dad worked the ranch I live on and his grandfather before that and his grandfather before that.

We're not as old as the Bannister ranch, but close. It's my heritage and I love it." He gave her a sheepish smile. "I'm just a basic guy. A cattleman born and bred."

"You're fortunate to have that legacy," she said, wondering if she could ever muster up the same passion for her work that seemed to be ingrained into his identity. Her work was something she'd stumbled into. Something she discovered she was competent at, and her career carried on from there.

For a moment, however, she wondered what her life would have been like if she'd followed through on Aunt Laura's suggestion. If she'd stayed in Saddlebank.

It was a moot point, she reminded herself. Her grandmother had needed her.

But still…

"Your dad's ranch goes back a few generations, as well," Vic said, breaking into her thoughts.

"Dad was never as much a rancher as you seem to be," Lauren said. "I think he only did it because he inherited it from his father. And though we stayed there, it never felt…like home. I always felt more like a guest in some ways."

"Did Knoxville feel like home?"

"Kind of. But there at least we were at our grandmother's home. She was kind enough, but it was still her place."

"So, no real home base? That's sad."

Lauren glanced over at him, surprised at his sympathy, surprised to see him looking at her.

Their gazes held, and when Vic smiled, once again she felt connection and possibilities. Her breath seemed hard to find and an unusual urge to reach across the truck overcame her. To touch his hand.

Her cell phone rang and he jerked his head aside. Lauren crashed back down to earth when she glanced at the name flashing on the screen.

Alex Rossiter. The ranch's potential buyer.

"Hello, Alex," she said, disappointed at how breathless she sounded. "What can I do for you?"

"Was wondering if I could come by next week Tuesday," he said, his voice booming in her ear. Alex was a large man with a large voice and matching attitude. "To look over the place. See what I'm getting into."

As he spoke Lauren drew in a shaky breath, feeling as if she had to find her balance.

"I think that should work," she said.

They made arrangements, but all the while she talked, she couldn't help feeling guilty. As if she was doing something wrong.

Alex abruptly said goodbye and Lauren lowered her phone, trying to find the right way to tell Vic what was happening. Straightforward was always best, she decided.

"That was the buyer of the ranch," she said, turning to Vic. "He wants to come out on Tuesday."

Vic just nodded, his jaw tight, his eyes narrowed as he stared straight ahead.

She put her phone in her purse and folded her hands on her lap, staring out the window.

But as they drove back to the ranch, she couldn't shake the sensation that she had caught a glimpse of another life. A life that held light and joy.

She shook off the capricious emotion.

She had a good plan. She had to stick with it. How it affected Vic shouldn't matter to her.

In spite of his approval of what she had done for her

grandmother, it was a reminder of the many times she had put other people first in her life.

It was time to take care of herself.

Chapter Four

"My girls." Aunt Laura tugged a green apron over her purple tunic as she grinned at Lauren and Jodie. The three of them had gathered in the back room of her florist shop to discuss the flowers for Jodie's wedding. "I'm so excited to help with this," she said, tugging on gloves before she pulled some white roses out of the large plastic tub. She laid them on the large butcher-block table, then pulled another tub closer to her.

The store was closed and after they were done Lauren knew they would be invited for tea. It was a ritual played out many times in their childhood when the girls were on their own because their father was busy with haying.

As Vic had been the past few days.

An image of Vic slipped into Lauren's mind along with their conversation in the truck yesterday. It had been a long time since she'd spent any amount of time with a man in a relaxed setting. He seemed like a nice guy and she regretted the fact that she couldn't sell the ranch to him.

He had come to the house again this afternoon but had

spent most of that time in the office. For which she was thankful. Being around him made her nervous.

A phone call from his brother cut his time short, and with an apology and a request to come back, he had left.

Trouble was, she and Jodie were going to Bozeman for the next few days to look at wedding and bridesmaid dresses and wouldn't be home.

"Lauren, can you grab some of those bells of Ireland?" Aunt Laura asked as she pulled some delphinium out of a tub.

Lauren frowned at her aunt's selection.

"Are you sure?" she asked, trying to visualize how the combination would look.

"Yes. Why?" The look that accompanied her aunt's question told Lauren that she had noticed Lauren's lapse and was wondering about it.

"Nothing. Just curious," she said, giving a quick smile that dismissed her aunt's curiosity. She didn't want to get into a discussion about Vic with her aunt and her sister present. She knew exactly what they would think.

Lauren entered the back cooler, enjoying the rainbow colors of roses, forsythia, tulips and dozens of other flowers whose names she slowly recalled. There in one corner, she caught the distinctive green of the bells of Ireland. She grabbed the container, shivering as she closed the cooler behind her.

"Now I know these aren't often put together in a bouquet," Aunt Laura said as she tugged a few out of the tub and slipped them into an arrangement. "But I think it could look dramatic. What do you think, Jodie?"

"I like it," Jodie said, but Lauren sensed she wasn't enthusiastic.

Aunt Laura tugged some baby's breath and wove it in.

"This might help," she said with a hopeful note.

"That does soften it a little."

But the forced smile told Lauren that Jodie had a different vision.

Lauren gathered up some of the discarded roses and lilies. She wove in some pussy willows and few hyacinths and added boronia, a cluster of small bell-like flowers.

"Oh, what's that?" Jodie said, moving over to where Lauren worked. "That's awesome."

"Oh, I was just fooling around," Lauren said, setting the bouquet on the table, self-conscious.

Her aunt looked from the flowers she had just put together, then at Lauren's bouquet. "You always did have a good eye for composition. I remember when you worked here, I couldn't keep up with the demand for your arrangements."

Lauren wiped her hands on her slacks. "It's fun. I just like trying different combinations."

"What would you do for bridesmaids?" Aunt Laura asked.

"I was just experimenting. You're the florist."

"And you're the one with talent. I'd like to see what else you would do." Aunt Laura's bright smile showed Lauren that she wasn't hurt. In fact, she seemed interested.

"Okay. How about we do this." Lauren reluctantly reached down to a tub of peonies and made a tight bouquet with them. She added a couple of the roses and some baby's breath this time. "This is a rough idea. We could frame it with banana leaves or, if you want to go more girly, with a circle of tulle."

"Oh, I like that," Jodie breathed, suddenly more animated.

"See, you have the gift," Aunt Laura said. "I think we should talk about you helping me out with the wedding flowers."

Lauren wasn't sure she would be able to help much. She would be in the middle of setting up her new business right before the wedding.

But as she looked over the flowers on the table, she felt a yearning she couldn't ignore. "We'll see" was all she said.

"And now I think we need to have tea."

They followed their aunt up the back stairs to her apartment. A few moments later they sat around her dining room table, munching on sugar cookies.

The lights were turned low, and the classical music Aunt Laura loved played softly in the background. For the first time since she'd come back to Saddlebank, Lauren felt at ease. Comfortable. Relaxed.

"So, tell me, have you girls heard anything from Erin yet?" Aunt Laura asked, sitting down across from them, her gray hair cut in a bob, her eyes looking from one to the other.

"I tried to call her, but she didn't answer her phone," Lauren said. "She sent me a text shortly after, though. She's been busy. At least that's her excuse."

"I'm just wondering why she won't talk to us," Jodie said, stirring yet another spoonful of sugar into her tea. "It's like she's avoiding us."

"She used to do that more often," Aunt Laura said, wiping a crumb of sugar from her lips. "I remember these intentional forays into melancholy she used to indulge in. She always was more introverted than either of you girls."

"I remember Dad getting so ticked at her when she would wander off into the hills and not come back for hours." Jodie released a light laugh that held little humor. "He could be so hard-nosed."

"Jodie. Careful," Lauren reprimanded. "Don't speak—"

"Ill of the dead," Jodie chimed in, giving her sister a sly wink to show her that her comment didn't bother her. "Gramma's mantra. I know, but it's still hard. Even in spite of the letters of apology he wrote both of us."

"Your father had his…moments," Aunt Laura said. "I just wish you could have spoken to him before he died. Gotten some of this stuff out of the way."

"Would he have said in person the things he wrote in our letters?" Lauren asked, taking a sip of her tea.

"Maybe. The actual words of apology were hard for him. He would do other things to show he was sorry." Aunt Laura gave them a sorrowful smile. "I hope you can appreciate that the letters he wrote you were a big deal for him. I know he spent hours sitting at his table in the café writing them. I hope it gives you a different view of him and, at the same time, a different view of the ranch. It's been in the family for decades."

Guilt suffused Lauren at her aunt's offhand comment.

"I know it's been handed down through the generations and I'm sorry none of us will be taking it over." Lauren glanced over at Jodie. "Finn doesn't want it, and well…" She let her comment fade away, not sure she wanted her aunt to know how important the money was to her.

Aunt Laura waved her hands as if erasing what she

had just said. "I wasn't saying you need to hang on to it just because it's a family heirloom. I want you to have some good memories of your father here. It was a part of your life and it's a good place. I know I have good memories from living there. I just wanted to know that you did, too."

Her aunt looked so distressed Lauren clasped her aunt's hands between hers to reassure her. "It's okay, Auntie. I do have good memories. It's just…"

"I'm so sorry I brought it up," Aunt Laura said. "I know your father was hard to live with. And, well, he had his reasons."

"Jodie told me you read her letter," Lauren said.

"Yes. I did."

"I hope that's okay," Jodie said to her. "Auntie was visiting one afternoon and it was on the table."

"Of course it is," Lauren said. "It was yours to show to whoever you wanted. But I guess I was thinking of what Dad said in Jodie's letter. About Mom cheating on him. Was that true?"

Aunt Laura pushed a few granules of sugar that had fallen off her napkin into a tiny pile as she seemed to ponder what Lauren had said.

"It was," she said. "Your mother wasn't a happy wife."

"Why not?"

"Your father never said anything in your letter, Lauren? About his marriage?"

"It was a lot of the same stuff that he told Jodie. That he was sorry he wasn't a better father. He said something in mine about his own struggles and he did say that he suspected Mom had cheated on him."

"I never wanted to say anything to you girls, and the truth was, it didn't matter so much." Aunt Laura carefully added a few more granules to her pile. "Your parents were already divorced. Like your grandmother said, I didn't want to cast any aspersions on your mother's character by speaking ill of the dead. But I think you need to know that your parents had to get married," she said.

"Had to?" Lauren's question broke into her aunt's statement. "As in, she was pregnant?"

"With you and Erin," Aunt Laura said, giving her an apologetic smile. "Your mom had just moved to Saddlebank and needed a job. I hired her at the flower shop and introduced them. She was fun and vivacious, and Keith, well, he'd always leaned toward the darker side, so I thought she would be good for him. Keith liked your mother well enough, but I don't think he ever planned to marry her. He had his own dreams. After our father died, Keith wanted to sell the ranch and join the marines. But when he found out your mother was expecting, he stepped up to his responsibilities. In retrospect, while it seemed the right thing to do at the time, it might not have been the best decision for either of them."

Aunt Laura paused, and Lauren glanced over at Jodie, gauging her reaction. She looked just as stunned as she felt.

"The cracks in their marriage started showing right away. They got worse after you were born," Aunt Laura continued, looking from one sister to the other. "Your mother would drive to Bozeman and go shopping, spending money your father didn't have. Your father wasn't a cattleman. He inherited the ranch from our father, so he rented it out and started working for the county as a sheriff's deputy. He loved his job. It was the closest he ever came to becoming a marine. But he didn't make a lot of money, so that caused other problems."

Lauren listened, trying to process what Aunt Laura was saying. She tried to balance it with her own memories of her mother, a sad woman who often complained about their father.

"Was their marriage all bad?" Jodie asked.

"No, honey. Not all bad." Aunt Laura gave both of them a smile. "Your father did love his family. And while he loved being in Saddlebank, ranching wasn't his first love. So I don't know if this helps you see your father in a different light. I'm hoping it makes you all a bit more sympathetic toward him. He may not have been the nicest person, but he was my brother and I miss him."

Lauren heard the choked note in her aunt's voice and both she and Jodie reached across the table and took her hand.

"Of course you do," Lauren assured her. "We do, too."

Aunt Laura gave them both a wavery smile. "I don't want to put anything more on your shoulders or influence your decision. I know you have your reasons and I'm sure they're good ones, but I am going to be sorry to see the ranch go to a stranger." She sat up and pushed her chair away. "And now we've had our confession time. You get to see a side of your parents you never did and I got to unload a secret that should have been told a long time ago. I think this calls for another cup of tea and some more cookies."

After she walked away, Lauren looked at Jodie, who had a puzzled expression on her face.

"Do we really need to do this?" Jodie whispered, leaning closer to Lauren.

"Do what?"

"Sell the ranch to that guy?"

"I'm not going to run it, you said Finn wasn't interested, and we both know Vic can't pay what Alex is offering. Besides, does it really matter who owns the ranch?" Lauren whispered back, shooting a quick glance to the kitchen, where Aunt Laura was making a fresh pot of tea. "You're established, Erin doesn't seem to want to come back and I'll be gone."

"I know. That's part of the problem."

"I'm not a rancher," Lauren murmured. "And I've no intention of becoming one. And while I'd love to stick around—"

"Would you?" Jodie asked, a pained note in her voice. "Would you really?"

"I would. Really," Lauren said, stroking her sister's shoulder. "I would love to be close to you. But I need to be realistic. I need to make a living. Take care of myself."

"I thought the same thing," Jodie said. "And then I met Finn."

"Well, you were lucky. I don't see that in my future."

"What about Vic?"

Lauren gave her sister an *oh, really* look that hopefully dismissed that idea. Then she smiled as their aunt came into the room, bearing a tray with more cookies and a fresh pot of tea.

"Are you talking about Vic Moore?" Aunt Laura asked.

"Yes."

"No."

Jodie and Lauren spoke at the same time.

"He's a wonderful young man," Aunt Laura said, ignoring Lauren's comment. "And so handsome and kind and loyal." She eased out a sigh. "I used to have the biggest crush on his father. He was just as good-looking. Just as nice."

"So why didn't you go for him?" Jodie asked, unwilling to let go of the topic of the Moore family.

"He had eyes only for Trudy, his wife." Aunt Laura sighed. "But Vic is still single, I understand," she said, looking over at Lauren. "He would make a fine husband."

"Nice try, Auntie," Lauren said. "But I think I'll pass. I need to focus on my business. That's my future." Last night she had called her partner, Amy, and listening to her enthusiasm for their new business had helped ground her back in reality.

"Be careful," Aunt Laura warned. "A business can be fulfilling, but I wouldn't want you to miss out on love."

"Love is overrated," Lauren said. But even as she dismissed her aunt's comment, she wondered if Aunt Laura was talking about her own life and running her flower shop.

"And how is your work with Maddie Cole going?" Aunt Laura asked Jodie, as Lauren poured them all more tea.

Maddie was a professional singer Jodie had accompanied at a concert held before Lauren came to the ranch. Maddie had been so enthusiastic about a composition Jodie had written, they'd been working together since then.

"We're working on a new set of songs that she wants to record, but I'm having trouble with a transition in one of them. Lauren and I are going to Bozeman tomorrow, and I'll stay a few more days after that to work with her. But I'd like to have it figured before I go. Maybe you could help me?"

"Sure. Let's go to the piano."

Jodie and Aunt Laura stood up, and Lauren grabbed a couple of cookies and followed them to the living room, dropping onto the couch. She munched on a cookie, happy to listen to her sister and aunt talk music.

But in spite of her resolve, as she listened to Jodie and Aunt Laura trying out a new melody, a dull lonely ache clenched her heart.

Her aunt had warned her not to miss out on love. So why did a picture of Vic shift into her mind? Too easily she remembered his gentle touch as he wiped the mud off her face. The crook of his smile that, somehow, didn't make her feel embarrassed at all.

She pushed the thoughts aside.

Don't go there. You have your plans. They're enough, and no man is worth sacrificing them for.

The noise of the people gathering in the fellowship hall of the church washed over Vic as he walked through the open double doors. He would have preferred to go directly home after church, but he had driven his mother to the service this morning and she'd expressed a desire to stay and chat.

Kids ran between adults, shrieking their pleasure as they played hide-and-seek or tag or whatever game they needed to burn off energy after sitting quiet for the past hour.

A little boy zipped past him, catching his toe in the carpet. He would have fallen if Vic hadn't caught him by the arm.

"Hey, little guy, you might want to slow down."

The little boy, his hair sticking up in spikes, his plaid

shirt open over a juice-stained T-shirt, flashed a gap-toothed grin at him, then ran off. A child on a mission.

Vic chuckled as he walked over to the table where a huge urn sat, and poured himself some coffee. He glanced around the people milling about, laughing and talking, his eyes unconsciously searching the crowd for a certain tall blonde woman who had attended church today.

According to Jodie, Lauren wasn't the most faithful churchgoer, so when he saw her come in and sit down in the spot where her father used to sit, across from where his parents always sat, he couldn't help a second look. He knew she and Jodie had been in Bozeman the past few days, so he was surprised to see her at all.

Trouble was, he glanced over the same time she did. He knew he didn't imagine the faint stir of connection between them. Or the fact that she didn't look away right away, either.

"So how is the haying going?"

Vic glanced up from his coffee just as Lee Bannister joined him.

Tall, with dark hair and deep-set, intent brown eyes, a square jaw and a demeanor that commanded respect, Lee tended to stand out in a crowd. But Vic knew him to be a humble, caring man who had learned some hard life lessons.

"Coming along. The usual dog and pony show. Breakdowns and rain. But we should be okay. I'm cutting again tomorrow." Vic stirred his coffee and set the used spoon in a bowl. "But should be a good crop."

"You put up hay on the McCauley place, don't you?" Lee asked as he poured some coffee for himself. "I heard you've been leasing it. How will that work now that

Keith's dead and the girls own the ranch? You able to make a deal with them?"

"It's all up in the air right now," he admitted, taking a sip of his coffee, wishing he could get a break from his own spinning thoughts.

"That's got to make your plans complicated. I know you had figured on that place for Dean."

"I did." Vic shrugged. "I guess I'll just have to take the pastor's words to heart."

This morning the pastor had preached on the need to trust and let go of the desire to control one's own life. Vic knew, especially the past few weeks, that he struggled with precisely that. It was hard to let go when his own brother depended on him to help.

"Don't we all," Lee said with a light sigh. "I know I've had to learn to let go of my own plans."

Vic nodded, acknowledging the wisdom he was sure Lee had gleaned from his time in prison for a crime he didn't commit. Yet the man wasn't bitter. In fact he seemed downright happy.

Probably had something to do with the pretty redhead who joined them. Abby Bannister granted Vic a quick greeting then gently tugged on Lee's arm.

"Sorry to interrupt, but I just got a call," she said. "That photo shoot I had planned for later this afternoon got bumped up and I have to leave right away."

"Of course. Let's go." Lee set his mug down and gave Vic a warm smile, clapping his hand on his shoulder. "I sure hope things turn out for you and Dean. He's had a rough go."

"He has," Vic agreed. "Take care."

As Lee left, Vic suddenly lost his desire for coffee and certainly didn't feel like chitchat. His conversation with Lee was yet another reminder of the things he had hoped to forget. At least for the morning.

But just as he was about to leave, his mother called out to him, hurrying to his side. "Vic. There you are. I've been looking for you." She rested her hand on the table as she caught her breath.

"You okay?" Vic asked, suddenly concerned.

"Just had to rush to catch you." She gave him a quick smile, her frizzy graying hair catching the light coming in from the large floor-to-ceiling windows from one wall of the room. Her glasses sat askew on her nose. Her shirt was bunched up over the belt she wore and her ruffled skirt, a throwback to the 80s, hung crooked.

His dear mother always said she didn't care how she looked and it showed.

"We've got company coming over for lunch," she said, moving her hand to indicate the woman who now joined them.

Vic's heart did a double flip as he took in Lauren's restrained elegance. Fitted brown dress, white belt, shoes and purse, and a fancy necklace that sparkled in the overhead lights. She wore her hair loose, but it was smooth and silky, and as she tipped her head toward him it slipped away from her face.

His mother's words finally registered. "Company?"

His mother gestured to Lauren. "Yes. I was talking to Keith's girl and said she should come over for lunch. She tried to object, but I wouldn't take no for an answer. I know her sister Jodie is gone to Bozeman this weekend and she doesn't know anybody here anymore, so I told her she simply had to come. No excuses."

"I'm sorry," Lauren apologized. "If it doesn't work out—"

"Nonsense," his mother said, patting her on the shoulder. "Nothing to work out. Dean's sulking at home and I could use some female company and we have lots of food. Besides, I promised her some daylilies and peony roots."

Vic could tell that Lauren was trying to find a polite way to get out of the invitation, though he knew it was futile. Once his mother set her mind to something, she would not let go. And of late she'd been complaining about being lonely. He guessed Lauren had mentioned her desire to clean up the flower beds on the Circle M and his plant-loving mother had probably jumped at the chance to talk botany with another woman.

"Just come for a while," he encouraged her. "It's got to be lonely sitting in that house by yourself. Unless you need to plant your flowers," he teased.

She smiled, which only served to make her more attractive.

"No. I'm letting them harden off before I put them in the ground."

"You won't need to do that," his mother said. "It's late enough that you could put them directly in. But we can talk more about that at home. You can follow us to our place. Just in case you don't know the way." Before anyone could make even the slightest objection, his mother bustled off again.

It was on the tip of Vic's tongue to let Lauren know that she didn't have to accept his mother's invitation, but he stopped himself. It might not hurt his cause if Lauren could meet Dean again. Put a face to the reason he needed to buy the ranch.

Chapter Five

"So what kind of work do you do?" Vic's mother pushed her empty plate aside and seemed more than happy to put off cleaning up until later. She tucked her curly hair back from her face and clamped it down with a hair clip that had been threatening to fall out.

Based on how casual Mrs. Moore seemed about her clothing choices, Lauren had suspected her home would be a reflection of that. But driving up to the two-story brick-and-sandstone home, Lauren shifted mental gears. The house was a beautiful mix of old and new. A wild array of flowering shrubs, perennials and potted plants softened the front of the house. Yet it didn't look stilted or planned.

The inside of the house was equally surprising. The appliances were basic white, but the wooden cupboards were an updated dark walnut with brushed aluminum hardware. The floor was a gray laminate and the dining room table and chairs were an elegant mix of wood and stainless steel.

Clearly Mrs. Moore cared more about her home than she did about how she looked. Lauren admired the woman, knowing that she herself had spent far too much of her own life worrying about the correct image she needed to project.

"I work as an accountant," Lauren said, wiping her mouth with a cloth napkin.

"My goodness. Numbers." Mrs. Moore fluttered her hands. "Benny always said I was horrible with numbers and he was right. Balancing the checkbook to me meant being able to carry it and my groceries without dropping either."

Lauren giggled, surprised at how comfortable she felt around the older woman.

"Good thing you don't need to balance the checkbook anymore," Vic chimed in, smiling at his mother. "Dean takes care of everything online," he said to Lauren.

"One of the few things I can do," Dean said, a grumpy note in his voice. He wore a plaid shirt that had seen better days, faded blue jeans with holes in the knees, a large leg brace and a sullen attitude.

The stubble on his handsome face didn't soften the hardened look he seemed to have adopted. Lauren remembered another Dean. Cocky. Self-assured.

This young man seemed to have lost that part of his persona.

"But you have a good job for now until you are able to work on the ranch again," his mother said with a smile for her youngest son.

"What do you do now, Dean?" Lauren asked, trying to draw the taciturn young man into the conversation. She remembered Dean well from the summers she'd spent here. He'd been a wild young man who lived a rough life. He'd also had a huge crush on Erin. But both Jodie and Lauren had warned her away from him. Thankfully she'd listened. Dean had hung out with David Fortier and Mitch Albon, both young men of questionable reputation. Now David was dead and Mitch was in prison. Dean, it seemed, had escaped that. Probably thanks to his stable family life.

"I work part-time as a finishing carpenter for Jan Peter. He's a big time contractor out here. But I guess I'll need to talk to him about full-time work."

Lauren shot Vic a puzzled look. "I thought you ranched with Vic." Hadn't Vic told her that he had figured on buying the Circle M for his brother?

"If you want to call what I do ranching." He released a bitter laugh. "And thanks to you, my life is going in a different direction."

"Dean. That's enough," Vic said. "Lauren is our guest."

Lauren's heart shifted as Dean's anger washed over her. Ranching wasn't in his future because she was selling the Circle M ranch.

She shouldn't have come.

Dean sighed, then turned to Lauren. "I'm sorry. I'm just in a lot of pain right now. That was out of line." Dean pushed his chair away from the table and grabbed a crutch. "I gotta go lie down."

He limped off, the thump of his crutch echoing in the silence.

Mrs. Moore watched him go, and Lauren saw the sorrow on her face. Poor woman, dealing with so many losses in one year.

"I'm so sorry," Mrs. Moore said. "But please, don't take it personally. He's been bitter since the accident and then his father's death." Her voice wobbled and Lauren felt a rush of sympathy for her.

"I understand," she said, reaching across the table to cover her hand in sympathy. "I have no doubt this has been a difficult time. For you, too."

Mrs. Moore gave her a grateful smile. "You're a sweetheart. It has been hard, but God has given us the strength to deal with it all. I don't know what I would do without knowing that He's watching over us." Mrs. Moore squeezed Lauren's hand. "I'm sure you feel the same way. What with your father's death and all. You girls had your own struggles, I know."

Lauren held her gaze, feeling a fraud by taking her concern, yet surprised at the affection she felt for this caring woman. Her own mother had been distant, dealing with her own sorrows. Yet here was this woman, a stranger to Lauren, feeling sorry for her.

"My faith has helped me through many of life's trials" was all she could say, unwilling to let go of Mrs. Moore's hand. It had been so long since someone other than her sisters, whom she seldom saw, had shown her affection. Had touched her like this. It warmed her soul.

Mrs. Moore gave her hands another squeeze, then sat back. "So tell me more about your work. You must be smart as all get-out if you work as an accountant."

Not smart enough to stay employed, Lauren thought with a too-familiar twinge of anger at her previous boss.

"I know how to work with numbers" was all Lauren could say.

"Will you be doing that here? In Saddlebank?" Mrs. Moore asked.

"No. I won't." Lauren couldn't help a quick glance Vic's way. She guessed from his mother's surprise at Dean's comment that Mrs. Moore didn't know of her plans.

"So you'll be supervising Vic's leasing the ranch?" Mrs. Moore asked.

"I can't make any decisions until I've stayed at the ranch for two months," she said, keeping things vague. No reason to bring up the topic of her selling the ranch.

"Saddlebank is a good place to raise a family," Mrs. Moore said with a melancholy smile. "Benny, my late husband, and I, were so thankful to be able to raise our boys here. I'm sure you would find the same if you gave it a chance. Being married and raising children is a wonderful thing." Mrs. Moore gave her an encouraging look and Lauren felt once again the twinge of sorrow that Harvey's breakup had caused her. The humiliation and the loss.

"Not everyone needs to find fulfillment in that," Vic said. "That was your choice and it worked for you."

"But it could work for you, too," Mrs. Moore said. The touch of sorrow in her voice made Lauren realize that Mrs. Moore's marriage comment was aimed at her son, not her. "That Tiffany girl was no good for either you or Dean. You were right not to go chasing after her."

Lauren saw Vic's lips thin and guessed his mother had brought up a painful topic. While part of her was curious, she knew it was none of her business.

"I understand you also had Finn Hicks living in your home awhile?" Lauren asked, steering the conversation to a safer topic. "Jodie told me that he moved in with you and your family when he was in his teens."

Vic's wry smile told her that he knew exactly what she was up to and that he was thankful for it.

"Yes. We did," Mrs. Moore said, latching on to the subject. "That poor boy's father had died and his mother was all over creation and he needed a home. But now he's got his own place, and he and Jodie are getting married. Things work out the way they're supposed to. And what about you? Any young man in your life?"

Mrs. Moore seemed determined to come back to marriage as a topic.

"No. No young man."

"Well, now, that's too bad." Mrs. Moore leaned her elbow on the table, looking past Lauren to the wall behind her, where she remembered seeing a series of framed pictures. "Having someone to share your life with is special. Benny was my life. My anchor." She paused and Lauren thought she might cry. According to Drake, her lawyer, it had only been about four months since Mrs. Moore's husband, Vic's father, passed away.

Then Mrs. Moore slapped her hands on the table and stood, as if putting her sorrow behind her.

"I need to lie down for a nap," she said, glancing from Lauren to Vic. "And I don't want to listen to the clatter of dishes, so I want you two to just leave them alone. Vic, why don't you take Lauren out and show her where the lilies are? The peonies are over by the garage and there's also some monkshood she's welcome to take."

"I don't think I'll need that much—" Lauren started to object.

"There's pots in the potting shed," Mrs. Moore continued, waving off Lauren's comment. "And you can use the narrow shovel to dig them up and the wagon to cart them around. You'll have to put them in your truck to bring them to her place. If you need help planting them, Lauren, let me know. And don't even think about doing the dishes."

Before either Lauren or Vic could say anything, she swept out of the kitchen and down the hall.

"Well, I guess I got my work cut out for me this afternoon," Vic said getting to his feet.

"You don't have to do this," Lauren demurred. "I feel kind of silly coming here and taking plants from your mother. Like she said, it's not the right time of the year anyway."

"I wouldn't fuss about that. My mother loves nothing more than to share the wealth of her garden and to know that the legacy of her mother lives on."

"Legacy?" she asked as she followed Vic out of the house.

"My mom got most of the plants in the yard from her mother, who, apparently, got them from hers. She claims to have single-handedly brought rare Marcher daylilies to Saddlebank County."

"Never heard of them," Lauren admitted as she headed out the back door of the house and through a pair of patio doors onto a deck.

And as she did, she came to a sudden stop, staring at the garden in front of her. Shrubs and trees edged two acres of verdant green lawn. They, in turn, were framed by bricked-in flower beds holding flowers of varying heights and color. An old bicycle covered in ivy rested among two-foot-high delphiniums, lilies, monkshood, bleeding heart, daisies, marigolds and pansies in another flower bed opposite.

In the shade of a white pergola, tubs with geraniums, million bells, lobelia and sweet potato vine nestled against wicker chairs. A small creek bisected the garden, flowing under an arched bridge that held pots of brightly colored aspermums.

It was like a sheltered oasis. An English estate garden transplanted to Montana. She could hardly take it all in.

"Impressive, isn't it," Vic said, standing with his hands on his hips as he surveyed the garden. "Took Mom about fifteen years, a lot of nagging and sweat equity from me, Dean and my dad to get it to this."

"It's amazing." Beyond the bridge Lauren saw a gazebo also hung with more pots. "How does she keep this all up?"

"It's what she does. And it's been good for her this spring. It's kept her busy after Dad died. Gave her a focus."

Vic wandered down the bricked path and over the bridge. Lauren followed him, but she felt the garden calling her to sit. Rest. Contemplate the beauty around her.

But Vic was a man with a mission, so she followed him past the gazebo, then through an opening in the row of trees at the far end of the garden. Once past the trees, the land opened up and she saw fenced pasture and fields rolling toward the mountains that cradled the basin.

Vic kept walking, following a pole fence that meandered toward a small garage. "Just wait here. I'll get the quad and trailer," he said as he pulled open the large double doors.

Lauren stayed where she was as she heard a small engine start up. Vic drove a small ATV out of the shop, pulling a trailer behind him.

"I'll just get a shovel and we're good to go," he said, disappearing inside again.

He came out with only one shovel.

"We'll need two," she said.

"I'll do the digging," Vic said as he tossed the shovel into the large, open trailer. "You can tell me what you want."

"Nonsense," Lauren said. "I can help."

"In that dress?"

"It's fine. Plus, I'm wearing flats."

"They're white."

"And washable."

Vic gave her another quick look and she felt suddenly self-conscious. She had chosen her clothes carefully. Though she didn't want to examine why, she had hoped, on one level, that Vic would be at church. But compared to his casual mother, she now felt like a vain fashion model.

She pushed past him, stepping into the dim interior. When her eyes adjusted she spied an entire array of gardening tools hanging neatly on one wall. She grabbed a shovel, stepped outside and gave him a look that dared him to say anything.

"Okay. I'll just get some pots and we can go," he said. He disappeared inside again and came out with a huge stack of empty pots nested inside each other.

She couldn't imagine that she'd take that many plants.

"So where next?" she asked.

"Hop on and we'll head over there."

Lauren looked from the seat of the ATV to Vic now swinging his leg over the seat and settling onto it. She doubted she would fit behind him. And how was she supposed to get on in her narrow skirt?

"You'll have to ride sidesaddle behind me," Vic said with a grin.

"I can walk," she said.

"Be easier just to ride. You're not scared of me, are you?"

He said it with a teasing tone, but at the same time Lauren heard an underlying challenge.

She stepped on the footrest of the quad and dropped into the seat behind Vic.

But she had moved too quickly and became unbalanced and the only way to recover was to grab Vic's shoulder.

His very large, muscular shoulder.

Vic took off and as she teetered on her precarious seat, wishing once again that she'd gone with her first choice of slacks and a blazer. But she'd wanted to look feminine this morning. Feminine and in charge. So she put on the dress that Amy called her power dress. The one she wore when she wanted to make an impression on clients.

Only she doubted it made any impression on Vic.

"I'm driving around to the side of the house," Vic said over the noise of the engine. "But we need to go through the fields first to get to the road leading there. Just in case you think I'm kidnapping you."

She laughed. "The quad and trailer were my first clue that you aren't," she returned. "Plus I could probably run faster than this machine."

"Oh, don't underestimate how fast this thing can go," Vic called back. "I've had it up to forty miles an hour."

"No, thanks," she said with a laugh.

"Then you'd really have to hang on," he said, shooting her a quick backward glance.

Lauren held his eyes a moment, then looked away, too easily imagining herself clinging to his broad back. The thought held an appeal that spoke to the loneliness of the past year.

You don't need a man, remember? You have your own plans and you need to stick with them.

But even as she repeated the mantra, it rang hollow.

Vic drove through an opening in a row of cottonwoods and shrubs, coming, as promised, to the side of the house. They came upon another large flower garden hidden from the driveway by more cottonwoods.

"This is what my mom calls her free-range garden," Vic said as he stopped and turned off the quad. "You can pick whatever you want from here."

This garden looked wilder, but at the same time Lauren could tell that it was cared for and nurtured.

The ground was still wet from the rain on Saturday and she was thankful she hadn't worn heels that would have sunk into the ground.

She stopped by a group of daylilies, the pink and purple blossoms waving in the light breeze.

"How many of these do you want?"

All of them, Lauren wanted to say as she took in the swath of color. It made her heart happy to see the glorious blooms and she bent down to have a closer look at one of the delicate flowers. "I've never seen one like this."

"That's the Marcher lily I was telling you about. Extremely rare, according to my mother."

"If there's enough to spare, I'd love one." She knew exactly where to plant it. The purple and pink of the lily would go well with the red geraniums she had chosen to plant in the flower bed on the side of the house.

"Your wish is my command," he said, slipping on his gloves and grabbing the shovel. With one quick push of his booted foot on the shovel, he cut into the ground around the plant she had indicated. She grabbed her shovel as well and helped to cut through the dirt, but she couldn't push down as far as Vic could. Even so, she kept going, determined to do her part.

A few moments later Vic was tipping a large clump of sod and plant over. Lauren grabbed a large pot and dragged it over, frustrated with the restriction of her narrow skirt.

With a twist of the shovel Vic lifted the mass of dirt and dropped it neatly into the pot. Lauren bent over to pick it up and with a heave, managed to get it into the wagon. She got dirt all over her dress, but she didn't care.

"You'll have to dig a big hole for that one," Vic warned.

"I'll be wearing more suitable gardening clothes when I do that," Lauren said, brushing at the dirt on her dress.

"Any other color you want?"

Lauren bit her lip, trying to decide.

"You know what, why don't you take one of each?" he said. "Get a bunch of pots and we can get working."

"I don't think I can take that many."

"I told you, my mom wants you to have them."

"But—"

Then to her surprise Vic pulled off his gloves and touched her lips as if to silence her. It was the merest whisper of a touch, but she felt as if her mouth had been branded. As if the air had been vacuumed out of her body.

Vic's eyes held hers and she saw confusion in their dark depths. As if he didn't know himself what he had just done.

She swallowed and looked away. "I guess… I could find space…"

"Sorry about that," he said. "It's a silly habit. I do it to my mom when she…when she talks too much."

"It's okay," she said, determined to sound casual but

at the same time unable to stop her eyes from seeking his again.

But he frowned at the plants as if his mind was already figuring out how to do this as he yanked his gloves on again.

Twenty minutes and sixteen pots later, the trailer was full of a delightful variety of plants in a rainbow of colors.

She wanted to go home right away and plant them all. She didn't know if she had space for that many plants, but Vic seemed determined to capitalize on his mother's generous offer.

Why bother planting them all? You won't even be around to enjoy them.

Lauren stilled the pernicious voice. Planting them gave her something enjoyable to do to fill her time.

"You look happy," Vic said as he lugged the last pot of peonies onto the trailer.

"I'm excited to get them in the ground."

Vic pulled a hankie out of his pocket and wiped off his face. "I know you're wanting to make the place look nice but truthfully, I can't think of any rancher I know that bought a ranch because it had peonies and lilies."

She heard the teasing tone in his voice, but at the same time her thoughts shifted to Dean—the true reason Vic wanted to buy her father's place.

"It gives me something to do."

"I can appreciate that," Vic said. He picked up his shovel and set it on the trailer. "Speaking of the sale, I'll be coming by tomorrow to finish up the haying. It should be dry after today. But it won't take me all day. I was hoping to go through the rest of your father's papers we didn't get to the last time I was there."

She looked into his eyes and her breath stilled, her heart slowed and everything around them faded away. It was just her and Vic in this idyllic setting.

He's getting too close. You have to be careful. Don't you ever learn?

And yet, she couldn't help a flicker of sympathy at his dilemma. Seeing Dean struggle, hearing his bitterness, was a tangible reminder to her of why Vic wanted to buy the ranch.

"I'm sorry that my dad didn't take better care of you and your brother," she said.

"I am, too." He pulled in a breath, then turned away. "I can take you home as soon as I load these up."

"No. That would be inhospitable," Lauren said, setting her shovel on the trailer. "In spite of what your mom said, I would like to go in and at least clean up if your mom or Dean aren't awake yet."

"Dean most likely didn't go to bed. I'm guessing he's out in the barn. Reading or resting his leg."

"I heard he injured it in a rodeo accident. How did that happen?" Jodie had made a brief mention of it but hadn't said how.

"Took a bad spill off a saddle bronc." He turned away. "Let's load up these plants."

His words were abrupt, and as he grabbed a few of the pots and brought them to his truck, Lauren sensed there was more to the story.

And for some reason she wanted to know what it was.

Vic pulled into the yard and parked by his brother's truck. Thankfully Dean was still home. He had delivered Lauren's plants as he'd promised his mother, but the entire time he was gone he had wondered if Dean would take off.

He had been in a lousy mood all morning and Vic suspected seeing Lauren and what she represented probably hadn't helped.

After the accident Dean had changed. Had become a bit more settled. And when he started working for Jan he starting talking seriously about working together with Vic and ranching together.

Then Lauren had come with her plans that changed everything.

He let his thoughts drift to her, confused at his changing reactions.

It had been easy to be with her this afternoon. Picking out plants. Laughing about how many she wanted and how he had to keep reassuring her that it didn't matter how many she took.

Then he'd touched her.

Vic winced at the memory. He still wasn't sure what had gotten into him, only that his gesture had been automatic. Instinctive.

At least she hadn't jerked away.

And don't read more into that, he reminded himself as he shoved the door of the truck open and clambered out, striding to the house.

After he and Lauren had finished digging up the plants, they had come inside, only to discover that his mother was still sleeping. Lauren insisted that they clean up as much as they could. But still his mother didn't wake. So they left.

His mother was up when he came into the kitchen, sitting at the table with a cup of tea and a gardening magazine. "So did you find enough plants?" she asked.

"More than enough. I think she'll be busy the next few days planting them all." He dropped into a chair across from her. "You have a good nap?"

"Yes, I did."

"Lauren wanted me to make sure to pass on her thanks once again. She felt bad that you weren't up when she came back into the house."

"I was sorry, too, but I was so exhausted. I haven't been sleeping right."

"Why did you invite her to come if you were so tired?" Vic asked.

"I was just being hospitable." His mother took a sip of her tea and flipped a page in the magazine. But Vic caught a hint of a smile and suspected that his mother was up to something else.

"She seems like a nice girl," she continued. "Not at all what I expected, considering how Keith used to complain about her."

"Keith complained a lot the last few years," Vic said as he took a cookie from the plate sitting on the table. It was hard not to sound churlish. Lauren's question about Dean's accident made him feel guiltier about what happened. And more determined to make it right.

"She's a lovely person. And attractive. I understand that she's single. Keith made some comment about her being left at the altar. He had planned to go to North Carolina for her wedding, then suddenly it got canceled."

As she spoke, the memory came back to him—Keith complaining about the change in plans, as if his daughter's canceled wedding was all about him. Now that he'd met Lauren, that moment took on a deeper meaning. While he had hoped seeing Dean would make her realize what was at stake, spending time with her made him aware of what she had lost, as well.

He didn't want to feel sorry for her. She had been on his mind too much already the past few days. He had to keep his mind on what he needed to do.

Keep his focus on his brother and his needs.

Chapter Six

Lauren sat back on her haunches, unable to stop smiling at the flower garden that was slowly rising from the tangle of weeds. Jodie was coming home this afternoon and Lauren was excited to show her the transformation.

The bare spaces left when she pulled out the endless weeds were now filled with a mixture of the flowers Mrs. Moore had given her and those she had purchased at the greenhouse the other day.

Though she knew cutting the blooms off would help establish the plant's root system, she couldn't. They looked so friendly and cheerful, adding a bright and pleasant note to the front of the house.

They made it look more like a home.

The thought drifted in her mind, and for a small moment she let it settle, then with a shake of her head dislodged it.

It's just the ranch.

She brushed the dirt off her pants and pushed herself to her feet, wiping her forehead with the back of her hand. The day had started out so fresh and clear, but now the heat of the afternoon sun beat down on her.

In the distance she saw Vic making his rounds with the tractor and baler. The field was large and he'd appear for a while, then as he moved farther on, disappear. He'd been here since midmorning, and from what she could see he was only half-done.

The tractor was an older one and every window was wide-open. If she was hot working out in the open, he must be cooking inside that tractor.

She set the empty pots back on the wheelbarrow, lifted it up and wheeled it across the yard to where Vic's truck was parked. In the bed of his truck sat the empty tubs the plants from his mother had come in.

Sweat trickled down her back and her hands, inside her leather gloves, were slick. Thank goodness she had worn a hat or she might have to worry about sunstroke.

Once again her eyes moved to where Vic worked. The tractor was stopped, the baler whining.

He must be winding the twine around the bale, she thought, remembering the sound from when her father had done the same work.

Another memory came to her—walking across the prickly hay field with Erin, bringing a container of lemonade to their father while he was working.

You should do that for Vic.

She shook off that thought. He had probably brought his own drink.

But it would be warm and gross by now. It would be a kind and neighborly thing to do.

Part of her knew that, but another part of her—the part that could still feel the touch of his finger on her lips, see the intensity of his expression—held back. Seeing Vic with his mother and brother, working alongside him digging plants, talking to him in church, had all added to a growing attraction.

She knew she couldn't get distracted. She had to keep her focus.

He dug up all those plants for you—surely you can do something kind for him.

She looked up at the cloudless sky, then at her watch. He would be out there for at least another couple of hours.

Before she could talk herself out of it, she strode to the house and went directly to the pantry, hoping the large canister of lemonade crystals her father always had on hand was still there.

She was in luck—she found not one but two containers. She pulled one down and brought it to the kitchen. It took her a few more minutes to find the insulated drink container they often used. When she pulled it out from the pantry, she felt a surprising touch of nostalgia, remembering bringing their father lemonade. How grateful he'd been.

She dropped ice into the container, added the lemonade crystals and poured the water in. She found a plastic bag, added some oatmeal-raisin cookies she had baked yesterday, grabbed two plastic cups, and a few minutes later was walking down the field. The increasing roar of the tractor told her that it was coming closer. She had timed it just right.

Shielding her eyes, she saw Vic in the cab, and as he came closer, she noticed him frowning.

Probably figured she had one more piece of bad news to deliver.

He slowed down as she approached and came to a stop right beside her.

She held up the container with lemonade and the bag of cookies.

"Thought you might want a break," she called out over the roar of the tractor.

His grin was a white flash on his dusty face. He shut the tractor off and climbed out.

"That sounds amazing," he said pulling his ever-present hankie out of his pocket. "I forgot to take extra water along today. I'm kind of parched." He wiped his face as best he could, then shoved the hankie back in his pocket. "Are you going to join me? Unless you're too busy making the flower garden magazine-worthy."

"It will never be anything like your mother's place," she said with a quick laugh. "And yes, I'll join you."

"I don't think any place will be or should be like my mother's," Vic returned, taking the container from her. "We can sit in the shade of the tractor. Unless the grass will be too scratchy for you."

"I may be from the city, but I'm about one-sixth country," she said with a challenge in her voice.

"Only one-sixth?"

"The two months of the year I spent here."

"Plus the time you lived here."

"Less the time I didn't."

"I should know better than to argue numbers with an accountant."

She chuckled as she found a place to sit.

He waited until she got herself settled on the ground before he sat down himself. She handed him a cup and he poured them both some lemonade. Then she held out the bag and he took a cookie from it. He took a long drink and then released a contented sigh. "That's amazing. Thanks so much," he said as he started munching on the cookie.

"You're welcome. I used to do this for my father."

"Ah. Country girl at heart."

"A bit."

"Did you ever ride when you were out here?"

"A bit."

He laughed at that. "If you ever feel the desire to go riding, the horses that Jodie has here are safe to ride. Finn has been working with them."

"So I heard. Jodie assured me I could take them out anytime I wanted."

"Have you?"

"I went out on my own on Saturday night," she returned, lifting her chin in a small gesture of defiance. "It was fun."

"I'd like to have seen that," he said. "Where did you go?"

"Just down the road to a trail leading to the river. Nothing dramatic."

"Those are usually the best rides," he said. He flashed her another grin and she returned it with one of her own, enjoying the easy give-and-take with this man. He was comfortable to be around.

She pulled her legs up to her chest, wrapping her arms around them as she took in the silence surrounding them. Far off she heard the lowing of the cows from the pasture across the road. The sound was an idyllic counterpoint to the chirping of sparrows and the croak of frogs from a creek splashing through the cottonwoods.

A few lazy flies buzzed around and Lauren released a long, slow sigh.

"You sound like you're decompressing," Vic said, pushing his cowboy hat farther back on his head.

"I feel like I am." She spoke softly as if afraid to disturb the moment. "I keep forgetting how quiet it is out here. How isolated."

"It's not that isolated. My ranch is down the road in one direction, the Bannister ranch in the other."

"I know, but in Chicago and New York we live stacked on top of each other, side by side. It's never quiet. Never."

She stopped, listening again, a smile lingering on her lips. A gentle calm and a desire to stay right where she was suffused her.

"I don't think I could handle that," Vic said, pouring some more lemonade for himself. He held the jug out to Lauren, but she declined a refill.

"I don't think you could, either," Lauren said, glancing over at Vic. She tried to picture him strolling down a city sidewalk, past office towers, in that rolling gait of his. The walk of a cowboy. It didn't jell.

"But you're used to it?"

"Got used to it," she admitted. "Don't forget, I've been living in large towns and cities ever since we left here."

A breeze started up just as she reached for the lemonade container to screw the lid down. Her hair was blown in her face, sticking to her lipstick, and she tried to shake it away but it wouldn't move.

She felt rough fingers on her face, tucking the strands of hair behind her ear.

It was a light touch. An innocent gesture that probably meant nothing to Vic, but it sent a thrill of awareness sparking down her neck.

She couldn't help how her head turned toward him

as he lowered his hand. She felt a sense of waiting. Expectation.

Then his phone beeped an incoming text and Lauren pulled herself back to reality. Vic glanced at his phone but chose to ignore it. He set it down on the ground between them.

"Don't forget to pick that up again," she said, pleased that her voice didn't sound as shaky as she felt.

"I won't. I don't go anywhere without my phone. My mom says it's unhealthy."

"It's unhealthy for me if I forget it."

"Why?"

"I get all jittery thinking I might miss some important call. Back in the city we call it FOMO—fear of missing out."

He chuckled. "I'm guessing you have your phone with you now?"

"Back pocket."

He smiled as he took another cookie, and she was thankful for the easy give-and-take between them. Just two people spending time together. Nothing more.

"You make these?" Vic asked.

"The only kind I know how to make, much to my grandmother's disappointment. She always said oatmeal-raisin cookies were the reason she has trust issues."

Vic's frown told her he didn't get the old family joke.

"She always thought they were chocolate chips and got disappointed. She never liked raisins. In anything."

"And yet you continued to make cookies with raisins?"

"Because I like them and it was the only recipe that turned out well for me," she returned, taking another drink of her own chilled lemonade. "Erin was the one who liked baking every kind of cookie and cake she found on the internet and in any cookbook my aunt had lying around."

"Jodie much of a baker?"

"No. She was the entertainer of the family."

"Youngest child," he said, taking another cookie out of the bag.

"You know of what you speak?"

"Dean's the same way. Or used to be."

"How is he doing today?"

"Better. He's helping Jan today, so that helps. Lets him feel useful."

Her thoughts shifted to the conversation they had at his mother's place. The abrupt way he had turned away from her when she brought up Dean's accident. She knew she should leave it alone, but her curiosity got the better of her.

"So how exactly did he get hurt?"

"He got dumped off a saddle bronc."

"And that's how he broke his leg?"

"No. That happened when he got tangled up in the gate he fell on."

Lauren winced. And couldn't help notice the harshness in Vic's voice. There was more to it than this.

"Has he been riding saddle broncs long?"

"Since he was a little kid." Vic raised one leg and rested his forearm on his knee as he stared off, as if returning to that moment. "It wasn't lack of experience that caused the accident. I should've paid attention."

His comment puzzled her. "What do you mean *you* should've paid attention?"

Vic's face grew hard and his eyes narrowed. In the

silence that followed, she wondered if he was going to say anything at all.

"I was riding pickup that evening," he said, his voice quiet. "I was supposed to be watching. I was supposed to grab him if he was in trouble. I didn't notice—"

He stopped, abruptly finished off the last of his lemonade and set the cup aside.

"So you think it's your fault that he got hurt?"

"I don't *think* it is, I *know* it is." Vic sounded angry.

Slowly things fell into place.

"You want the ranch for Dean because of what happened," she said.

Vic's eyes latched on to hers and Lauren wondered if she had pushed him too hard, said too much.

But as he held her gaze, his shoulders seem to slump and he leaned back against the tractor tire. He moved his hand over his chin, as if debating what to say next. "No secret I want the ranch for Dean. I told you that from the beginning."

"No. But I didn't know it was because you felt guilty. About what happened to Dean."

"I don't feel—" He stopped himself, blew out a breath and released a harsh laugh. "You're the first person that seems to have put all that together."

"Not the first. You have, too. And I wonder if Dean has."

"Doesn't matter. I have to do this. I have to try," he amended. "And I know it won't work for you if I find that agreement, but I still need to try."

She understood completely, recognizing the burden of every firstborn child. The need to take care of everyone, to take on the responsibility of everyone. Once again doubts assailed her.

Stop overthinking this. For once put yourself first. It's what you want, what you need.

The little mental lecture centered her. But at the same time she was sorry the topic of Dean had come up. For a few moments she'd felt a connection with Vic. For a few moments she'd shared ordinary conversation with an appealing man. It was nice.

Dangerous, but still nice.

Then her phone rang and all hope of any normal conversation with Vic fled.

It was Alex Rossiter.

Vic finished off the last of his cookie as he tried not to listen to Lauren's phone conversation. He knew she was talking to her buyer.

"I know you told me you were coming tomorrow," she said, her voice sounding strained. "But I forgot to make plans." She nodded as Vic faintly heard the chatter of a male voice.

The buyer.

The man with all the money.

Then she said goodbye and slipped the phone into her back pocket again.

"So what does he want?" Vic asked, wiping the remnants of cookie crumbs off his pants.

"He asked me last week if he could come tomorrow." She scratched her chin with her forefinger as if thinking. "He wants me to show him around the ranch, but…"

"You don't know that much about it," he finished for her, remembering the phone call she got when he brought her to town.

"I know something, but I haven't been here for over ten years. And I thought—"

"You want me to show him around."

She looked over at him, her eyes pleading. "I would feel better if someone who knew the ranch could talk to him about it."

He exhaled, shoving his hair back from his face in a gesture of frustration. What irony. Escorting the future buyer over the ranch he had counted on buying himself.

Though he hoped to go through more of the papers in Keith's office tomorrow, he was starting to see the futility of it all. All they had found so far was an old lease agreement Keith had drawn up with Rusty Granger—frustrating that he had protected Rusty's interests but not his—and a host of grocery lists and to-do lists, but that was about it.

He doubted that a further search of the office would yield anything more. And yet he knew he had to give it one more try.

"I know it's a lot to ask and I'm sorry—"

"I'll do it," he said as he got to his feet.

She stood as well, looking sheepish. "Thanks. I appreciate it."

"What time is he coming?"

"About noonish tomorrow. Does that work?"

"I'll be done haying today, provided I don't get any more distractions." In spite of his irritation with the situation, he couldn't help smiling at her. He appreciated the lemonade and cookies, and the fact that she had taken the time to think about him.

"I won't bug you anymore," she said, returning his smile.

"Bringing lemonade and homemade cookies hardly constitutes bugging." He looked over at her and to his surprise she didn't turn away. As their eyes locked, he felt an age-old emotion rise up in him. The beginnings of appeal and connection. The hesitant looks. The careful dance between a man and a woman signaling a shift toward attraction.

Be careful. This one isn't for you. She's not sticking around. She created a host of problems for you.

But in spite of the very wise and practical voice warning him, he kept his eyes on Lauren and she on him.

He wanted to touch her face, brush his fingers over her flushed cheek. The impulse was so strong, he felt his hand rising.

Then she turned away—the moment was gone—and he clenched his fist, frustrated with how she was insinuating herself into his life. Yesterday, after he came back from delivering her plants at the ranch, he'd found his thoughts returning to her again and again.

Reliving that moment when he had touched her.

He gave himself a shake, then bent to pick up his phone.

He frowned when he saw two identical black phones lying in the cut hay, neither of them with covers.

"Which one of these is yours?" he asked, picking them both up.

She looked as puzzled as he was, then took one. "I think it's this one," she said, hitting the home button.

A picture of his mother and Dean flashed on the screen and she handed it over to him. "Sorry. I didn't mean to intrude."

"That's okay," he said, handing her the other phone. "It was a perfectly innocuous picture."

She shoved her phone in her back pocket and gave him a wistful smile. "It's sweet."

Somehow the compliment fell awkwardly between them.

Sweet.

"So I can tell Alex to come tomorrow?" she asked.

"Yeah. Sure." Vic dropped his phone in his shirt pocket. "Tell him two is probably best. I should be done by then." Then he climbed back in the tractor.

Lauren was already walking away, carrying the lemonade container in one hand and the bag with the cookies and the cups in the other. He started up the tractor, backed up and lined himself up with the swath of hay and moved ahead.

But before he started moving, he glanced over at Lauren again.

Only to see her looking at him. She lifted her hand holding the bag, waggled her fingers at him, turned and walked away.

What was that about?

You're being all high school. Don't read too much into that.

And yet, as he started working, that simple gesture stayed with him.

As did her smile.

Chapter Seven

"We generally put the cows out on these pastures first thing in the spring," Vic was saying as he walked with Alex Rossiter past the fenced fields across the road from the ranch house. The cows in the pasture were just brown and black dots farther back, closer to the hills. "Then, as the snow retreats on the mountains and the grass starts growing farther up, we move them to the higher pastures."

Lauren followed a few steps behind, feeling useless but at the same time thankful Vic had agreed to this. She knew that her father moved the cows partway through the summer. She and her sisters had participated in a pasture move years ago.

It had been one of those idyllic days. Sunlight poured from blue sky devoid of clouds. A faint breeze kept bugs at bay and the rhythmic plod of the horses they rode had lulled the McCauley sisters and their father into a good mood.

The memory made her smile.

But it wasn't the kind of information you could pass on to a prospective buyer.

"How many head can you run?" Alex was asking, punching something into his phone, which never left his hand.

"Two hundred in this pasture with proper pasture management."

"Management as in?"

"Rotation. Moving them around more frequently."

"Sure. Whatever," Alex muttered as his fingers flew over the screen's keyboard.

The conversation drifted past Lauren, again somewhat familiar but not information she knew.

She sensed an edge of tension to Vic's voice. He most likely wasn't the most objective guide, she realized, but he was the one who knew the place the best.

"How long has this ranch been operating?" Alex asked, turning to Lauren. "You're the owner, after all—you should know that."

He winked at her. The last time she met Alex Rossiter, it was at her office. He had worn an open-necked shirt, a gold chain, a blazer and blue jeans that were artfully faded and distressed. And expensive. As were his John Lobb tasseled loafers.

Today he had gone with the more down-home cowboy look. Plaid shirt, plain blue jeans, cowboy boots so new they still shone, and topping it all off, a straw cowboy hat, crisp and gleaming.

Then there was Vic, with his twill shirt rolled up at the sleeves, stained leather gloves shoved in the back pockets of blue jeans faded at the knees and ragged at the hem, worn over scuffed cowboy boots. His hat was weathered and sat easily on his head, almost an extension of himself. Authentic. Man of the land.

He looked rooted. Grounded.

Alex was a nice guy, a pleasant man, in fact, but compared to Vic he seemed insubstantial.

His money wasn't. And she needed every penny of it.

"The ownership of this ranch goes back many generations," Lauren said. She leaned against a fence post, dredging up the history lessons her father gave them whenever he thought they needed reminders of their past. "My father inherited it from his father, whose wife was related to the Bannister family of Refuge Ranch, which is farther up the valley. Before that it's a tangle of Bannister and McCauley ownership. I think I ran across a family tree going through my father's papers. I can show it to you if you're interested."

Alex waved off the offer. "No. I was just making conversation."

His comment was throwaway, but she couldn't shed it that easily as her gaze traveled over the fields she had ridden on as a young girl, the fields her father and his father and grandfather had owned.

She would be breaking that chain.

The thought affected her, and she felt the beginnings of regret and dangerous second thoughts.

"So what would you like to see next?" Vic asked as Lauren dragged herself back from her precarious thoughts.

"What do you recommend?" Alex addressed his question to her, seeming to ignore Vic.

"We can drive farther down the road to show you some of the other places and a few outbuildings," Lauren suggested.

"I thought we could go farther up into the hills on horseback. Get a feel for what that would be like. I was hoping you could come along," Alex said.

He slanted her an arch smile and added a touch on her arm that telegraphed his meaning.

He was flirting with her.

She was taken aback but recovered. She had to keep things professional.

Besides, his attention wasn't welcome or appreciated. She looked past him to Vic, who stood with his thumbs hooked through his belt loops in a classic cowboy pose.

Only she knew it wasn't fake. His hat was pulled low, shadowing his features. She couldn't read his expression, but she guessed he wasn't impressed with Alex.

"What do you think, Vic? Do you have time to saddle up some horses and go into the backcountry?" she asked.

"Sure. As long as Alex is up to an hour-long ride."

"I'll be okay," Alex said, still looking at Lauren, his smile deepening. "Especially if you come along."

Lauren tried not to roll her eyes. Instead she gave Alex a tight nod, then pushed herself away from the fence post. "Let's go, then."

Half an hour later, as she and Vic were saddling the horses, Alex wandered around the yard, looking at the house, the barns. But it seemed half his attention was on her.

As she slipped the cinch strap through the ring, she caught Vic looking at her over top of Roany's saddle. "So what's your take on the guy?" Vic asked.

"What do you mean?"

"I think he's not interested in the Circle M as a ranch."

She tugged on the strap and threaded it through a last time, pulling as she did, striving to find the right words to express her own uncertainties and yet not give Vic false hope. "I know. I think he sees it as an investment, though I don't think he realized how large it was."

"You told him how many acres it was."

"When lots the size of your mother's garden are considered huge, you can't imagine how much land a ranch can encompass." She sighed, glancing back at Alex, who now stood, hands on his hips, smiling up at the house as if it met with his approval.

She had talked to Amy yesterday to reassure her that she would, indeed, send her share of the investment to her in a couple of months, once the will was satisfied and Alex had transferred the money.

Which he had assured her was not a problem.

"And you must do what you must do," he said, his voice quiet.

Lauren wasn't sure if he was mocking her or simply acknowledging her circumstances. Trouble was, she didn't like to think that he would want to hurt her.

She lowered the stirrup and rocked the saddle horn to make sure everything was secure, then ducked under the horse's lead rope to get the bridle.

"I'm sorry," Vic said as she passed him. Then, to her surprise, he caught her by the hand and turned her to look at him. "I shouldn't put pressure on you. It's just—I'm thinking that you're starting to like it here."

She suddenly found it difficult to breathe.

"I am. It's peaceful here," she said finally, fully aware of the callused warmth of his hand and how reluctant she was to remove hers. This was getting to be dangerous, she reminded herself even as she kept her hand where it was. The subtle connections between them were luring her into a place she had promised herself she would never go again.

"It can be," he said, his thumb making slow circles over her hand, making her heart speed up. "Winter can be harsh and wild, though. When the wind whips up snow and piles it into snowbanks, blocking off roads."

"I've never been here in the winter, except when I was a little girl," she said, her breathless voice struggling to find equilibrium.

"It has its own beauty, though," Vic continued. "Its own moments when the sun comes out and the world looks like an endless blanket of white."

His voice and the pictures he sketched with it were beguiling, and Lauren imagined herself tucked away in her father's ranch house, looking out over blinding fields of white, a fire blazing in the hearth, a book on her lap.

It's a dream, her practical self told her. A foolish dream. How would she survive? How would she make a living?

She tugged her hand free and pulled herself away from Vic. She hurried to the tack shed, and in the quiet and gloom she caught her breath and regained her perspective.

She was growing dangerously attracted to Vic.

She couldn't allow this. Letting another man into her life was dangerous. Her father. Harvey. She had known them longer than she had known Vic and they both had proved to be untrustworthy. No way could she allow herself to be vulnerable again.

But unbidden came the questions Vic had asked her when they were coming back from the greenhouse. Questions no one had ever asked her—why she did what she did. Why she was an accountant.

She was good at it. It was her job. Her dream to start her own business.

But even as she repeated the words in her head, standing in this tack shed, the scents of old leather and saddle soap and the musky smell of horse blankets stirred other memories of rides into the hills. The freedom she felt here.

The peace.

She shook off the thoughts, grabbed Roany's halter and took a steadying breath. It was losing her father, she thought, that was making her feel so nostalgic. So vulnerable. She couldn't let herself get all emotional.

And with that pep talk fresh in her mind, she stepped out of the shed and ran straight into Alex.

"Whoa, there," he said, grabbing her arms to steady her. "There's no rush."

She gave him a tepid smile, pulling back. "Sorry. I don't want to keep Roany waiting," she said, holding up the bridle.

"I guess we don't want antsy horses on our ride." Then, thankfully, he lowered his hands.

She walked over to Roany and felt a moment's hesitation. It had been many years since she had bridled a horse, but she knew Vic and Alex were watching and she wanted to prove herself competent.

Take your time, analyze the situation, then move with confidence.

Her father's advice returned to her. She took the headstall in one hand, the bit in the other, and with the hand holding the bit, inserted her finger and thumb on each side of Roany's mouth. She put pressure on his mouth, then he obligingly opened it and she neatly slipped the bit inside.

A few seconds later the bridle was on and buckled and Lauren felt in control of her world.

She led Roany to Alex, showed him how to get on, then returned to where Vic was buckling up Spot's bridle.

"Is she ready?"

Vic nodded, avoiding her eyes, and she wondered if he regretted that moment he had touched her.

As she mounted and followed Vic and Alex, she couldn't help but think how Alex's touch had done nothing for her.

But Vic's had left her breathless.

"From here you can see across the valley." Vic pointed out the Saddlebank River meandering through fields and groves of trees. "Just to our right, about two miles down, is where Refuge Ranch starts, and beyond that the Fortier spread."

The land spread out below them and Lauren rested her hands on the horn of the saddle, letting her eyes sweep over the vista with its varying shades of green. The shadows of clouds moved over the undulating land. She heard the trill of a song sparrow, the eerie cry of a hawk circling overhead. And blended through it all the occasional lowing of cows.

An unexpected tranquility came over her and a peculiar happiness followed.

"I always loved coming up here," Lauren said to Vic, drawing in a cleansing breath and releasing it slowly.

"It's a beautiful view."

She glanced over at Alex, but he was frowning at his phone, reading something on the screen.

"The land goes right down to the river, doesn't it?" she asked, turning back to Vic.

"Some of the richest pastureland is right along the Saddlebank River. And it can carry a lot more cows than it does, but your dad would've needed more help to run them all. It's a great ranch, lots of potential."

Lauren was surprised at the admiration in Vic's voice. The way he leaned forward in the saddle, as if getting a better look at what lay below, showed a connection to the land that she envied. He was rooted here. He belonged here.

"What would you do with the ranch that my father didn't?" As soon as she asked the question, regret flashed through her. As if she was encouraging him to verbalize dreams that would never take place now.

But Vic smiled and pointed to the land below. "I'd break that pasture along the river and turn it into cropland."

"Wouldn't that leave you short on pasture?"

"The ranch isn't running to capacity. I've been holding back heifers to increase our herd over time. And when I get to the herd size I want, I would break the existing pastures into smaller ones and utilize rotational grazing to get more out of them." He glanced over at her and then gave her a laconic look. "But I guess that's all just a dream now, isn't it?"

Lauren didn't look away as regret and second thoughts scrabbled at her. She wanted to apologize, but that seemed moot. "Do you have the same view from your place?"

"No. Our ranch is on the other side of the road."

"It's beautiful, isn't it, Alex?" Lauren avoided Vic's eyes, glancing over at Alex, but he was still busy with his phone.

She felt a moment's irritation and he must have sensed it, because he suddenly glanced over at her and slanted her a sheepish grin. "Just checking with my partner. He's shifting some stocks for me."

Lauren only nodded, recognizing his need to keep his finger on the pulse of his business.

Something she'd been neglecting the past two days. This morning she'd checked her phone and seen four text messages from Amy. She'd quickly answered them but left her phone in the house when she went out to help Vic.

She didn't want to be distracted on this ride, and she didn't want business to intrude.

"So, tell me some more about the ranch," Alex asked, dropping his phone back into his shirt pocket.

"This ranch can carry about eight hundred cow-calf pairs," Vic was saying, "and it currently has about four hundred acres in hay, which I was thinking—"

"What about the horses we saw on the yard? Would they come with the ranch?" Alex asked, interrupting Vic, turning to Lauren.

"I don't think so," Lauren said, shifting gears with Alex's change in topic. "Jodie and Finn have been working with the horses, and I believe Finn wants to move them to his place when the ranch sells."

Jodie had been adamant that the horses not be sold with the ranch, and Lauren could understand her objections. They had good bloodlines. Her father had invested more money in the horses than in cattle, and Jodie and Finn were hoping to breed some more horses and train them.

"Too bad. Maybe I should talk to him. See if he'll sell me some. Be a good idea to have some horses available for when me and my friends come and stay here." He turned back to Vic. "How hard would it be to get some cabins built? Who could I talk to about that?"

"Jan Peter is a contractor based out of Saddlebank. He does good work," Vic said. "My brother works for him."

"Where would be a good place to build them? I don't know if I want to have guest cabins right on the main property."

"There is another yard site farther down the road," Vic said. "It used to be a separate ranch before Keith's father bought it out. There's an older house there. It has power and a well. That place could work."

As Vic spoke, Lauren had to dig back into her memory, vaguely recalling visiting another yard site to do some cleanup around a house. She and her sisters had wanted to go exploring inside, but their father wouldn't let them. They'd had work to do and there had been no time for fun.

When they were a little older, she and Erin had saddled up the horses and gone riding down there. But the door of the house was locked, and the curtains were drawn over the window, and they were too afraid to break in. Erin had always said that someday she was going to live in that house, tucked in her own corner of the world.

Guess that isn't happening now, she thought, the weight of other people's expectations hanging on her shoulders. But Erin had remained uninvolved. It was up to her and Jodie to make the decisions. If Erin didn't want Lauren to sell, she hadn't made that known to her.

"I'd like to have a look at that place, too," Alex said as he took out his phone again. But this time he held it up and took a picture. He fiddled with his phone some more and looked up at Vic and Lauren. Smiling.

"This place would be a great investment." He nodded with a satisfied grin. "Now, let's go see that other yard."

* * *

Alex drove away, his shiny truck roaring off the yard, and honked the horn once as if saying one last goodbye.

Vic pushed his hat back on his head, trying hard not to begrudge the guy his fancy truck, his easy talk of getting financing to close the deal. As if it was simply a matter of shuffling money from one account to another.

But what bothered him most was his attitude toward the ranch. As if it was simply an investment. Some place to park his money until it increased.

He hadn't made a firm commitment to buying the place, and Vic knew he was dreaming, but part of him hoped Alex would change his mind.

He glanced at Lauren, who stood beside him, one arm folded over her stomach. Her other hand twisted a strand of her blond hair around and around her finger as she watched the dust cloud Alex's truck left behind waft over the yard.

"You seem disappointed," Vic said.

"Disappointed? No. Not really. I think he got a good idea of what he's getting into."

"He didn't give you an offer, though."

"Not yet, but I'm sure he'll take it. He told me that it's the most promising property he's seen yet."

"He's looking at other places?" The thought ignited a tiny spark of hope.

"Just one other smaller ranch closer to Missoula. But he likes how this place is closer to the mountains. Likes how the land around here has increased in value."

Lauren and Alex had spent some time talking by his truck as Vic unsaddled the horses and brushed them down. He wasn't privy to that conversation, but he was surprised at the jealousy he felt when he saw Alex hug

Lauren, hold her by the shoulders and give her another one of his flirtatious smiles.

Then he kissed her on the cheek and the jealousy began smoldering.

Stupid, he knew. She was never going to be part of his future in any way. But there it was.

He glanced at his watch. He had a couple of hours yet.

"I was wondering if I could have one last look through Keith's papers," Vic said, looking over at Lauren again.

"Of course," she said. "There's a few folders I haven't gone through, and yesterday we finally cracked the password on his computer."

"Really? What was it?"

"Our names." Lauren gave him a wistful smile. "Kind of touching."

"He did talk of you girls often."

"He wrote us each a letter before he died," Lauren told him.

"A final goodbye?" Vic asked.

"In a way. Apologies, as well. From a man who wasn't the easiest father, it's been an adjustment to read his regrets laid out in black and white. This from a man whose mantra was never apologize, never show weakness." She laughed. The sun caught glints of light in her hair. "My aunt gave us a bit of his background, however. And it helped us see him in a different light."

Her words seemed to fade. "Anyway, let's go through the rest of the papers first, then the computer. Hopefully…" Again her words drifted off and he wondered what she meant by *hopefully.*

Hopefully they would find something that would help him?

Or hopefully they wouldn't?

He pushed both thoughts aside as he followed her into the house. They went directly to the office and started sorting through the last of the files she had pulled out.

Twenty minutes later all the files had been gone through. Nothing.

"So, I guess we'll try the computer next," Lauren said, pulling up a chair to the desk, sensing Vic's disappointment. "Like I said, Jodie and I checked it out but couldn't find anything. You might have a better idea of what you're looking for."

Vic pulled the chair he'd been using beside hers. As he sat down, a stock picture of mountains came on the screen.

"Dad wasn't the most organized with the computer, and it's kind of old and has never been updated. But Jodie and I tried doing a search of lease agreements..." While she spoke, her fingers flew over the keyboard, and when she hit Return, a small beach ball–looking icon showed up and spun away.

Finally another window showed up with a list of files.

"You can see that some of these are emails and some of them are PDFs and a few documents. We looked through all of them but couldn't find anything resembling an agreement. Some of them are searches he's done on the internet that he might have bookmarked, so it looks like he was putting something together."

Vic leaned forward, as if getting six inches closer would give him more insight into what he was looking at.

"Would you have any idea of any other search terms we could use?"

"'Rent to own'?" Vic asked, scratching his forehead with his finger, trying to drag up any references Keith might have made that could help.

Once again Lauren's fingers flew over the keyboard.

"You clearly know how to handle a computer," Vic said, unable to keep the admiration out of his voice.

"What?" Lauren shot him a curious glance. "I'm just typing."

"Well, my typing is of the biblical sort," Vic said.

Lauren gave him a confused look.

"Seek and ye shall find," he said.

She laughed and the sound echoed in the office. It transformed her features. She held his gaze a beat longer than necessary and once again Vic felt the attraction he sensed was growing between them rise up.

"Did you enjoy yourself this afternoon?" he asked, hoping he didn't sound as breathless as he felt.

"I did. I've been out a few times by myself, but I never dared go that far. Not on my own and not on such a long ride." She smiled. "It was wonderful to see the valley looking so lush and green. To see all that space. I forgot how big the ranch was."

"It's a good size." He wanted to make a comment about Alex having lots to work with but didn't want to bring him into the moment.

"I never asked my father much about the history of the ranch. But was it this large when he inherited it from my grandfather?"

"Yes. It was. Your dad didn't expand it. He seemed content to let it be."

"Aunt Laura said he wasn't a rancher at heart."

"It wasn't what he wanted to do, but maybe he felt the pressure…maybe he thought it was what he was supposed to do."

She stopped, looking suddenly troubled.

And Vic's mind shifted back to the conversation

they'd had when they were in the truck on the way back from the greenhouse. How she talked of her work as an accountant as something she'd fallen into. Something she had to do. When he'd asked her about her passion, it wasn't accounting that she spoke of.

This afternoon, working with the horses, riding the trail, looking out over the valley, he'd seen a peace come over her features that he'd only caught glimpses of before.

And he couldn't fight the feeling that whether she wanted to admit it or not, she belonged here more than she belonged anywhere else.

He took a chance.

"Is that what this accounting business will be for you?"

Leaning back in her office chair, she shot him a puzzled glance. "What do you mean?"

"Do you see it the same way your father saw the ranch? Something you feel you should do, not something you have a passion for?"

She sucked in a quick breath, her eyes growing wide, a blaze of anger flashing in her eyes, and he thought he had gone too far.

But then she seemed to sag back against the chair, her hands clutching each other, her eyes looking away.

"It's an opportunity…it's a good business deal…" But her faltering words didn't hold the same assurance as the first time she had spoken them.

It sounded like she was working hard to convince herself of the rightness of her choices.

Then she shot him a wary glance. "Please don't tell me you're trying to make me doubt my decision because it will help you."

Vic knew how it must look to her. His sowing of doubt in her mind could work to his advantage.

He shook his head and took another chance, reaching out to touch her cheek. "I'm wondering if you're making a decision with your head or your heart. And I'm trying to put my opinions aside."

"Well, you'd be the first man in my life to do that." The bitter tone in her voice caught him by surprise.

"What do you mean?"

She waved off his question. "Nothing. Doesn't matter."

"Were you talking about your father?" He knew he was prying, but he wanted to know more about her. To deepen the connection he sensed building between them.

He leaned closer to Lauren, his arm resting along the back of her chair.

"Him and, well…a guy I was engaged to."

The canceled wedding.

"His name was—is—Harvey," Lauren continued. She didn't look away, but he saw the tightening of her jaw. Clearly it still bothered her.

"So what happened?" He kept his voice low and nonthreatening, his fingers lightly brushing her shoulder in commiseration.

Lauren looked away, concentrating on her hands wound tightly around each other. "Plans changed."

Her vague comment only increased his curiosity. "In what way?"

She lifted her chin, her eyes now hard, and Vic worried he might have gone too far. Pushed too hard.

"He got a chance to move to London and he suddenly decided that he didn't want me to come with him. So a week before our wedding, he called it off. Jodie was with me when it happened." She shot him a frown. "She didn't tell you?"

"Guess it wasn't mine to know." Vic let his hand rest on her shoulder and gave it a light squeeze.

She sighed, her fingers unwinding from each other. "It happened two years ago. We'd been engaged for four. I kept waiting for him to commit. Kept pushing him to make a decision. He finally decided on a date, then he got this job opportunity." She paused, then shook her head. "I wasn't a part of the decision. He decided that he wanted to go on his own. Dropped me and—" She stopped there. "However, he only managed to reinforce a lesson that I learned the hard way from my father and my last boss."

"And that was?"

She tilted her head to one side, as if examining him, deciding what she should or shouldn't tell him.

"That I have to take care of myself. That no one else is going to do that for me."

Vic heard the steely conviction in her voice. He sensed there was more to the story, but he also sensed he wasn't going to get anything else from her.

At least not now.

But it gave him an insight into her need to sell the ranch.

"Well, you need to know that not all men are the same," he said, his hand still cupping her shoulder.

She looked at him. Really looked at him, her features softening as their eyes met. "I'd like to believe that. I really would." Her words were quiet, and as their eyes held, Vic felt the attraction growing between them.

Then he gave in to an impulse, leaned closer and gently brushed his lips over hers.

She didn't move. Just sat perfectly still. Had he misread the situation? But to his surprise and joy, she slipped her hand around his neck and returned his kiss, her fingers tangling in his hair, her mouth warm and responsive.

Slowly they separated and he laid his forehead against hers. Her breath was warm on his face.

He knew he had shifted much with this kiss.

Trouble was, he wasn't sure where it would end.

Chapter Eight

Lauren knew she should pull back. At least her logical self knew she should. But the part of her that yearned for Vic's presence kept her close to him, one hand on his neck, her other on his broad, warm shoulder.

Now what?

The question swirled through her mind and she wasn't sure what to do with it. Alex had just left with a promise to call her. Her plans hadn't changed and yet…

She drew away, her hands drifting down over his chest, her fingers trailing over his shirt, and then, reluctantly, she pulled back.

She didn't want to feel confused. Didn't want to feel vulnerable. Things were moving too quickly. Too much was happening at once. And yet all she wanted was for him to kiss her again.

She turned away, swallowing down her misgivings, focusing on the computer screen. "So let's try…" She cleared her throat and tried again. "Let's try that other search term you were talking about."

She typed in "rent to own" and again the spinning beach ball came up, followed by a list of files.

Lauren scrolled through these as well, slowly shaking her head. “Sorry. No documents, no PDFs, just a few internet searches he bookmarked. But I can’t find anything.”

“And you’re sure we’ve gone through all the papers?”

“I’m sure.” Lauren leaned forward a moment, then shook her head, looking again. “Sorry. Nothing.”

Lauren typed in a few more search terms, giving it a few more tries, but she couldn’t find anything. She wished she could. Wished that something would turn up.

After her ride with Vic and listening to him talking about the ranch, her doubts about her plans had been intensified. She wasn’t so sure she wanted Alex owning this ranch. Turning it from a working ranch into a vacation spot for him and his friends for only a few weeks of the year. Looking at it as strictly an investment that he could get rid of to another rich friend if the time was right. Though her father hadn’t wanted to be a rancher, she’d heard about the legacy of the Circle M. And seeing the place through Vic’s eyes gave her another perspective.

She turned her chair to face him, giving him a careful smile.

“I’m sorry, but I can’t find anything.”

He shoved his hand through his hair in what she assumed was a gesture of frustration.

“So, what now?” he asked, his voice taking on a hard edge.

“I’m not sure,” she said, surprising herself with her vague answer. When she first came to the ranch she’d been so sure of what she wanted.

But now?

"But I do want to thank you for taking me and Alex around on the ranch. I enjoyed it."

A vague smile teased his lips. "I'm glad. I don't know how much Alex enjoyed it, though. He seemed more interested in his phone than in what we were showing him."

"When you're running a business, you need to stay in touch." Which was a reminder to herself to get in touch with Amy. Find out how things were going with the business.

But not now, she thought, feeling a wistful sweetness at being with Vic. For the first time in a long time, she felt as if the cycles of frenetic activity in her life had been put aside. She felt she could slip through the day, enjoying the moments as they came instead of always looking ahead to the next one and worrying how it would turn out, tweaking, adjusting and shifting so it could.

"At any rate, I was thankful for the tour. It was fun to go out riding."

"You seemed comfortable around the horses," he said. "Maybe we should go out again sometime."

She grinned at the thought. "I think I would enjoy that."

Then he reached to brush her hair away from her face, tucking it behind her ear.

It was a casual gesture but spoke to a growing intimacy between them that she wasn't sure what to do with.

But for now, she didn't want it to end. His eyes seemed to smolder and she sat perfectly still, expectation humming between them.

His head moved a fraction, and before she could stop herself, she moved to meet him.

Then the porch door crashed open and a voice called out, "Hello? Anybody home?"

Jodie.

Lauren stifled a sigh of annoyance, then gave Vic a regretful smile.

"Guess my sister is back."

"Lousy timing," he said, his finger trailing down her cheek.

Then he pushed himself to his feet and grabbed his cowboy hat from the filing cabinet. "So, I guess we'll see each other around?"

"I sure hope so," Lauren said, standing up, folding her arms over her stomach.

"You coming to the rodeo on Friday?"

"Absolutely," she returned.

"I'll see you then." And the smile he gave her was like a promise.

"So did you and Vic find anything connected to that lease agreement he's been looking for?" Jodie asked later, after Vic had gone and Lauren had helped her cart in all the groceries and wedding stuff.

Lauren dropped the last of the bags on the kitchen counter and began putting the groceries away in the cupboard and refrigerator. "No. Unfortunately."

"Unfortunately. That's an interesting choice of words."

Trust her sister to pounce on a single comment and braid an entire conversation out of it.

"Unfortunately for Vic," Lauren amended. "I think the computer was his last hope at finding something to substantiate his claim."

Jodie sighed as she set a handful of shopping bags

on the kitchen table. "And did your guy Alex Rossiter come today?"

"Not my guy. Just the potential buyer."

It wasn't too hard to see by the grim set of Jodie's mouth what she thought of it, but as quickly as her grimace came, it left. Lauren felt again the weight of expectation and behind that, doubt over her decision. She knew Jodie supported her, but she also knew that the longer Jodie stayed here, the less inclined she was to sell the ranch.

Trouble was, Lauren felt the same. And the memory of Vic's kiss didn't help her resolve any.

"Did Vic get the haying done?" Jodie asked, moving on to safer topics.

"Yes. He did. He said he had to haul the bales back to his ranch, but that would probably happen next week."

"The garden is looking good," Jodie said as she unpacked the bags she had set on the table. "I love how they brighten up the place. You have a real knack for that. Makes the place look more like a home. I should get you to do some landscaping on Finn's place—my future home," she said. Her voice took on a dreamy tone that used to make Lauren feel a mixture of happiness for her sister blended with a touch of envy.

But now?

She reached up to touch her lips, as if to see if she could still feel Vic's lips on hers.

"I think that could be fun" was all she said. "Now show me what you decided on."

Jodie gave her a searching look, then a slow smile crawled over her lips. "You seem happier today. Was it because you spent the day with Vic?"

Lauren's heart jumped in her chest. She wasn't sure

she was ready to bring all this out into the open. Not sure she wanted to discuss with her sister the confusion that gripped her.

She knew exactly what Jodie would say and on which side she would come down on. Lauren knew she needed to make her decision on her own without any outside influence.

"I'm just glad that our tour with Alex went well" was all she said.

Jodie's smile faded and she nodded. "Of course."

Lauren felt like a fraud, but she couldn't talk about Vic. Not yet. Not when she didn't know herself what she wanted.

"So tell me what you found for the table decorations."

With a bright smile Jodie grabbed the first bag and pulled out a box of flameless candles. And then some fabric for table runners and a host of other items.

The wedding was being held at Finn's place. It was to be a small affair in December with a Christmas theme, but Jodie still wanted it to be classy, she'd said.

"We still need to decide what you and Erin are wearing," Jodie said. "And I wanted you to come with me to Aunt Laura's to make a final decision on the flowers. I also need to make a payment on that wedding dress we found."

"Too bad I didn't keep my dress. You could have worn it," Lauren said with a wry tone.

Jodie bit her lip and rested her hand on Lauren's shoulder. "I'm sorry. I keep forgetting that this is hard for you."

Lauren just shook her head. "I'm happy for you. Truly. And every day I'm away from Harvey I realize how wrong he was for me."

Mostly because she now had another standard by which to judge him. A man who, even though it put her in conflict with him, put the needs of his family first.

A man of integrity who was willing to help.

Who kissed her.

A flush warmed her cheeks and she looked away, frustrated that such a simple thing could create this reaction. She'd been kissed before. Nothing new.

But not by a man like Vic.

"Harvey was wrong for you, and though I'm so sad that he called off the wedding, better that than a divorce like Mom and Dad had to deal with."

Lauren turned a roll of ribbon over in her hands, trying to formulate her wayward thoughts.

"Do you worry if you're able to do this? Get married?"

Jodie grinned, but when she caught Lauren's eyes, she grew serious. "What do you mean?"

Lauren turned the ribbon over again, picking at the price tag with her index finger. "Mom couldn't manage. I couldn't. Your old boyfriend Lane dumped you. Erin claims she never wants to be married…"

She let the last of the sentence fade away as she thought of the most recent text she had received from her twin sister a couple of days ago. Talking about faithless men and how marriage was a farce.

Oh, Erin, what is going on in your life? Why won't you tell us?

Jodie took the roll of ribbon away from Lauren and took her hands in her own. "Of course I'm concerned. Getting married is a big commitment. I haven't had the best experiences with guys, either. But I believe in Finn and I especially believe that God has blessed our relationship. That's what holds us together. And the fact that I know that together we can go to God in prayer with the things that concern us. That we can hold hands and put everything in God's care."

Jodie squeezed Lauren's hands. "From what I hear about Mom and Dad, that didn't happen, and I know that Harvey didn't go to church. And Lane, well, he attended church, but I can't think of any time we prayed together. But Finn and I do. I think that's what makes the difference, and that is what helps me believe this will work."

Lauren held her sister's earnest gaze, sensing her conviction and recognizing the truth in what she was saying. "I know that you love him and that he is a good person..." She stopped herself, knowing that she had to be careful.

"There's a *but* hovering there, waiting to come out, except in your case it would be a *however*," Jodie said with a quick laugh.

Lauren gave her an apologetic smile. "Doesn't matter."

"Spill it," Jodie urged.

Still Lauren hesitated, knowing she would be showcasing her own insecurities if she continued.

"Please. You never said much after Harvey canceled the wedding and took off for London. I remember helping you cancel events, return stuff, sell your dress. I know it was hard for you, but you never complained at all."

"What good would it have done?" Lauren asked, putting the red ribbon she'd been toying with back in the bag. "It was over. I made a monumental mistake."

"What mistake? Dating Harvey?"

"Trusting Harvey." She shrugged. "I don't know if I dare let myself do that with any man again."

Jodie gave her a sympathetic look. "I can understand that. But trust is a major part of any relationship. And I can guard my heart and keep it to myself, or take a chance and trust Finn. And I have chosen to trust him. Because I know I can. Because I know Finn will do anything for me. Make a sacrifice for me."

Lauren was envious of her sureness, but as she listened to her sister, a cold reality unfurled.

"What?" Jodie prompted. "You look like you've had a major breakthrough.

"I just realized that none of the men who had been important in my life have ever done that," Lauren said. "None of them have ever made any kind of sacrifice for me. Not Dad. Not Harvey. Interesting."

"Interesting and kind of sad, isn't it?" Jodie said. "I could say the same thing until I met Finn."

Then Jodie got up and gave her a quick hug, pulling back and holding her shoulders. "When the right man comes along, I believe you'll know you can trust him."

"Maybe," Lauren said in a noncommittal tone. And unbidden came a memory of Vic driving her to town, helping her with her car.

She shook off the memory, knowing how dangerous it was. She had to stay focused on her plans.

"So where do you want to store this stuff?" she asked, gathering up the spools of ribbon and putting them back in the bag.

But that night she lay in her bedroom, staring up at the ceiling, thinking about what Jodie had said. Thinking about trust, reliving the day. Smiling as she thought of their ride up into the mountains, feeling her heart shift in her chest as she kept returning to that moment in the office when Vic kissed her and her world tilted.

You can't let yourself be vulnerable again, she told herself. *You can't let anyone else determine the direction of your life. You're in charge. Have to be.*

But somehow those words taunted her with their empty certainty. She thought of the sermon she'd heard on Sunday. How the pastor had spoken of how we want to control our lives and what a foolish notion that is. How little control we actually have.

And, at the same time, how important it was to place every plan we make in God's perspective and see it through the eyes of eternity. What will last, what will persevere?

And what will glorify God?

Lauren tossed over onto her side again. Was she being selfish? Was she focusing too much on the things of this earth and not seeking God first?

She turned onto her back, staring up the ceiling of the room that had belonged to her over two months of the year for nine years. She remembered the many dreams she had spun here. Dreams of being on her own, away from family and obligations, and trying to keep everyone happy.

Was it so wrong to want to take care of herself? Trusting other people to do so had been a huge mistake. She knew Jodie wanted her to keep the ranch, but Jodie didn't need it. Erin didn't seem to care. So it was up to her.

And Vic wanted it for his brother. Needed it for his brother.

But surely that couldn't be reason enough for her to give up on her own dreams and plans. Dean had Vic to take care of him. Whom did she have?

She closed her eyes and breathed out a prayer, the only thing she knew she could do right now.

Guide my decisions, Lord, she prayed. *Help me to make decisions that will glorify You.*

But even as she prayed, part of her held on to her own ideas. Trouble was, she wasn't entirely sure she trusted God, either.

Chapter Nine

Vic tightened the cinch on his horse, checked the rigging, rope and bridle. Once he was sure everything was secure, he adjusted the padded leather chaps he wore to protect his legs. Behind him he heard the clang of horses' hooves against the metal fences outside, the bawling of steers, waiting to be ridden.

The day was rodeo perfect. Plenty of sunshine and enough of a breeze to keep the bugs off the animals.

Ahead of him, he heard the crowd gathering in the stands, the country music echoing in the arena.

Ten minutes before showtime.

Then a sudden attack of nerves was unwelcome and surprising, as memories slammed into his mind.

Dean falling off the horse. The cry of agony as his leg got caught in the fence.

That one moment that changed everything.

Could he really do this?

Every time he rode out into the arena, he felt the responsibility of the care of the cowboys and the stock. But Lauren would be in the crowd this evening.

Distraction or welcome presence?

He paused before getting on, taking in the building's energy, the contestants gathering, the whinny of horses, the bellowing of steers and bulls.

The energy and the possibility that things could go well or go very wrong.

Help me be strong, Lord, he prayed, resting his head on his saddle before he mounted. *Help me stay focused. Help me to keep my concentration on what I need to do.*

Because knowing Lauren was in the crowd made a difference whether he wanted to admit it or not.

He drew in a deep, calming breath, the smells of dirt, horses and hot dogs bringing up older and better memories. Those were the ones he had to cling to, he reminded himself. The cowboys he rescued. The horses and bulls he got safely into the back pens. His unsung successes that were part of every rodeo pickup man's story.

"Vic Moore. Glad to see you here," a high-pitched voice called out.

Vic turned around to face a young man in his late twenties. Tall, lanky, his upper lip curved over a chew of tobacco, his black cowboy hat square on his head, wearing a plaid shirt and Wrangler blue jeans—Walden Proudfoot was the embodiment of a rodeo cowboy and one of the best pickup men in the business.

Walden slapped Vic on the shoulder, nodding his approval of his presence. "So glad you're working with me. I missed you."

"I missed being here."

"When I found out you were partnering with me, I knew I was in good hands."

Vic laughed, thankful for the confidence Walden had in him.

"How's Dean doing?"

"Still a struggle."

"He miss rodeoing?"

Vic shook his head. "He's never mentioned it." The focus of Dean's anger and bitterness seemed to be his disability more than his inability to ride broncs again.

"That's too bad. He was a solid rider."

"And what about you? When are you going to quit this game?" Vic asked, steering the conversation to a safer topic.

"I don't know. Hauling five horses around from rodeo to rodeo gets tiring and expensive. I'm done by the end of the season, but each time spring rolls around, I get the itch."

"It's in your blood or not," Vic admitted. "How's your brother Ziggy doing? Has he ever finished in the money?"

"Nope. Still a donator."

Vic had to laugh at the term given to cowboys who never made any money but kept competing. He asked after a few more friends who had ridden the circuit with them, swapped a few more stories about other rodeos.

And then a voice booming over the mic called out the individual competitors of the events. They each came out to stand in a circle facing the audience.

Vic rode out with Walden when their names were announced, cantering their horses around the arena, hats lifted in greeting.

He scanned the crowd, heard his name and saw a woman with dark hair, standing, waving both arms, cupping her hand around her mouth and whistling. Jodie.

What a character.

But it was the reserved blonde beside her who snagged

his attention. He inclined his head toward her and then, a second later, she was out of his sight.

Then the singing of the national anthem was announced. Two members of the drill team came out, cantering around the ring, the Stars and Stripes and the flag of the association following.

After the anthem was sung, the cowboys all ran out, and with a roar and a blare of music, the rodeo was underway.

Vic took up his position to the right of the bareback chutes, pulled his hat down, recoiled his rope and quieted his horse.

Then with a clang of the gate, the first horse and rider burst out of the chute.

The next hour was a combination of waiting, anticipation humming through him and his horse, and an eruption of action, watching, reading, pacing the animals, and getting the rider on the back of his horse and setting him down if need be.

Vic settled easily back into the routine, surprised at how much he had missed the excitement. The expectation. The sudden quick moves as he paced the broncs.

He switched horses when the calf ropers and the steer wrestlers worked from the other end of the arena, hazing the steers. He helped chase a few of them back to the pens and between times managed to catch a few glimpses of Lauren. She was leaning forward, watching, intent.

Just like she did everything else, he thought, shifting on his horse as he returned to his position while the horses were brought into the bucking chutes.

He wondered if she thought about the kiss they'd shared as much as he had.

The announcer called out the next event.

Saddle bronc.

The one that had put his brother in the hospital.

He shoved his hat down on his head and, as he usually did before any cowboy was ready to go, uttered a quick but sincere prayer.

Lord, help me to do my job, stay focused, and keep the cowboy and horse safe.

Then the cowboys holding the chute gate got the nod from the cowboy on the horse. The gate swung open and with a lunge the horse exploded into the arena.

Vic pulled his horse back to give the bronc room, watching as the horse bucked, keeping his attention on the rider and the movements of the horse. The bronc sunfished, spun, and just before the buzzer went, Vic and Walden rode alongside the horse to release the bucking strap and get the rider off. But Vic could see the rider was in trouble. His foot had slipped too far into the stirrup.

Vic's heart jumped; adrenaline kicked in. He signaled to Walden to take care of the horse as he came up abreast of the rider, now dangling down from the saddle.

Vic moved his horse in as close as he could get, trusting his horse to do his job while Vic did his.

"Grab my hand," he called out to the cowboy. He reached down, almost coming off his own saddle as his horse paced the bucking horse, not fazed by its tossing head and frantic movements.

The cowboy tried, but the erratic actions of the horse made it impossible.

"I got ya, I got ya," Vic called out in encouragement.

Then he leaned down again just as the bronc took a sudden turn toward his own horse, and he and the dangling cowboy were crushed between the two racing animals.

* * *

"What's happening? What's going on?" Lauren stood, leaning closer, watching the frightening scene unfolding below. All she saw were horses racing alongside each other, cowboys scattering as the horses came toward them. Vic was leaning so far over she couldn't believe he could stay in his saddle.

"The rider got his foot hung up," Finn was saying, his voice tense. "He can't get out."

The other pickup man was hauling hard on the lead rope to pull the horse back. He leaned back and snapped the bucking strap off the animal, but still the horses ran around the arena in a clump of legs and bodies.

"Where's Vic? Where's Vic?" Lauren wanted to run down and leap over the walls to help, even though she knew she could do nothing.

Her heart thundered in her chest. Her hands grew clammy. What was going on? Why wasn't Vic coming up?

Then another cowboy on horseback came into the arena, followed by a group of other competitors.

"Stay with him. Vic, stay with him," she heard Finn muttering over the fearful cries from the audience around her.

She couldn't watch, but she couldn't look away. It all happened so fast and yet it seemed it would never end.

Finally the horses slowed down and as they did, Vic sat up, his hand clutching the bright red shirt of the bronc rider, dragging him onto the back of his horse. While the rider clung, Vic reached down again and then, amazingly, the cowboy's foot was free. The saddle bronc gave a shake of his head as if to say this was all in a day's work, then trotted off, led by Walden, the other pickup man.

Lauren sat back on the bench, her heart still banging like a drum in her chest. He had come so close, she thought, remembering the sight of the horse's dangerous hooves flailing about, inches from Vic's head. It could have ended so badly.

Thank You, Lord, she prayed, pulling another breath. *Thank You for saving Vic.*

Everyone in the crowd cheered as the competitor slipped off the back of Vic's horse and raised his hat to the crowd.

Then limped off to the chute area.

Vic patted his horse and Lauren saw his shoulders come up as if pulling in a deep breath of relief. His head turned just enough, his eyes scanning the crowd, and then he seemed to see her. He gave her a quick nod and then turned his horse back, ready for the next competitor.

"That was too close," Lauren said, her hands pressed to her chest, her heart racing. "I thought Vic was going to fall off that horse. That was so scary."

"Vic's one of the best riders I know," Jodie assured her, putting her arm around her shoulders as if in support. "He knows what he's doing. See how he managed to get that guy off the horse? Bet he hardly broke a sweat."

Lauren nodded, knowing Jodie was right, but her terror surprised her. Watching Vic now, adjusting his rope and tugging on his gloves, settling himself in his saddle, he seemed the epitome of calm. A quiet center in the middle of the madness going on in the arena.

But her hands and knees were still weak, her legs still trembling.

Then she caught Finn's grin.

"That's rodeo," he said. "Ten minutes of prep followed by eight seconds of panic."

"The panic seemed longer than eight seconds," she said, her voice shaky.

"Vic was in charge the whole time," Finn assured her.

Lauren felt herself relax, but at the same time the depth of her reaction surprised her. Even dismayed her a bit. Vic meant more to her than she realized.

"He's good at what he does," Jodie said. "You don't need to worry."

"I wasn't…worried." But her heart wasn't slowing down, a solid testament to her concern.

"Well, you seemed worried." Jodie nudged her with her elbow. Then she got up. "But all this excitement made me hungry. I'm getting some fries. Anyone else want some? Lauren?"

"We just ate," Lauren said, giving her a frown.

"Soup and salad." Jodie wrinkled her nose and shot Finn a pained look. "Lauren made me eat carrot and chickpea soup and quinoa salad, if you can imagine. No bread. No dessert. I need a major infusion of starch and fat. You sure you don't want any?" she asked Finn.

Finn shook his head, as well. "I'm good. Had a delicious veggie burger at the Grill and Chill."

"You did not," Jodie said with an incredulous tone, giving him a poke.

"I did. Brooke told me she was going to get George to cook more healthy options and give people more choices on the menu."

"A veggie burger? My fiancé is eating a veggie burger? Can't believe George got convinced to do that."

"Brooke has some pull these days with him."

"Do you think she has enough to get him to pull an engagement ring out of his pocket?"

"Oh, goodness, not that soap opera again?" Finn asked, a pained note in his voice.

Lauren frowned at Finn as he rolled his eyes. "What soap opera?" she asked.

Jodie just smiled her indulgence at her fiancé, giving him a patronizing look. "He's talking about the ongoing relationship between Brooke and George Bamford. Owner of the Grill and Chill."

"Brooke Dillon?"

"Yes. Gordon and Brooke's romance has been years in the making. Everyone in Saddlebank has been watching it develop."

"I think I remember her. She's good friends with Keira Bannister, isn't she?"

"Yep. And I worked with her decorating for the concert last month."

Lauren couldn't help but feel some guilt at the mention of Jodie's concert. She should have come, but she'd been hanging on to her job by her fingernails, working late all the time to satisfy her boss, doing everything she could to keep her job.

Not that it had done her any good.

"Anyhow, it looks like things are on between them again," Jodie continued. "And I have to go get some fries before I faint from carb deprivation." Then she jogged down the stairs toward the concessions, her dark hair bouncing behind her.

Lauren smiled at her sister, then turned her attention back to the arena, thankful for the little interlude that helped settle her racing heart.

Vic was loping his horse around the arena, chasing the last bronc toward the chutes.

Then he turned his horse around, head up, as if he was looking for her.

Their eyes met and she felt a tingle. Then he turned and got ready for the next competitor.

A few more cowboys competed, and while they did, Finn explained some of the finer points of the event. How the cowboy had to be positioned when they came out of the chute. How they were marked for their spurring and how the horses were marked for their bucking.

"The combined points gives the cowboy his score," he said, just as another cowboy was bucked off.

Thankfully the following rides were less dramatic, though Lauren had to admit they were all thrilling. She cheered as hard as anyone when a cowboy made his eight seconds and called out her disappointment when one didn't.

But as interesting as the rides were, her eyes consistently shifted to where Vic was working. The flash and drama came from the cowboys with their decorated and fringed chaps, their dramatic rides and dismounts or dumps. But the entire time Vic and Walden rode along the edges of the area, swooping in on their solid and unfazed horses, coming alongside to help a cowboy off, chase horses away.

"I noticed Vic is riding a different horse this time," she said to Finn. "When he first started he was on a pinto horse."

"And he'll probably be riding a couple more before the events are all done," Finn said, leaning forward, his elbows resting on his knees, his program rolled up in his hands as he scanned the grounds. "Those horses get a good workout, and you need them fresh and alert. It's not uncommon for a pickup man to go through four or five horses over the course of the evening."

"They seem so calm," Lauren commented as she watched Vic and his horse, waiting at the end of the arena. "The horses."

"They have to be," Finn said. "But they also need a bit of kick to them."

Lauren was confused. "What do you mean?"

"They have to run alongside a snorty horse full of adrenaline and stay in charge. Not be afraid to push back if the saddle bronc or bareback bronc wants to challenge them. And they have to be able to do all that in a noisy arena with all kinds of other things going on and still respond to what the rider wants."

"Does Vic work as a pickup man often?" she asked, watching as he successfully roped a horse that wouldn't come back and led it around the arena toward the alley leading to the back pens. With a skillful flip of his wrist he got the rope off and was now coiling it up, his movements slow, unhurried.

"Only once in a while since Dean's accident," Finn said.

"Vic seems to blame himself for that," Lauren said.

"When a cowboy gets hurt, I think the pickup men always look back and wonder what they could have done differently. In Vic's case it was his own brother that got hurt. But from what I heard, I doubt Vic could have changed the outcome no matter what he did."

Then Finn nudged her with his elbow. "And why does this matter to you so much?"

Lauren knew the flush warming her neck and face was a giveaway, but she kept her eyes on Vic. "I hate to see someone take responsibility for something that they don't have to."

"Especially if his name is Vic?"

Lauren wasn't going to get pulled into that tangle. So she said nothing.

"I think he likes you," Finn added, rubbing his square jaw with his forefinger and giving her a knowing look. "And Vic's not the kind of guy to show his hand too quick. Not when it comes to women. Not since Tiffany."

Lauren pressed her hands between her knees, reminding herself that it shouldn't matter to her if he'd had a romantic past. She did, too, after all.

But she was also a weak woman, and the memory of Vic's kiss, the touch of his hand on her face, elicited emotions she hadn't felt in a long time.

"Who was Tiffany?" The question slipped out before she could stop herself.

"A girl that caused a lot of complication in Vic's life," Finn said. "She was dating Dean for a while. Then she dumped him, hoping to get together with Vic. She and Vic had dated a few years before that. She was in the arena the day that Dean had his accident. But she left right after that."

"Why?"

Finn shook his head, tapping the rolled-up program on his knee. "Vic wasn't interested in her after that. But between getting dumped and the accident, Dean became a bitter young man. And it kept Vic shy of women since then." Then Finn gave her a wry smile. "Until you."

Lauren swallowed down a surprising jealousy, but at the same time she felt a renewed flutter at Finn's insinuation. She wanted to brush it off and tell him he was crazy.

But just then Vic rode past. The event was over and he was walking his horse along the fence. And he was watching her.

She saw a faint smile on his lips, and her heart gave an answering beat. She had to catch herself from lifting up her hand in a wave.

"Next up, ladies' barrel racing," Jodie announced as she plonked herself down between Lauren and Finn. She carried a large cardboard tray loaded with French fries topped with a bright red mountain of ketchup. "And don't you dare touch my fries," she warned, glancing from Finn to Lauren.

"Trust me, the way you've bathed those in ketchup, I'm not tempted," Lauren said.

"So you got over your scare?" Jodie asked, popping a fry in her mouth.

"What scare?" Lauren pretended not to know what her sister was talking about.

"Oh, c'mon. When Vic dived down to get that rider, you turned as white as a marshmallow."

Lauren wasn't sure how to respond to her sister's teasing. On one hand it made her smile. She and her sisters used to tease each other mercilessly if there was any hint of attraction to any guy. Usually it became a chance to huddle up in someone's bedroom when Gramma was asleep. Or, when they were at the ranch, while their father worked the night shift.

They would giggle, analyze and rhapsodize, and either encourage if they approved or discourage if they didn't.

She knew Jodie approved of Vic. And that she hadn't cared for Harvey. Somehow that seemed to add another layer to her changing emotions for Vic.

"Oh, look, there's Aunt Laura finally come to join us."

"Where?" Lauren asked.

"Look for the fluorescent plaid shirt and pink shorts," Jodie said, standing up to wave.

And sure enough, there Aunt Laura was, making her way up the stairs, holding down her purple cowboy hat with one hand, a bag of popcorn in the other.

"Where does she find getups like that?" Finn asked as Aunt Laura slipped past the people at the end of the row. "I didn't know boot companies even made purple cowboy boots."

"Hey, Auntie," Lauren said, when their aunt joined them.

"Hello, my dear girls. And Finn," Aunt Laura said, giving Lauren a quick hug and Finn a salute with her bag of popcorn.

"How was your day?" Lauren asked.

"Not too bad. More lookie loos at the shop than buyers, unfortunately." Aunt Laura sighed, giving Lauren a nudge. "I should get you to make up some arrangements for me. I'm sure they'd fly out of the cooler. You have a knack."

Lauren waved off her compliments, then Jodie spoke up.

"The horse Finn trained is going to be competing next," Jodie said to her aunt. "You came just in time."

"Excellent. Is it competing on its own, this well-trained horse?"

Jodie gave her an arch look, catching the irony in her aunt's voice. "Yes. Sans rider. Finn trained it so well it can run barrels on its own."

"This I have to see," Aunt Laura said, folding her hands on her lap, winking at Lauren.

Then a woman sat down behind Finn, and as she leaned forward, Lauren saw a flash of blond hair and caught the scent of almond perfume.

"Hey, Finn, do you think your nag stands a chance against the one I trained?" the woman teased.

Lauren glanced back and grinned when she saw who it was.

Her distant cousin Heather also trained barrel-racing horses. Lauren guessed that Finn and Heather had some healthy competition going on.

"Hey, Heather," Lauren said, lifting her hand in a wave of greeting. "It's been a while."

"No kidding," Heather said, patting her on the shoulder. "I heard you were back in town. So great to see you. We'll have to catch up sometime."

"That sounds like a plan," Lauren said. The sight of her cousin brought back many good memories of times spent at the Bannister ranch.

"I not only think my well-broke and intelligent horse will do better than the one you took under your wing, I know it," Finn said, a challenge in his voice.

"You two do realize that someone has to ride these trained animals," Aunt Laura chimed in. "And that a good rider can make a poor horse compete better and that no amount of training can make up for a poor rider."

"Aunt Laura, shush," Heather said, placing her finger on her lips. "You start spreading those kinds of rumors and you'll put me and Finn right out of a job."

They all chuckled, then turned their attention to the first competitor. In spite of the teasing, they all cheered each competitor on as the girls went racing down the arena, guiding their horses around the barrels, leaning so far in that Lauren thought they might fall off.

"Sounds like the horse you trained is up next," Jodie said to Finn, giving him a thumbs-up as the announcer called out the name of the next competitor. "Here's hoping it doesn't balk."

"Don't even say that word out loud," Finn warned.

Jodie pressed her finger to the wrinkle above the bridge of his nose, then fluttered her fingers. "Frown, be gone."

And when Finn laughed and gave Jodie a quick kiss, Lauren felt another tinge of envy.

That's what she wanted, she told herself. What Jodie and Finn had. That easy give-and-take. She looked back at Heather and John, who were sitting close together, then at her aunt sitting on the other side of her. She felt surrounded by people she knew. A community.

She wanted this, too.

And what about your business? Isn't that what you really want?

Panic swirled up in her at the questions. She couldn't be wrong about the business, could she? Because if she didn't have that, what did she have?

She looked away from Finn and Jodie, her hands clenched as she glanced around the arena.

Then she saw Vic. Perched on the top rail of the fence by the bucking chutes to watch the barrel racing. He wore his hat pushed back on his head, his gloves in his hands, his elbows resting on his knees as he leaned ahead.

He looked over to where she was sitting and straightened, a smile slipping over his features.

Lauren felt a shift in her perspective. The hum of possibilities.

Did she dare put it all in this man's hands?

Chapter Ten

Vic led the last of his horses into the trailer, ran its lead rope through the metal loop on the side and secured it with a bowline knot. He gave it a tug to make sure it was solid, then walked around the horse, running his hands over its rump to make it aware of his position. The other horses whinnied, sensing they were headed home.

Vic jumped out of the trailer and as he grabbed the door, he saw a welcome sight.

Lauren, followed by Finn and Jodie, was walking through the dusty temporary pens toward him. Her blue jeans were snug, her white shirt loose and her hair hung around her face in a blond cloud, softening her features.

As did her welcoming smile.

"Great job tonight, Vic," Finn said as they joined him. "That catch was one in a million. It's probably all over the internet already."

Vic just grinned as he closed the squeaking back gate of the horse trailer and latched it shut. "I doubt that."

"You kidding?" Finn said, clapping his hand on Vic's shoulder. "I'm sure there were at least a dozen phones trained on you. You'll be a YouTube wonder."

Vic just laughed, looking past Finn to Lauren, who had hung back but was watching him.

Just like he was watching her.

"You bringing your horses back to your ranch tonight?" Jodie asked, tucking her arm through Finn's. "Aren't you working again tomorrow?"

"Just for slack. Devlin is coming in tomorrow night, so I'm off."

"Big plans for tomorrow night, then?"

Vic wished his eyes didn't slip toward Lauren, and when he caught Finn's smirk, he wished he had more self-control.

"Jodie and I should go," Finn was saying. "I need to go congratulate Adelaide on her win tonight."

Then they were gone, and Vic and Lauren were alone.

In the ensuing quiet, Vic felt suddenly self-conscious. Like some goofy teenager in the presence of his crush.

"That was quite something tonight," Lauren said. "The way you rescued that rider."

Vic shrugged off her praise, uncomfortable with his moment of fame. The young bronc rider had stopped him a few moments ago and given him an uncharacteristic—for a cowboy—hug. Then thanked him again and again.

"Just doin' my job, ma'am," he said, putting on his best *aw, shucks* attitude and voice.

"Well, you went above and beyond. Finn said you guys are the unsung heroes of the rodeo, and I guess you proved that tonight."

Her praise warmed his heart and his smile grew as their gazes held. "That means a lot to me."

"I was glad I could witness it." She took a step closer and then stood up on tiptoe and brushed a kiss over his cheek. "Your reward."

Vic caught her by the hand as she drew back. "That means more to me than the hug I just got from the cowboy."

"He gave you a hug? Hmm. I didn't know that was an option," Lauren teased. Then her expression grew serious. "I'm so thankful you're okay. That cowboy was lucky to have you around."

"Walden was there, too."

"I know, but you were the one who put your life on the line."

Her approval and admiration did much for his self-esteem even as he tried to minimize what he had done.

"So, are you heading home?" she asked as the horses in the trailer expressed their impatience by hitting their hooves on the aluminum sides.

"Yeah. I should get them out on pasture. And fed good for tomorrow."

"Well, I hope it goes well for you tomorrow."

"It would go even better if you agreed to go out with me tomorrow night."

She hesitated, and for a beat he thought he had misread her, pushed too far. Then she smiled and nodded. "That would be lovely."

"I thought we could go to Mercy. There's a new restaurant there, not too city, not too country. A good mix of both."

"So…champagne with the burgers," she said.

"Or soda with the oysters," he countered.

Her resounding laughter was like a cool breeze that washed over him.

"Great. I'll come by about five thirty to pick you up. If that's okay?"

"More than okay," she replied.

He touched her cheek with his finger, then swooped in and stole a quick kiss.

The flush on Lauren's cheeks was encouraging and adorable at the same time. He hadn't thought he could have that affect on her.

"I'll see you tomorrow," she said, her voice husky, her smile coy.

Then she walked away from him, but just before she turned down the alleyway where Jodie and Finn were, she shot a glance over her shoulder.

And gave him a smile that dived straight into his soul.

"Are you sure you don't want dessert?" Vic asked, reaching across the table of the restaurant and taking Lauren's hand.

She liked the casualness of it. The give-and-take of a comfortable relationship.

The restaurant was quiet for a Saturday evening, and she and Vic were tucked away in one corner. The lights were low, the music soft and candlelight cast Vic's chiseled features into shadow.

"I'm delightfully full," she said with a touch of regret as she glanced at the dessert menu lying beside her. "Though I have to say the pavlova cake and the lemon tart are tempting."

"We could split them?"

Lauren thought a moment, then shook her head. "No, thanks, but I will have some more coffee."

She wasn't ready to leave yet, to go back home and end this magical evening. At the ranch she was always reminded of what he might gain or lose and what was at stake for her and her future.

Here it was just her and Vic, with no decisions hanging over her head. She had shut her phone off to stop the increasing flurry of texts from Amy. She didn't want to think about anything but Vic.

"So Jodie was telling me that you might be doing the flowers for her wedding?" he asked.

"I might help out Aunt Laura."

"You girls used to work with your aunt in her shop, didn't you?"

"Mostly it was just me. Erin often had her nose buried in a book and Jodie would be upstairs in my aunt's apartment above the shop, plunking away on the piano."

Vic still held her hand, his fingers caressing hers. "That sounds great."

"My aunt's place was a small refuge for us. A place we could relax and be ourselves. Being at her flower shop brought back some wonderful memories."

"Any other good memories of being here?" Vic asked.

Lauren twisted her fingers around his, looking down at them as she combed through her thoughts. "I remember going for trail rides up into the hills with Dad a few times. He could be patient when he chose to be." She looked up at him. "Going riding with you on the ranch brought back some of those memories. Reminded me of how beautiful the ranch is."

"So it wasn't always horrible to come here every summer?"

A peculiar tone had entered his voice. As if he needed to know how she felt about being here.

"No. It wasn't. In fact, we had a freedom here that we never had at our grandmother's place. Dad would give us a list of chores to do and then either go off to work or do other things on the ranch. Once we were done with our list, we could do our own thing. A benign neglect at times, but I think he didn't know what to do with three young girls all summer. Sometimes the chores took longer than we wanted them to and occasionally, if we rushed through them, he would make us do them over again if we didn't do them properly."

"What kind of chores did you have to do?"

"Believe it or not, we had chickens. Had to gather the eggs. Brush and groom the horses. Put halters on them and lead them around to get them used to being handled. Clean the house. Do laundry. Weed the flower beds, but that fell mostly to me. Jodie had to practice her piano. Erin was usually in charge of making supper. She was the better cook." Lauren's mind sifted back to that time, old memories coming out of being on her own with her sisters, laughing and joking and teasing each other. And, to her surprise, they made her smile. Then she turned her attention back to him. "What kind of chores did you have to do?"

"I can tell you Dean and I had it much tougher than you did," Vic said, his fingers making light circles on hers. "We had heavy-duty chores. Hauling and stacking square hay bales, moving large round ones. Helping move cows. Tractor work. Some field work. Manly stuff."

Lauren laughed at his mock seriousness. "Are you and Dean close? Finn told me that when he lived with you after his father died that he loved being at your parents' place."

Vic's expression grew pensive, then he gave her a wry smile. "Dean and I were close. Until..." His sentence faded away and a pained look crossed his features.

"Until the accident?" she prompted.

"Partly. But mostly until Tiffany."

She'd heard about her from Finn and Jodie. Now she wanted to know more.

"Who was she?"

"A girlfriend we had in common." He pulled his hand away, crossing his arms over his chest, his body language fairly crying out *no trespassing*.

But Lauren sensed that things were changing between her and Vic. She couldn't let this go. She felt as if they were on the cusp of something important. And she wanted to know everything about him before she dared move forward.

"What do you mean?"

"I'd liked her, and we dated for a while. But she was more attracted to Dean. So we broke up and she dated Dean for a couple of years," he said. "But then things weren't working out for them. Dean found out that she wanted to go out with me again. She didn't like the life Dean was living. Partying, drinking. You know what he was like."

She did. Dean always drove the fastest, partied the hardest and talked the toughest. Those were many of the reasons why they'd talked Erin out of dating him when he'd asked her out years ago.

"Anyway, she got tired of it, so she said. She came to talk to me about him and in the process told me that it was me she really cared for. That dating Dean was a mistake." Vic sighed and shook his head. "I told her that she had to end it with Dean. That it wasn't fair to him. So she did. Trouble was, she told me she had done it the week before. So the night of the rodeo, she called me. Told me she was going to be in the audience. Watching me."

He shook his head. "Dean's horse was taking a while to settle down and I kept looking for her in the stands.

Then I heard her call out to me. I turned to look at her just as Dean's horse jumped out of the chute. It was in that distracted moment that Dean was injured."

"What happened?"

"He made a turn away from where I was. His horse made a spin, not a bad one. Nothing Dean couldn't have handled, but for some reason Dean lost his balance. His leg was crushed against the fence and caught between the bars as the horse pulled away."

Lauren winced, thinking of how close some of today's riders had come to the fence. "So you've always thought Dean's injury was your fault?"

"I should have paid attention. I shouldn't have looked when Tiffany called me."

Lauren heard the pain in his voice. The regret. Then something Vic had said caught her attention. "But you just said Dean could have handled the spin his horse gave him."

"It's not my job to assume that. It's my job to watch out for the cowboys. Always. And what made it worse was that Tiffany lied to me. She hadn't broken up with Dean the week before. She had just broken up with him that night. Right before he had to ride."

"How cruel of her."

"Not the best timing, but then, neither was mine."

"So in reality, Dean was even more distracted than you were," Lauren said.

"What are you saying?"

"Dean's frame of mine was probably worse than yours when he climbed on that horse. Just before he's supposed to ride, his girlfriend breaks up with him? He surely can't have had all his attention on what he had to do."

"Doesn't excuse my carelessness."

"Maybe not, but Dean's concentration should have been on his ride. I'm sure it wasn't. So most likely he wasn't performing the way he usually did. Even if you had been watching him the entire time, I doubt you could have prevented his accident."

The puzzled look on Vic's face told Lauren that he might not have considered this possibility before.

"When I saw you working today, I saw a man who was in charge. A man who knew exactly what he was doing all the time. The way you handled that cowboy caught up in his stirrup showed skill and foresight. You know what you're doing, and I don't think that one moment of distraction was the problem."

"So you're thinking Dean is as much to blame as I am."

"I'm not thinking it's a matter of who's to blame. I'm thinking the whole mess is a series of circumstances that were beyond your and Dean's control. It was an accident."

Vic sat back, frowning, as if mulling it over.

"I have a feeling that you and I are more alike than we realize," she continued. "I often felt guilty over what happened to Jodie—when she and Dad got into that awful fight and she injured her hand. I felt I should have been there to talk reason into both of them. But I wasn't and I doubt I could have. I think as oldest siblings we feel like we have to take care of our younger sibs. And if something happens, we think it's our fault."

"Maybe."

He didn't sound convinced.

She leaned forward, reaching out to him. "I don't think it's right of you to take all that on yourself. Tiffany doesn't sound like she's a real class act. No offense." She realized too late how catty and jealous that might sound.

A wry smile crawled across Vic's lips. "She wasn't the best choice for either Dean or me. My mother never liked her, which should have been my first clue."

"At any rate, I think you've been putting too much of the blame on your shoulders, when I don't think it belongs there."

Vic took both her hands in his. Squeezed them hard. "Thanks for saying that. I don't agree with you one hundred percent, but I appreciate the sentiment."

"It's not a sentiment. You're a good man and you take good care of your family. You can't let this one event that wasn't even your fault take all the good parts of you away." She squeezed his hands back.

Then, to her surprise and pleasure, Vic lifted her hands to his lips and pressed a kiss to each one. He gave her a tender smile, his eyes glowing in the low light. "I think it's time to ask for the check."

A small thrill shivered down Lauren's spine. "I think I agree with you."

A few minutes later they were walking out of the restaurant across the darkened parking lot. The sun had set and the overhead lights cast captivating shadows.

They got to his truck, but before he opened the door, Vic pulled her into his arms, his hand cradling the back of her head. "You're a special person, Lauren McCauley," he said, his voice all husky.

Lauren slipped her hands around his neck, her fingers tangling in his hair. Then they drew closer, their lips meeting in a warm, tender kiss.

They pulled back after a few moments, looking into each other's eyes.

"I'm glad we did this," Vic said. "Took some time for just the two of us."

"I think we'll have to do it again."

"Are you going to church tomorrow?" he asked.

"Yes." She smiled at the thought. "It's been a while since I've attended regularly, but I liked going last week."

"You mean you didn't always enjoy it?"

Lauren gave him a look of regret. "We went with my father because it was expected, which created some resentment."

"But you'll be coming tomorrow?"

"Yes. I will."

"Would you like to go out on a picnic? After church?"

"That sounds wonderful."

"Then it's a date."

Lauren smiled at him and contentedly laid her head on his shoulder, her arm slipping around him as she held him close. This felt so right, she thought, her head resting on the warmth of his chest, possibilities dancing through her mind. Tentative plans. Hopeful dreams.

You thought the same about Harvey. And you were engaged to him for four years. Can you trust this guy?

The insidious voice was like a serpent, wriggling into the moment. Lauren tried to ignore it, but she couldn't get rid of it completely. And as she drew back, looking into Vic's face, she felt torn. Confused.

Emotions she didn't want in her life.

Certainty and solidity. That's what she was looking for.

Could Vic give that to her?

She wished she could be sure.

Chapter Eleven

"That was delicious," Lauren said, wiping her mouth with her napkin, then folding it up and setting it on the paper plate.

"You do realize that'll get thrown away," Vic teased her, leaning back on one elbow beside her. He twirled a blade of grass between his fingers, a feeling of utter contentment washing over him.

They had come back to his place after church and he had packed up the truck and driven to a spot where he, his father, Dean and Finn used to go.

Few people knew about it, even though it was on Bureau of Land Management land. He wanted Lauren to see it. To fall in love with the land.

To change her mind about leaving?

He realized that if he were honest with himself, that was part of his reason. The other was he simply wanted to share with her something he enjoyed so much. To give her a small gift of peace.

"Force of habit," she said, brushing her hair back from her face as she continued tidying up.

Vic let her work, watching her, enjoying this small

taste of domesticity. She had taken off the gray blazer she had worn to church; the scarf she had around her neck lay in a silky puddle on top of it. The simple blue T-shirt she wore enhanced the blue of her eyes, and her jeans were a surprisingly casual touch.

"Oldest-child syndrome," he teased, reaching over and running the blade of grass down her arm.

"Something you're not suffering from right now."

"I never had to do the dishes. Woman's work."

She grabbed the napkin package and bopped him on the head with it. He sat up, caught her arm and pulled him to her, dropping a kiss on her lips.

"You're not playing fair," she said.

"I didn't know we were playing a game," he returned, slipping his fingers through her hair.

"All of life is a game," she intoned in a mock-serious voice.

"And it doesn't matter if you win or lose—"

"It's how you play the game," she finished for him. "I wish more people played by the rules."

Her comment came from nowhere and he wanted to challenge her on it. But she pulled away and put the garbage into a bag, then set it in the cooler they had packed the lunch in.

"Now that you're done," he said, getting to his feet, "I have something I want to show you."

Lauren sat on her haunches, her head tilted to one side. "That sounds intriguing."

"Come with me." He held out his hand and she gave him a coy smile.

"Can I trust you?" she teased him.

He thought of what Jodie had told him. About her ex-fiancé.

And he grew suddenly serious.

"Always," he said.

Her expression softened and her eyes were intent.

"You know, I believe I can." She put her hand out and he pulled her up.

Vic led her out of the clearing over a narrow, worn path. Tree branches slapped at them and he pushed them aside best he could. A few bugs followed, buzzing around their head. That, the faint rushing of water and their footfalls on the packed dirt were the only sounds in the stillness surrounding them.

"I can't get over how quiet it is up here," Lauren said, her voice lowered as if in reverence.

"I don't imagine you have much quiet living in the city."

"No. I didn't."

"Do you miss it yet? City living?"

She didn't reply and he glanced back again to catch her looking at him. "No. I haven't." Then she gave him a smile, and the glimmer of hope that had been ignited when she sat down beside him in church this morning grew.

He wanted to ask if she would consider staying in Montana, but he was afraid to hear her answer.

They eased down the narrow trail and then, as the sound of rushing water grew louder, he led her out onto a large, flat rock. Droplets of moisture from the water tumbling down over large boulders cooled the air, the water it fell into roiling from the force. But then as it flowed away from them, it settled into a quiet, deeper pool.

"This looks like something out of a movie," Lauren breathed, clinging to his hand.

"I spent a lot of happy times here," he said.

She hugged her knees, looking pensive.

"What are you thinking about?" he asked, sitting down beside her.

"I was just remembering today's sermon. How hard it can be to trust God and, even more, people, when trust has been broken."

"Are you thinking of your fiancé?"

"Very much *ex*-fiancé," she corrected, looking at him. "And not only him, but other men in my life."

Vic felt a shiver of apprehension, but at the same time sensed they were slowly moving themselves to a place of trust. Much as he didn't like to think of her with other guys, this had been her reality.

"I've heard the verse that Pastor Dykstra preached on before," she said, resting her chin on her upraised knees. "But it seemed to hit home today."

"'Trust in the Lord with all your heart and lean not on your own understanding,'" Vic quoted from Proverbs.

"I've spent a lot of my life leaning on my own understanding," Lauren said, her voice growing quiet, contemplative. "I always figured I was the one who had to be in charge." She turned her head toward him, giving him a wry smile. "Always had a hard time accepting help, let alone asking for it."

"I got that from the first moment we met."

She granted him an apologetic smile. "I'm sorry about that. I was feeling uptight. Tend to feel that way around guys I'm attracted to."

"That sounds encouraging."

She grew serious again. "Harvey did a real number on me—you may as well know that. I was going to marry him. I had made a huge commitment to him. And he broke that trust."

"Did he give you a reason for the breakup?"

Lauren released a harsh laugh. "He said he'd never really loved me. And, looking back, I believe that."

"Did you love him?" As soon as he spoke, he wished he could take the words back. He wasn't sure he wanted to know if she had. But more importantly, it wasn't his business.

But it is your business. You care for her. You need to know what she's dealing with.

"I thought I did. At first." Her quiet words rested lightly in the air. "We were supposed to be business partners. And I think it got hard to separate the two relationships toward the end. We spent more time arguing about business than we did talking about wedding plans. I think I knew the truth, but I was too afraid to act on it. I figured he was my only chance. He was my first boyfriend. I'd never dated much before that. I didn't think you could break up with a boyfriend, let alone a fiancé. I took the idea of being faithful very, very seriously."

"I have a hard time believing he was your only boyfriend," he said, brushing his fingers over her knuckles.

"It's true. I was kind of uptight and smart and nerdy, and I took on the burden of caring for my sisters and grandmother. I was always mature for my age, and I think guys didn't know what to do with that," she said with a light shrug.

He leaned in and gave her a kiss. Then another. "Then I have a lot to make up for, don't I?"

Her eyes crinkled at the corners as she smiled. "You're a special guy, Vic Moore."

Her comment was both encouraging and, if he were honest, not precisely what he hoped to hear.

Vic felt the precariousness of his own changing feelings. She was growing more and more important to him.

And he wanted her to know that.

So he kissed her again.

A shiver trickled down Lauren's spine as Vic's lips slowly left hers. Her lips grew cool and she wanted to kiss him again.

But she felt a warning niggling at her.

Men don't put your needs first.

Even as she looked into Vic's eyes, part of her sensed that this man was different.

She glanced down at her watch. She had promised Amy she would call her this afternoon. They needed to talk. Her plans for the future, which were once rock solid, had been shaken up by this man sitting next to her.

And she wasn't sure what to do about it.

"Do you need to go?" Vic asked.

"Sorry. I have to make a few phone calls this afternoon."

"Of course." He gave her a careful smile and she wondered if he sensed what those phone calls would be about.

He got up and started walking toward the path. She hesitated, looking at the pool, how restful it was, and yet it was a result of the turbulence of the waterfall.

Please, Lord, she prayed, *let me find my own place of rest. Help me to trust that You will watch over me and bring me where I should be.*

The drive back to the ranch was silent. As if each of them was lost in their own thoughts.

But all the way there, Vic held her hand. They exchanged the occasional glance, reinforcing what was growing between them.

She couldn't pass it off or ignore it anymore.

But she wasn't ready to face it head-on, either. The thought of putting her life into any man's hands… It made her tremble inside.

Lean not on your own understanding.

Could she trust God and believe, as the passage said, that He would direct her paths?

The thought of changing everything created a mixture of fear. But behind that lay an excitement and expectation she couldn't deny.

But which one would win out? She was taking charge of her own life with this new business venture.

Was it worth it?

The question seemed to rock her crumbling certainty.

Help me, Lord, she prayed. *I truly don't know what to do.*

"You okay?" Vic asked as he parked the truck beside her car. "You seem…pensive."

"That's a sensitive word for such a manly cowboy like you," she teased, taking refuge in humor. Deflecting and retrenching.

"I know how to use the thesaurus app on my phone," he said, his own tone light. Breezy.

She was comfortable with him in a way she'd never been with Harvey. And it was that, combined with her changing feelings for him, that was creating so much confusion in her life.

They got out of the truck. Lauren grabbed the blanket and Vic took the cooler. As they carried them up the walk to the house, Lauren looked past it to the corrals beyond.

"Is that Dean?" she asked.

Vic turned in the direction she was pointing, then abruptly stopped.

"That idiot is trying to get on that horse," he said, dropping the cooler on the sidewalk. "He hasn't tried to mount one on his own yet."

Lauren set the blanket down on the cooler and followed Vic as he jogged around the house. He skirted the edge of his mother's garden at the back of the house and headed to the corrals.

Just as Vic thought, Dean stood beside a horse that had already been saddled. His crutches leaned against the fence.

"Dean. Stop. Don't," Vic called out as he came closer.

Dean ignored him and, hobbling alongside the horse, led him to a box that stood by the fence.

"Let me help you," Vic said, climbing over the fence.

"Leave me alone," Dean called out. "I have to do this."

Vic walked over to Dean just as Dean struggled to get on top of the box. The horse shifted away from Dean, turning his head as if to see what was happening.

"You're distracting the horse," Dean called out.

Lauren heard the anger in his voice. And something else she couldn't identify. She was tempted to tell Vic to leave Dean alone, but she could also see from the way the horse was shifting around that Dean would need Vic's help.

Vic caught the halter rope and, moving closer to the horse, managed to get it to move sideways.

"You can probably get on now," Vic was saying.

But Dean didn't move.

"Dean?" Vic said, frowning at his brother.

"Why do you always think you have to take care of me? Why are you always fixing everything?"

Dean carefully stepped off the box and tossed Vic the reins. "I don't feel like riding now."

"But it would be so good for you," Vic said. "I think it's great that you want to go riding. I can help you make it happen."

Dean grabbed his crutches and fitted them under his arms. "I'm sure you can. But I need to do this on my own." He shot Vic an angry look. "There are some things in life you just can't fix."

He limped through the gate, then past Lauren. He gave her a cursory look, added a tight nod and headed toward the house.

Vic patted the horse on the side and, without another word, turned it around and tied it back up. With quick, sure movements he undid the cinches, slipping the saddle and blanket off the horse in one movement.

A few moments later the horse was unbridled and released. It shook its head, then moved to the middle of the pen, lowered itself to the ground and then, with awkward and ungainly movements, began to roll.

In spite of the tension that still shivered through the air, Lauren had to smile at the undignified sight.

And, thankfully, so did Vic when he came back from the tack shed.

"You goof," Vic said to the horse as he walked past it to open the gate. "You didn't even get sweated up."

"I've always wondered why they do that," Lauren said as Vic returned to her and climbed over the fence. It seemed easier to discuss the horse than to address what had happened between him and his brother.

"It's like scratching your back," Vic said. "Feels good."

The horse stood, shook off the dust, tossed its head at them and trotted off through the open gate to join the other horses.

Vic watched it a moment, his hands resting on the fence, then he looked over at Lauren. "Sorry about that. About Dean. I think he's just...frustrated."

Lauren nodded, acknowledging his comment but wondering if maybe Dean was right. She recognized the need to help. To jump in and try to fix. She had done it many times with her own sisters.

"You look like you'd like to say something more," he said.

He was too astute.

"It's okay," he prompted. "I've got thick skin."

"I'm an older sister and I know what you're trying to do," she said, choosing her words with care. "And it's wonderful that you want to help him, but I think Dean was right. He needed to do this on his own."

"He would have fallen and hurt himself," Vic said. "He's been doing so well with his rehab, I didn't want to see him lose all his progress with one stupid mistake."

"He was being careful," Lauren said. "He's a big boy."

"But what if..." Vic shook his head as if he understood what he was doing.

"What if he fell? He would get hurt. But I don't think he wanted to fall, so I doubt he would have taken any huge risk." Lauren stopped herself, realizing she was lecturing him.

Vic seemed to consider her comment. "I think you're right. I'm going to have to learn to leave things be with him."

Lauren laid her hand on his arm and gave a gentle squeeze. "Remember, it's not your fault, what happened to him. You don't have to work overtime to make up for it."

Vic gave her a grateful glance. "I suppose," he said. He cupped her face in his hand and she thought he was about to give her a kiss when her cell phone rang.

She looked down at the screen and her smile faded away.

It was Amy.

"I better take this," she said, holding up the phone.

She touched the screen, accepting the call as she walked away from Vic. But as she lifted the phone to her ear she heard nothing. She was too late.

A momentary reprieve, she thought, noticing that a text message had come in while her phone was ringing.

It was from Alex Rossiter.

Events and decisions were crowding in on her. She needed to make choices soon.

But as she turned back to look at Vic, she knew she couldn't put off her decisions any longer.

Chapter Twelve

"So, how was your date?" Jodie asked as Lauren dropped onto the deck chairs Jodie and Finn had found tucked away in one of the garages.

From her seat Lauren could look over the flower beds that now held splashes of red and purple, yellow and blue.

There were buds on the lilies, and though Nadine at the greenhouse had told her to cut them off, she had kept the flowers on. Next year they would bloom even more.

Next year.

I want to be here next year.

"You've got your thinking face on. Was the date that bad?" Jodie sat up, dropping her bare feet onto the wooden deck with a thump, her blue eyes wide. "Don't tell me—"

"The date was fantastic, if you must know, and that's all I'm going to tell you." Lauren held up her hand to forestall any further questions from her sister.

"So, what's making you look so serious?"

Lauren kicked her shoes off and tucked them under her, leaning back in the chair, her eyes sweeping over the yard. Beyond the barn she saw fields rising to hills rising to mountains, purple edged against a sky slowly turning pink as the sun set.

"It's beautiful here, isn't it?" she said.

"Yeah. It is." Jodie inhaled a deep breath, then blew it out. "And you're thinking of moving back to the city. Living the dream."

"I don't know if I've ever thought of it as the dream," Lauren said. "I think owning my own business with Amy was a means to an end."

"The end being independence."

"Sounds kind of empty now, doesn't it."

"It is. Independence is overrated. You can't tell me that you'd prefer to own your own business, live in an apartment downtown and head off to work in an office every day. Wearing high heels? Every day?"

Lauren chuckled at the disgust in her sister's voice. "I can wear flats, too."

"Is that what you want? Compared to this?" Jodie swept her hand out, encompassing the view.

Lauren shook her head. She didn't.

"Then can't you stay?"

"I want to," she whispered, thinking of Vic and what they had shared. His love for his brother. His solidity. "But what would I do here? I wouldn't have my own life."

"I know that's important to you."

"You have your music, your composing. You have your own place and a future with Finn."

"You could start an accounting business here."

"Maybe. But I would have to start from scratch."

"Would you want to do it? For Vic?"

"The idea of making that kind of sacrifice for another

man scares me to death. I did it with Harvey, and while I know Vic is nothing like Harvey…"

She let the sentence drift off, knowing that Vic was ten times the man Harvey was.

"I know exactly how this works," Jodie said, pulling her chair closer and taking Lauren's hand in hers. "Finn made me nervous, too. But I learned to trust him. Vic is a good guy. I know you can trust him."

Lauren nodded, her head doing battle with her heart.

"What's going on behind that cool, calm facade of yours?" Jodie pressed.

"Obligations. Promises. And the fact that what Amy and I are planning gives me control over my life."

"You know that none of us ever can control our lives," Jodie said. "I had to learn that lesson long ago. So many things come along that can toss over that particular apple cart."

Lauren heard the wisdom in her words.

"But here, in Saddlebank, you have a community you can be a part of. A church that's dynamic and welcoming. You have me and you have a man who, I believe, truly cares about you."

"Maybe," was all she said.

"I've seen a real change in you since you've come back," Jodie continued. "You seem more relaxed. Less uptight. You've lost that frown line between your eyebrows, and your mouth isn't as pinched. I've seen you smile more the past few weeks than I've seen in a long time."

"I am happier," she admitted, giving her sister one of those smiles that did come easier than they had before.

"And you look happier now than you did with Harvey." Jodie gave her a pensive look. "I sometimes wonder if you really loved him."

"I've wondered the same thing." She toyed with her sister's engagement ring, turning it so it caught the sun, emitting sprinkles of light. She'd had a ring just like it. In her mind it represented success and security, but it had all been a lie. "I think Harvey became a habit after a while. It was easier to stay with him than to think about what my life would be like if I left him."

"And Vic? How do you feel about him?"

Lauren's heart turned over in her chest as thoughts of Vic overshadowed the vision of independence she'd carried with her since getting laid off.

"I care about him more than I want to think about," she said. "He makes me feel like I want to be a better person."

Her phone rang, and with a feeling of anticipation she reached for it. Vic had asked her to text him when she got home. Just to make sure she made it safely, he had said with a teasing grin.

But as she glanced at the screen, her heart dropped. It wasn't Vic. It was Amy.

"I've got to take this," she said as she got up. "I missed her last call. Please excuse me." But as she walked into the house, she realized that at one time texts and calls from Amy about their plans had created a sense of excitement.

Now they created a sense of dread.

"Well, I guess that's the last of it." Vic leaned back in the office chair, tamping down his fear as they set the file containing Keith's personal papers aside.

Though nothing had emerged from the last few times

he was here, he'd felt an urgency to try one last time. The problem was now he wasn't only looking to protect his interests in the ranch—he was hoping to give Lauren a reason to stay.

After their last date, he felt even more strongly than before that Lauren belonged here. He just wished he could convince her of that.

"I'm sorry we couldn't find anything," Lauren said, reaching over and turning the computer off.

"Me, too." He glanced at his phone lying on the desk as the time registered. "And I gotta go. Dwayne is coming to pick up your dad's truck."

"It's still at your ranch?"

"Yeah. Since your father's accident."

He pushed up from his chair, fighting to resign himself to that reality. He held his hand out to her to help her up and she took it. She stood in front of him now and lifted one hand, resting it on his shoulder.

He studied her features, wondering what she would say if he asked her to stay, knowing that if he did, he was heading down a one-way path himself.

Because asking her to stay meant sticking his neck out.

The last time he had done that, with Tiffany, the results had been disastrous.

That wasn't your fault.

And yet, he felt as if his pushing Tiffany away had been the flashpoint that turned his and Dean's lives around.

He didn't want anything to happen with Lauren. He wanted her to decide for herself.

"You look like you've got heavy things on your mind," she said as her phone buzzed yet again.

It had been ringing all morning, but she'd ignored it. He knew things were coming to a head.

"Are you going to get that?"

She shook her head.

He fought down a sudden beat of frustration. "I'm sure Alex doesn't appreciate being strung along like this."

She gave a noncommittal nod.

"Are you going through with the ranch deal with Alex?"

"I don't know."

"What about us?"

"Us?" Her frown wasn't encouraging, and it didn't help his growing frustration, either.

"I thought there was an *us*. I though we were moving toward that."

"I think we are—"

"Think?" He took a step back, the words he wanted to speak clogging up his throat. "You *think* we are? After all what we've shared? I *know* we have something special."

The anger in his voice masked the fear that she was considering leaving.

"I did. I really did."

"Did." He pounced on that word. "So what happened? I thought we were creating a relationship, you and me."

"I'm sorry," was all she could manage.

His fear grew, which only stoked his anger more. "Sorry. What does that mean?"

"It means I'm sorry."

"For what? For spending time with me? For leading me on? For making me think that something was happening between us?"

He knew he should stop, but he rushed headlong, heedless, afraid.

Then he saw a spark of anger kindle in her eyes, saw her lips thin, her hands clench.

And he knew he had pushed her too hard.

His anger was a surprise and, at the same time, it ignited hers.

How dare he accuse her of leading him on?

She straightened to her full height. There was no way she was going to let him have the advantage of height, towering over her in his anger.

Though in spite of that, she still had to look up at him.

Still had to look up into those eyes, which only a few moments ago had looked at her with such affection, but now were narrowed in antagonism.

"I was never leading you on," she shot back, still trying to figure out how things had shifted so quickly.

"So something was happening between us."

"*Is* happening." The words slipped out and she could see from the way his expression shifted, he had caught it, as well.

"Then why is Alex still texting you? Why are you taking a job I'm sensing you feel obligated to? Is it the money?"

"That helps."

"So that's what this all comes down to?" He released a short laugh and her back stiffened.

"You know, it's so easy for you to judge me," she said, trying to keep her own rising emotions under control. "You have a mother who cares about you. People who you matter to you. You've probably never had to scrabble for your next dollar."

"I can't imagine you doing that," Vic said. "You've had a good job for many years. Don't tell me you haven't managed to save up."

In spite of her resolve, her anger grew. "Okay, I won't tell you how Harvey smiled at me, all the while bilking thousands out of the joint business account that took us years to set up. An account that he emptied in days. How I thought I trusted him and as soon as he had a choice between work and me, he chose work and he took our money. You know, he not only left me at the altar. He left me flat broke. It's not something I'm proud of. Not something I let anyone know. I'm supposed to be so smart, so good with money, and some lying, sneaky… man took everything from me. You talk about buying this place, and while I'd love to sell it to you, I told you that I can't afford to. I need every penny of it to pay for this business."

"Which you're still leaving to run."

How could she explain to him what this meant to her without making it look as though she wanted to leave him? She wanted the security and independence of her own business, but she wanted him, too.

But she couldn't have both. Choosing the business meant losing him. Choosing the ranch meant losing herself.

"What about Jodie? And Erin? You seem to be able to make your decisions in your own little world."

"Because that's what I learned," she shot back. "All my life I've had to be in charge. When we left this ranch, my mother was a wreck. We moved into my grandmother's house on sufferance. I had to take care of my sisters because my grandmother barely tolerated us. After my mother died, even more so. We were shunted here in the summer to give my grandmother a break. My father didn't know what to do with us so, once again I was in charge. When my grandmother got sick, guess who took care of her? Even Harvey required sacrifices from me. Saving money so we could build up our business and our future together. I've given everything I have to give to everyone I've ever known."

Her voice caught as the humiliation of that crashed in on her again. But she wasn't going to let that determine her future. "All of my life it's been about other people. Taking care of everyone else. Watching out for everyone else."

She drew in a slow breath, her anger slowly easing out of her. "Just for once, I'd like to think of me. Make a decision for me."

Though he held her angry gaze, his own eyes narrowed, she sensed a shifting in his attitude. As if he was at least considering what she had to say.

And just then a muffled ringtone sounded in the office.

She pulled her cell phone out of her back pocket and glanced at it with a sigh of resignation. "It's Alex."

"Of course it is." Vic drew back, and anything she thought she'd seen there was replaced with an icy stare. "Then I better go."

He gave her a curt nod, grabbed his hat and dropped it on his head as he spun on his heel.

Then he left.

Chapter Thirteen

"Hey, Alex, what can I do for you?" Lauren said, wearily dropping into her father's office chair. Her hands were still trembling from her fight with Vic.

How had things gone so badly so quickly?

He was pushing her. He wanted a decision and she wasn't ready to give it to him.

She pressed her fingers against her temple.

"You've been hard to get hold of," he said. "You sure you still want to do this deal? 'Cause you seem to be less than enthusiastic." He sounded testy and Lauren wondered if he would back out. The idea created a sliver of fear. But behind that was a surprising sense of relief. If Alex didn't buy the ranch…

Amy would be left hanging. And her own plans would change. Everything she'd been working toward would disappear. Swept out of her life.

She thought back to the fight she'd just had with Vic. The angry words she'd thrown at him.

How she'd told him things she'd never wanted to reveal.

He had goaded her into it, she told herself. Pushed her into a corner.

"I still want to make this happen," she said. "But I'm curious, would you run it as a ranch? Would you be willing to lease it to Vic?"

"I could care less one way or the other. To tell you the truth, buying the ranch is just a way to dump some money," Alex said. "More of an investment for me than anything."

An investment. Jodie's words about Alex returned and Lauren wondered why it mattered.

But it did. Vic had long-term plans for this place. He would nurture it. It was part of the Saddlebank legacy. Refuge Ranch had just celebrated 150 years of continuous ownership. That was a huge feat in this day and age. There was history in this place, she thought, leaning her elbows on the desk, looking out the window over the land that had been cared for and nurtured for generations of her father's family.

And your family.

"Anyhow, gotta run," Alex said. "My people will talk to your people in the next few days." And before she could say anything, he hung up. Off to another business meeting, amassing more money to invest in other properties.

Then she had something else that needed her attention, because her phone had beeped while she was talking to Vic.

Amy. Sending another text. Wondering what was going on.

The pressure of other people's expectations dragged her in so many directions. Vic. Alex. Amy.

Maybe she should let Vic purchase the ranch. Maybe she and Amy could make a lesser offer on the business. Get creative about financing for the rest.

So you can move to the city and live the dream?

The thought, once so enticing, now seemed empty and depressing.

As the thought of leaving Vic, of not having him in her life, registered, she felt a sharp, dull pain beneath her breastbone. Sharper than any pain Harvey had ever dealt her.

She closed her eyes, pressing her hands to her face.

Help me to trust, Lord. Help me to know what to do. Help me to see You as my all in all.

The passage from Sunday alighted into her mind.

Trust in the Lord... He will direct your paths.

But the thought of letting go of all her plans still spooked her. Made her feel untethered. Lost. She had hitched her wagon to other men's stars before and had been left hanging. Been disappointed.

Vic is not Harvey. He's not your father.

Confused and frightened, she grabbed her phone and dialed Amy's number.

"Thank goodness you called, girlfriend," Amy said, breathless. "I've been getting all panicky. The sellers have been putting major pressure on me. How are things progressing on the sale?"

"I just talked to Alex. He still wants to go ahead."

"That's great news. Did he give you a date for closing the deal? We're going to need those funds soon."

"No. I have to talk to my lawyer." She let her eyes scan over the land. "I just wish Alex didn't see it as only an investment. I wish he wanted to see it run as a working ranch."

"What do you care about that?" Amy asked. "You just want the money."

Did she? Really? Was the ranch that disposable to her?

Once again she wished she could talk to Erin. Really talk to her. Not just terse text messages. Find out where she was. But the last phone call she'd had with Erin was a brief conversation about how things were going. Erin hadn't wanted to know about the ranch. She'd just said that she'd be fine with whatever they decided.

And while Lauren knew how Jodie felt, she had been surprisingly supportive.

"Speaking of money, do you think the sellers would take a lesser offer?" she asked, floating the idea. "I was thinking we could talk to the bank and increase our long-term loan."

"Why are you talking about this at the last minute?" Amy said. "You know we went over and over this. We'll need every penny from the sale of the ranch to add to what I've got to make this work. The bank will only carry us for so much. And that's thanks to your credit rating."

Lauren once again felt the sting of Harvey's betrayal. The disgrace of having her credit rating go from stellar to ugly with a few swipes of an already overcharged credit card that he had neglected to tell her about. A card in both their names that he had maxed out and then left her responsible for.

"You can't back out now, friend," Amy warned. "You just can't. You know how much this means to me."

"I'm not backing out. It's just…"

"You've been sounding weird the last few calls," Amy said. "Is there something going on that I need to know about?"

Vic, Lauren thought, pressing her fingers against her temples. Vic's need to take this ranch on.

"You're not thinking of backing out, are you?"

Lauren hesitated.

"You know you owe me, Lauren."

And there it was. The card that Amy had said she would never play. The debt was finally getting called in.

"I know." Lauren was quiet, thinking of those darker days. After Harvey had left her and she'd had less than nothing, Amy had taken her in. Had given her a place to live and told her it didn't matter that she was unable to make rent. Jodie had been dealing with her own stuff and was unable to help out. And she couldn't go to Erin.

But Amy had been there every step of the way, letting her stay while Lauren paid off the credit-card debt Harvey had left her with.

Though she'd managed to repay Amy most everything, she could never repay her kindness. Now the piper needed to be paid, Lauren thought.

"This isn't because of this guy, is it?" Amy asked. "This guy who wants to buy the ranch instead of Alex?"

Lauren's wants and needs fought with each other in her head. "He's got good plans for this place. He wants to buy it for his brother."

"Are you falling for this guy?" Amy said, a faintly accusing tone in her voice.

Lauren wanted to deny it, but she couldn't. Because she knew she was past that point. In spite of the angry words they had traded just a few moments ago, she knew she was far more connected to Vic than she wanted to admit.

The anger he had thrown at her hurt. If he hadn't mattered, his words couldn't have wounded her so deeply.

"Girlfriend, do I need to remind you of how lost you were after Harvey dumped you? How I would listen to you talk about your dad? And your last boss? You know what they all have in common? They're guys. And you know better than anyone that you have to take care of yourself. That you can't count on a guy to do that for you."

Her words flew at Lauren, striking with deadly accuracy, resurrecting insecurities that still hounded her.

"I know I do. And you know how grateful I am to you for everything." Still she hesitated, torn by her conflicting desires.

I thought we were moving to an us.

Her heart stuttered as his words resonated in her mind.

She pressed on. "Please talk to the bank anyhow. See if they can work with the numbers I'm going to text you. Just float it past them."

"Okay. Just so you know, if they decline, we're still a go, correct?"

"I understand."

"Stay the course," Amy reminded her, repeating words that Lauren had often lobbed her way when they were making these plans. "No guy is worth sacrificing your independence for."

They said goodbye, then Lauren tossed her cell phone on the desk, spinning her chair around, a reflection of her own mind.

Stay the course. No guy is worth it.

She pushed herself out of her chair. She needed to get out of here. To think.

She strode out of the house, got in her car and headed out. She didn't know where she was going. The only thing she knew was that she had to get away.

Clear her head.

* * *

What had he done?

Vic slammed his hand on the steering wheel, frustrated and furious with himself.

He always prided himself on being even-keeled and steady. The sudden flashes of anger and fury had always belonged to Dean.

But this?

He groaned aloud as he relived the things he had said to Lauren. The pain he might have caused.

It was fear that drove him to it, he told himself. Fear that things were coming to a head.

Fear that he would lose Lauren.

He wanted to call her and apologize.

For what?

Telling her how he felt? Laying out what he had hoped was happening?

Unconsciously he reached in his pocket to get his cell phone.

But his pocket was empty. He dug in his other shirt pocket, then he remembered. The last time he had used his phone was in Keith's office at the Circle M Ranch. He must have left it there. He stopped the truck and drew in a deep breath.

Though he didn't want to go back, maybe this was a chance to make amends for his behavior.

He turned the truck around, gunned it and headed back.

Lauren's car was gone when he arrived, which gave him a mixture of relief and regret.

No second chances here.

And though he knew no one was home, he still

knocked on the door, then he stepped into the house, an echoing silence greeting him. Then he heard a faint ding.

Notification that a text message was coming in on his phone. Probably Dwayne telling him when he was coming to pick up Keith's truck. He followed the sound back to the office and saw his phone sitting on the desk beside the computer, the screen lit up with the message.

Echoes of the fight he and Lauren had had lingered. Words he wished he could take back hovered. And in spite of that, part of him still clung to the hope that Lauren wanted to stay.

He shook them off, grabbed his phone and swiped across the screen to read the text.

Deal is a go. Terms as originally planned. Excited to start working together. Here's to a future free from men.

He glanced at the sender, confused. Someone named Amy.

As he read it again, the puzzling words finally registered. As did the fact that the screen on this phone was pristine. His was scratched with a small crack in the corner.

He was holding Lauren's phone. And this text had come from the partner Lauren was going into business with.

Lauren was going through with the sale.

That was it. It was over. Done.

He put the phone down and as he did, he saw his own phone, half-hidden under a stack of papers. He pulled it out and shoved it in his back pocket, waves of sorrow and anger rising up in him.

Lauren was leaving.

He strode out of the house toward his truck, got in and drove back toward his place, his heart heavy in his chest.

He didn't want to think about it but couldn't stop.

He wanted to pray but didn't know what to pray for. As he drove, he stared at the road stretching ahead of him. Empty. Lonely.

Stop writing country songs. Get a grip. She's just a woman.

But she wasn't just a woman. She was Lauren. And corny as it sounded, he knew that her leaving would create an emptiness in his life he didn't know he could ever fill.

Help me through this, Lord, he prayed. *Give me strength to deal. Help me to lean on You. Not on my own understanding.*

Pulling in a deep breath, he felt his emotions steady, his anger and exasperation with himself and with Lauren push to the back of his mind.

At the same time, the words she'd thrown out rose up again.

Just for once I'd like to think of me.

Coming from someone else, that could have sounded selfish. But even before he met Lauren, he had heard Jodie say how selfless her sister was. How she had done so much for her and Erin.

Lauren's admission about Harvey added another layer.

But behind that came his own reality. It was time to tell Dean that it was over.

And as he turned his truck into the driveway of the ranch, he felt his heart sink at the thought.

Then he saw Dwayne's tow truck, parked by the barn.

He had other things to deal with. Vic hopped out of his truck, to give Dwayne directions where to go.

Vic had pulled Keith's truck back behind the hay barn after the accident and hadn't looked at it since. He couldn't. Each time he saw the busted-in window and the crumpled cab, he thought of Keith. He was thankful that he had put it where it was so Lauren hadn't had to see it the few times she had come to his place.

His stomach twisted at the thought of Lauren.

The ranch would be sold to an absentee owner. Another ranch become victim of wretched excess.

And the worst part of this was that it meant Lauren was leaving. He had shown her what he could and told her what he dared. And she was still going.

Help me to let go, Lord, he prayed. *Help me to be happy for her. To know that if this is what she wants, then this is good.*

But even as he prayed, he couldn't rid himself of the idea that maybe this wasn't entirely what she wanted. But he had to let go. Let her do whatever it was she thought she wanted to do. Give her the space to do it.

"Did anyone come and get the registration papers from the truck?" Dwayne asked as he jumped out of the cab of his truck, ready to hook up the winch cable.

"Insurance company didn't need them. They had everything on file."

"I might need them. Just in case," Dwayne said, pulling on his gloves.

While he got ready, Vic walked over to the truck and yanked on the passenger door. It took a few tries, but he finally jerked it open. The glove box proved just as unwieldy. He pulled his jackknife out of his pocket and fiddled with the latch, then finally managed to get it open. The insurance papers and registration card were tucked in a black vinyl folder inside. He pulled the folder out and as he did a stained and wrinkled envelope came with it and drifted to the floor of the truck.

Vic bent over and picked it up. Then frowned.

The envelope had his name scrawled across the front. In Keith McCauley's handwriting.

A chill feathered down his spine as things came together. Keith McCauley had been on his way to Vic's place when he had his accident. Had he been coming to deliver this?

He thought of the letters Lauren and Jodie had mentioned. Letters that spoke of regrets and sorrow and offered apologies. Was this letter one of those?

"Got the stuff?" Dwayne asked as Vic slowly closed the door, still staring down at the envelope.

"Yeah. Here it is." He handed him the folder but folded up the letter and tucked it in the back pocket of his blue jeans.

Dwayne flipped open the folder and shot Vic a puzzled glance. "You look kinda pale. You okay?"

"I'm fine. Let's get this truck loaded up and out of here."

Twenty minutes later the truck was on the flat deck, Dwayne was headed back to town and Vic was finally alone. He tugged the envelope out of his pocket, trudged over to the corrals and sank down on a hay bale. He held the letter a moment, thinking of Keith. Remembering.

Then he ripped opened the envelope and tugged out two pieces of paper.

The first was a letter.

Dear Vic,
I want you to know that I hope to get to the lawyer and do this right but for now this note will have to do. We never signed anything permanent so until we do, I want you to have this. Keith.

Vic read over the letter once again, then set it aside and glanced quickly over the second piece of paper.

Across the top of the letter, Keith had written, "Lease Agreement Between Keith McCauley and Vic Moore."

Vic swallowed, and his heart did double time, pounding in his chest. This was the documentation he had been looking for all this time.

This document verifies that I, Keith McCauley, am leasing my ranch, the Circle M, to Vic Moore. This is a lease-to-own agreement.

Vic dragged his hand over his face and continued. The agreement went on to state that Keith agreed to sell Vic the Circle M Ranch for a set amount of money in the first year he leased it, then a set amount if he bought it in the second year.

Vic had leased it for three years, so the second number applied. And it was exactly the amount Keith and Vic had agreed upon. The amount he had figured on when he spoke with Lauren at Drake's office the first time he saw her.

The amount that didn't come close to what Alex, the current buyer, was offering her.

He leaned back against the fence as the implications of this letter sank in.

He would have to talk to Drake. See if it was legitimate. But he guessed it would be as legal as the will Keith had drawn up in his own handwriting.

Would Lauren contest it?

She could stay now. Would have to. She couldn't buy the business if he exercised his rights to the ranch.

But was that what he wanted? To force her hand? He wanted her to choose of her own free will. He thought of what she had told him about her ex.

He could only imagine how humiliating it must have been not only to be dumped the week of her wedding but also to be so duped by a man you thought you were going to share your life with.

Just for once I'd like to think of me.

"Hey, honey, what's up?"

His mother's voice behind him made Vic jump. He spun around in time to see her walking toward him, her hat hanging to one side, as she pulled off her gardening gloves.

"I was working out in the garden and saw you sitting here. What's going on?" she asked, lowering herself to the bale beside him.

Vic wasn't sure he was ready to talk about what had happened, but he knew the facts would come out some time or other.

"I just found this in Keith's truck," he said, holding out the papers for his mother to look at. "It's the lease agreement I've been looking for all this time."

"You found it?" His mother took the papers and glanced over them, her eyes flying over the words. "All this time and they were right here. You could have saved yourself so much trouble."

And a broken heart.

His mother handed Vic the papers back. "Is something bothering you?"

Vic folded up the papers and slipped them back in the envelope. "This agreement means I can probably stop Lauren from selling the ranch to Alex." Vic turned to his mother and gave her a wan smile. "Which means I'll have dibs on the ranch. For Dean. It means I can finally take care of him."

"I know how much that means to you," she said, slipping her hat off her head. "But I think you need to know that we never expected you to take care of Dean. I know that you seem to think it was your fault Dean got hurt. That you should have stopped it."

She gave Vic a caring look. "I don't think Dean ever expected you to take care of him. I know I certainly didn't, and I think it's time you let go of that notion."

Vic heard his mother on one level and understood, but months and months of thinking he had to take care of his brother were hard to shake.

"Maybe not. Maybe my reasons for buying Keith's ranch were tied up with him. But I still think it's a good opportunity."

"It is. And I'm sure Dean would be happy if you ended up with it. But I think it's time you make this decision for yourself. Not for Dean. You've taken on too much. You have to let Dean take care of himself. Live with the consequences of his own actions."

As Vic listened to his mother, he felt an easing of the burden he'd been carrying all this time. But at the same time, while one weight had fallen off his shoulders, it was as if another one had replaced it.

Now it was entirely up to him to decide what to do for his own reasons.

And as he thought of what Lauren had told him and what the repercussions of this agreement would be for her, he knew exactly what he had to do.

Chapter Fourteen

"So I've kept my mouth shut for the past five minutes, but now you have to tell me about that sad face of yours," Aunt Laura said as she placed a delicate fern in the floral arrangement she was working on.

Fifteen minutes ago, two hours after she drove away from the ranch, Lauren had walked into her aunt's flower shop. As she stepped inside, a bell above the door tinkled. The muted drone of the refrigerated case holding an assortment of arrangements and the mixed scents of flowers, potpourri and candles enfolded her in a familiar embrace. Sighing with relief, Lauren had followed her aunt's tuneless humming to the back room, where Aunt Laura was perched on a stool at the butcher-block table. A huge mug of coffee was parked beside her and a glorious spill of flowers in front of her.

Lauren grinned as she sorted through the flowers she was working with. "I should have guessed you wouldn't miss that."

"I just know my girls," Aunt Laura said, twisting a red silk ribbon into a bow and tying some wire around it. "And as soon as you came into the shop, I knew something was wrong."

But, bless her aunt's heart, she didn't say anything. Didn't press. Just gave Lauren some flowers and directions and time.

Lauren snipped a rose, then carefully cut the thorns off before inserting it in the block of Oasis that would hold the arrangement. "It's been a bad morning," she said as she picked up a white lily and pared it down. She felt a quiver of sorrow rise up her throat and she swallowed it down. She didn't want to cry.

She had done enough of that on her drive around the county. She'd stopped at the lookout point and sat a moment, overlooking the valley and the Saddlebank River, letting the beauty wash over her. A love and appreciation for this place had been easing its way into her heart and soul ever since she arrived. Looking out over the valley, she'd felt a sense of continuity from the only place in her life that had always been there. Had always been a part of her life.

And now someone else had found a place in her heart.

She had tried not to think of Vic, but every word they spoke, every emotion that had spilled out, washed over her again and again.

Thankfully she'd forgotten her phone at the ranch, so she didn't have to deal with Amy and Alex and their incessant demands.

But still her aunt said nothing.

"Vic and I had a fight," she said after a long pause.

"Oh, dear. That's not good." She didn't press for details.

But Lauren knew she needed to talk this through.

"It was about the ranch and the business I want to buy."

"What did you fight about?" Aunt Laura asked.

"I think he was hoping I would stay."

"Why would he hope that?"

Her aunt's comment seemed artless, but Lauren heard the other question behind that.

And why didn't you want that?

I do want it, she thought.

But Alex and Amy and expectations and dreams of independence clung with tentacles she was afraid to pull away from.

"Because we've been spending time together. Because we've..." Her voice faltered.

"We've?" her aunt said, her tone encouraging.

Lauren ripped a tiny strip off a banana leaf, twisting it around the flowers she arranged, the words rising up her throat, demanding to be articulated.

"We've kissed. We've shared dreams. We've talked about our faith," she said, her voice wavering with sudden and unwelcome emotion. But once she started it was as if the words rose up, needing to be spoken aloud. "We've spent enough time together that I dared to think I was able to let someone into my life again. But I've got all this other stuff going on and I can't sort it out. Alex. Amy. The business. My plans for the future."

She twisted up another leaf, inserting it in the arrangement. "Trouble is, I don't know if I want that anymore. I don't know what I want." She picked up another lily, catching her breath. "And yet my practical self, the part of me that helped me survive living with Gramma, taking care of my sisters, my mother, working my fingers to the bone so that Harvey and I could get set up and then getting dumped—that part of me tells me not to be foolish. To take care of me first."

Her aunt calmly snipped another carnation and placed it in the piece she was working on.

"That sounds serious," she said, not meeting Lauren's eyes.

Lauren was surprised at the relief she felt at finally being able to speak about what had been tangled up in her mind the past few hours.

"Do you care for Vic?" her aunt asked, finally looking directly at her.

Lauren held her gaze and then her shoulders slumped. "More than I want to admit. More than I've ever cared for anyone."

"If you could let go of expectations from other people and demands and old dreams you've clung to, if you could set them all aside and narrow everything down to you, what would you choose?"

"It's not that easy. Everything is so wound around everything else, I don't know how to untangle it."

"Have you prayed about this?"

Lauren split off another piece of the banana leaf, turning it over in her hands, trying to do exactly what her aunt suggested.

"I'm not sure what to pray."

"I think you have to be careful not to expect that God will suddenly show up with a bolt of lightning and give you the answer. I think you have to acknowledge that you need to place your life in His hands and trust that the people He has placed in your life will also, if they are faithful, watch over you."

"Other than you, I don't know if that's ever happened."

Her aunt came to stand beside her, slipping her arm

around Lauren's shoulders. "Ever since you were a little girl, you've always watched over your sisters. Always been watching out for someone else. I know that. I heard a saying once and I think you should try to apply it now. Sometimes the place where your head and your heart intersect is the place where your best decision is made. So think of where that happens. Think of what you want and what you need and see if there's a connection."

Lauren shot her aunt a puzzled glance as what she said seemed to settle. Take root.

"I think I just want something that belongs to me. A place and business of my own…but I don't want to be on my own." She drew in a slow breath as a new realization grew. "I want to be with Vic. If everything else was stripped away, I'd want to be with him. But I'm afraid that if I do…"

"He'll have control over you."

Lauren nodded, surprised at her aunt's ability to see past the trees and identify the forest.

"That's something you'll have to deal with," her aunt continued. "Trust is a huge part of any relationship, and if you can't trust, then the foundation is weak." Aunt Laura squeezed just a little harder. "So my question to you is, can you trust Vic?"

"My heart tells me I can."

"And your head?"

Lauren thought of everything Vic was willing to do to secure the ranch for his brother. How he put up with her own initial antagonism. How regularly he showed up to go through papers and the computer, always hoping something would happen. All for his brother.

How attentive he could be. How caring.

"My head tells me that Vic is a good man. That he would take care of anyone in his life. And he has."

Lauren felt a flicker of fear even as she spoke the words. The thought of what she could be leaving behind if she went through with her plans with Amy.

What she could lose.

Then the store's phone rang just as a bell above the entrance announced a new customer.

"You take care of your customer," Lauren said. "I'll get the phone."

"Floral Folly," she said, tucking the handset under her ear as she turned back to the arrangement she'd been working on.

"Finally," Jodie said, breathless. "I've been calling and calling your cell phone. I thought Aunt Laura might know where you are and here I get you. Where have you been?"

"I've been driving around," she said. She didn't want to talk to Jodie right now. Didn't want to talk about what Vic might have told Finn, who might have told Jodie.

"Have you talked to Vic?"

Nothing like coming directly to the point.

"When?" she asked, preferring to see where her sister was going before she blindly stumbled along behind her.

"In the last half hour or so?"

"No."

"Have you talked to Drake? He's been trying to call you, too."

"No. I haven't."

"You should call Drake. Then Vic."

"I don't feel like it right now."

"Well, then I'll let you know what happened. Are you sitting down?"

"Yes." A prickle of fear trickled down Lauren's neck. "It's not Erin, is it?"

"What? No. Not Erin. It's Vic. He went to see Drake. Apparently he found that lease agreement he was looking for. It laid out the terms of the lease and the buyout."

Lauren's heart rate, already increasing, now began pounding in earnest. She knew the buyout amount from the figure Vic had quoted her. And it was less than what Alex was willing to pay. "What does that mean? Is it legal?"

"Apparently. Dad signed it and Drake verified it."

Lauren swallowed, confusion warring with happiness for Vic and fighting with concern over how this would affect her.

"So, what do we do now?"

"Well, we don't do anything. Vic told Drake he wasn't following through on it. He didn't want to claim his legal rights to first purchaser of the ranch at the amount Dad had written in the agreement."

Lauren struggled to keep up with the words her sister was breathlessly tossing at her.

"What?"

"Vic has the lease agreement. It's legal. But he's not exercising his rights of first refusal," Jodie said again. "You do know what this means, doesn't it?"

Lauren still wasn't sure. Her head was spinning as she tried to absorb this startling turn of events.

"Where did he find it?"

"Apparently in the glove box in Dad's truck. He was driving to Vic's place when…when he rolled the truck." Jodie stopped there, her voice breaking just a little.

Lauren felt as if her brain was exploding with all the information she'd just heard.

"So he brought the agreement to Drake?"

"Yeah. To have it verified, I guess. And then he changed his mind."

"Did Drake say why?"

"Nope. You'll have to talk to him."

That was going to be her next call.

"So nothing's changed, has it?" Jodie said, her voice rising with a faint note of hope that begged Lauren to negate what she had just said.

"I don't know what to think," Lauren said truthfully. "I can't believe he did this."

She ran her hand through her hair, pushing it back from her face as she blew out her breath.

"Well, I'll let you go. Make your phone calls," Jodie said. "Let me know how this all works out."

"I will."

Lauren ended the phone call, looking at the unfinished arrangement sitting in front of her, the implications of what Vic had just done slowly settling into her soul.

He had found the document he knew existed.

And once he found it, he'd given up the rights laid out in it.

Why would he do that?

Had Dean changed his mind about ranching? She pushed herself away from her stool and walked to the front of the store, where her aunt was just handing Jane Forsythe her receipt.

"Hey, there, Lauren," Jane said, smiling, as Lauren stopped by her aunt. "How are you doing?"

"I'm good. I understand Vic Moore was at the office today?"

"Yeah. He just left half an hour ago."

"Did he say where he was going after that?"

"I imagine back to the ranch. He said something about having to work with one of his horses."

"Thanks." Lauren couldn't call him, because his number was plugged into her phone, which was sitting on her desk at the ranch. She turned to her aunt, touching her shoulder. "I need to go" was all she said.

"Of course. Thanks for coming."

Lauren gave her a quick hug. "Thanks for your help."

"Where are you going?"

"I'm going to talk to Vic."

The colt turned away from Vic and once again he waved his rope at it and sent it around the round pen in the arena, the dust from its hooves settling in the warm summer air trapped in the building.

Stubborn horse simply wouldn't give.

When Vic had come back from town, he'd needed to keep busy doing something. Anything. He hadn't talked to Dean yet, explained to him what had happened and what he had done.

Working with this colt was a way of putting that conversation off.

A couple of times he'd felt a chill of regret at what he'd done, but each time he did, he thought of what Lauren had told him.

How she'd given up everything for everybody. He heard the pain in her voice. Sensed the depth of the sacrifices she had made.

Keith had often mentioned how frustrated he was with his daughters. But when Vic sat and talked with Drake today, after making his decision to rip up the lease agreement, he'd found out more about Keith's expectations of young girls whom he'd barely known and barely gotten to know.

He, who had grown up with loving parents and a caring community, couldn't imagine the loneliness and responsibility that must have haunted Lauren.

The colt whinnied at him, lowering its head, tonguing its mouth.

He stopped and let the colt come toward him, waiting for its response, ready to reward it.

"It's okay," he said, his voice steady, even, while his thoughts spun and doubled back in his head.

Why had he done what he had? What would happen to Dean? Why had he ruined their one big chance?

He stilled the noisy voices in his head as he reached out and gently touched the colt's withers. It flinched and he drew back, but then the colt came close again.

"It will be all right," he told the colt, gently stroking its side, rewarding the movement toward him.

Please, Lord, let that be so.

And as he prayed, the noisy, accusing voices grew still.

He heard the creak of a door and he half turned, expecting to see Dean come storming in to accuse him of ruining his future in yet another way.

But the blond hair and lithe figure belonged to someone else. Someone who had been on his mind since the first time he had seen her sitting in Drake's office.

She stood silhouetted against the light dancing through her hair, casting her features in shadow.

He couldn't read her expression.

So he waited for her to come closer. To make the first move.

Just like the colt he'd been working with.

She stood there, then, slowly, she started walking toward him.

He waited until she came to the metal door of the round pen, then joined her.

She stood in front of him, looking bemused.

"I talked to Jodie about what you did," she said. Her voice was quiet. "I can't believe… I don't know…" She stopped there, her voice fading away, and then, to his shock and surprise, he saw her eyes well up.

He'd thought he would be able to keep his cool. Keep his distance.

But the silent slide of tears down her cheek melted his already shaky resolve.

He closed the gap between them in two steps, took her in his arms and drew her close to him. Her arms slipped around him, her head tucking under his chin.

They stood there, the moment lengthening, words unnecessary.

Vic stroked her hair, absorbing the fact that she was here. She had come to him.

Finally she drew back and wiped her cheeks, releasing a self-conscious laugh. "Sorry."

"Nothing to apologize for," he said, smoothing away a few tears from her cheek.

She looked up at him, a question in her eyes.

"Why didn't you follow through? With the lease agreement. Why did you rip it up?"

"That sounds dramatic," he said. "I just got Drake to run it through the shredder."

She gave him a tentative smile. "Why did you let him do that? It was what you've been looking for ever since I got here."

He paused, giving himself time to choose the right words.

"I did it because I wanted you to be able to do what you wanted. I did it for you."

She slowly shook her head, as if trying to figure out what he was saying. What he had done.

He had to tell her. Now he really had nothing to lose by her knowing.

"I did it because I love you," he finally said. "I wanted you to be able to decide your own future and take your own path."

Lauren's eyes grew wide; her lips parted as astonishment crept over her features.

"You love me?"

"I do. I love you."

She grabbed the back of his neck, pulled his head down and kissed him, her fingers tangling in his hair, her other arm clinging to him.

His first reaction was surprise, his second a shivering warmth.

He pulled her closer. Finally they drew back.

"I can't believe this," she whispered, her hands stroking his face, her fingers trailing over his features. "I can't believe you would do this for me. No one has ever done anything like that."

"Like I said, I did it because I love you. I had no expectations."

"I know you didn't." She rested her hands on his shoulders. "But it meant so much to me. It showed me something deep within me that took some time for me to acknowledge."

"Which is?" he gently prompted.

She looked up at him again, a warm smile curving

her lips. "That you are the best person I've ever met. That you are a wonderful, caring man. That I know I can trust you with my life. With my heart." She stood up on tiptoe and brushed a welcome kiss over his lips. "I love you, too, Vic Moore."

Her words created a rush of joy in his heart.

"I'm glad. Makes it easier to talk about a future."

"We have a future?" she asked, her smile turning adorably coy.

"I want a future. With you. I want you by my side and I want to be by your side."

"I want the same," she said.

He kissed her again, sealing their promises. But as he drew away, another reality intruded.

"And what about your business?" he asked. "Your partnership with Amy."

"I've done more phoning the last hour than I've done since I got here," Lauren said, curling her hands behind his neck, leaning back to hold his gaze. "I wanted everything decided before I came here to you. I told Alex the ranch wasn't for sale, but I directed him to Amy. Put them in touch. I talked to Amy on the way here and I believe they are setting something up. She's disappointed I won't be working with her. We are good friends and have always gotten along well."

"That won't change," Vic assured her.

"I don't think so. I think Alex is willing to invest in the company and let her direct how things will be run."

"So once again you've taken care of the other people in your life," he said in a teasing tone.

"It's what I do." She gave him another smile. "And you shouldn't complain, because I hope to do the same for you."

"That doesn't make you very independent," he said. "I know that was important to you."

"I think I have a solution. I wouldn't be surprised if Aunt Laura would be willing to let me take over her flower shop. Maybe sooner than later."

"Would you be okay with that?"

Lauren nodded, her expression growing softer. "I think I would like it more than running an accounting business."

"You look happy just thinking about it," he said, another concern fading away.

"I've always loved helping her."

"And you love flowers and plants."

"Not as much as I love you," she said.

Vic kissed her again and then felt a nudge behind him. He turned to see the colt he'd been working with, head hanging over the gate, trying to get his attention.

"Looks like someone's ready to work with me," Vic said, half turning to touch the colt's head. Acknowledge its presence.

"Some things just take time," Lauren said, touching the colt herself. "It's a matter of trust, I think."

Vic grew serious and turned back to Lauren. "I know you've been burned in the past. But I want you to know that you can trust me."

Lauren gave him a warm smile, then kissed him again. "I know that, and I do. I trust you with my heart and my life."

"I won't let you down." He slipped his arm over her shoulder, pulling her close. "And now I suppose we'll have to go talk to our family. Let them know what's happening."

Lauren's smile grew even broader. "Our family. I sure like the sound of that."

"So do I."

And together they walked out of the barn and into their future.

* * * * *

THEIR RANCH REUNION

Mindy Obenhaus

For Your glory, Lord.

Acknowledgments

A big thank-you to Captain Glen Vincent, Village Fire Department, for your twenty-nine years of service as a firefighter and for your willingness to share your knowledge.

Thanks to Wendy Jilek at Colorado Kitchen and Bath Design, Montrose, Colorado, for your input on the kitchen-design process.

Much appreciation to Catrina at ServePro of Montrose and Telluride.

And I couldn't have done any of this without the love and support of my incredible husband. Thank you for being my rock.

Forget the former things; do not dwell on the past.
See, I am doing a new thing! Now it springs up;
do you not perceive it? I am making a way in the
wilderness and streams in the wasteland.

—*Isaiah* 43:18–19

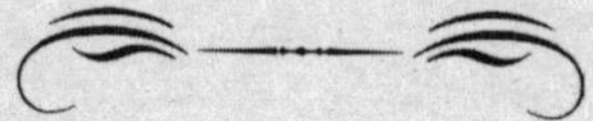

Chapter One

If she had to look at one more spreadsheet, she'd go batty.

Overdue for a break, Carly Wagner pushed away from her laptop at the oak kitchen table, poured another cup of tea and wandered into the parlor of her Victorian home. The late morning sun filtered through the windows, bathing the somewhat formal though still cozy room in warmth. Taking a sip of her Cream Earl Grey, she glimpsed the photo of her great-grandmother on the mantel and smiled. Granger House was more than just her home. The bed-and-breakfast was a way of life.

She let go a sigh. If only she didn't have to keep taking in these bookkeeping jobs to help build up her savings. But if she hoped to send her daughter, Megan, to college one day…

She was just about to sit in the powder-blue accent chair when something outside caught her attention. Easing toward the side window, she noticed a vehicle in the driveway next door. She fingered the lace curtain aside and peered through the antique glass pane.

That truck did not belong there.

Her neighbor, Olivia Monroe, Livie to everyone who knew her, had been dead for six months. Since then, no one had set foot in that house without Carly's knowledge. Until now.

Narrowing her gaze on the ginormous black F-350, curiosity mingled with concern. After all, Livie's house now belonged to her. Well, maybe not completely, but Lord willing, it would, just as soon as she convinced Livie's grandson, Andrew, to sell her his half. That is, once she finally mustered the courage to call her old high school boyfriend. Then she would finally be able to act on her dream of expanding Granger House Inn and kiss bookkeeping goodbye.

Allowing the curtain to fall back into place, she paced from the wooden floor to the large Persian rug in the center of the room and back again. What should she do? She hated to bother the police. Not that they had much to do in a quiet town like Ouray, Colorado. Then again, if it was nothing, she'd look like the nosy neighbor who worried over everything.

No, she needed to do a little investigation before calling the cops.

She headed back into the kitchen, depositing her cup on the butcher-block island before grabbing her trusty Louisville Slugger on her way out the back door. The cool air sent a shiver down her spine. At least, that's what she told herself. Realistically, it was rather mild for the second day of March. Perhaps the sun would help rid them of what remained of their most recent snowfall.

Making herself as small as possible, she crept across the drive and around the back of Livie's folk Victorian. Banging echoed from inside. Or was it her own heart slamming against her rib cage?

With Livie's house key clenched in her sweaty palm, Carly drew in a bolstering breath and continued a few more feet. She soundlessly eased the metal storm door open just enough to insert her key into the lock of the old wooden door. Then, thanks to the ongoing hammering sound, she slipped inside undetected.

The seventies-era kitchen, complete with avocado-green appliances and gold countertops, looked the same as it had every other time she'd been there in recent weeks. Pathetic. She still couldn't understand why Livie would do such a horrendous thing to this charming house. Carly could hardly wait to get rid of that ugly old stuff and replace it with a look that was truer to the home's original character.

Bang. Bang. Bang.

Carly jumped, sending her renovation ideas flying out the window. At least until she took care of whoever was in the parlor.

Raising the bat, she tiptoed into the short hallway, past the closet, until she could see who was making that racket.

She peered around the corner, nearly coming unglued when she spotted the male figure crouched beside the wall on the other side of the kitchen, using a hammer and a crowbar to remove the original trim moldings.

She slammed the tip of the bat onto the worn wooden floor with a crash. "*What* are you doing to my house?"

The man jumped. Jerking his head in her direction, he hustled to his feet until he towered over her.

Carly gasped. *What is he doing here?*

Eyes wide, she simply gaped. The perpetrator wasn't just any man. Instead, Andrew Stephens, Livie's grandson, stood before her, looking none too pleased.

Heat started in her belly, quickly rising to her cheeks. Though it had been nearly twenty years since they'd dated and she'd seen him a few times since, her mind failed to recall that the boy she once knew so well was now a man. A very tall, muscular man with thick, dark brown hair, penetrating brown eyes and a stubble beard that gave him a slightly dangerous, albeit very appealing, look.

His surprise morphed into irritation. "Your house?"

She struggled for composure, jutting her chin in the air while trying to ignore the scent of raw masculinity. "You heard me." Aware she wasn't acknowledging the complete truth, her courage suddenly waned. "Well, half of it anyway."

Andrew eyed her bat. "I'm not sure where you're getting your information, Carly, but this house belongs to me." Shifting his tools from one hand to the other, he moved closer. "And I have a copy of my grandmother's will that proves it."

Oh, so he thought he could intimidate her, did he? Not to mention call her a liar?

She laid one hand over the other atop the bat. "That's odd. Because I received a letter from Livie's lawyer, along with a copy of her will, and it stated that the house passes equally to both you and me." And while her plan was to offer to buy out his half, this probably wasn't the best time to bring that up.

He cocked his head, his expression softening a notch. "Are you okay? You haven't hit your head or something, have you?"

She sucked in a breath, indignation twisting her gut. Wasn't it enough that he'd broken her young heart? Now he thought she was crazy. Well, she'd show him.

Resting the bat on her shoulder, she whirled and started for the back door.

"Where are you going?"

"I'll be *right* back." She stormed out the door and marched over to her house, kicking at a dwindling pile of snow along the way. Did he really think she was going to let him plead ignorance when she had proof? That house was half hers and she refused to be bullied.

Once inside Granger House, Carly went straight to her bedroom, opened the small safe she kept tucked in the corner and pulled out the large manila envelope. Let Andrew argue with this.

Leaving her bat in her kitchen for fear she might actually be tempted to use it, she again made her way next door, irritation nipping at her heels. She would not let Andrew stand between her and her dream.

When she entered this time, he was in the kitchen, arms crossed, leaning against the peninsula that separated the eating space from the food-prep space, looking better than an ex-boyfriend should.

She removed the papers from the envelope and handed them to him. "Page three, last paragraph."

She watched as he read, noting the lines carved deeply into his brow. So serious. Intense. And while he had never been the carefree type, it appeared the big city might have robbed him of whatever joy remained.

When he glanced her way, she quickly lowered her gaze. Just because she hadn't seen him in forever didn't give her the right to stare. No matter how intriguing the sight.

"I don't get it." He flipped back to the front page. "This will was drawn up only a year and a half ago." He looked at her now. "The one I have is at least five years old. Meaning this—" he wiggled the papers—"supersedes that."

Carly rested her backside against the wood veneer table, her fingers gripping the edge. "So, are you saying you *didn't* receive a letter from your grandmother's lawyer?"

He shook his head. "Not that I'm aware of."

This was her chance to make her move. Before she chickened out. "I'm sorry to hear that. However—" she shoved away from the table "—we can take care of this quite easily." She lifted her chin. "I'd like to buy out your half. I've been looking for a way to expand my bed-and-breakfast, and this house is the perfect solution. Besides, you're never in Ouray—"

"I love this house. Always have. You know that."

While she knew that Andrew the boy had loved the house, she could count the times Andrew the man had set foot in Ouray since moving to Denver right after graduation. A move that was supposed to be the beginning of their future together. Instead, it had torn them apart.

Refusing to let the painful memories get the best of her, she crossed her arms over her chest. "Until today, when was the last time you were in this house?"

"After my grandmother's funeral."

"And the time before that?" She awaited a response.

After a long moment, he shoved the papers back at her. "This house has been in my family for four generations. And I'm not about to let that change anytime soon. Even for you."

Andrew hadn't been this bowled over since Crawford Construction, one of Denver's largest commercial builders, offered to buy out his company, Pinnacle Construction. Even then, he hadn't been totally unaware. He'd heard rumors. But this revelation about his grandmother's house took him completely by surprise.

There was no way he was going to sell Carly half of the house that rightfully belonged to him. There had to be some mistake. He hadn't even been notified of the change to Grandma's will.

Watching out the kitchen window as Carly made her way back to Granger House, her blond curls bouncing with each determined step, he could think of only two explanations. His grandmother was crazy, or Carly had somehow coerced her into changing her will, giving his high school sweetheart half of the house that had been promised to him from the time he was a boy.

He continued his scrutiny, chuckling at the memory of Carly holding that baseball bat. Coming into the house, not knowing who was inside, took a lot of guts. Apparently the shy girl he'd once known no longer existed. Then again, that was a long time ago. She'd since become a wife, a mother, a widow… Not to mention one of the most beautiful women he'd ever seen.

Shaking off the unwanted observation, he waited for her to disappear inside her house before digging the keys out of his jeans pocket and heading out the door. He had to get to the bottom of this and fast. For months, he'd been looking forward to updating this old home to use as a rental property. Now, as he awaited the closing on his next business venture, he had eight weeks to do just that.

He climbed into his truck and fired up the diesel engine, daring a glance toward Granger House. With its sea foam green paint, intricate millwork and expansive front porch, the historic Victorian home looked much the way it would have when it was first built nearly one hundred twenty years ago. Today's guests must feel as though they're stepping back in time.

His gaze drifted to the swing at the far end of the porch. Back when he and Carly were dating, they spent many an evening there, holding hands, talking about their plans for the future. Plans he once thought would include her.

But that was then. This was now.

He threw the truck into gear and set off for his grandmother's lawyer's office, only to discover the man was out of town for the week. Frustration burrowed deeper. He didn't know what to do. Perhaps his father would have some insight.

Andrew's shoulders slumped. Seeing his father meant a trip to the ranch. Something he hadn't planned to do just yet.

If he wanted answers, though, it was his only option.

He maneuvered his truck onto Main Street, past the rows of colorful historic buildings, to continue north of town, beyond the walls of red sandstone, on to the open range. A few minutes later, he passed under the arched metal sign that read Abundant Blessings Ranch. Why his parents had named the place that, he'd never understand. Their lives were far from blessed, working their fingers to the bone with little to nothing to show for it.

He'd never live like that again.

Bumping up the gravel drive, he eyed the snow-capped mountains that stretched across the far edge of the property, beyond the river where they used to fish and swim.

A couple of horses watched him from the corral as he passed the stable. Red with white trim, it was the newest building on Stephens' land. Apparently the trail rides his father and oldest brother Noah offered during the summer months had been successful. That, in addition to the riding lessons Noah taught, had likely funded the structure.

The old barn, however, was another story. Closer to the house, the rustic wooden outbuilding had seen better days. The roof sagged, the pens on the outside were missing most of their slats and the ancient shingles were in sore need of replacing. Better yet, someone should just bulldoze the thing and start fresh.

A task he could easily take care of once they were well into spring. But he'd be back in Denver by then, the proud owner of Magnum Custom Home Builders.

He pulled alongside his father's beat-up dually, killed the engine and stepped outside to survey the single-story ranch house.

Though the sun was warm, a chill sifted through him. He wouldn't have believed it possible, but the place looked even worse than it had six months ago when he was here for his grandmother's funeral. The cedar siding was the darkest he'd ever seen it. The house, along with the large wooden deck that swept across one side, could use a good power-washing. Not that Dad, Noah or his younger brother, Jude, had the time. Before the cancer took its toll, the house had always been Mama's domain. And with five sons eager to please her, she was never at a loss for help.

The back door opened then, and Clint Stephens stepped outside, clad in his usual Wrangler jeans and chambray work shirt. "I thought I heard an engine out here." Smiling, his father started toward the three short steps separating him from Andrew, the heels of his well-worn cowboy boots thudding against the wood.

"How's it going, Dad?"

"It goes." His father cocked his graying head and peered down at him. "You no longer feel the need to tell your old man when you're coming back to Ouray?"

Andrew pushed the mounting guilt aside. "Maybe I wanted to surprise you." Hands shoved in his pockets, he perched his own booted foot on the bottom step. "I was planning to do some work on Grandma's house, but it seems she changed her will. You wouldn't happen to know anything about that, would you?"

"I do. I'm kinda surprised you don't, though."

"Why?"

"Didn't you get a copy of the new one?"

"No, sir."

"Hmm..." His father rubbed the gray stubble lining his jaw. "Guess we'd better have a talk, then." He turned back toward the house. "I just put on a fresh pot of coffee. Care to join me?"

After toeing out of their boots in the mudroom, they continued into the family room. Though the mottled brown carpet Andrew remembered from his childhood had been replaced with wood laminate flooring, the room still looked much the same with its oversize furniture and wood-burning stove.

He eyed the large Oriental rug in the middle of the room. Mama had been so tickled when he'd given it to her the Christmas after the new flooring had been put in. Said the rich colors made her simple house feel more grand.

While his father moved into the kitchen that was more like an extension of the family room, or vice versa, Andrew stood frozen, held captive by the wall of framed photos at the end of the room. Baby pictures of him and his brothers. Graduation photos. Milestones and achievements. There had never been a prouder mama than Mona Stephens.

Guilt nearly strangled him. He hadn't even had the respect to be here when she died.

"You still take it black?"

Turning, Andrew cleared his throat before addressing his father. "Just like you taught me."

The corners of Dad's mouth twitched. "There's some roast beef in the fridge." He motioned with a nod. "Help yourself if you're hungry."

Considering Andrew hadn't eaten anything since he pulled out of Denver well before sunup…

He spread mayonnaise on a slice of white bread, recalling his last visit before his mother's death. Despite chemo treatments, she still had his favorite foods waiting for him. From homemade apple pie to beef stroganoff, the most incredible aromas filled the house.

He glanced around the dated L-shaped kitchen. This old ranch house would never again smell so good.

"If you didn't get a copy of the new will, how'd you find out about the change?" Dad eased into one of the high-backed chairs at the old wooden table near the wall.

"Carly paid me an unexpected visit." He picked up his sandwich and joined the old man. "So, what gives? Grandma promised her house to me. I have a copy of her will that proves it. Why'd she make the change?"

Dad set his stained mug inscribed with #1 Dad atop the table. "Carly meant a lot to Livie. She was a friend, a caretaker and the granddaughter she never had."

"Okay, but Carly isn't family."

"Not by blood. But like I said, Livie thought of her as family. They were very good friends, you know."

"No. I didn't know." Andrew took a bite. Sounded like Carly went to great lengths to worm her way into his grandmother's life, all to expand her bed-and-breakfast.

"After Carly lost her husband, she and Livie grew even closer. Your grandmother understood what Carly was going through."

Something Carly probably used to her advantage.

"No one can understand the pain of a young widow better than someone who was also a young widow." Dad lifted his cup and took another sip of coffee. "That aside, your grandmother had her concerns that you might sell the place." His gaze settled on Andrew. "Making Carly half owner might have been her way of ensuring that the house remained with someone she loved."

"But I've always wanted that house. That's why Grandma left it to me in the first place." That and the fact that none of his brothers were interested. "I would never consider selling."

"You were in Denver, hardly ever came home."

Guilt wedged deeper. Even if he'd found the time to come back, he wasn't sure he could face the judgmental looks he was bound to receive from his brothers. As though he'd betrayed them for not getting here before Mama died.

"What are you planning to do with the house, anyway, son?"

His appetite waning, Andrew wrapped his suddenly cold fingers around the hot cup his father had given him. "Open up the bottom floor, add an extra bath, update the kitchen… I was hoping to have it ready by the high season to use as a rental."

"Sounds like quite an undertaking."

Andrew shrugged, still suspicious of the relationship

between his grandmother and Carly. "You know, Carly mentioned something about wanting to expand Granger House Inn. You don't suppose she shared those plans with Grandma in hopes of getting her hands on that house, do you? I mean, it is right next door."

His father's brow furrowed. "It's possible she made mention of it. But Carly's not the scheming type. You know that."

Did he?

"Apparently she's pretty determined," Andrew said, "because she offered to buy my half of Grandma's house."

Lips pursed, Dad nodded in a matter-of-fact manner. "You gonna take her up on it?"

"No." Andrew shoved his sandwich aside. "What was Grandma thinking?"

Dad chuckled, lifting his cup. "Doesn't really matter, son. You and Carly are just going to have to find a way to work it out."

Chapter Two

"Yes, we do have an opening for Easter weekend." Sitting at her kitchen table that afternoon, Carly settled the phone between her ear and shoulder, grateful for the distraction. Her mind had been reeling ever since her encounter with Andrew.

She brought up the reservations page on her laptop. "The Hayden Room is available. It has a queen-size bed, a private bathroom and a spectacular view of Hayden Mountain."

"Oh, yes. I think I saw that one on your website." Excitement laced the female caller's tone. "It's beautiful."

Carly couldn't help smiling. Actually, all of their guest rooms were on the website. Something that had garnered Granger House many a booking. The problem she most often encountered, though, was when a group of people or a family required more space or multiple rooms she didn't have available. That was exactly where Livie's house would benefit her. Not only could she book the three rooms there individually but also market the entire house to those larger parties. Whatever the case, the addition of Livie's house would virtually double her income.

"I guarantee you won't be disappointed." She took hold of the phone. "Would you like to reserve it?"

"Yes, please. For Friday and Saturday night."

Ah, yes. There was nothing Carly loved more than a fully booked weekend. Especially this time of year when things tended to be a little sparse. Looked like she'd better get her breakfast menus planned. Though it was still a few weeks away, Easter weekend was extra special. There'd be ham to prepare, biscuits, scones…

She took the caller's information, hanging up as the kitchen timer went off.

Standing, she grabbed a pot holder and moved to the commercial-style range to retrieve a large baking sheet from the oven. Within seconds, her kitchen was filled with the aromas of cinnamon and vanilla.

She crossed the wide expanse of original hardwood and deposited the pan on the island. Until learning she'd inherited half of Livie's house, Carly had been saving to remodel the kitchen at Granger House. While the room was large, it had one of the worst layouts ever, with the stove by itself at one end of the room and the refrigerator clear over on the other. Not to mention the lack of counter space. But since she'd be using that money to buy out Andrew's half of Livie's house, she'd just have to live with it a while longer.

Too bad Andrew had to be so difficult. Okay, so the house had been in his family for generations. She'd give him that. But unless he was planning to move back to Ouray, what possible use could he have for it? The place would just sit there empty.

Nope, no matter how she looked at it, there was no

way this co-owning thing was going to work, and she couldn't help wondering why Livie had set things up that way. Unless…

She picked up her spatula to remove the cookies, then stopped. Oh, say it wasn't so. Livie had never tried to play matchmaker for Andrew and her while she was alive. Why would she do it in death?

No, no. Carly refused to believe it.

Still shaking her head, she shoveled the cookies from the baking sheet to the cooling rack. Regardless of Livie's intentions, no matter what they might have been, Carly would simply have to figure out how to convince Andrew to sell her his half. She would not let him rob her of another dream. Not when this one was so close.

Back when she first took over Granger House from her parents seven years ago, she had grand ideas and had expressed an interest in expanding when the house on the opposite side of them came on the market. Her late husband, Dennis, had never been fond of the idea, though, so she'd tucked those dreams away. After his death two years later, she was too busy caring for Megan and simply trying to keep up to even think about anything other than what was absolutely necessary. But as Megan got older, Carly would occasionally revisit her daydreams. Still, with the other house no longer available, that's all they were.

Until Livie's death. Suddenly it was as though God had granted the desires of her heart in a way she never would have imagined. After all, just like Granger House, Livie's house was only a block off Main Street, affording guests easy access to just about everything in town. And the fact that a narrow drive was all that separated the two houses made it the perfect candidate for her expansion.

At least until Andrew showed up, thinking he was going to claim his inheritance.

She let go a sigh. How was she, a simple small-town girl who'd spent her entire life in Ouray, going to convince some bigwig businessman like Andrew? It wasn't as if their romantic history would score her any brownie points.

Her gaze drifted to the cookies. And plying him with food wasn't likely to do the job, either.

Lord, show me what I should do. Because right now, it looks as though Andrew and I are at an impasse.

The back door opened then, bringing a surge of cool air as nine-year-old Megan bounded inside.

"Mmm…cookies." Her daughter dropped her backpack on the wooden floor.

"You're just in time. They're fresh out of the oven."

Without bothering to take off her coat, Megan rushed over and grabbed one. "Yay, snickerdoodles!" She took a big bite.

Carly snagged her own cookie, pleased that her daughter appreciated her culinary skills. And running a bed-and-breakfast, she was almost always cooking something. If not directly for her guests, then she was trying out new recipes. Something her friends benefited from, making it a win-win for Carly. They gave her feedback and she didn't have to worry about her waistline. Well, not as much, anyway.

"How was school?"

With the cinnamon-coated treat sticking out of her mouth, Megan shrugged out of her coat. "Good." She dropped the puffy thing on a hook near the door before plopping into one of the Windsor-style chairs at the table to finish her snack. "Who's at Ms. Livie's house?"

Carly glanced out the window to see Andrew's big black truck once again in the driveway. With all the noise that thing made, she was surprised she hadn't heard him pull in.

Why was he back, anyway? After watching him leave this morning, she'd hoped he'd decided to stay away until they reached an agreement.

"That would be her grandson, Andrew." She grabbed a glass from the cupboard and continued on to the refrigerator for the milk.

"Do I know him?" Megan's blue eyes followed Carly as she moved toward her daughter.

She set the glass, along with another cookie, in front of her. "He's the one who played cards with you, me and Livie a couple of years ago."

"When Ms. Livie's daughter died, right?"

"That's him." She ruffled Megan's straighter-than-straight strawberry blond hair, a trait she definitely didn't inherit from her mother. But after decades of fighting her natural curls, Carly had finally learned to embrace them. "You have a good memory."

"Why is he at Ms. Livie's house now, though?" Megan picked up the second cookie. "I thought she gave it to you."

Carly cringed. She'd had no business mentioning that to Megan until the estate had been settled. Yet in her excitement over the news all those months back, she'd blurted it out without thinking.

"She gave me half of it. And she gave Andrew the other half."

"Which half is yours?"

Carly puffed out a laugh. She could only imagine what was going through her daughter's nine-year-old mind. As if Carly and Andrew could just slap a piece of tape down the middle.

"Unfortunately, it's not quite that simple." And if she couldn't get Andrew to sell her his half, she'd be stuck taking in people's accounting books until Megan graduated college.

Megan stood, dusting the crumbs from her hands. "Can I go over there?"

"I don't think that's a very good idea right now." If ever. At least, not with Andrew there. Mr. Serious likely wouldn't tolerate kids.

Still, she couldn't help wondering what he was up to. Not after catching him removing baseboards this morning. Baseboards he'd better plan on putting back, because she wasn't about to stand by and let him strip the home of its character.

"On second thought, maybe we should go over there and say hi." And if their presence happened to remind him that she was keeping tabs on him, so be it.

Megan paused at the island, looking very serious. "We should take him some cookies."

Hand perched on her hip as she watched her daughter, Carly wasn't sure how she felt about the suggestion. However, it was Livie who'd always said you caught more flies with honey than with vinegar. And right about now, there was one big fly Carly was interested in catching.

"I think that's a terrific idea."

"Well, that's just great."

Andrew dropped his phone on the counter in his grandmother's kitchen. He'd been calling his attorney's cell all afternoon. When he finally decided to try the office, he learned that the man was in court and wouldn't be available until tomorrow.

He blew out a frustrated breath. This was not how he'd envisioned this day playing out.

Pushing away from the cabinet, he paced the ugly gold-and-brown vinyl floor while he waited for a pot of coffee to brew. He knew it was a long shot, but perhaps Ned could find a way to get Grandma's will overturned and the original reinstated. Then all of his problems would be solved.

You and Carly are just going to have to find a way to work it out.

Hmph. Dad always did look at things simplistically. The only thing simple about the dispute between him and Carly was the fact that they both wanted this house.

As the coffeemaker spewed out its last efforts, Andrew grabbed a mug from the cupboard. If it hadn't been for Carly, he could have had at least one wall taken down by now. Enough to give him an idea of how the house was going to look with an open concept. Instead, he was left with a whole lot of nothing to do.

Leaning against the counter, he took a sip. He'd loved his grandmother dearly, but leaving her house to both him and Carly had to be the craziest idea she'd had since she went white-water rafting down the Uncompahgre River at the age of eighty-three. Except for sharing a game of cards after his mother's funeral, he and Carly had barely spoken in seventeen years. Not since the day she turned down his marriage proposal and walked out of his life forever.

Relegating the unwanted memories to the darkest corner of his mind, he scanned the sorry-looking kitchen. While he wasn't about to give up on getting his grandmother's old will reinstated, he could still be proactive, just in case things didn't work out the way he hoped. Near as he could tell, there were only two ways out of this predicament. And since selling his half to Carly was out of the question, that left him with only one option—he'd have to buy out Carly's half of the house. Something that chafed him more than he cared to admit.

Aside from paying for something that was rightfully his to begin with, he'd have to come up with an offer better than hers. Sweeten the deal, so to speak, making it too good to refuse. Much like the company who'd just bought him out. And left him with a tidy chunk of change. Carly would be able to do whatever she liked with Granger House and leave this house—and him—alone.

"Hello, hello." As though he'd willed her to appear, Carly pushed open the back door, knocking as she came.

Try as he might, he couldn't ignore the fact that she was still one of the most gorgeous women he'd ever seen. The kind that could take your breath away with her natural beauty.

Her blond curls brushed across her shoulders as she held the door, allowing a young girl to enter first.

Her daughter had grown quite a bit since the last time he'd seen her. What was her name? Maggie? No, Megan.

"Hi." The girl smiled up at him with blue eyes reminiscent of her mother's and waved. In her other hand she held a small plate covered with plastic wrap. "We brought you cookies." She handed them to him.

So these were Carly's weapons of choice. Children and food. Ranked right up there with little old ladies.

His conscience mentally kicked his backside. Dad was right. Carly wasn't the type to try to steal his grandmother's house. However, that didn't mean he was simply going to hand it over.

While Megan wandered off as though she lived there, he set the plate on the counter and helped himself to a cookie. "Snickerdoodles. How did you know I was in need of a snack?" He took a bite.

The feisty blonde watched him suspiciously. "What brings you back here?"

He chased the first homemade treat he'd had in a long time with a swig of coffee. "I'm—"

"Uh-oh." Megan's voice echoed from the next room. "Somebody made a mess."

After a moment, Carly tore her gaze away from him and started into the front room.

Andrew set his cup on the counter and followed.

Rounding the corner into the home's only living space, he saw Megan pointing at the small stack of baseboards he'd begun to remove this morning. Before his plans were rerouted by Carly.

"I was doing a little work."

Carly lifted a brow. "I'm not sure what kind of work it was, but you need to put those back."

Irritation sparked. Who was she to start giving him orders?

"Whose is this?" Now on the other side of the room, Megan rocked back and forth in his grandmother's glider, pointing to the duffel he'd left by the front door. He wouldn't go so far as to call the kid nosy, but she was definitely curious. Not to mention observant.

"That would be mine." He turned to find Carly watching him.

Both brows were up in the air this time. "Planning to stay a while?"

This was ridiculous. He should not be interrogated in his own house. "As a matter of fact, I am. For several weeks. Which reminds me—" he crossed his arms over chest "—I think we need to set up a time to talk." Glancing at Megan, he lowered his voice. "Privately."

Mirroring his stance, Carly said, "I was thinking the same thing."

"At least we're in agreement about something."

"I'm going upstairs." A sigh accompanied Megan's announcement, quickly followed by the clomping of boots on the wooden steps.

Andrew knew just how she felt.

With Megan gone, Carly addressed him. "I'm curious. Before you learned that you were not the sole owner of this house, what were your intentions for it? I mean, were you planning to move in?"

"Temporarily, yes. I'm going to update the place and use it for rental income."

Seemingly confused, she said, "Where will you be?"

"Denver, of course."

Lines appeared on her forehead. "Let me get this straight." She perched both hands on her hips. "You don't want me to use Livie's house for my bed-and-breakfast, yet you want to turn it into rental property?"

"In a nutshell, yes."

"Why not just rent your half to me?"

It wasn't that he didn't like Carly. He wasn't purposely trying to thwart her plans. But this house was supposed to be his and his alone.

He dared a step closer. "Because, should I come back to Ouray, I want to be able to stay here. *Without* having to share it with someone else."

She shook her head. "So you'd rather pay me half of the rent money you get? That makes no sense."

"Pay you? Why would I—?"

"Mommy?" Megan hopped down the stairs, one loud thud at a time.

Carly seemed to compose herself before shifting her attention to her daughter. "What is it, sweetie?"

The girl tugged on Carly's sleeve, urging her closer, then cupped a hand over her mother's ear. "We should invite him for dinner." For all her implied secrecy, Megan had failed to lower her voice.

A look that could only be described as sheer horror flitted across Carly's face. Her eyes widened. "Oh, I'm sure Andrew already has plans for—"

"Nope. No plans at all." Fully aware of her discomfort, he simply shook his head, awaiting her response.

Clearing her throat, Carly straightened, looking none too happy. "In that case, would you care to join us for dinner?" She practically ground out the words.

He couldn't help smiling. "Sure. Why not?"

Watching them leave a short time later, he knew good and well that Carly was no more excited about having him for dinner than he was about sharing his grandmother's house. But as Grandma was fond of saying, it is what it is.

Who knew? Maybe they'd have an opportunity to talk. And if all went well, by the time this evening was over, Grandma's house would belong to him and him alone.

Chapter Three

Carly removed the meat loaf from the oven and put in the apple pie she'd tossed together at the last minute. Throw in some mashed potatoes and green beans and it was comfort food all the way. She'd need all the comfort she could get if she hoped to make it through an evening with the man who had once been able to read her every thought.

Using a pot holder, she picked up the pan of meat and headed for the island. *Nope. No plans at all.* She all but flung the pan on the counter, sending spatters of tomato sauce across the butcher-block top.

She grabbed a rag and wiped up the mess, knowing good and well that Andrew was simply trying to get her goat. And enjoying every minute of it, no doubt. Just like he did back in high school. Only she was no longer the timid girl who was afraid to stand up for herself.

After throwing the rag into the sink, she returned to the stove to check the potatoes. Fork in hand, she lifted the lid on the large pot.

It irked her that Andrew was planning to use Livie's house as a rental. Why wouldn't he just let— Wait a minute.

Steam billowed in front of her.

She was half owner. That meant she had a say in what went on next door. He couldn't use it as a rental without her permission.

Smiling, she poked at the vegetables. Yep, they were done.

She replaced the lid and carried the pot to the sink. This whole dispute would be over if Andrew would simply agree to sell. Unfortunately, for as eager as she was to discuss purchasing his half of the house so she could move forward with her expansion plans, she wasn't at liberty to talk business with Megan in the room. Which meant this whole evening was a waste of time.

That is, unless her idea of plying Andrew with food actually worked.

Holding the lid slightly off-center so as not to lose any of the potatoes, she drained the water from the pot. Maybe he'd be in such a state of gastronomic euphoria by the end of this evening that it would be impossible for him to say no when she again extended her offer.

Dream on, girl.

"Can I help?" Megan emerged from the adjoining family room at the back of the house, directly off the kitchen. Carly's parents had built the addition when she was young as a private space for the family. Now Carly appreciated it more than ever, because it allowed her to keep an eye on her daughter while she worked in the kitchen.

"Of course you can. Care to set the table?"

"Okay."

Carly opened the cupboard to grab the plates.

"Not those plates, Mommy."

"What?" She glanced down at her daughter.

"We need the guest plates." Meaning the china she used for the bed-and-breakfast. And this time of year, guests were predominantly limited to weekends.

"Sweetie, we don't use those for regular meals."

"This isn't a regular meal. Mr. Andrew is company, so we need to eat in the dining room with the pretty dishes."

Oh, to be a child again, when everything was so simple.

Lord, help me make it through tonight.

"Okay. Let me get them for you."

They moved around the corner into the dining room, and Carly retrieved the dishes from atop her grandmother's antique sideboard. Meat loaf on china. That'd be a first.

Leaving Megan in charge of the table, Carly returned to the kitchen to mash the potatoes. She pulled the butter and cream from the large stainless steel refrigerator.

"Which side do the forks go on?"

Closing the refrigerator door, Carly grinned, recalling how she used to help her mother and wondering if Megan would one day take over Granger House Inn. If so, she'd be the third generation to run the B and B. Not that she was in any hurry for her daughter to grow up. Carly was already lamenting Megan's occasional usage of Mom instead of Mommy.

"On the left."

A knock on the back door nearly had Carly dropping the dairy products she still held.

Megan must have heard it, too, because she raced past Carly and threw open the door.

Carly deposited the butter and cream on the counter and hurried behind her daughter. "Young lady, what have I told you about looking to see who it is before you open the door?" Not that there was much to worry about in Ouray. Still, a mother could never be too cautious in this day and age.

"Sorry."

"Evening, ladies." A smiling Andrew stepped inside, looking far too appealing. His hair was damp, and he smelled freshly showered.

Closing the door behind him, Carly eyed her flour-speckled jeans. Clearly he'd done more primping than she had. An observation that had her as curious as it did bothered.

"Welcome to our home." Megan swept her arm through the air in a flourish.

"Thank you for inviting me." He stooped to her daughter's level. "This is for you." He handed her a small brown paper gift bag with white tissue sticking out the top.

Megan's eyes were wide. "For me?"

"Yep. And this one—" straightening, he turned his attention to Carly "—is for your mother."

Carly's heart tripped as she accepted the package. A hostess gift had been unexpected, but the fact that he'd thought of both of them had her reevaluating their guest. At least momentarily.

"Th-thank you."

"Can I open it?" Megan looked as if she was about to explode with anticipation.

"Of course. What are you waiting for?" Andrew looked like a kid himself as he watched Megan pull out the tissue, followed by a small rectangular box. "My own cards!"

"Did my grandmother ever teach you how to play Hearts?"

"I don't think so." Megan eyed him seriously.

"Looks like I'll have to carry on the tradition, then. Perhaps we can play a game after dinner."

"Okay." Megan excitedly removed the plastic wrapping. "I can practice shuffling now, though, can't I?"

"You sure can." Andrew looked at Carly again. "You can open yours, too."

Her stomach did a little flip-flop as she removed the tissue and pulled out a small box from Mouse's Chocolates. "Ooo..."

"I hope you like truffles."

She lifted a shoulder. "No, not really."

His smile evaporated and, for just a moment, she felt bad for messing with him. Then again, after the way he'd coerced her into this dinner invitation, why should she care?

"Oh, I'm sorry. I thought most women—"

"I love them."

The corners of his mouth slowly lifted as he wagged a finger her way. "You had me going for a second."

Looking up, she sent him a mischievous grin. "Good."

She moved back toward the island, glad she had potatoes to keep her busy for a few minutes. Was it her imagination or did Andrew's brown eyes seem a touch lighter tonight? Like coffee with a splash of cream. Maybe it was the blue-gray mix in his flannel shirt. Whatever the case, it might be best if Megan kept him occupied for a while.

When they sat down to dinner a short time later, Andrew surveyed the table. "This is quite the spread." His gaze settled on Carly. "I wasn't expecting you to go to all this trouble."

Again, her insides betrayed her, quivering at his praise. "No trouble."

"Yeah. My mommy cooks like this *all* the time."

Suspecting her daughter was attempting a little matchmaking, Carly added, "Not all the time. And we rarely eat in the dining room."

He glanced about. "That's a shame. This is a nice room."

"Oh, it gets plenty of use with the bed-and-breakfast." She eyed her daughter across the table. "Shall we pray?"

After dinner, Andrew followed through with his promise and taught Megan Livie's favorite card game while Carly cleaned up the kitchen. Not only was she surprised by his patience with Megan and the gentle way he encouraged her, she greatly appreciated it. While Dennis had been a good father, he always seemed to have more time for his work than he did for his family. A fact that had Carly practicing the art of overcompensation long before his death.

With the dishes done, Carly joined them in the dining room.

She smoothed a hand across her daughter's back. "I hate to put the kibosh on your fun, but tomorrow is a school day."

"But I'm beating him. Please, can we finish this game?"

As much as Carly wanted to resist, to tell Megan it was time for Andrew to leave, she didn't have the heart. "Go ahead."

Fifteen minutes later, with her first win under her belt

and promises of a rematch, a happy Megan scurried off to get ready for bed.

Andrew pushed his chair in as he stood. "Think we could talk for a minute?"

"Um…" Carly's body tensed. While she had planned to reissue her offer to purchase his half of Livie's house, she wasn't sure she had the energy tonight. Then again, maybe he'd had a change of heart and was willing to accept her offer. "Okay. Let's go out front."

He followed her through the living room, past the carved wooden staircase and Victorian-era parlor chairs. "You've got a bright kid there. She's a fast learner."

Carly tugged open the heavy oak and leaded glass door. "I've always thought so."

Outside, the chilly evening air had her drawing her bulky beige cardigan around her. Moving to the porch swing, she sat down and stared out over the street. Once upon a time, she used to dream of finding someone who would sit with her and hold her hand while they talked about their day, the way her parents always had. Like she and Andrew used to do. And Dennis was too busy to do.

Now she knew better than to dream.

To her surprise, though, Andrew joined her on the swing. Close enough that she could feel the warmth emanating from his body.

"This has been a full day," he said.

If she thought her mind was muddled before he sat down… "Yes, it has." And she could hardly wait for it to be over.

He stretched his arm across the back of the swing, his long legs setting them into motion as he surveyed the neighborhood without saying a word.

For a split second, she wondered what he would do if

she were to lean into him and rest her head on his shoulder. Would he wrap his arm around her and hold her close, the way he used to? Or would he push her away?

Feeling the cold seep into her bones, she pushed to her feet. “What was it you wanted to talk about?”

He hesitated a moment before joining her. Took in a deep breath. “I’m willing to pay you the full value of the house for your half.”

Her jaw dropped. “Do you have any idea how much property values have risen around here?”

He shrugged. “I can afford it.”

His words sparked a fire in her belly. He hadn’t changed a bit. With Andrew, everything was about money. Making it, having it… Just like her late husband had been.

Well, he’d sorely underestimated her.

“I don’t care if you offer me a million dollars. There are some things that just can’t be bought. Including me.”

Refusing to listen to another word, she stormed into the house and slammed the door behind her.

By noon the next day, Andrew was at his wit’s end. Carly’s adamant refusal last night, coupled with his former admin assistant’s acknowledgment that a certified letter from Ouray had indeed come for him a few months back and was left on his desk, had him more confused than ever.

Tucked in a corner booth at Granny’s Kitchen, a local diner he remembered as The Miner’s Cafe, he listened to the din of the early lunch crowd and pondered what remained of his burger and fries. One would think he’d be used to Carly’s rejection by now. At least last night’s dismissal hadn't stung as much as when she'd refused to marry him.

He sighed, dipped a french fry into some ketchup and popped it in his mouth. Seventeen years later, he still wasn't sure what had gone wrong. But last night revealed something he hadn't expected. Despite everything, Carly still held a very special place in his heart. Simply being near her stirred up what-ifs and could-have-beens.

Rather absurd, if you asked him. They didn't even know each other anymore. Besides, he was headed back to Denver just as soon as he finished Grandma's house. And he knew all too well how Carly felt about the big city.

His phone vibrated in his pocket. He wiped his hands and slid out the device, happy to see his attorney's name on the screen.

He pressed the phone against his ear. "Hey, Ned."

"Judging from all the missed calls I have from you, I'm guessing you're eager to talk to me."

"Yes." He straightened in the wooden bench. "I was beginning to think you were avoiding me."

Ned laughed. "Sorry, buddy. I didn't think you'd be in need of my services so soon. Don't tell me you're bored with Ouray already."

Surprisingly, Ouray had been anything but boring this time around.

"No, but I do have a problem." He pushed his plate aside and proceeded to explain the change to his grandmother's will. "Is there any way I can get this will revoked and the original reinstated?" He reached for another fry, awaiting his lawyer's response.

"Was your grandmother of sound mind? Did she have dementia or anything?"

"Not that I'm aware of." Though given her decision to split the ownership of the house, he was beginning to wonder. If it had been one of his brothers, he could understand it. But Carly wasn't family.

"Then it's highly unlikely you'd be able to get it overturned."

Andrew wadded his napkin, tossed it on the high-gloss wooden tabletop and raked a hand through his hair. He'd anticipated as much. Still…

"Can I get you anything else?" Beside him, the waitress smiled down at him.

"One minute, Ned." He eyed the unquestionably pregnant blonde. "I'm good, thank you."

She slid him his check. "My name is Celeste if you need anything else. Otherwise, you can pay at the register on your way out."

"Good deal. Thank you." He again set the phone to his ear. "Sorry about that." He grabbed the ticket as he slipped out of the booth. "So, what are my options?"

"You could—"

The town's emergency siren shrieked to life just then, making it impossible for Andrew to hear anything. "Hold on again, Ned." He stepped up to the register and paid his tab as the high-pitched wail of fire trucks added to the discord.

When the madness finally settled, he stepped outside and resumed his call. "Okay, let's try this again." The cool midday air had him zipping up his jacket.

"And here I thought Ouray was just a sleepy little town."

Andrew looked up and down the historic Main Street. "Apparently not today."

Ned chuckled. "As far as options, you could offer to buy out the other person's half."

Crossing the street, Andrew let go a sigh. "Already did."

"And?"

"She slammed the door in my face." A quick glance heavenward had him noticing the plumes of thick, black smoke billowing into the air a few blocks away. Pretty significant fire, if you asked him. And fairly close to his grandmother's house.

A wave of unease rolled through him. "Uh, Ned, I'm gonna have to call you back."

He shoved the phone in his pocket, quickening his pace until he reached the corner. When he did, he peered to his right.

Dread pulsed through his veins as every nerve ending went on high alert. The fire trucks were in front of his grandmother's house.

He broke into a run. One block. Adrenaline urged him forward. Two blocks.

"Oh, no." Heart sinking, he came to a halt.

Across the street, smoke rolled from the back of Granger House Inn. Flames danced from the kitchen's side window, lapping at the sea foam paint, threatening the historic dentil moldings and clapboard siding.

One of the firemen barked orders, orchestrating the chaos, while others flanked the corner of the house, their hoses aimed inside.

But where was Carly?

"Andrew!"

He jerked his head in the direction of his brother Jude's voice.

A police officer for the city of Ouray, his younger brother vehemently motioned him across the street.

Andrew hurried toward him.

"We need you to move your truck out of Grandma's drive."

"Sure thing." He tugged the keys from his pocket and threw himself into the vehicle, the smell of smoke nearly choking him.

As he backed into the street, he spotted Carly's SUV in front of her house. Where was she? Was she safe? Could she have been trapped inside? Oh, God. Please, no.

He quickly parked on the next block before rushing back.

People had gathered on the opposite side of the street, watching the horror unfold.

He scanned the faces, looking for Carly. She had to be here somewhere.

He again eyed the flames, feeling helpless. Sweat beaded his brow as panic surged through his body. *God, she has to be all right.*

Spotting Jude in the middle of the street, Andrew jogged toward him. "Where's Carly?"

"In the ambulance."

Ambulance?

He ran past the cluster of onlookers to the emergency vehicle parked a few houses down.

Drawing closer, he finally saw her, standing near the rear bumper, attempting to pull off the oxygen mask while the female EMT fought to keep it over her face.

Andrew had never been so glad to see someone.

He slowed his pace as Carly ultimately ripped the

mask from her face. "I don't need this." She coughed. "That's my house." More coughing. "I need to—"

Andrew stepped in front of her then. "You *need* to let the firemen do their job. And you *need* to get some good air into your lungs." He pulled the mask from her hand, noting the resignation in her blue eyes as she looked up at him, her bottom lip quivering. "At least for a little bit."

The fact that she didn't resist when he slipped the respirator over her head still surprised him. But when he reached for her hand, she quickly yanked it away.

He groaned. Stupid move. Who was he to try to comfort her?

Only then did he notice the way she cradled her hand, holding it against her torso. The redness. She'd been burned.

"I think we'd better get you into the ambulance."

She shook her head. "I want to see what's happening." The words were muffled through the plastic mask.

Andrew eyed the male and female EMTs. "Can she sit here while you look her over?" He gestured to the rear bumper.

They nodded.

He looked at Carly. "You promise to let them do what they need to do?"

A cough-filled moment ticked by before she finally agreed.

The female EMT checked Carly's vital signs as the man went to work on her hand. All the while, Carly's tearful gaze remained riveted on Granger House.

Andrew could only imagine the flurry of emotions threatening to swallow her at any moment. The uncertainty, the grief… He wished he could make it all go away.

He sat down beside her as the man wrapped her hand

in gauze. "What happened there?" Andrew pointed to the injury.

"I had gone to the bank." She coughed. "When I got back—" looking up, she blinked repeatedly "—I opened the back door and the…flames were everywhere."

His eyes momentarily drifted closed. Thank God she was okay.

Unable to stop himself, he slipped an arm around her shoulders and pulled her close. Despite wearing a jacket, her whole body shook.

Returning his attention to the house, he saw that the smoke had started to turn white, a sign that the fire was almost out. However, there was no telling what kind of damage it had left in its wake. Granger House was more than Carly's home. It was her livelihood. Without it—

As if she'd read his thoughts, Carly lifted her head, her eyes swimming with tears. "What am I going to do?"

Chapter Four

How could this have happened?

Carly stood beside the towering conifer in front of Livie's house a couple of hours later, her arms wrapped tightly around her middle. Staring at Granger House, she felt as though she were fighting to keep herself together. In only a short time, the fire had ravaged her majestic old home, leaving it scarred and disheveled.

At the back of the house, where the kitchen was located, soot trailed up the once beautiful sea foam green siding, leaving it blackened and ugly. Windows were missing and, as she strained to look inside, all she could see was black.

She breathed in deeply through her nose, trying to quell the nausea that refused to go away. If only they would let her go inside. Perhaps she'd find out things weren't as bad as they seemed.

The loud rumble of the fire engine filled her ears as firemen traipsed back and forth, returning hoses to their trucks. Carly eyed her gauze-wrapped hand. At least it didn't sting anymore. The smell of smoke would be forever seared into her memory, though. Not to mention the heat of those flames.

Tilting her head toward the cloud-dotted sky, she blinked back tears. Save for a few years, she'd spent her entire life at Granger House. It was more than her home…it was family. An integral part of her heritage. Now she could only pray that the whole thing wasn't a loss. Even insurance couldn't replace that.

But what if it was a total loss? What would she do then?

"Can I get you anything? Are you warm enough?" The feel of Andrew's hand against the small of her back was a comfort she hadn't known in a long time. From the moment he appeared on the scene, Andrew had yet to leave her side. For once, she was grateful for his take-charge attitude. His presence was an unlikely calm in the midst of her storm.

"No, thank y—"

"Oh, my!"

Carly turned to see Rose Daniels, a family friend and owner of The Alps motel. Hand pressed against her chest, the white-haired woman studied the carnage. Beside her, Hillary Ward-Thompson, a former resident who'd recently returned, appeared every bit as aghast.

Carly knew exactly how they felt.

The dismay in Rose's blue eyes morphed into compassion as she shifted her attention to Carly, her arms held wide. "I came as soon as I heard." She hugged Carly with a strength that belied her eighty years. "You poor dear. Are you all right?"

She nodded against the older woman's shoulder, tears threatening again, but she refused to give in. She needed to stay strong.

After a long moment, Rose released her into Hillary's waiting embrace.

"I hate that this happened to you." Hillary stepped back, looking the epitome of chic with her perfectly styled short blond hair and silky tunic. Then again, Carly wouldn't expect anything less from the former globe-trotting exec.

"How can we help, dear?" Rose shoved her wrinkled hands into the pockets of her aqua Windbreaker. "Just tell us what you need."

"Besides food, that is," Hillary was quick to add. "Celeste has already talked to Blakely and Taryn. They're planning to bring you dinner." Her daughter, Celeste Purcell, owned Granny's Kitchen.

Carly hated that she'd added to their already hectic lives. "They don't have to—"

"Nonsense, darling." Hillary waved a hand through the air. "That's what people do in Ouray. You know that."

All too well. She'd been on the receiving end when Dennis died. Since then, she was usually the one to spearhead donations. A role she was much more comfortable with.

"There's also a room for you at The Alps should you and Megan need a place to stay," said Rose.

Carly felt her knees go weak. In the chaos, she'd forgotten all about Megan. What kind of mother did that? How would her daughter react? Would she be scared? Sad?

Andrew moved behind her then. Placed his warm, strong hands on her shoulders. "Thank you, Rose, but that won't be necessary. Carly and Megan can stay in my grandmother's house if need be."

Hillary's gaze zeroed in on Andrew. "Do I know you?"

Andrew shook his head. "I don't believe so." He extended his hand. "Andrew Stephens."

The woman Carly suspected to be somewhere around sixty cautiously accepted the offer. "Hillary Ward-Thompson." She let go, still scrutinizing Andrew. "You wouldn't be related to Clint Stephens, by any chance?"

"Yes, ma'am. He's my father."

Hillary's espresso eyes widened for a split second. "You favor him a great deal."

"So I've been told." Seemingly distracted, Andrew shot a glance toward the house before peering down at Carly. "It looks like the chief might be ready to talk with you."

"We won't keep you, dear." Rose's smile was a sad one as she moved forward for another hug. "I'll touch base with you later. Until then—" she let go "—you're in my prayers." Turning to leave, she patted Andrew on the arm. "I'm glad you're here."

"Thanks, Rose. So am I."

Carly was glad, too. Without him, she'd be curled up in a corner somewhere, bawling like a baby, clueless about what to do or where to turn. But why was *he* glad?

As the two women continued down the sidewalk, Ouray's fire chief, Mike Christianson, approached. "Good to see you again, Andrew." The two men briefly shook hands.

"You, too, Mike. I just wish it were under better circumstances."

Carly swallowed hard as her former schoolmate turned his attention to her. Now married with three kids, Mike was a good guy. She knew he wouldn't sugarcoat anything. Though the harsh reality was what she feared the most.

His features softened as his weary green eyes met hers. "The good news is that the fire never made it to the second floor."

Her shoulders relaxed. That meant her guest rooms were okay. But what about her and Megan's rooms on the first floor? The kitchen, parlor and family room?

"Most of the damage was confined to the kitchen and family room."

"How bad?" She absently rubbed her arms.

He hesitated, his gaze momentarily falling to the ground before bouncing back to hers. "I'm afraid you're not going to be able to stay here for a while, let alone host any guests. Kitchen is a complete loss."

So far, Carly had managed to keep her nausea in check. Right about now, though, she was quickly losing that battle. She didn't know which was worse—not being able to stay at Granger House or not hosting any guests. No guests meant no income, but to have her home taken from her…

Where was that oxygen mask?

As though sensing she needed help, Andrew slipped his arm around her while he addressed Mike. "Do you know what caused the fire?"

Mike nodded, his lips pressed into a thin line. "As most often happens, it was a cooking fire."

Confused, Carly shook her head. "Cooking? But I wasn't— Oh, no." She felt her eyes widen. Stumbled backward, but Andrew held her tight. Her hand flew to her mouth, horror flooding her veins. "The chicken." The earth swirled beneath her. Sweat gathered on her upper lip. "I forgot." She looked at Mike without really seeing him. "And I went to the bank."

A churning vortex of emotions whirled inside her. A feeling she'd experienced only one other time in her life. The night she learned that Dennis had died. And just like that time, this was all her fault, and poor Megan would be the one paying the price for Carly's mistake.

Andrew recognized the self-reproach that settled over Carly the moment she learned the cause of the fire. He was all too familiar with the hefty weight of guilt. He'd carried it for the last two years, since the day he'd given work a higher priority than his dying mother. When he'd finally made it to her bedside, it was too late. He never got to say goodbye or tell her how much he loved her.

He shook off the shame as the fire trucks pulled away. He had to do everything he could to help Carly. He could never turn his back on her. Especially now.

Still standing in his grandmother's front yard, he eyed his watch. School would be letting out soon. And if Megan came walking up here, unaware of what had happened, Carly would blame herself even more.

He wasn't about to let that happen. "What do you say we go meet Megan?"

Carly's deep breath sent a shudder through her. "I guess that would be best. Give me an opportunity to prepare her before she sees the house."

As they walked in the direction of the school, the extent of Carly's nervousness became clearer. The constant *zip*, *zip*, *zip* sound as she fiddled with the zipper on her jacket was enough to drive anyone crazy.

Still a block away from the school, he touched a hand to her elbow to stop her. "Anything you care to discuss?"

Her blue eyes were swimming with unshed tears as she peered up at him, her bottom lip quivering. "What am I going to say to her? I mean, what if she hates me?"

Seeing her pain made him long to pull her into his arms. "Hates you? Why would Megan hate you?"

"Because the fire was my fault." She crossed her arms over her chest and held on tightly. "Because of me, my daughter won't be able to sleep in her own bed tonight. Won't be able—"

"Now hold on a minute." Using their height difference to his advantage, he glared down at her. "It's not like you meant to start that fire. Being absentminded one time does not make you a bad mom." Softening his tone, he reached for her good hand. "Instead of focusing on the bad, play up the good. She's nine years old. Kids that age love sleepovers, don't they? Tell her she gets to have an extended sleepover at my grandmother's."

Lifting only her eyes, she sent him a skeptical look. "That's the only good thing you could come up with?"

It did sound kind of lame. "Well, I haven't seen the extent of the damage yet, but it sounds like you might be getting a new kitchen, too."

"Like Megan's going to be impressed with that." She started walking again, shoving her hands into her pockets. "I'm just going to have to trust God to give me the words."

When they met Megan at the school, she was her typical exuberant self. Obviously no one had mentioned anything to her about the fire. In a town as small as Ouray, that was unusual. Good, but unusual nonetheless.

The kid walked between them, her purple backpack bouncing with each step. "Did you make cookies today?"

He glanced at Carly to find her looking at him, her

expression teetering somewhere between nervous and petrified. Did she really believe her daughter would hate her?

Hoping to reassure her, he offered a slight smile and nodded, as if to say, *You can do this.*

She nodded back. "No, sweetie. There was a little problem at home today." Stopping, she looked into her daughter's eyes. "A big problem, actually. There was a fire. In the kitchen."

Confusion marred Megan's freckled face.

"The fire chief said we're going to have to stay somewhere else for a while."

Megan looked up at her mother through sad eyes. "Where?"

"At Livie's."

The girl turned to Andrew then. "But where will you stay?"

"At the ranch."

Her eyes went wide. "You have a ranch?"

"No. It's my dad's."

"Oh." Her gaze drifted away, then quickly shot back to him. "Can I see it sometime?"

He couldn't help laughing. Whoever said kids were resilient was right. "Sure."

Several minutes later, with gray clouds moving in from the west, hinting at snow, the three of them stood at the back of his grandmother's drive, staring at Granger House. The charred back door stood slightly ajar, windows in both the kitchen and family room were gone, and soot marked the window frames where the flames and smoke had attempted to reach the second floor.

Carly rested her hands upon Megan's small shoulders. The girl's blue eyes were wide, swimming with a mixture of disbelief and fear, her bottom lip showing the slightest hint of a tremor.

Poor kid. The fire hadn't just robbed her of her home. It had robbed her of her security, as well. He had to find a way to make her feel safe again. To protect both her and her mother from any more pain. And standing here staring at the ruins of their beloved home wasn't going to do that.

He rubbed his hands together. "It's getting chilly out." He stepped between the two females and Granger House. "I'll tell you what. Why don't you two go on inside my grandmother's house and make yourselves at home while I survey things at your place?"

Both sent him an incredulous look.

"The fire chief said it was fine. I'll just see what kind of damage we're talking about."

"I want to go with you." Carly looked at him very matter-of-factly. "I'm going to have to see it eventually. Might as well get it over with so I know what I'm up against."

"Okay." He still didn't think it was a good idea, but… "What about Megan?"

"I want to go, too."

Carly smoothed a hand over her daughter's strawberry blond hair. "Are you sure, sweetie?"

The girl nodded, not looking at all sure of anything.

"All right, then." Still skeptical, he went to his truck to retrieve some flashlights from the toolbox in the bed. With the electricity out, it was likely to be pretty dark in there. "We'll go through the front door. Perhaps you'll each want to gather up a few things."

"Such as?" Carly watched him as he pulled out the flashlights.

"Whatever you can think of. Clothes. Toiletries." Assuming they hadn't been consumed in the fire. "Things you use day to day." He closed the lid on the large metal box. "Okay, let's go before it gets dark."

The trio climbed the wooden steps onto the front porch.

As soon as Andrew pushed the antique door open, they were met with the strong odor of smoke.

"Eww..." Megan held her nose. "It stinks."

Carly put an arm around her. "I know, sweetie."

Inside, the parlor looked unscathed for the most part, save for the slight tinge of soot on the walls. He turned on his flashlight and aimed the beam around the room for a better look.

"Don't worry." He glanced at Megan now. "They have people who can take care of that and make everything smell like new."

"Really?"

Killing the light, he gave her his full attention. "Have I ever steered you wrong?"

That earned him a smile.

They moved collectively into the dining room, where all the antique furniture appeared to be intact. But as they neared the door to the kitchen—

"Can I check my bedroom?" Megan's room sat off one end of the dining room, while Carly's was on the opposite end.

Carly glanced his way. "Would you mind going with her while I grab some things from my room?"

The fact that she trusted him with her daughter meant a lot. "Not at all."

Megan turned on her own flashlight and slowly moved into her room.

Andrew followed, relieved to see that, like the parlor and dining room, the mostly purple bedroom remained intact, though perhaps a little damp from all the water the firemen had used.

"Go ahead and take some clothes. I know they're probably wet or smell like smoke, but we can toss them in the wash."

While she opened drawers and pulled out items, all of which seemed to be purple or pink, with one random blue piece, he tugged the case from her pillow to hold the clothes.

"Oh, no."

He stopped what he was doing. "What is it?"

Head hung low, the girl frowned. "My cards. I left them in the family room."

If cards were her greatest loss, he'd count himself blessed. Still, they were important to her. "No worries. I'll pick you up a new deck tomorrow."

Her gaze shot to his. "Really?"

"Cross my heart—" he fingered an X across his chest "—and hope to die."

She threw her arms around his waist. "You're the best, Andrew."

The gesture stunned him. Or maybe it was the intense emotions her hug evoked in him. He'd never had much interaction with kids. But this one was definitely special.

A few minutes later, when he and Megan returned to the dining room with a pillowcase full of clothes and shoes, he dared what he hoped was a stealthy peek into the kitchen. And while it was too dark to see everything, what little he did glimpse didn't look good. Or even salvageable.

"Ah, good. You got some clothes." He jumped at the

sound of Carly's voice. Turning, he saw her standing beside the table, holding a large tote bag.

"We did, so it looks like we're ready to go." He did not want to allow Carly in the kitchen. At least, not now. Maybe tomorrow, after the shock had a chance to wear off.

"Not yet." Carly set her bag atop the dining room table. "I'd like to see the kitchen."

"Let's do that tomorrow. It's getting dark outside anyway, so you won't be able to see much."

Leaving her bag behind, she took several determined steps toward him and stopped. "I want to see it. Now."

Chapter Five

Talking tough was one thing. Putting words into action was another. And try as she might, Carly couldn't persuade her feet to move across the wooden floorboards of her dining room. Still, she had to do this, had to see her kitchen, because not knowing left far too much to the imagination.

She drew in a bolstering breath, the sickening smell of smoke turning her stomach. At least her great-grandmother's dining room set and sideboard had been spared, as had the antique pieces in the parlor and her bedroom. Her gaze traveled to the opening that separated the dining room from the kitchen. Based on the charred swinging door, she doubted things on the other side of the wall had fared so well.

"You're sure you want to do this?" The uncertainty in Andrew's voice only solidified her determination.

"Yes." She eyed her daughter. "Megan, you stay with Andrew."

Willing one foot in front of the other, she eased toward the kitchen door, her mouth dry. Her heart thudded against her chest as though it were looking for escape.

The closer she drew to the kitchen, the more bleak things became. She reached out a steadying hand, only to have her fingers brush across the scorched casing that surrounded the door. Trim that was original to the house, now burned and blackened. And she had yet to see the worst of it.

Two more steps and she rounded into the kitchen. She clicked on the flashlight Andrew had given her.

Her heart, which had been beating wildly only seconds ago, skidded to a stop. The space was almost unrecognizable. Soot-covered paint peeled away from the walls, dangling in pathetic strips. Floors and countertops were littered with water-soaked ash and all kinds of matter she couldn't begin to identify or explain. She always kept a clean kitchen, so how could—?

Looking up, she realized the ceiling was gone. Over a hundred years of drywall, plaster and who knew what else now strewn across the room, exposing the still-intact floor joists of the bedroom above.

How could she have been so careless? This would take forever to fix. Where would she even begin?

The once dark stained cabinets that Carly had painted white shortly after taking over the house were blistered and burned. The butcher-block island top, salvaged from the original kitchen, had met a similar fate.

Noting her commercial range at the far end of the room, she tiptoed across the wet floor, tears welling as she ran her hand over the soot-covered stainless steel. It had been only two months since she'd paid it off.

"Mommy?"

She blinked hard and fast. She couldn't let Megan see her like this.

Turning, she saw her daughter standing in the doorway, lip quivering, holding up a blackened, half-melted blob of blue-and-white fur.

A sob caught in Carly's throat. Boo Bunny, Megan's favorite stuffed animal. The one her father had given her, the one she still slept with every night.

As the cry threatened to escape, Carly pressed a hand to her mouth and quickly turned away. She'd failed her daughter not once but twice, throwing her life into a tailspin from which she might never recover.

"Megan," said Andrew, "why don't we go outside and get some fresh air?"

Out of the corner of her eye, Carly saw Andrew escort her daughter from the room. She appreciated his intervention, as well as everything else he'd done for her today. Without his steadfast presence and guidance, she would be an even bigger mess.

After pulling herself together and taking a quick perusal of the partially burned-out family room, she joined Andrew and Megan on the front porch. The two were sitting in the swing, and Carly was pretty sure she overheard something about another game of cards. If it made her baby happy, she was all for it.

"Ready?" Andrew stood and handed Carly her tote.

"Yes."

"I'm hungry." Megan hopped out of the swing.

Peering at the sky, Carly was surprised to see that the sun had already dipped below the town's western slope. Though it wasn't dark yet, Ouray lay bathed in shadows. And her daughter had yet to have her after-school snack. Carly shook her head, disgusted. Add that to her list of failures.

A black, late-model SUV pulled alongside the curb just then, coming to a stop behind Carly's vehicle.

"Cassidy!" Megan bounded down the stairs as Celeste Purcell and her two daughters, Cassidy and Emma, got out.

Carly glanced back at Andrew, then tugged her tote over her shoulder and followed.

The three girls hugged and were practically giddy by the time she reached Celeste.

Her very pregnant friend met her with a sad smile. "Oh, Carly." They hugged best they could with Celeste's swollen belly between them. Then, with a final squeeze, Celeste stepped back, her brown eyes focused on Carly. "How bad is it?"

"Pretty bad." She drew in a shaky breath, still clueless about how to move forward. "At least the major damage was confined to the kitchen and family room."

Celeste pointed to Carly's tote bag. "Mom and Rose said you're going to stay next door."

"Yes, at Livie's house." She poked a thumb toward the home. "Andrew said— Oh, wait." She twisted to find Andrew standing behind her. "Celeste, this is Andrew Stephens. Andrew, Celeste Purcell."

"You were in the diner today." Celeste smiled.

He rocked back on his heels, Megan's pillowcase full of clothes at his feet. "I was. Good food, by the way."

"Speaking of food…" Celeste started toward the back of her vehicle, moving past the chattering trio of girls, to open the hatch.

The girls' giggles warmed Carly's heart. Perhaps her daughter would be okay after all.

Celeste tugged at a large box. "I brought you some enchiladas, chips and salsa for dinner and a pan of Granny's cinnamon rolls for breakfast." She started to lift the box, but Andrew intercepted her.

"Let me get that." He took hold of the cardboard container. "Smells fantastic."

Carly reached to close the hatch. "You didn't have to do all that, Celeste."

"Sweetie, if the roles were reversed, I know you'd be doing the same thing for me."

The crunch of gravel under tires drew their attention to the street.

The approaching Jeep eased to a stop in front of Livie's house. Blakely Lockridge, Rose's granddaughter, and Taryn Coble, Celeste's sister-in-law, soon emerged.

"Sorry we're late." Taryn tossed the driver's door closed behind her before falling in alongside Blakely. "I had to feed the baby."

"How is the little guy?" Carly eyed the new mother.

Taryn blushed. "He's just perfect."

"You won't be saying that once he starts walking." Blakely had a toddler herself, as well as an almost-teen. And Carly was pretty sure she'd heard recent mention of another one on the way. Her strawberry blonde friend addressed her now. "How are you holding up?"

"I'm still standing." Though given the opportunity, she was certain she could collapse at any moment.

"And we thank God for that," said Blakely.

"Mommy—" Megan tugged on Carly's jacket "—I'm hungry. Can the girls and I have a treat?"

Carly looked down at her daughter, her heart twisting. Other than what Celeste had brought, she had no food. Nothing to give her daughter, no—

"Oh, I almost forgot. There are some cookies in the box, too," said Celeste. "Help yourselves."

As Andrew pulled a plastic container from the box

and handed it to Megan, Taryn said, "Blakes, that sounds like our cue to unload."

"Unload?" Carly watched the two women as they returned to Taryn's Jeep.

"We thought you might be in need of a few groceries." To emphasize her point, Blakely lifted two brown paper bags from the backseat.

Andrew nudged Carly with his elbow and nodded toward Livie's. "Would you mind catching the door?"

Celeste and her girls said goodbye as the rest of them made their way inside. In no time, every horizontal surface in Livie's kitchen, countertop and tabletop, was covered with bags and boxes. And the aroma of those enchiladas wafting from the oven had Carly's stomach growling.

Blakely emptied butter, eggs, fruits and vegetables from one bag and put them in the fridge. "We'll let everyone know where to find you, because there will be plenty more food."

"Oh, and Dad said to tell you he'll be by first thing tomorrow morning." Taryn folded an empty bag. Her father was Carly's insurance agent. "He was stuck in Grand Junction today. Otherwise he'd be here now. However, he's already contacted a restoration company out of Montrose, and they should be here anytime."

The outpouring of support had Carly feeling overwhelmed. She was blessed to have such wonderful friends. Yet as they continued to work, small arms worked their way around her waist, and she gazed down into her daughter's troubled blue eyes. Carly couldn't help worrying. While Megan had been able to laugh with the girls, reality had again taken center stage. Now it was up to Carly to make things better. And she'd do whatever it took to make that happen.

Andrew had forgotten how generous the people of Ouray could be. When cancer claimed his mother two years ago, the donations of food were almost more than his brothers and dad could eat. A scenario that had played out again when his grandmother died last fall.

He eyed the goodie-covered counter in his grandmother's kitchen, recalling that summer his dad had gotten pneumonia. Andrew was only fifteen at the time, his brother Noah, eighteen. That was the worst summer ever as the two of them worked the ranch without their father. Thanks to the town's generosity, though, their family never went hungry.

Now, seeing Carly the beneficiary of their goodwill warmed his jaded heart. He couldn't think of anyone more deserving. The outpouring of support also reminded him of how different Ouray was from the big city. Everyone banding together for the common good.

While Carly put Megan to bed, Andrew called his father and brought him up to speed, telling him about the fire and letting him know that he'd be staying at the ranch. Then he went to work, trying to clean up the kitchen and put away as many things as he could. Whatever would help Carly.

People had been stopping by all evening, dropping off casseroles, baked goods and groceries. Some had even gone so far as to bring clothes and toiletries—those things people used every day but didn't give much thought to until they didn't have them.

Glancing around the outdated room, he could hear the sound of a generator coming from next door. Per the insurance company, the restoration team had arrived from Montrose shortly after Blakely and Taryn had left. So when more people arrived with food, he took the opportunity to slip over to Granger House. The crew had immediately gone to work assessing the extent of the damage, not only from the fire but from smoke, soot and water, as well. They'd also begun the water removal process to prevent further damage and boarded up the back door and broken windows. This was only the beginning, though. Getting rid of all traces of smoke and soot would likely take weeks.

He shoved two more boxes of cereal into the already overstuffed pantry. Had it really been only yesterday that he left Denver? Closing the door, he shook his head. So much had transpired since then. Just thinking what lay ahead for Carly had his brain spinning. Though he doubted she had a clue.

Instead, her sole focus was her daughter, and rightfully so. But come tomorrow, she was going to be bombarded with a lot of things that would need to be addressed right away. And with Carly teetering on the brink of collapse, he couldn't help feeling that he should step in and help guide her through the aftermath. After all, he was a contractor, and she was…the woman he'd once planned to marry.

He closed the pantry door and leaned against it. They'd dated the last two years of high school and had their future planned out. Or so he'd thought. He went off to college in Denver, and she followed the next year. Then he left school in favor of the construction job he'd taken over the summer. The money was good, meaning they could marry sooner and start on a solid foundation, instead of struggling the way his parents had.

But between his work schedule and her classes, they rarely saw each other. Before he knew it, she was ready to go back to Ouray. Hoping she'd stay, he proposed. But she wasn't interested in building a life in Denver. And he had no interest in coming back to Ouray. His dreams were far too big for this small town.

Movement had him turning to see Carly coming into the kitchen. She looked like the walking dead. Only much prettier, of course.

She stopped abruptly, her weary gaze skimming the kitchen. "Where did everything go?"

"Pantry, cupboard—" he pointed "—pretty much anyplace it would fit." He paused, suddenly second-guessing the decision. Who was he to organize someone else's kitchen? A woman's, no less. He was just a single guy whose refrigerator had more empty space than actual food. Besides, Carly probably had her own way of organizing. "You're welcome to move things wherever you like, though."

"No. I'm sure they're just fine where they are." Her tired blue eyes found his. "Thank you for doing that for me." Her praise did strange things to his psyche.

"Megan go to sleep okay?"

"Surprisingly. I was afraid we might have a problem without Boo Bunny, but she barely lamented not having it. At least, not once I told her I'd let her pick out a new stuffed animal at the toy store."

"I take it Boo Bunny was the blue-and-white blob she found at the house."

"Yes. Her father gave it to her."

"No wonder she was so attached." After a silent moment, he said, "They're still hard at work next door, so don't be surprised if you hear noises."

"How can they do that? I mean, there's no electricity."

Smiling, he eased toward her, wanting to prepare her for tomorrow. "That's what generators are for."

"Oh, yeah." She covered a yawn with her gauzed hand. "I forgot about that."

She was beyond exhausted.

Whatever he'd planned to talk to her about could wait until morning. Right now she needed sleep.

Moving into the living room, he picked up his duffel. "I should go so you can get some rest."

She didn't argue but followed him outside. "I figure one of two things will happen. Either I'll be asleep as soon as my head hits the pillow, or my mind will be so busy thinking about things that I won't get any sleep at all."

"Well, for your sake, I hope it's the first one." He looked up at the full moon high in the sky, illuminating the snow on the surrounding mountaintops.

The hum of the generator next door filtered through the cool air.

"What a difference twenty-four hours can make, huh?" There was a hint of hoarseness in Carly's voice.

Curious, he faced the woman who was now beside him.

"Last night at this time, I was slamming the door on you."

"Oh, that." He adjusted the duffel in his hand. "Well, this hasn't been what I would call an average day."

"No. Me, either." She rubbed her arms. "I appreciate everything you did for us today, Andrew."

"I didn't do much."

She peered up at him. "You were there for me. I needed that." With two steps toward him, she pushed up on her toes and hugged him around the neck. "Thank you." Her words were a whisper on his ear, soft and warm. And he felt his world shift.

Releasing him, she turned for the door. "Good night."

Still stunned, he managed to eke out "Night" before she disappeared into the house.

Climbing into his truck a few minutes later, he shoved the key in the ignition and waited for his breathing to even out. Carly stirred something inside him that he hadn't felt…well, since they were a couple.

That was not good. Because despite today's events, there was still the issue of his grandmother's house. And that was a battle he intended to win. Even with this little hiccup.

Shifting his truck into gear, he headed in the direction of the ranch. He had only eight weeks before he was needed back in Denver. After that, he didn't know when he'd be able to break away to work on Grandma's house. Which meant he had to settle the question of ownership quickly. Something Carly wasn't likely to discuss until Granger House was up and running again. Meaning he'd have to see to it that the repairs didn't take any longer than necessary. And that left him with only one option.

He'd have to do the work himself.

Chapter Six

The air was crisp the next morning as Carly walked a seemingly rejuvenated Megan to school. After much reassurance that Granger House would not forever smell like smoke, her daughter was quick to offer up suggestions for both the kitchen and the family room. Starting with turquoise cabinets and a purple sofa.

Now, sitting at Livie's kitchen table, Carly couldn't help but chuckle. While those were indeed beautiful colors, they weren't exactly appropriate for a historic home such as Granger House.

Nursing her fourth cup of tea, she stared out the window at the large blue spruce that swallowed up much of the backyard. She'd spent half the night second-guessing her refusal of Andrew's offer to pay her full price for her half of this house. That would pay for Megan's college and then some.

But it would also mean giving up her dream. Something her brain was too muddled to think about right now. At this point, her mind couldn't fully process anything.

Regardless, her daughter's attitude this morning had

apparently rubbed off on her. She was ready to roll up her sleeves and get busy on the repairs. Because the sooner that happened, the sooner she'd be back in business.

Her phone vibrated, sending it dancing across the table's wood veneer.

Picking it up, she saw her mother's number on the screen. She'd called her parents last night, after Andrew left, to tell them about the fire. So why was Mom calling now? Carly hoped she hadn't added to her mother's worry. After all, with Carly's father recovering from back surgery, the woman had enough on her plate.

"Hi, Mom." She pressed the device against her ear and took another sip of the English breakfast tea Blakely had so graciously brought her.

"Morning. I just wanted to check in and see how you were doing. Please tell me you were able to get some sleep. You sounded absolutely exhausted last night."

"I was." Too many crazy thoughts running through her head for any real sleep, though.

"You're still at Livie's, I take it."

"At the moment. I'm waiting for Phil so we can go over the insurance stuff."

"Oh, I so wish I could be there to help walk you through this mess."

"I'll be fine, Mom. Dad's health is far more important than holding my hand. Besides, I've got Phil and Andrew to help me."

"Be sure to tell Andrew we said thanks for letting you and Megan stay at Livie's."

"What do you mean thank him? I am part owner, you know."

"Okay, then tell him I appreciate all the support he's

given you. Not every man would be willing to do that. Especially one you have a history with."

"Point taken." She still didn't know what she would have done without him and was grateful she didn't have to find out. "Just so you'll know, I did thank him for his help."

"That's my girl."

The doorbell rang.

"I need to let you go, Mom." She stood and started toward the front door.

"Call me later?"

"I will."

"Love you."

She paused at the front door. "Love you, too." Ending the call, she shoved the phone in the back pocket of her jeans and tugged open the solid oak door. "Hi, Phil."

"Good morning." He wiped his feet on the mat before stepping inside. "Sounds like the restoration guys are hard at work next door."

She nodded, pushing the door closed. "I'm pretty sure they were here all night. Either that or they left late and were back at it by the time I took Megan to school."

"That's good. The sooner we jump on this, the better off you'll be."

"Amen to that." She pushed up the sleeves of her sweater, grateful her folks took care of the asbestos back in the eighties. Otherwise she'd have to wait weeks on abatement alone. "I am ready to put this behind me ASAP."

"In that case, shall we head next door?"

"Oh. Okay."

"You sound disappointed."

"No. I guess I just thought we'd have to go over my policy or something."

Feet shoulder width apart, the silver-haired man thumped his tablet against his thigh. "I've already done that. The damage and contents are covered, minus your deductible, of course."

"How much will that be?"

"Two percent of whatever the total is. I won't know for sure until I've assessed the damage."

Nodding, she mentally crunched some numbers. Looked like she'd have to tap into the money she'd planned to use to purchase the other half of Livie's house. Money that had originally been set aside for a kitchen reno. Talk about irony.

"You also have business interruption. That covers whatever profits would have been earned during the restoration process."

"Yes, I remember Dad insisting I put that in there."

Phil lifted a brow. "Aren't you glad he did?"

"Definitely." She again reached for the door. "I guess we'd best head on over to my house, then."

Outside, the restoration company's generator echoed throughout the neighborhood. The sun had risen higher in the sky, chasing away the early morning chill. As she approached Granger House, though, a dark cloud settled over her. Things had looked pretty bleak when she surveyed the damage last night. Now, in the light of day, they'd likely appear worse. She wasn't sure she could go through that again.

Do you want Granger House up and running or not? She didn't have to think twice.

Drawing from the steely reserve that had served her in the past, she pushed through the front door. After a brief discussion with the restoration crew, she and Phil stood in her burned-out kitchen. With no heat and blowers going since last night to dry things out, the place was freezing. For now, at least, the blowers had been turned off.

A high-powered floodlight connected to a generator illuminated things as Phil moved about the room, taking measurements and making notes on his tablet. "I don't suppose you have an inventory of your belongings, do you?"

"Only the antiques." She rubbed her arms. "Why? Is that bad?"

"No." He sent her a reassuring smile. "It just means you'll have a little homework to do."

"Such as…?"

"You'll need to walk through each of these spaces mentally and write down everything that was in them. Everything from appliances to salt shakers. Storage containers, pots, pans, utensils…anything that was lost."

"I can do that."

"By the way, did you have any reservations on the books?"

Reservations? "How could I have forgotten something so important? I have bookings for this coming weekend and just about every weekend after that."

"I'm afraid you'll need to contact those people."

She blew out a frustrated breath. "I've got their information on my—" She gasped. Her laptop?

She hurried to the heavily charred table that now rested on two legs. "Where did it—?" Lowering her gaze, she spotted the half-open computer lying on the floor. Her heart sank as she lifted the partially melted, soot-covered device. The business she'd worked so hard to build was crumbling before her very eyes.

Feeling a hand on her shoulder, she looked into Phil's warm gaze.

"Do you have remote backup?"

Obviously she hadn't had enough tea. Or sleep. "Yes." Dennis had been a computer guru, so the concept of remote backup had been engrained in her.

Thank You, God.

"Good. We'll cover a new laptop." He took hold of the one she still held in her hand and set it aside. "In the meantime, I have one you can borrow. I'll bring it by later today." Turning, he continued. "The restoration company will clean everything in the house, from carpets to draperies to anything else that was affected by the smoke or water."

"That's good to know."

"Did you have a contractor in mind?"

"For what?"

"To do the work on your kitchen. Looks like you'll be getting a new one."

"Oh." While she supposed that was good news, she never realized there would be so many things to consider. "No. I—"

"Hello?" Andrew stepped into the kitchen. "I thought I might find you here." He continued toward them. "Phil. How's it going?" The two men shook hands.

"Good. How 'bout yourself?"

"Not too shabby." Wearing a lined denim jacket over a beige Henley, he rested his hands on his hips. "You two been going over everything?"

"Actually, I was just asking Carly about contractors."

"I guess I showed up at the right time, then." He

smiled at Carly. "Since you and Megan will be staying at my grandmother's, that leaves me with nothing to do. So—" he shrugged "—I'd be happy to offer my services."

"Uh…" Working with Andrew? That would mean seeing him every day.

"I'd be able to start right away."

Phil's gaze darted between Carly and Andrew before settling on Carly. "A good contractor who can start immediately? That's pretty rare."

Probably. But still…

She crossed her arms over her chest. "What do you think it'll take? Two, three weeks?"

"More like five or six," said Andrew.

"Weeks?" Granger House couldn't be closed for that long. And she definitely wasn't willing to spend that much time with Andrew. She glanced at Phil, hoping he'd concur that five weeks was far too long.

"Sounds about right to me."

She felt her body sag. If that were the case, waiting for another contractor would only mean the project would take even longer. And she didn't want Granger House out of commission any longer than necessary.

But working with Andrew?

Seemed as though she didn't have a choice.

Squaring her shoulders, she looked him in the eye. "Have at it, then. The sooner things get started, the better off we'll both be." Because seeing Andrew, day in and day out, was the last thing she wanted to do.

Sunday afternoon, Andrew stood in the shell of Carly's kitchen, the space illuminated by portable floodlights he'd hooked up to a generator, awaiting her thoughts on her new kitchen layout. With the help of his younger brothers, Matt and Jude, along with Carly and even Megan, they'd gutted the space, removing everything from cupboards to appliances, debris, you name it. They salvaged what they could and tossed the rest into the Dumpster he'd had brought in.

On Friday, he went to the city to see about permits. To his surprise, they said he'd be able to pick them up Monday afternoon. Something that never would have happened in Denver. He grabbed his travel mug from atop his toolbox and took a swig of coffee. He was proud of Carly, the way she'd pulled herself up by her bootstraps and dug in to get the job done. Not everyone would have been able to bounce back so quickly. Then again, most people didn't have a kid like Megan to spur them on. She'd definitely kept things lively during the demo, chattering almost nonstop about school, her friends and how the fire had practically made her a celebrity.

Shaking his head, he chuckled. Megan was a great kid. In some ways much like her mother, while in others quite different. Like her outgoing personality. Growing up, Carly had definitely leaned more toward the timid side. Something she'd obviously grown out of.

He was glad he was able to help them. Even if his motives weren't as pure as they should have been. Working on Carly's place also gave him an excuse not to be at the ranch. It wasn't that he didn't love his father. On the contrary, he rather enjoyed spending time with him. The old man was always up for a good conversation. But the ranch was so...depressing. Sometimes he felt as though the place just sucked the life right out of him. Like it had his mother.

Shaking off the morbid thought, he turned off the

noisy blowers the restoration company had kept going almost from the moment they arrived, then glanced at his watch before strolling into the dining room. Where was Carly?

He'd told her that, since they were starting from scratch, she was free to do just about anything she wanted in terms of layout. Instead of sharing her thoughts, though, she'd paced the wooden floor virtually the entire weekend, tapping a finger to her pretty lips as she hemmed and hawed.

Well, now he needed some decisions so he could get the ball rolling first thing tomorrow.

Just when he was about to head next door to check on her, she strolled through the front door, looking much cuter than most of his clients.

"Sorry I'm late." Her blond curls bounced around her shoulders. "Someone called wanting to make reservations for this summer."

With Granger House Inn's landline out, she'd been able to get calls forwarded to her mobile phone.

Hands tucked in the pockets of her fleece jacket, she shrugged. "It felt good to *book* a reservation instead of canceling." Reluctantly she'd contacted all of her upcoming clients, letting them know about the fire and offering them a discount on a future stay. Even though her insurance policy had coverage for business interruption, he knew she was worried about Granger House Inn's reputation and felt the incentive might help smooth things over.

"Well, then, I guess we'd better get going on things. Can't have a bed-and-breakfast without a kitchen." Besides, the faster he finished Carly's house, the faster he could move on to his grandmother's. Though he still might not complete it before heading back to Denver.

Of course, that was assuming he and Carly could come to an agreement. But that was a discussion for another day.

"Where's Megan?" he tossed over his shoulder on his way into the kitchen.

"At a friend's."

Once inside the space that had been stripped to the studs, some of which were damaged by the fire and would have to be replaced, he clapped his hands together and rubbed them vigorously. "Okay, so what are we doing?"

Carly opened her mouth as though she were ready to share her vision, then snapped it shut, her shoulders drooping. "I don't know."

He tamped down his rising frustration. "Carly, you spend a lot of time in this room and do a *lot* of cooking. Haven't you ever dreamed of having more counter space or better lighting? More storage?"

"Yes. At one time, I was even saving to have the kitchen remodeled. Then I got the news from the lawyer about your grandmother's house and my plans changed." She met his gaze. "Still, I never had any really cohesive plans."

"But it's a starting place." He took a step closer. "Tell me what some of your thoughts were. Some of the things you were wanting."

"That's just it. My thoughts are too jumbled together right now for me even to begin to sort them out. It's like somebody just dumped a five-thousand-piece puzzle in front of me and told me to put the thing together without ever looking at the box cover. The only things I know for sure are that I want a kitchen that is efficient and looks like it belongs here. Nothing ultracontemporary or trendy." Suddenly a bit more animated, she started to pace. "I want classic. And white. Something nice and bright."

Efficient and classic. Now they were getting somewhere. "Hmm… Megan's going to be one disappointed little girl."

Carly turned to look at him.

"She's pretty stoked about the turquoise, you know?"

That earned him a laugh. And hopefully lightened her mood.

"Now let's talk layout," he continued. "Where would you like to put the sink?"

Her brow puckered in confusion. "Right where it's always been. I mean, you can't just move a sink."

He couldn't help smiling. "Yes, believe it not, you can. Especially in a situation like this, when you're starting from scratch. All we have to do is move the plumbing."

"You can do that?"

"With the help of a licensed plumber, yes." He crossed the room, his work boots thudding against the floorboards. "What would you think about putting it here, under the window?" He stood in front of the currently boarded-up opening. "That way, instead of looking at a blank wall while you're doing dishes, you can look outside."

Her nose scrunched. "That would be better. But then, what would I put where the sink used to be?"

Good grief. Had she never watched HGTV?

He moved back to where she stood. "Are you familiar with the kitchen work triangle?"

"Sort of, yes. Sink, stove, fridge, right?"

"Exactly. So rather than having your stove way over on the other side of the room—which was an obvious afterthought—what if we put it where the sink used to be?"

Her blue eyes scanned the room. "What would you think about using some vintage and reclaimed pieces? Cabinets, perhaps?"

He kept his groan to himself. The search for those items could take forever, leaving him no time to work on his own planned renovations. Watching Carly wander the kitchen, though, her thoughts finally taking flight, he couldn't help being drawn in. The sparkle in her eyes made it impossible. Instead, he found himself wanting to make her dreams come true. Even if she wasn't sure what those dreams were.

"What would you think about adding a pantry? And a bigger island? One people could sit at."

Her expression unreadable, she simply blinked. "That would be amazing. But how?"

"Carly, this is a *big* space." He stretched his arms wide. "Don't confine yourself to the way things used to be. You said you wanted to expand the B and B. Here's your starting point." Considering he still had no plans to budge on Grandma's house, he probably should have phrased that differently. But the faster she moved, the faster he could get back to working on his own project.

"We can do this, Carly. Together." He took a step closer. "So what do you say? Shall we take a chance on something new and fresh?"

Chapter Seven

Thanks to the wonderful people at the local internet provider, Carly no longer had to tote Phil's laptop to the local coffee shop for access. Instead, she could remain at Livie's and surf the web to her heart's content. And ever since her meeting with Andrew last night, she'd done just that. However, her heart was anything but content. On the contrary, the countless hours spent staring at the computer screen, looking at Victorian-era kitchens, trying to decide what she wanted, had only confused her more. Sure, she'd seen a lot of things that looked great, but how would they work for her?

Having Andrew breathing down her neck wasn't helping any, either. She knew she needed to make a decision, but a kitchen was a long-term commitment. One she had no intention of rushing into, regardless of how hard he pushed. A well-thought-out kitchen took a lot of careful planning. After all, it wasn't simply a room. It was an extension of her. And if past experience was any indication, it's where she'd be spending most of her time. So she was determined to get it right.

If only she were able to envision what the finished

product would look like. The images she'd seen online gave her some clue, but she had yet to find a kitchen the size of hers. And that only added to her frustration.

In the meantime, Andrew was awaiting her decision. "Cabinets alone can take up to six weeks to come in," he'd said.

Did he think she was purposely dragging her feet? That she wasn't eager to get back into her house?

Pushing away from Livie's kitchen table, she went to the counter and poured herself another cup of tea. *God, I could really use a heaping helping of clarity here.*

A knock sounded at the door.

Cup in hand, she made her way to the front door and tugged it open to find a smiling Andrew. As if she needed any more pressure.

"What are you doing?" He followed her back into the kitchen.

Tucking her irritation aside, she pointed to the laptop. "Same thing I've been doing for two days."

"Any progress?"

She set her mug on the table and glared at him. "No. And I'd appreciate it if you would stop bugging me about it. When I make a decision—"

"Get your coat. We're going to get you some help."

Her gaze narrowed on him. "What? You're taking me to a shrink?"

"No. I'm taking you someplace where they will help you visualize your new kitchen."

He was taking her. Did he think she was incapable of making a decision on her own? Not that she didn't appreciate all of his hard work and persistence. Without his take-charge attitude, her kitchen would still be in shambles.

Still, she'd learned the hard way that the only one she could truly count on was herself. She was the one who had to live with her choice, not Andrew. Besides, all of this togetherness was getting a bit unnerving.

What are you afraid of? Andrew is nothing more than an old friend.

Yeah, a really cute old friend.

You wanted to know what your new kitchen was going to look like.

She huffed out a breath. "Okay, let's go."

Forty-five minutes later, he pulled his truck up to a kitchen design showroom in Montrose.

Inside, there were kitchen vignettes, all in different styles. Some were sleek and contemporary, while others were rustic. Still others leaned more toward the classic look.

"Welcome to Kitchen and Bath Showcase." A petite saleswoman Carly guessed to be not much older than her thirty-six years approached, her high-heeled pumps tap, tap, tapping against the gleaming tile floor. "I'm Marianne."

"Hi, Marianne." Andrew extended his hand. "Andrew Stephens. We spoke earlier this morning."

"Yes." Her gaze moved to Carly. "Andrew tells me you're having some problems visualizing your new kitchen."

"I'm a bit overwhelmed, yes."

"That's entirely understandable. And exactly why we're here." Marianne gestured toward the kitchen displays to their left. "Let's take a stroll over here." She led them into the maze of sample kitchens. "I understand you have a Victorian home."

"That's correct. So I don't want anything contemporary."

"Oh, no. A Victorian demands something timeless."

Timeless? That would work.

Marianne led them past a vignette with knotty wood cabinets, black countertops and a rustic wood floor. "Are you thinking stained or painted cabinetry?"

"Painted. I want light and airy."

"Something like this?" Marianne motioned to an all-white kitchen with a dark wood floor that warmed the whole space.

"Wow." Carly stepped onto the hardwood. Smoothed a hand across the beautiful island topped with Carrara marble. The cupboards were simple. Classic. And she liked the white subway tile backsplash.

"Marianne, did you receive the pictures and dimensions that I emailed you?" Andrew was beside Carly now.

"I did, and I already have them plugged into my computer. Once we settle on a few things, we can get to work."

"What do you think, Carly?"

She tried to ignore the feel of his hand against the small of her back and concentrated on the kitchen. "It's exactly what I want. But I still can't envision the layout."

"Come with me." Marianne motioned for them to follow.

On the opposite end of the showroom, Carly and Andrew settled in on one side of a long desk while Marianne pecked away at her computer on the other side until she'd pulled up a screen with the outline of Carly's kitchen. Everything from windows to doors was marked out.

"What I was thinking—" Andrew pointed at the large monitor "—was that we put the sink under the window on this wall, the stove over here—" he pointed again "—and then in this corner, a nice walk-in pantry."

"Were you wanting an island?" Marianne addressed Carly.

"Definitely. Granger House is also a bed-and-breakfast, so I need lots of counter space for prep work."

"I was thinking a large one about here." Andrew circled his finger in the open space across from the sink. "Perhaps with some seating."

"I have an idea." Marianne moved her mouse to direct the cursor on the computer screen. "Where does this door lead?"

"To the dining room," said Carly.

"If we put the sink on that wall under the window, your guests will be able to see the dirty dishes."

Carly leaned in closer. "You're right. I hadn't thought about that." Not exactly something she wanted her guests to see.

"So what if, instead of putting the sink here—" the woman made a few clicks on her mouse "—we leave that as a long counter you can use as a staging area?"

Carly straightened. "That would be amazing. But what about—?"

"The sink?" Marianne smiled. "You've definitely got enough room for an oversize island." She drew that out on the screen. "You could have seating on the far side. Over here, across from the stove, you could have your sink and dishwasher, and you'd still have plenty of countertop between the two for prepping food, rolling out dough, whatever."

Carly was getting more excited by the minute. But

never had she been more thrilled than when Marianne typed everything into her computer and showed her an image of her new kitchen. No more guesswork or wondering. She could see everything for herself.

"That's amazing. I never would have thought I could have something like that. I won't know what to do with all that storage."

"Believe me, you'll figure it out." Marianne pushed away from her desk. "Let's go look at some door samples and colors."

On the drive back to Ouray, Carly felt as though the weight of the world had been lifted off her shoulders. "I'm so glad you took me there, Andrew. Thank you."

"You're welcome." Hands on the steering wheel, he stared straight ahead.

Watching him, Carly realized he'd been the answer to her prayer. This trip had given her the clarity she'd asked God for this morning. She pressed against the leather seat of his truck, wondering again where she would be without him. He'd been her rock this past week, supporting her, guiding her through all the chaos. Something she never would have expected. Even from her husband.

Suddenly sullen, she turned away and looked out the window at the mountains that loomed in the distance. By their fifth wedding anniversary, Dennis had lost interest in their marriage. In her. Even with Megan in the picture, his work at a local internet technology firm took a higher priority than family. Customers demanded his time and got it. Leaving little to nothing for her and Megan.

Never again would she take second place in someone's life. If she ever fell in love again—which she had no intention of doing—she'd take first place or nothing at all.

* * *

Andrew awoke Tuesday morning, ready to get to work on Carly's kitchen. He was glad he'd taken her to the design showroom. He understood that some people had trouble visualizing things. And when talking about something as expensive as a kitchen, you wanted to get it right. But thanks to Marianne, Carly now knew exactly how her new kitchen was going to look.

He'd need to stop by the hardware store before he could get started, though. At first he thought that would require another trip to Montrose. Then his brother Noah reminded him there was now one in Ouray.

Armed with electrical wire and boxes, he exited the store, feeling more invigorated than he had in a long time. Probably because he'd spent far more time in the boardroom than on the job site this past year.

The cool morning air swirled around him as he eyed the snow-covered peaks that enveloped the town and the rows of historic buildings up and down Main Street. For the most part, Ouray looked the same as it always had. Growing up, he'd felt as though Ouray held him back. There was a lot he wanted to achieve. But the tiny town had so little to offer that he couldn't wait to break free. Yet something about the town now felt…different. Less constricting.

Shrugging off the weird vibe, he loaded the supplies into his truck and headed for Granger House.

Aided by the floodlights, he spent the rest of his morning swapping out the damaged studs and marking off the layout of the new kitchen. Since Marianne had flagged their cabinet order as expedited, he hoped they'd be able to shave some time off the six-week turnaround. Before cabinets, though, the kitchen's original hardwoods would need to be sanded, stained and sealed. Something that would prevent anyone from working in the kitchen for as much as a week while things dried.

However, there was plenty to do before then.

With the studs in place, he began drilling holes for the new wiring. He sure hoped Carly showed up soon. He was starving. But also grateful that she'd volunteered to feed him. Otherwise he'd have to make a run somewhere to grab something, and that would only take more time.

Since he'd turned off the blowers, he was able to hear when the front door opened.

"Get it while it's hot." Carly entered the kitchen carrying a brown paper bag in one hand and a thermos in the other.

He stopped what he was doing and set his drill on the floor. "You don't have to tell me twice."

"Good." Looking particularly pretty in a soft purple sweater that brought out her eyes, she set the items atop his makeshift worktable that consisted of two sawhorses and a sheet of plywood. "I've got grilled cheese on rye and some homemade tomato soup."

"Perfect." Especially since the house was still without heat.

She pulled two foil-wrapped sandwiches from the bag. "I didn't know how hungry you'd be, so I made you a second if you want it."

His stomach chose that moment to rumble.

Carly grinned, reaching for the old-fashioned thermos she must have found hidden away at his grandmother's. "It's in the bag whenever you're ready." She removed the lid, which functioned as a cup, and poured in the hot, steaming liquid. "Here you go."

"Thanks." His fingers brushed hers as he took hold

of the cup. Their gazes collided, triggering the strangest sensation. Something akin to an electrical jolt. And judging by the way Carly quickly pulled away, her cheeks pink, he guessed she'd felt it, too.

He took a bite of his sandwich, chalking the whole thing up to static electricity.

Looking at everything in the room except him, she picked up her sandwich, peeled back the foil and took a dainty bite.

"I'll be starting on the electrical shortly," he said between bites. "If everything goes according to plan, drywall should be going up by the end of the week." He was rambling when he needed to shut up and eat.

"What about windows?" Setting her sandwich on the work table, she pointed to the boarded-over spaces where the windows and the back door once were.

"Thanks for the reminder. I was going to ask if you wanted to stick with the same size windows or, in the case of the one over here—" he moved to where he'd once suggested they put the sink "—would you like to go with something bigger?"

"Wouldn't bigger look out of place with the rest of the house?"

"Yes. So rather than go bigger with the actual window, we would simply add another window or even a third, like they did in other parts of the house."

"But what about the inside? The casings and such?"

"Not to worry. I spoke to Jude about it when we were doing the demo, and he said he could easily duplicate what's there now so everything would be seamless." When not on duty, his policeman brother was an extremely talented woodworker.

Carly didn't respond. Merely roamed the space, one

arm crossed over her midsection, her other elbow resting on it as she tapped a finger to her lips. A stance that meant she was thinking about something. And usually spelled trouble for him. Was it the window she was thinking about or something more?

"I don't know about having the sink on the island. I mean, it's always been over here." She gestured to the wall behind her.

"Facing a blank wall." Sandwich in hand, he stepped closer. "Now you'll be able to see your entire kitchen when you're at the sink. Not to mention into the family room. You'll be able to see Megan."

"True. But I'm not sure how I feel about having the refrigerator at the far end of that counter. I'm used to having it closer to the dining room."

"It's not that much farther. And remember, you've got a bigger island now." Wadding up the foil from his first sandwich, he moved beside her. "It's a little late to start second-guessing things, Carly. The cabinets are already on order."

"Yes, but better to make changes now than later."

Why did she have to make any changes at all? "I thought you liked the new design." She was so excited when she saw the mock-up on the computer.

"I do. But it's so…different." She started pacing again. "What if I don't like it?"

"Look, I know you're afraid of change, but believe me, change can be good."

She whirled toward him then. And if looks could kill… "I am *not* afraid of change. But we're talking about a lot of money here, and I want to make sure I get things right."

"Whoa, easy." Holding his hands up, he took a step

back. Why was she suddenly so defensive? "I'm not trying to cause any trouble."

His ringtone sounded from his jeans pocket.

He tugged out the phone and looked at the screen. His attorney. "Excuse me." He turned away. "Hey, Ned."

"I've got the latest numbers for Magnum Custom Home Builders."

Just what he'd been waiting for. "And?"

"Looks good. Matter of fact, real good."

"Gross profit?"

"Seven figures."

"Impressive." He glanced behind him to find Carly still wandering. "What kind of debt are we looking at?"

Ned rattled off the numbers.

"Not bad. Any property for future development?"

"Yes, though I don't have the details."

This time when he turned, he found Carly glaring at him. "Hey, I need to go, Ned. I'll touch base with you later." He ended the call and drank the last of his soup before approaching Carly. "Now, where were we?"

Arms crossed over her chest, nostrils flared, she said, "Everything is about money with you, isn't it?"

"What are you talking about? I'm purchasing a new business."

"Even back in high school, you were consumed with money."

"Yeah, so I could help my parents. You know better than anyone how they struggled to make ends meet."

"So you say."

He wasn't sure what had gotten under her skin, but she sure seemed eager to push his buttons.

He took a step closer until they were toe to toe. "Noah and I worked ourselves to death. Yet it wasn't enough. So forgive me if I refuse to struggle like my parents did." He turned away then, trying to ignore the pain and regret welling inside him.

"Funny, I never heard your parents complain. And why would they? I mean, five sons, a thriving ranch… Sounds to me like your folks had a pretty good life."

He jerked back around. "Then why did my mother die so young?"

Chapter Eight

Gray skies and freezing temperatures were the perfect match for Carly's mood. Standing outside Ouray's one and only school, she burrowed her hands deeper into the pockets of her coat, trying to get warm while she waited for Megan. More than three hours after she stormed out on Andrew, she still felt like a heel. She'd foolishly lashed out at him after he accused her of being afraid of change. He had no idea that those words would haunt her to her grave. That those same words were the reason she lost her husband.

She huffed out a breath and watched as it hung in the air. Somehow she had to make things right. Because the anguish on Andrew's face when he mentioned his mother still gnawed at her. She'd wanted to hurt him the way he'd hurt her. Apparently she'd succeeded. Now she was wrestling with herself, trying to come up with some way to make up for being so callous.

"It's f-f-freezing," said Megan several minutes later on their walk home.

"I told you it was going to get cold. But no...you refused to listen to your old mother and chose to wear your spring jacket."

Megan giggled. "Come on, Mom. You're not old."

Did the kid know how to get on her good side or what? "Well in that case—" she wrapped an arm around her daughter "—I've got some hot cocoa for you when we get home."

"What are you waiting for, then?" Megan took off running. "Come on."

When they reached Livie's house, Andrew was loading his truck. After a quick glance their way, he turned and stalked up the front steps and into Carly's house, shoulders slumped, looking every bit as miserable as he had when she left him.

She patted Megan on the shoulder. "You go on in. I'll be there shortly."

"What about the cocoa?"

"It's in the pan on the stove."

Megan's eyes widened. "Mom, you didn't—"

"No, I didn't leave the stove on. Pour some into a mug and then heat it in the microwave for a minute and a half."

"One, three, zero?"

"You got it."

Her daughter darted toward the house.

"There are some cookies on the counter, too."

A smiling Megan shot her a thumbs-up as she pushed through the door.

Carly tugged at the crocheted scarf around her neck and started next door as Andrew emerged from Granger House, carrying his toolbox. "How's it going?"

He shrugged. "Wiring's done."

"Sounds like progress." She shuffled her feet, waiting for him to respond, but he didn't. So much for small talk.

What do you expect after the way you went after him?

She moved to the far side of the truck where he stood, arms resting on the side of the pickup bed. "Look, I'm sorry for what I said earlier. I had no right to attack you like that."

He looked at her now, pain still evident in his dark eyes. "So, why did you?"

She swallowed hard. She couldn't tell him about Dennis. That she was the reason he was dead. Hands shoved in her pockets, she toed at the gravel in the drive. "Stress, I guess."

He nodded. "I can understand that."

He could?

"I know I can't take back what I said, but I'd like to make a peace offering in the form of dinner."

He lifted his head to stare at the darkening clouds. "I'm not really in the mood—"

"I brought you some hot cocoa, Andrew."

They turned to see Megan moving ever so slowly toward them, now wearing her winter coat, a steaming mug cradled in her mitten-covered hands.

He whisked past Carly to her daughter and took hold of the cup. "I was just thinking how nice it would be to have a hot cup of cocoa. How did you know?"

Megan's smile grew bigger by the second. "I don't know. I just did."

He took a sip. "Mmm…this is really good."

"My mommy makes the best cocoa. She says it's a secret recipe."

Carly felt herself blushing when he glanced at her.

"I was just asking Andrew if he'd like to join us for

dinner." She knew she was playing dirty, basically suggesting her daughter help coerce him, but she couldn't help herself.

True to form, Megan bounced up and down, hands clasped together. "Oh, please say yes. I want to play cards again."

Carly had been grateful, if not a little surprised, when Andrew presented Megan with a new deck the day after the fire. Megan had told her he said he would, yet Carly still doubted. The gesture had taught her that, among other things, Andrew was a man of his word.

He looked at Carly for a moment as though weighing his options. Or trying to come up with a way out. Finally he met Megan's gaze. "What time should I be here?"

Carly was glad he accepted her invitation. However, when he showed up at Livie's shortly after six, as opposed to the six thirty she'd suggested, she could have kicked herself for allowing Megan to go to a friend's. Because if she knew her daughter, she'd be home precisely at six thirty and not a minute before. Leaving Carly alone with Andrew until then.

"Make yourself at home," she tossed over her shoulder on her way back through Livie's parlor after answering the door. Her steps slowed as she approached the kitchen, though. This *was* his home. Half of it, anyway. Seemed her thoughts of a buyout and renovations had taken a backseat since the fire. Still, that didn't mean she was ready to give up on her dream.

Standing at the avocado-green stove, her back to him, she could feel him watching her. Normally being alone with him wouldn't have been a big deal. They'd actually been getting along quite well. But after putting her foot in it this afternoon…

"So, you're buying another business?" She turned.

He stood at the end of the peninsula, making an otherwise bland brown flannel shirt look incredible. "Yes. A custom home builder."

She retrieved three plates and three bowls from the cupboard, feeling like an even bigger jerk for tearing into him. "I imagine you're grateful to have some time off, then." She breezed past him on her way to the table. "You know what they say about all work and no pla—"

One of the so-called unbreakable plates slipped from her hand then, crashing to the floor and shattering into a million tiny pieces.

Gasping, she slowly set the remaining dishes onto the table and stared at the shards splayed across the gold-and-brown vinyl floor, all around her socked feet.

"Don't move." Andrew was beside her in a flash. "Are you okay? You're not cut, are you?"

She shook her head, still shocked. That plate had virtually exploded. "I don't think so."

"Good." He studied the mess. "Let's try to keep it that way."

She sent him a curious glance. "What do you have in mind?"

"Only one thing I can think of." With that, he scooped her into his arms and started into the living room, the pieces of glass grinding beneath his work boots.

"Really? This is your only solution?" Resting one hand against his chest, she could feel his muscles. "You couldn't have simply swept up the stuff around me?"

His grin was a mischievous one. "Why would I do that when this is so much more fun?"

"Fun for you, maybe. For me, it's just—" *Torture* was

the only word that came to mind. Being in Andrew's arms felt so…good.

"Just what?" In the parlor, he had yet to put her down.

"I—I…"

His playful smile morphed into something different. More intense. His gaze probed hers, questioning. As if…

Her gaze drifted to his lips, though she quickly jerked them back to his eyes. The corners of his mouth tilted upward as if he knew what she was thinking.

The front door burst open. "It's snowing!"

They turned to see a stunned Megan.

Andrew quickly set Carly's feet on the hardwood floor.

Carly smoothed a hand over her sweater. Lost in Andrew's embrace, she'd forgotten all about the time.

A quick glance at Andrew revealed how red his face was. And if the heat in her own cheeks was any indication, she was just as crimson.

Megan's eyes narrowed for a second before she crossed her arms. "Were you guys kissing?"

"No," said Andrew.

"Of course not," Carly added.

Without further discussion, Andrew promptly returned to the kitchen and went to work sweeping up the broken glass, allowing Carly to get dinner on the table. And, fortunately, Megan let the subject drop. Likely because she was more interested in the card game Andrew had promised her after dinner.

"Come on, Mom. You need to play, too." Megan dutifully wiped off the freshly cleared table.

"But what about the dishes?" Carly turned on the water at the sink.

"Don't worry." Sitting in his chair, Andrew shuffled

a deck of cards. "They'll still be there when we're done." His grin had her narrowing her gaze.

"Great." She turned off the water, and returned to her seat. "You'll be able to help me, then." Or maybe not. That would only keep him here longer, and they'd had enough togetherness today.

"Megan—" he watched Carly as she tossed the dishrag into the sink "—would you mind grabbing a couple of spoons?"

"What for?"

"I'm going to teach you a new game."

Her daughter's nose wrinkled. "With spoons?"

"I remember that game." Carly had played it many times with Andrew's family. "There are only three of us, though."

He leaned closer. "Figured we'd start her off slow."

Recalling the oft raucous times they used to have at the ranch, she said, "Good idea."

Andrew dealt the cards and explained the rules to her eager daughter. The first person to get four of a kind and grab a spoon was the winner.

Things were rather timid the first couple of rounds. Then it was a free-for-all until Megan and Andrew were fighting over the same spoon. Carly watched with amusement as her daughter stood beside him, wrestling the utensil from his hand.

"No…" He threw his head back. "It's mine, I tell ya. I was first."

Megan giggled, tugging with all her might. "Uh-uh."

Finally he relinquished the trophy, as Carly knew he would. What she hadn't counted on, though, was his laughter. Carefree and unrestrained, like when they were kids.

Making her laugh, too.

Gasping for air, he looked at her, his smile pensive. "Do you know how long it's been since I've done that?"

She wasn't sure if he was talking about the game or the laughter. Nonetheless, she said, "It's often the simple things that bring us the greatest pleasure."

"In that case, this is the greatest pleasure I've had in a long time."

She believed him. And that made her very sad.

Three days after Andrew had literally swept Carly off her feet, the aroma of her tropical shampoo still lingered in his mind.

And that was not a good thing. He was still thankful Megan had walked in when she did. Otherwise, he might have done something foolish, like kiss Carly. And that would have been a mistake. A relationship between them would never work. He was Denver, she was Ouray, and that's the way they would always be.

Yet as he pulled up to his grandmother's house Friday morning, he couldn't stop thinking about that game of Spoons and the pleasure it had brought him. It had been a long time since he'd done something just for fun. Work consumed most of his time. Then he'd go home to an empty house and collapse into bed. But now he found himself wondering—what if he had someone to go home to? A family. How different might his life look then?

Not that it mattered. He was a confirmed bachelor. One who needed to pull himself together, gather his thoughts and concentrate on today's mission. He was taking Carly and Megan, who was out of school for a teacher in-service day, on another trip to Montrose. This time they'd be looking at appliances, lighting, carpeting for the family room and such. Unlike yesterday, when they'd gone to choose the marble slabs for her countertops, nothing was needed immediately, but knowing how overwhelming the process could be, he thought it would be a good idea to get Carly started now.

A fresh dusting of snow covered the ground as he stepped out of his truck into the chilly midmorning air. Though with the sun coming out, it was likely to be gone by afternoon. Just as it had vanished earlier in the week.

It still surprised him that Megan wanted to go with them. Then again, after walking in on him and Carly the other night, she might have thought they needed a chaperone.

He continued up the walk and knocked on the door.

Megan opened it a few seconds later, already wearing her coat. "Hi."

"Hi, yourself. Looks like you're ready to go." Movement had his gaze shifting past her to her mother.

"We sure are." Wearing her puffy white jacket, Carly joined them.

"Okay, let's get on down the road, then."

They piled into his truck and pulled out of the drive.

He'd just turned onto Main Street when his phone rang through the truck's speakers and the name Dad appeared on the dashboard's touch screen caller ID.

He pressed the button on his steering wheel. "What's up, Dad?"

"You still in Ouray?" His father's deep voice boomed through the cab of the vehicle.

"Yes, sir."

"Carly and Megan with you?"

He glanced at Carly in the passenger seat and smiled. "Yes."

"Hi, Mr. Clint," yelled Megan from the backseat.

The familiarity surprised Andrew. Between Grandma and church, he supposed their families had always been intertwined.

"Morning, darlin'. Tell Andrew he needs to bring you and your mama by the ranch on your way to Montrose. I got somethin' I want to show you."

Andrew struggled to come up with what that something might be. His father was gone when he left that morning, and they hadn't spoken. But recalling how eager Megan was to visit the ranch…

"Okay, Dad. We're on our way."

"Abundant Blessings Ranch." Megan read the sign as they pulled onto the property. "This is where you grew up?"

Unfortunately. "I did."

She scooted to the driver's side of the truck and pressed her hands against the glass. "Cool. You have horses."

"Well, my brother and my dad do, anyway."

Megan's head poked between the two front seats. "Where's your mom?"

The question took him by surprise. Somehow he managed to keep it together, though. "She died."

"Oh, yeah." She lowered her head. "I forgot." When she looked up again, she said, "My daddy died."

He was taken aback by her candor. Not a hint of sorrow or regret. Then again, she was young when her father passed away. Not old enough to have regrets.

"Looks like the barn could use a fresh coat of paint." Leave it to Carly to take the subtle approach.

He glanced her way. "Or a demolition crew."

Dad emerged from the barn as Andrew pulled his truck up to the house.

Megan was the first to open her door and hop down onto the gravel. “Hi, Mr. Clint.” She waved.

His father coughed as he approached. “Young lady, I think you’ve grown six inches since the last time I saw you.” Which most likely would have been at church.

The kid grinned, straightening to her full height. All four-foot-whatever inches of her.

Carly stepped forward to hug the old man. “How are you, Clint?”

“Not too bad.” Releasing her, he smiled, his dark gaze sparkling as it met each one of theirs. “Come with me. I’ve got something to show you.”

Andrew couldn’t help wondering what his father was up to. Whatever it was seemed to have the old man pretty stoked.

The trio followed him into the rundown barn.

The smell of hay, earth and manure filled Andrew’s nostrils as he eyed the old gray rafters overhead. The place looked a little better from the inside, but not by much. The roof was still shot.

Dad led them to one of the stalls, the wooden gate creaking when he opened it.

Megan gasped when she saw the two brand-new foals. “They’re so *cute*.”

“Easy, sweetie. We don’t want to scare them.” Carly kept her voice low and slipped an arm around her daughter’s shoulders. “But they are adorable.”

Andrew had to agree. The twins were chestnut colored, and each had a white blaze that stretched from the tops of their heads to their noses. It had been a long time since he’d seen a newborn anything.

"Where's their mother?" asked Carly.

Andrew suspected the answer but waited for his father to respond.

The old man coughed, his expression grim. "She had a tough time with the delivery."

Carly eyed him now, understanding lighting her baby blues. "So they're orphans?"

Dad nodded.

Andrew stepped closer and reached a hand into the pen to pet the soft fur of the first foal. "Remember when you and I used to help feed the calves way back when?" He looked at Carly now.

"How could I forget?" She moved beside him to pet the other foal. "They were so sweet, so little."

Megan looked perplexed. "Did you used to work here, Mommy?"

"No. But I used to hang out here a lot."

"How come?" Megan tilted her head, looking very serious.

Pink crept into Carly's cheeks. "I just liked being here."

"Your mama and Andrew used to be very good friends," said Dad.

Andrew caught his father's smirk before the old man went into another coughing fit. The sound was eerily familiar, reminding him of that summer Dad battled pneumonia. And how protective his mother had been from then on whenever he caught something as simple as a cold.

Urging Megan to pet the foal in his stead, Andrew moved toward his father. "Have you been to see a doctor about that cough?"

"I don't need no doctor. It's just a little chest cold." He

leaned against the stall and changed the subject. "You know, these foals are going to require a lot of care and feedings. Unfortunately, time is one of those things I don't have a lot of."

"I can help, Clint," said Carly. "Matter of fact, I'd be happy to."

"Me, too." Megan bounced beside her mother.

Andrew wasn't sure how he felt about them spending time at the ranch. It reminded him too much of when he and Carly were dating. Ironically, some of his best memories were of their experiences together at the ranch.

"I thought I heard voices in here."

They all turned to greet his older brother, Noah. After years on the rodeo circuit, he now lived at the ranch and helped his father with the cattle, though his main focus was on the horses, as well as the trail rides and riding lessons they offered in the summer. Which made Andrew wonder…

"How come you've got the foals in here? I'd think you'd want them down at the stable."

"I asked him the same thing." Noah glared at the old man.

"And I told you, I want them close to the house." When Dad looked Andrew's way, his eyes shimmered. "They were Chessie's babies."

Mama's horse. The one Dad had given her. Now Andrew understood.

While Dad went over the details of feeding the foals with Carly and Megan, Andrew took Noah aside. "How long has he been coughing like that?"

"A couple days, I guess."

Andrew mentally kicked himself for not paying closer

attention. Just because he didn't like being at the ranch didn't give him an excuse to ignore his father. From now on, he'd have to keep a closer watch.

Chapter Nine

Carly breathed in the scents of the ranch as she made her way into the barn late Monday morning, armed with two feeding bottles. While some people might think the barnyard smells offensive, she found them rather comforting. Until Andrew brought her and Megan here on Friday, she'd never realized how much she missed the place.

During her high school years when she and Andrew dated, there were days when she spent more time at Abundant Blessings Ranch than she did at her own house. It was here that she'd learned how to fish and milk a cow, shimmy under a barbed wire fence without getting cut. And she was thrilled that her daughter would now get a chance to experience at least some of what the ranch had to offer. Abundant blessings indeed.

Too bad Andrew didn't feel that way about his own family home. She still didn't understand why he thought the place so abhorrent. Did he really believe the ranch had caused his mother's early death?

The babies were standing when she made it to their

stall. One even tried to whinny, though it sounded more like a series of happy grunts.

"You guys know I've got food, don't you?" She swung open the gate and stepped inside the hay-covered space.

Immediately both foals nudged her hands with their velvety noses, eager to eat.

"Hold on a second." She positioned herself between them and lowered the bottles, one on each side of her.

Elsa and Anna—she still couldn't believe Clint had let Megan pick the babies' names—wasted no time latching on, behaving as though they hadn't eaten all day. In fact, this was their sixth feeding since midnight.

Noah and Andrew had taken turns, insisting their father sleep. The man's cough had grown increasingly disconcerting, and they'd also heard him wheezing. So, despite his father's objections, Andrew had taken him to the doctor.

She looked from one chestnut foal to the other. "You two need to slow down or you'll get a tummy ache."

While the twins continued to eat, she leaned against the wooden wall and contemplated all the crazy twists and turns her life had taken recently. Inheriting Livie's had meant she was one step closer to her dream coming true. But between Andrew's refusal to sell and the fire at Granger House, she'd once again been forced to relegate her dream to a back burner. Even if she could talk Andrew into selling, would she still be able to afford to buy him out?

After finally making it to the one-stop home improvement center late Friday, her eyes were opened to just how much everything was going to cost. Even little things like cup pulls and knobs for the kitchen cabinets, a sink, and pendant lights for over the island were more than she'd expected. Sure, she had good insurance, but that money would only go so far.

She let go a sigh, wondering why all of this was happening now. Was she not supposed to expand the bed-and-breakfast? Did God want her to keep taking in bookkeeping?

The thought made her cringe.

About the time Elsa and Anna finished draining their bottles, she heard the sound of gravel crunching under tires outside. That, coupled with the sound of a diesel engine, told her it was Andrew and his father.

She exited the stall, pausing to make sure the old latch was securely in place. "You girls take a nap. I'll be back later."

When she departed the barn, both father and son were getting out of the truck.

She shielded her eyes from the sun as Andrew tossed his door closed.

"So, what'd the doctor say?" Noah hollered as he jogged from the stable, his concern evident. He must have seen them drive up.

Andrew waited until they were all at the back of the truck. "He's got pneumonia. And he's been sentenced to bed rest."

"Oh." Her gaze drifted to the older man making his way up the steps, looking none too happy.

Noah shook his head. "He's not going to like that."

"Sputtered about it all the way home," said Andrew.

"Probably would have been better if they'd just put him in the hospital. I mean, what are we going to do?" Noah glanced from his brother to his father. "Hog-tie him?"

Andrew followed his brother's gaze. "I think we

might have to hire someone to look after him. Besides, he wouldn't listen to us, anyway."

"That's silly." Tucking the two empty bottles under her arm, Carly brushed a windswept hair away from her face. "Why not just let me take care of him?"

Both brothers sent her the strangest look.

"At least during the day. I'm here helping with the foals anyway. And with Granger House out of commission, it's not like I have a whole lot to do."

She turned her attention solely to Andrew. "Besides, I want to help. Your family has always been so good to me, this is the least I can do."

"Are you sure you can handle him?" Noah's dark brow lifted. "He can be pretty stubborn, you know."

"I'm not worried." She watched the older man shuffle into the house. "Clint and I get along fine. He's a good man."

The brothers looked at each other as though sharing a silent conversation before turning back to her.

"Thank you, Carly," said Noah.

"If he gets to be too much, though," said Andrew, "you just let us know."

She smiled. "I will. But I doubt that'll be necessary." She took two steps toward the house, paused and turned back around. "Come on. I'll fix you guys some lunch."

After a quick meal of canned soup and roast beef sandwiches, Andrew headed back to town to work on Granger House, and Noah returned to his work in the stables. Clint settled into his recliner and willingly agreed to the breathing treatment the doctor had ordered. He fell asleep shortly thereafter, so she took the opportunity to sneak out and feed the foals.

When she returned, Clint was still sleeping, so since

Andrew had offered to pick up Megan from school and bring her to the ranch, Carly pushed up her sleeves, ready to give the ranch house some much-needed TLC. The Stephens men weren't necessarily messy, but there was something to be said for a good, thorough cleaning. Especially in the kitchen.

She cleared the off-white Formica countertops of clutter before scrubbing them down with bleach, along with the sink and stove. Next she cleaned out the refrigerator, wiped it down, then grabbed a package of chicken from the freezer. All the while, she'd periodically poke her head around the corner to check on Clint, pleased to see he was still asleep. Rest was exactly what he needed to get better.

While the meat thawed in the microwave, she searched the cupboards, trying to figure out what she could make the guys for dinner. Their pantry didn't have a whole lot of variety. Canned soup and veggies, some tomato sauce, pasta… A casserole, perhaps.

Inspired, she put the chicken on to boil. No sooner had she set the lid atop the pot when the sound of Clint's raspy breathing drew her into the adjoining family room. He was awake now, his forest-green recliner upright, and he was looking a bit pale.

"How are you feeling?" She knelt beside his chair, resting a hand on his forearm.

"I know my boys asked you to stay here. But there's no need to fuss over me, young lady. I've been taking care of myself for a long time."

She bit back a laugh. While Clint Stephens might indeed be capable of taking care of himself, his wife, Mona, was the kind of woman who went above and beyond when it came to her men. Tough when she had to be, but not afraid to spoil them, either. Something Carly had always admired.

"I understand. I'm pretty good at taking care of myself, too. But everyone needs a little help now and then. If it hadn't been for Andrew and other folks around town, I never would have made it through these last couple of weeks." She patted his arm. "Now, what can I get you?"

He clasped his hands over his trim belly. "I reckon I could use a cup of coffee."

She was thinking more along the lines of juice or tea.

"I like it black. And strong." A man's man through and through.

"Coming right up." She pushed to her feet. "And just for the record, Andrew and Noah did not ask me to stay with you. I volunteered."

The older man seemed a little more amicable after that. He turned on the television situated in the corner of the room and watched some police show while she assembled the chicken spaghetti casserole. She put the pan in the oven and washed her hands before going to check on him again.

His chair was empty.

"Clint?" Her gaze darted around the room. She checked the hall to see if perhaps he'd gone to the restroom. Then she heard sounds coming from the mudroom.

She entered to find the man wearing his coat and hat and heading out the door.

Suddenly grateful for being a little on the small side, she darted around him to block the opening. "Just where do you think you're going?"

"I have a ranch to tend to."

"Not under my watch, you don't." She held her ground. Even when he closed what little distance there was between them, to tower over her. Though she had no doubt he could push right past her if he really wanted to. She could only hope that—

"Young lady, I suggest you get out of my way." Determined dark eyes bored into hers.

But she had no intention of letting Andrew and Noah down. One way or another, she would win this battle.

Clouds gathered over the mountains to the west as Andrew's pickup bumped over the cattle guard at the entrance to Abundant Blessings. He couldn't remember ever being this eager to get to the ranch. Not that it was the ranch spurring him on. Instead, he was worried about his father.

Why had it taken him so long to notice Dad's cough? If he hadn't been there, would Noah have picked up on it? He didn't want to cast stones at his brother, but what if Andrew hadn't been in town? Suppose Dad had gotten sick and Noah hadn't realized it until it was too late?

What if his father had been at the end and Andrew didn't get a chance to say goodbye?

Truth be told, that was the part that had bothered him all afternoon. What if something happened to his father and he wasn't there? What if he never got to say goodbye?

He drew in a deep breath, refusing to let that scenario play out again.

Then there was Carly. He and Noah had practically dumped the old man on her. It wasn't her responsibility to take care of him. No, either he or Noah should have stayed with their father until they could hire someone.

"I hope Mommy hasn't fed the foals yet." Megan's words as she squirmed in the passenger seat pulled him out of his thoughts. She was every bit as impatient as he was to get to the ranch, albeit for different reasons.

"Are you kidding?" He glanced her way. "You saw how much they ate this weekend. Even if she did feed them, they'll be ready to go again in no time."

She giggled. "Yeah, they were *really* hungry."

Since both Noah's and Dad's trucks were parked close to the house, he pulled up to the far end of the deck. He shifted into Park, his gaze suddenly drawn to the entrance to the mudroom. Why was Carly standing in the open doorway? And why was her stance so rigid, her arms crossed?

Beyond her, he glimpsed his father. Cowboy hat atop his head, he glared down at Carly, looking fit to be tied.

Andrew's heart twisted. How could he have been so naive? He should have known better than to leave her alone with the old man. Clint Stephens was as stubborn as they came. No one except his wife had ever tangled with him and come out a winner. And from the looks of things, Dad had every intention of winning the battle of wills brewing between him and Carly.

Andrew exited the truck and grabbed Megan, tucking her behind him as they climbed the three steps onto the deck.

"Clint Stephens, you get back in that recliner right now or I'll have Noah and Andrew here so fast it'll make your head spin." Apparently neither Carly nor his father had noticed them.

A bone-chilling breeze kicked up as he moved beside the house, lifting the collar on his jacket. Looking down at Megan, he touched a finger to his lips.

Eyes wide, she nodded, seemingly understanding his silent request.

Peering around the corner, he continued to watch. A part of him was ready to rush to Carly's side and give his father a piece of his mind. But the other, more rational part told him to stay put and let her handle things. Because despite his father's intimidation tactics, she was doing a good job of holding her own. Much like his mother had done.

The thought made him smile.

His father continued to stare Carly down, but she wasn't budging. Dad started coughing then, his body convulsing. The cold air must have gotten to him.

Showing no mercy, Carly said, "You might think you're ready to go out there, but your body is telling you otherwise."

The old man continued to cough.

She stood her ground, though. "You gonna be stubborn and ignore it? Or are you man enough to listen to what your body is trying to tell you?"

Andrew had to smother his laugh. She had his dad's number, all right.

His father removed his hat and turned around.

"Okay, then." Carly's posture eased. "Let's get you settled." She stepped away from the door, closing it behind her. She'd obviously won the battle of wills. Just like his mama.

He breathed a sigh of relief, another thought niggling his brain. He'd underestimated Carly. Not to mention his father. It irked him to no end to think that his father had tried to bully her.

He glanced back at Megan. "Your mama's one tough cookie, you know that?"

The kid grinned. "Can we go see the foals now?"

"Sure."

The foals attempted to nicker as he and Megan made their way into the barn. He pushed the door closed, glad that the dilapidated structure still blocked the wind.

While Megan petted and talked baby talk to Elsa and Anna, he tried to wrap his brain around the wayward thoughts that were suddenly bombarding him. Until now, he'd always thought of Carly as the girl he once loved. But seeing the tough yet tender way she dealt with his father had him realizing she'd become an amazing woman.

"I thought I saw you two sneaking in here." Noah closed the door, armed with two bottles. "Megan, you think those babies are hungry again?"

She nodded, her smile morphing into a giggle as one of the foals nuzzled her neck.

Grinning, Noah handed her one of the bottles. "Looks like we'd better hurry before they decide to make a snack out of you."

"Have you been in the house yet?" Leaning against the side of the stall, Noah offered the second bottle to Elsa.

Andrew shook his head. "No. Though we did witness an interesting exchange between Carly and the old man."

His brother's eyes narrowed. "How so?"

Andrew explained what had transpired.

"Maybe Carly isn't the right person to watch Dad, after all."

"Are you kidding? She's perfect," said Andrew. "I mean, when was the last time you were able to get the old man to back down?"

"Good point."

"Besides, Carly volunteered. It's not like we coerced her or anything."

"True."

"I talked to Jude. He's working a double shift today but should be in tonight."

"That's good. I'm going to need him to help me with the cattle." Noah smirked. "That is, unless you'd like to help me."

Andrew held his hands up. "Don't look at me. I've got plenty to do at Granger House."

"Excuses, excuses." His big brother dragged the toe of his well-worn boot through the dirt. "I called Matt."

Their middle brother and Dad had always had a volatile relationship, but even more so after Mom passed away. She was the glue that had kept things together. Without her… "How did that go?"

Noah shrugged. "You know Matt. He doesn't say much. Just that things are busy at the Sheriff's department, but he might stop by." They shared a knowing look, neither believing that Matt would actually show.

"What about Daniel?" Their baby brother was the adventurer of the family and currently white-water rafting in South America. "You need me to contact him?"

"Nah, I'll email him tonight, let him know what's going on. It's not like he can do anything anyway." Noah pushed off from the wall. "Mind taking over for me? I need to run back up to the stable."

The two traded places.

"Guess I'll see you at supper," said Noah on his way to the door.

"Who's cooking? You or me?"

One side of his brother's mouth lifted. "Neither. I checked in with Carly earlier. Said she's got us covered."

When the foals finished eating, Andrew and Megan made their way to the house. Stepping inside, he was overcome with the most incredible aromas. Food the likes of which this house hadn't known since his mother's passing.

Moving from the mudroom into the main part of the house, he was taken aback. His father was in his recliner with a plastic mask over his mouth, looking very pale.

Beside him, Carly turned off the machine that provided the breathing treatments. "Feel better now?"

Dad nodded and removed the mask, his hesitant gaze drifting to Carly's. "Thank you."

Andrew almost fell over. If he hadn't heard it for himself, he never would have believed it. Carly had definitely won the old man over.

And Andrew couldn't say he blamed him.

Chapter Ten

By midday Tuesday, Carly had cleaned just about everything she could clean at the ranch house. She fixed herself another cup of tea, scooped up the mug and leaned against the pristine counter, watching Clint sleep in his recliner. His continued wheezing was cause for concern. She'd hoped there would be some sign of improvement, yet things were, perhaps, even a little worse. Then again, it had been only twenty-four hours. She prayed he might turn a corner tomorrow. In the meantime, she'd do her best to keep him comfortable, well rested and nourished.

The timer she'd set on her phone vibrated in her back pocket since she didn't want to risk waking him.

She set her cup on the counter and turned off the timer before retrieving two large baking sheets of oatmeal raisin cookies from the oven. Chocolate chip had been her first choice, but since there were no chocolate chips to be found at the ranch house... Maybe she'd pick some up for tomorrow.

Spatula in hand, she transferred the cookies to the cooling racks she'd laid out on the long wooden table.

It felt good to cook for other people again. That's one of the things she missed the most about Granger House Inn being out of commission.

She was off the hook for tonight's dinner, though. Rose Daniels had gotten wind of Clint's illness and called Carly earlier, wanting to know how the townspeople could help.

Carly had thanked her and then, as tactfully as she could, went on to express her concerns about Clint's health and potentially exposing him or any visitors to unwanted germs. To which Rose replied, "You're right, dear. I'll just let everyone know that the Stephens have got you to cook for them, so no meals are needed." And then the woman promptly volunteered to bring them some pulled pork for tonight.

Setting the empty baking pans in the sink, Carly chuckled. She could only hope to have a heart as big as Rose Daniels's.

After washing the baking sheets and moving the cooled cookies to a storage container, she glanced around the room. Surely there was something productive she could do. She wasn't one simply to sit and twiddle her thumbs. Maybe she should start bringing her laptop so she could knock out some bookkeeping while Clint was asleep.

Cup in hand, she wandered down the hallway to see if she'd missed anything. She'd washed Clint's sheets as well as dusted and vacuumed his room but had vowed not to enter any of the brothers' rooms. Noah had moved back in after leaving the rodeo circuit a few years back; Jude still spent much of his time here, helping his father with cattle; and Daniel kept his room for the rare occasion he wasn't traveling. Which he was currently doing, so Andrew was occupying the space.

Continuing to drift, she entered the small room that had been Mona's crafting space. Spools of colorful ribbon still hung from dowels attached to the wall, while decorative papers and fabric had been tossed into baskets and boxes and pushed against the walls, as though someone had cleaned up the space without really knowing where things went.

On the far side of the room, a long countertop stretched the length of the wall with shoe boxes and a stack of books piled in one corner. Moving across the worn beige carpet, she realized that they were scrapbooks. She set her cup down and lifted the cover on the top one. The first page was blank, as were the second and third pages. They all were.

Perplexed, she closed the scrapbook, set it aside and reached for the next one. Also empty. Three, four and five, too. Hmph.

Picking up her tea, she took another sip. Maybe they were just extras.

As she lowered the cup, her gaze fell to the boxes beside the scrapbooks. Just regular old shoe bo—

What was that?

She leaned in for a closer look at the one on top. There was a handwritten *N* in one corner.

Returning her mug to the counter, she tugged the box toward her, casting a glance over her shoulder to make sure no one was coming. She had no business doing this. These could be Mona's most cherished possessions. Yet something compelled her to look.

With the first box in front of her, she glimpsed the corners of the second box, finally spotting an *A*. Nudging it aside, she moved on to the third box. Sure enough, there was an *M* on one of its corners.

She grabbed the box with the *A*, set it atop the one already in front of her and lifted the lid to discover dozens of photos. A smile played on her lips at the sight of a baby Andrew staring up at her. All that dark hair. Simply adorable.

Picking up the photo, she turned it over. It was labeled Andrew—4 months old.

As she continued to look through the box, she saw that some photos had been grouped together. Each bundle was tied with ribbon and had a slip of paper tucked on the top, describing what the photos were about. Labels such as Andrew—Ranch Photos, Andrew—Scouts… In addition, every picture had extensive notes written on the back.

She returned Andrew's photos to the appropriate box before checking the other four. Each was organized in the exact same manner, and there was a separate box for each of Mona's five boys.

Carly could only imagine the time this must have taken. Talk about a labor of love. But that was so like Mona.

She glanced at the empty scrapbooks. Five scrapbooks, five boxes. Had Mona intended to put together a scrapbook for each of her sons?

Except her plans never came to fruition. Carly leaned against the counter. Could she pick up where Mona left off?

She quickly put everything away, tucking it all back the way she had found it, and returned to the family room with a renewed sense of purpose.

Later, after Clint woke up and had accepted another

breathing treatment, she brought him some cookies, settled on the overstuffed loveseat next to him and told him what she had found.

"That's all she did during those last months." Clint leaned back in his recliner. "All she could do, really. She always liked to give the boys something sentimental at Christmas. Those scrapbooks were supposed to be their gift that year." His voice cracked. "The cancer got her before she could make them, though."

Carly battled her own emotions, covering by retreating to the kitchen to get him some more juice.

When she returned, she set the glass on the table beside him before taking her seat again. "What would you think about me completing the scrapbooks in Mona's stead?"

"No." He shook his head. "It wouldn't be the same."

"I'm afraid I'd have to disagree." She stood and started toward the hallway.

"Where are you going?"

"You'll see." Determined to overcome his objection, she grabbed Andrew's box and brought it to his father. Opening it up, she said, "Just look at how orderly and detailed Mona left everything. As though she were hoping someone would pick up where she left off."

Tears filled the older man's dark eyes as he fingered his wife's handwritten notes. "She did all this?" He sniffed and continued to dig through the box.

After examining the contents, he looked over at Carly. "You might be right." He placed the lid back on the box and handed it to her. "It would be a shame to let all of my wife's hard work go to waste." He smiled then, his cheeks wet with tears. "I believe she would be very appreciative if you completed this project that was so near to her heart."

"I would be honored to do it, Clint."

He dabbed his eyes with a napkin before reclining again. "I know I haven't been the easiest patient, but I thank you for taking care of me, Carly."

She smiled, grateful that they'd managed to come to an understanding yesterday.

"And for giving Andrew a reason to hang around a while, though I'm sorry it had to be at your expense."

She blinked away the tears that threatened. "Believe it or not, Clint, your sons still need you. Which is precisely why you need to get well."

Things were looking up by Wednesday afternoon. At least in Andrew's mind. His father was doing better, Carly's new windows and door had been installed, and Marianne had called from the design studio to say that the cabinets would be shipped sooner than expected.

Now, as he made his way to the ranch with Megan, his mind was reeling. Since the timeline had been bumped up, he needed decisions from Carly. Namely appliances. They'd looked at tons of them this past weekend, but aside from the special-order commercial range, Carly was still mulling things over. The time had arrived to make those purchases.

Walking into the ranch house, he was again greeted with the smells of home. An aromatic dinner and a hint of something sweet. He could get used to coming home to Carly. A beautiful woman, great company, fantastic cook…

While Megan went on inside, he paused in the mudroom, confused by the train of thought his mind had taken. After all, he'd soon be headed back to Denver to embark on the next phase of his life. And Carly would never leave the life she'd built for her and her daughter.

He gave himself a stern shake before meeting her in the kitchen. "Good news. Your cabinets are arriving early." He followed her from the stove to the refrigerator. "So we need to get your appliances on order ASAP."

Carly poured a short glass of milk and put three snickerdoodles on a plate. "Sorry, but I can't think about the kitchen right now." She crossed to the table and set both in front of Megan and her homework. The woman was like a well-oiled machine.

She faced him now. Worry puckered her brow as she shoved the sleeves of her black sweater to her elbows. "Your father's fever is up."

"What?" The old man seemed to be doing so well this morning. How could things change so quickly?

"I've already contacted the doctor. Trent's going to drop by on his way home, possibly give him a shot of antibiotics." She heaved a sigh. "If that doesn't work, he's going to the hospital."

Andrew's heart skidded to a halt. "But… I thought he was doing better." He eyed his dad in the recliner, thanking God that he was in Ouray and not Denver. Though if he were, he'd have come immediately. He'd learned that lesson the hard way. Still, what if he lost his dad? What would he do? They were getting on so well.

No, he wouldn't let anything happen. He couldn't.

He watched as Carly went to his father, touched a hand to his cheek, then returned to the kitchen with his empty glass.

"Why isn't he in bed?" Andrew practically barked out the words as Carly returned to the kitchen.

Carly's blue eyes narrowed. "Because he refused. If he's more comfortable in his chair, then let him be in his chair." She glanced at the empty glass in her hand. "I need to get him some more juice."

"I'll get it." Andrew took the cup from her and headed to the fridge for some apple juice. His hands were shaking as he tipped the carton. He bumped the glass, spilling the juice all over the linoleum floor.

He let out a frustrated growl.

Next thing he knew, Carly was at his side. She laid a hand on his arm and smiled up at him, as if understanding more than just his frustration over the juice. "I've got this." Taking hold of the glass, she turned to her daughter. "Megan, why don't you take Andrew out to feed the foals? I think he could use some fresh air."

He hated to leave. Still, he knew Carly was right. He'd thought things were on the upswing. Now he needed to come to terms with this latest turn of events. Apparently Carly knew him better than he thought. Not that that was anything new.

While he and Megan fed the foals, he raked a hand through his hair and stared at the holes in the ancient roof. Dad was only sixty-five. Too young to die. He should have been enjoying retirement, not spending all his time worrying about this stupid ranch.

God, why is this happening? First Mama then Grandma... Are You ready to take Dad, too?

Lowering his gaze, he shook his head from side to side. Who was he to be questioning God?

Nobody, that's who. He had no power. He didn't cause the sun to rise and set. He didn't tell the rain and snow to fall from their storehouses.

No, he was a mere man. One who often failed to recognize that he wasn't in charge. That he didn't always get his way. Life was always changing. And not always according to his plan, amplifying the conviction that his job was simply to have faith. Even when he didn't understand.

When the doctor arrived a short time later, Andrew, Megan and Noah joined everyone inside. The doctor gave Dad a shot of antibiotics, along with instructions for Carly to call tomorrow with an update on his progress.

Andrew walked him out. "Thank you for coming out, Dr. Lockridge."

"No thanks necessary. I pass right by here on my way home." He reached for the door of his truck. "And call me Trent."

Andrew nodded. "Thanks, Trent."

Between the doctor's visit and a dinner of homemade chicken noodle soup, Andrew's mood was much improved. Then again, that was the kind of meal that was therapeutic on so many different levels. Throw in a few snickerdoodles and he happily agreed to take care of the dishes while Carly gave his father another breathing treatment.

The fact that she'd stayed so late said a lot about her concern for his father. It was a school night, after all, and Megan would need to get to bed soon.

When Andrew and Noah finally convinced her that they'd take turns monitoring their father, Carly donned her coat, telling Megan to go say good-night to the foals.

The cold night air fell around them as Andrew walked her to her SUV. He eyed the starry sky. "They're saying we might be in for a snowstorm."

"Not surprising. It is only March, you know." Stopping beside the vehicle, she shoved her hands in the pockets of her fleece jacket and looked up at him. "How are you doing?"

"Better, thanks to you."

"I didn't do so much. It's Trent who saved the day."

He couldn't argue that. Just knowing he was willing to stop by after hours meant a lot. Thanks to him, Dad was resting comfortably and, Lord willing, the shot would have him feeling better tomorrow.

He dragged his fingers through his hair. "I sure hope so."

As he lowered his hand, she took hold of it. "I know you're scared."

His eyes searched hers, a weight settling in the pit of his stomach. She knew him too well. But did she have any idea just how scared he was? Did she understand why? Did she know that he'd ignored Noah's repeated pleas for him to come and allowed himself to become so busy that he wasn't even there when his mother died?

Then, as if reading his thoughts, she dropped his hand and wrapped her arms around his neck. "You're a good man, Andrew. And a good son." She kissed his cheek before letting go. "Megan, come on, sweetie. Time to go."

A flurry of emotions swirled through him as he watched her drive away. He was grateful God had brought her back into his life. Because with Carly around, he suddenly didn't feel so alone.

Chapter Eleven

Talk about a dilemma.

Carly awoke the next morning, eager to get to the ranch to check on Clint. Yet not quite as eager to see Andrew. Why on earth had she hugged him last night? That made twice in recent weeks she'd allowed herself to get caught up in her emotions. This time she'd even kissed him. On the cheek, but still… When he'd had the opportunity to kiss her that night at Livie's after she'd dropped the plate, he hadn't taken the chance.

To make matters worse, when she did arrive at the ranch shortly after dropping Megan off at school, he'd barely said goodbye before he was out the door. As if he couldn't bear to face her.

Fine by her. She was feeling a little sheepish herself. Obviously Andrew's only interest in her was as a friend, client and caretaker for his father. As it should be. So why did it bother her so much?

At least she could take heart in the fact that Clint was doing better. She'd prayed all night that he would show some sign of improvement by this morning, and from what she could tell, he was. He had more color and seemed to be more alert. Best of all, his fever was down.

Now it was up to her to make sure it stayed that way. Forward progress was good. Going backward wasn't. She couldn't let her guard down with either Clint or Andrew.

As for Clint, she'd have to monitor his temperature, bump up the number of breathing treatments, and make sure he got the fluids and rest he needed. Whatever it took to keep him out of the hospital.

"It's downright freezing out there today." Eyeing Clint, she added two more split logs to the wood-burning stove that kept the common areas of the house nice and toasty. "And from the looks of those clouds—" she nodded toward the picture window "—we might be in for a little snow, too."

"Glad I don't have to worry about going out there, then." Clint burrowed deeper into his recliner, adjusting the blanket over his legs. A hint, perhaps, that he still had a long road to recovery.

"No, you do not." She closed the glass doors on the stove, smiling, then slipped her hands into the back pockets of her jeans as she straightened. "The only thing you have to worry about is getting well. So you just relax and take it easy."

She retrieved the remote from the arm of the couch and punched in the numbers for Clint's favorite channel. The one that played all the old Westerns.

Seeing the cowboy-hat-clad hero that appeared on the screen, she couldn't help noticing how similar his attire was to Clint's when he was working the ranch. Then it dawned on her. These were the shows Clint would have watched as a kid growing up in Ouray. No wonder he'd wanted to become a rancher. She could only imagine the childhood dreams he'd fulfilled since he and Mona bought the land that was Abundant Blessings Ranch all those years ago. They'd been partners in every sense of the word. Something Carly admired.

Her parents had been the same way about Granger House Inn. So when they passed it on to her, she'd envisioned Dennis and her fulfilling the same role. But his interest in the B and B was limited to income. Everything else seemed to fall on her.

Not much of a partnership.

Now, as she finished cleaning up the kitchen from breakfast, Clint was asleep, so she took the opportunity to head into Mona's craft room to start working on the scrapbooks. Every time she so much as thought about them, she got excited.

Talk about an awesome responsibility. Thankfully, Mona had all of the details written out. Even so far as to state how the pictures were to be arranged.

Standing at the long counter with the first blank scrapbook open, she took a deep breath and lifted the lid on Noah's box of photos. Such a cute baby. Though, truthfully, the Stephens boys all kind of looked the same. Dark hair, dark eyes…until you got to Daniel. Blond, blue-eyed…a complete departure from the rest of them. That boy definitely favored his mama.

Once she had removed all of the photos from the box, she noticed the colorful papers and cutouts used for scrapbooking tucked in the bottom. She picked up a small envelope and found that it was unsealed. More instructions, perhaps?

She pulled out the note card adorned with Colorado columbines, opened it and read.

My dearest Noah…

Carly covered her mouth with her hand, a lump forming in her throat. Mona had even written them letters… when she knew she was dying.

The first time I held you in my arms, I knew I was created to be a mother. You were my sunshine on cloudy days, always quick with a smile. But that smile faded when Jaycee died—

Carly blinked away tears. Noah had lost his wife when she developed an infection after miscarrying their first child. And a grieving Noah returned to the rodeo circuit, as though daring God to take him, too.

Closing the card, she tucked it back into its envelope. It wasn't hers to read. Though she was more determined than ever to complete this task.

Lord, thank You for allowing me to find these boxes. Please guide me and help me bring Mona's vision to life for her boys—

Uh-oh. Voices echoed from the main part of the house. Andrew. Noah.

Drat. She must have lost track of time. Was it lunchtime already?

She scrambled to put everything back into the box, praying neither of the brothers would find her and spoil this magnificent surprise.

Shoving the box alongside the others, she hurried down the hall, pausing to take a deep breath before rounding into the family room. Sure was a lot of commotion going on. Didn't they realize they were going to wake Clint?

When she continued into the family room, she saw Noah adding more wood to the already more-than-sufficient stack along one wall and Andrew hauling in multiple bags of groceries. Surely this wasn't the end of the world.

"Looks like you guys are preparing for the worst." She crossed to the kitchen, where Andrew had begun unloading everything from pantry staples to milk, eggs, meats and cheeses. "It's just a little snow."

They looked at each other before Noah addressed her. Something that was really starting to bug her. If they had something to say— "Storm's moving in quicker than expected."

Andrew pulled two boxes of cereal from one bag. "And a Pacific disturbance is giving it lots of fuel."

Okay, even she knew that wasn't good. After all, she'd lived her entire life in Ouray.

Arms empty, Noah moved toward her. "We're under a blizzard warning from this evening until tomorrow or the next day."

"I had no idea." She should have paid closer attention to the weather this morning. Because if this came to fruition, keeping both Clint and the foals safe would be a challenge. Particularly if the electricity went out. She just hoped the guys were up to the challenge. "I guess I'd better plan to leave early today so I can pick up Megan. We'll have to hunker down at Livie's."

"Actually…" Andrew came alongside her then. So close she could feel the warmth radiating from his body. Though that was nothing compared to the warmth she saw in his coffee-colored eyes. "I'd feel better if the two of you stayed here."

Did he really think her that helpless? Or did he simply want her here to take care of Clint? Well, he was a big boy and *she'd* been taking care of herself and Megan for a long time, so she didn't need—

"I need to know that you and Megan are safe." He caressed her cheek with the back of his hand, rendering her virtually speechless.

There wasn't a thing she could do except swallow the lump in her throat, look up at him and manage to say, "Okay."

By the time Carly served up a hearty dinner of beef stew and homemade bread, the wind had really kicked up and snow had begun to fall, right along with the temperature. Now, as Andrew burrowed deeper under the quilt his grandmother had made, the winds howled, rattling the bedroom windows.

Staring at the blue numbers on the alarm clock, he was surprised that the electricity had stayed on past midnight. Typically they would have been plunged into darkness by now. At least until someone fired up the generator.

He breathed a sigh of relief that Carly and Megan were here, safely down the hall in Jude's room. Since his policeman brother was needed in town, he'd opted to stay at Matt's. Even if he hadn't, though, Andrew would have gladly given up his room—well, Daniel's room—and slept on the couch. Whatever it took to make sure that Carly and Megan were comfortable and taken care of.

A loud crack sounded from outside, sending Andrew bolting from his bed. More cracking, followed by a crash.

Confused, he lifted the blinds on the window and

looked outside, but the snow was coming down too heavy to see anything else.

A million scenarios ran through his mind as he rushed from the room.

Noah was already in the mudroom, coat in hand.

"What was that?" Andrew asked his brother.

"I have no idea, but I intend to find out."

Andrew grabbed his own coat, put that over the Henley and sweatpants he'd worn to bed and shoved his feet into his boots, the actions reminding him of when they were kids. Always wanting to keep up with his big brother. "I'm coming with you."

Outside, the snow was coming down sideways, propelled by the force of the wind. Even with the floodlights, it was nearly impossible to see.

Noah looked left, then right. "We'd better check the barn." He had to yell to be heard over the wind.

Andrew followed him through the snow. "What's that noise?" There was something else besides the wind. Something…alive.

Noah stopped in front of him. Turned his head. "I hear it, too."

Andrew squinted, trying hard to see past all of the white.

Suddenly his eyes widened. "The barn!" Or rather, what was left of it.

"The foals!" Noah darted ahead.

Andrew was on his heels. Drawing closer, he could see that the entire section where the foals were had caved in. But they were still alive. That was the sound he heard.

Together, he and his big brother examined the collapse, trying to determine where the horses were and how to get to them.

"I'll be right back." Andrew sprinted to his truck for some flashlights. Once he returned, it didn't take long to find the animals. Unfortunately, they were wedged between the wall that still stood and a large amount of debris. And they were too spooked to come out on their own.

Noah ducked under the wreckage in an effort to reach them.

"Andrew!"

He turned at the sound of Carly's voice. "What are you doing out here? Get back—"

She put one booted foot in front of the other, her eyes widening. "The foals? Are they—?"

"No." Noah emerged from the rubble then. "But they're trapped."

"Where?" Beside Andrew now, she stooped to look.

Both men shone their flashlights, the snow pelting their faces.

"That timber—" Noah motioned with his light "—is holding things up." Lowering the beam, he looked at Carly. "It's also preventing me from getting to them. I can't get past it. I'm too big."

"I'm not."

Andrew recognized the expression of determination on her pretty face.

He looked at his brother, his heart constricting. With this kind of wind, it was only a matter of time before that timber went down, too. And when it did, the foals would likely be crushed. So the thought of sending Carly in there didn't settle well.

Noah stared at him as if waiting for Andrew's approval.

Carly clutched his arm. "We can't let them die."

He knew that. Didn't mean he had to like it, though.

He met her gaze now. "You'd better be careful. Things could topple at any second."

"I will." A hint of trepidation puckered her brow. "I promise."

Andrew and Noah kept their flashlights aimed on the foals, providing as much light as possible for Carly as she made her way into the barn.

Andrew's heart wrenched, his breath hanging in his throat. *God, please keep her safe—*

Before his prayer was finished, she had shimmied under the timber, all the while talking to the foals. Coaxing them. How she managed to keep a soothing tone to her voice amid this chaos was beyond him.

One horse tentatively moved toward her, then the other.

"Come on, babies." Beside him, his brother cheered them on, though not loudly enough to scare them.

A few seconds later, Carly managed to slip behind the foals and urge them to safety.

"Better get ready to grab one." Noah positioned himself in front of the opening.

Elsa came out first, and Noah scooped her into his arms.

Andrew moved into place and duplicated his brother's move with Anna.

Suddenly, a loud crack ripped through the air.

"Carly!"

The timber had given way.

She was just about out when boards and shingles began raining down on her. She covered her head with her hands and arms. Then she went down.

He started to put the horse down, but she saw him.

"No!" Lying on her stomach, she struggled to break free. "I'm okay." A grimace belied her words. She grunted. "I'm just stuck."

He couldn't bear the thought of leaving her.

"Andrew?"

Over the raging wind, he looked at her again.

Her blue eyes pleaded with him. "Go!"

Noah nudged his arm. "Let's get them to the stable."

The stable? Carrying a hundred-pound weight? That would take forever. But with no bridle or rope to lead them, he held the foal tight and made his way to the stable as quickly as possible, willing God to propel his every step.

Once the horses were settled into a stall, he left Noah to take care of them and rushed back out into the blinding snow.

He ran as fast as he could. His lungs were burning, his face numb despite the sweat that beaded his brow, but it didn't matter. Carly was all he cared about.

Anger burned in his gut. Dad had no business keeping those animals in that decrepit barn. Even after Noah had suggested they move them for the duration of the storm, the old man insisted they remain near the house. Now Carly might have to pay for his foolishness with her life.

Approaching the barn, he skidded to a halt. Through almost whiteout conditions, he saw his father pulling Carly from the rubble.

Somehow she managed to stand, but she was limping.

Andrew rushed to help.

"I'm fine," she said. "My ankle was caught, that's all. Just get me inside."

Megan met them at the door, her blue eyes wider than he'd ever seen. "Mommy? Are you okay?"

"I'm fine, baby." She hugged her daughter.

"What about the foals?" Megan fretted. "Are they okay?"

"Yes, they are." Andrew dusted the snow from his hair. "They're in the stable with Noah."

"That's a good girl you've got there, Carly." His father patted Megan on the back. "Stayed put, just like I asked her to."

Andrew felt his nostrils flare. "The foals should have been kept in the stable to begin with. It's safer, more secure…"

His father's gaze momentarily narrowed before he began to cough.

"Andrew, I need you to stoke the fire for me, please." Carly's expression told him she was none too happy with him for calling his father out. He didn't care, though. It needed to be said. He'd seen enough pain and suffering here at the ranch to know that there was no room for poor choices.

He dutifully tended the fire while Carly helped the old man to his chair.

"I think it would be wise to do another breathing treatment." She reached for the nebulizer.

"Oh, if I have to," the old man wheezed.

"Yes, you have to. But what do you say I reward you with some hot cocoa when you're done?"

Hands clasped in his lap, the old man gave a weak smile. "I'd say things are looking up. Care to join me, Megan?"

"For cocoa? Oh, yeah."

With his father settled, Carly headed into the kitchen.

Andrew followed, noting there was still a slight hitch

in her step. Her ankle had to be killing her. She shouldn't even be on her feet. "You're sure you're okay?"

She pulled the milk from the fridge. "I'm fine. I just needed a little help getting out from under all that weight." At the stove, she poured the milk into a pan. Added some sugar, cocoa and cinnamon.

He came up behind her, laying a hand against the small of her back. "You know, if it hadn't been for you, those foals would have been crushed."

She continued to whisk the mixture as though trying to ignore him. "I'm just glad they listened to me."

He tucked her damp curls behind her ear. "You're their mama. They know your voice."

She peered up at him now, her tremulous smile warming him from the inside out.

What would he have done if something had happened to her? Because if there was one thing tonight had shown him for sure, it was that his feelings for Carly had moved far beyond friendship.

Chapter Twelve

Carly opened her eyes several hours later and stared into the predawn darkness of Andrew's brother's bedroom. Beside her, Megan's even breathing confirmed that she was still sound asleep. No wonder, with all the excitement they'd had last night. Or rather, earlier this morning.

Unfortunately, excitement was becoming all too familiar to Carly. The last two weeks of her life had hovered somewhere between a nightmare and a dream. First the fire, then planning the perfect kitchen, caring for Clint and spending time with Andrew. Time that had involved a plethora of emotions, everything from fear to bliss. Andrew made her feel things she hadn't felt in forever. Things she'd vowed never to feel again.

So, as she eased out from under the covers now, careful not to disturb her daughter, she couldn't help wondering what might be in store for her today.

The freezing-cold air sent a shiver down her spine as she tugged her bulky cable-knit sweater over the base layer she'd slept in. The electricity must have finally fallen prey to the storm. Fortunately, when she'd picked up Megan from school yesterday, they'd had time to stop by Livie's to grab some toiletries and extra clothing.

Stepping into her jeans, she was pleased to discover that the ankle caught in the collapse no longer bothered her. Curious, she put all of her weight onto it.

No pain at all.

When the barn came crashing down on her, she'd feared the worst. Instead, God had protected her and the foals.

She eased into the chair beside the door, sending up a prayer of thanks as she shoved her feet into a pair of fuzzy socks. She also lifted up her concerns for Clint, praying that being out in the wind and freezing temps last night hadn't set back his recovery. The man needed to be healthy again so he could return to doing the things he loved so much. Such as tending this ranch.

With that in mind, it appeared her mission for today was clear. To see to it that the Stephens men and Megan were taken care of. This blessed assignment had filled that void left by the B and B, giving her purpose once again. One far better than bookkeeping.

Emerging from the bedroom, she softly closed the door behind her so as not to wake Megan and padded silently down the hall.

The faintest hint of light appeared through the picture window in the family room while flames danced behind the glass doors of the wood-burning stove, as though someone had recently stoked the fire. And the aroma of fresh-brewed coffee filled the air.

"Good morning." The sound of Andrew's voice sent her heart aflutter.

Rubbing her arms, she turned to see his silhouette approaching from the kitchen. "Morning."

"Noah went out to fire up the generator." Andrew stopped in front of her now, coffee mug in hand, the soft glow from the fire illuminating his amazing eyes. "So we should have some lights soon."

"Lights are good." But she was more interested in heat. She moved closer to the stove. At least it was warmer out here than in the bedroom.

Then she noticed Clint's empty recliner. She prayed that he was warm enough in his room and that he was sleeping well.

Turning, Andrew went back to the kitchen. "How's the foot?" He opened one cupboard, then another, though it was difficult to make out what he was doing.

"Believe it or not, it doesn't hurt at all."

"Really?" He continued whatever it was he was doing. "That's good." A minute later he returned to her side with a second mug. "One English breakfast tea."

"Thank you." She took hold of the cup with both hands, savoring the warmth from both the tea and the gesture. She liked the way Andrew anticipated her needs. And that he'd wanted her and Megan to ride out the storm here at the ranch.

"You have no idea how terrified I was when that barn came down on you." His expression took on a more simmering mood. His eyes narrowed, his nostrils flared. "This stupid ranch is nothing but a source of trouble." His gaze bore into her. "I don't know what I'd do if I lost you again."

Carly froze.

Lost? To lose, one must have possession in the first place. Did he have her? Or her heart, anyway?

Uncomfortable with the intensity of his stare, she took a sip, peering out the picture window at a sea of white.

"Looks like things are improving out there." The ferocious winds of last night had died down, though they still had the capability to send snow drifting across the open range, hindered only by the mountains that stood in the distance.

"Thankfully." His agitation seemingly waning, he retreated to the overstuffed sofa and motioned for her to join him. "Did you sleep okay?"

After an indecisive moment, she eased onto the comfy cushions. "Like a rock. How about you?"

"Ditto." He reached his arm around her then, as though it were the most natural thing in the world, caressing her no doubt reckless curls with his fingers. The gesture, as opposed to the cold this time, sent a wave of chill bumps skittering down her arm. "Because I knew you and Megan were safe."

Her heart raced with anticipation. A thousand what-ifs played across her mind. Were these the actions of an old flame turned friend? Or did Andrew truly feel something more for her?

Movement caught her eye before she could assess things further. Megan shuffled toward them in her fleece pajamas, her strawberry blond hair in full bed-head mode.

"Good morning, sunshine." Andrew inched over, allowing her to sit between them.

Her daughter gave a sleepy smile as she snuggled between them.

"Sleep well?" Carly laid her head against her daughter's.

These were the moments she cherished. The quiet times with just her and Megan.

Except it wasn't just them. Andrew was there, too.

And in that moment, it was as if they were a family. Her, Megan and Andrew.

Her heart rate accelerated again. Did she dare to dream? Dare to consider a future that consisted of something besides just her and her daughter?

With Andrew it would be so easy.

But she wasn't cut out for marriage. Or rather, marriage wasn't cut out for her.

No, there would be no fairy-tale endings for her. She gave up on dreams when Dennis lost interest in her as his wife. He no longer wanted her. When he died, they were simply two people existing in the same house. Definitely not the kind of marriage she'd envisioned.

She wasn't about to travel down that road again. A road littered with broken promises and shattered dreams. Besides, Andrew was going back to Denver in a few weeks, anyway. So the sooner she got back to town, back to Livie's house, back into the B and B, and back to her old life, the better off she'd be.

The lights in the kitchen came on then. The timing couldn't have been better.

She pushed to her feet. "Breakfast will be ready soon." And, Lord willing, she and Megan would be on their way back to town shortly thereafter.

Thanks to a gas stove, they'd just finished a breakfast of pancakes and bacon when Jude called from town to let them know that the power was out all over Ouray proper. Information that suited Andrew just fine. Because the more reasons he had to keep Carly and Megan at the ranch, the better. And since his grandmother's house had neither a working fireplace nor a generator, there wasn't any room for Carly to argue.

While she gave his father a breathing treatment, Andrew took Megan to the stables to feed the foals. Now that the wind had died down, things weren't too bad outside.

"Whose snowmobile?" Megan pointed to the machine Noah had parked outside the stable. Evidently his brother had been too lazy to walk this morning.

"That would be Noah's."

"Oh." She frowned, adjusting her shimmery purple stocking cap.

"What's wrong?"

"I was just thinking how fun it would be for you, me and Mommy to go for a ride."

"I see." He couldn't say he blamed her. Being cooped up inside was never fun. Especially when you were a kid. And there were no other kids around.

He reached for the door to the stable. "You know, we have two more back at the house."

"Really?" She stepped inside, her entire face lighting up. "Could you take us for a ride? Oh, please, please, please." She clapped her purple mittens together.

The sight made him chuckle. Come to think of it, he hadn't been snowmobiling in forever. Odd, since it was something he'd always enjoyed.

Surrounded by the smell of hay and horses, he looked down at Megan. How could he turn down such a cute plea?

"It's okay with me. But it's almost lunchtime, so we'd better wait until after that. And only if your mama agrees."

"Yay!" She threw her fists into the air like Rocky Balboa and danced around.

"But first we need to feed Elsa and Anna."

While Megan gave the rapidly growing foals their bottles, he found Noah adding fresh hay to the stalls and put a bug in his ear about her request. He knew good and well that Carly wouldn't leave his father unless someone was there to look after him.

By the time they arrived back at the house, Carly was at the stove, working on grilled ham-and-cheese sandwiches and tomato soup.

In her eagerness, Megan practically stumbled right out of her boots trying to get to her. "Mommy, Andrew said he would take us for a snowmobile ride. Please, please, can we go?"

Carly flipped another sandwich. "We're about to have lunch."

"No, *after* lunch."

Turning ever so slightly, her mother narrowed her pretty blue eyes on him while addressing her daughter. "Sweetie, we'll need to go home soon."

He didn't get it. Carly had seemed fine when she woke up this morning. But ever since breakfast, she'd been more…standoffish. And he didn't have the slightest clue why.

"Not as long as the electricity is out." He grabbed a carrot stick from the bowl on the counter and bit off the end. "You two will freeze."

She pursed her lips, returning her attention to Megan. "Okay, you can go for a short ride after lunch."

"What about you?" Megan cocked her head, her bottom lip slightly pooched out. "I want you to go, too."

"I have to take care of Mr. Clint."

"I can do that." Noah's timing couldn't have been better. "You go on and have fun with Andrew and Megan."

Now that all of her objections had been overcome…

Andrew lifted a brow. "What do you say, Carly? You used to enjoy snowmobiling when we were kids."

She removed one sandwich and added more butter to the pan before answering. "I suppose a short ride wouldn't hurt."

He wasn't sure what she considered short, but he planned to make the best of it.

When lunch was over and the kitchen was clean, Andrew and Megan went outside while Carly settled Dad in for a nap. Andrew needed to make sure the largest of the machines, one all three of them could ride on, was gassed up and ready to go.

"This is going to be so much fun." Megan watched his every move.

He sure hoped so. The whole notion of a snowmobile ride didn't seem all that appealing to Carly. Something he found rather strange considering she used to plow circles around him when they were younger. A fact she never let him forget.

After returning the gas can to the shed beside the house, he fired up the machine. Revving the engine, he looked at Megan. "Shall we take 'er for a test run?"

No having to ask her twice. She hurried off of the deck and hopped on behind him.

He handed her a helmet. "Safety first."

She tugged it on, and he helped her fasten it before taking a spin around the house.

When they returned, Carly was waiting on the deck, helmet tucked under her arm as she pulled on her gloves. "Are you purposely trying to wake your father?"

He glanced back at Megan, who was wearing the same uh-oh expression he was. "Did we really wake him?"

"No. But with all that racket, you could have." She

slipped her helmet on, then climbed aboard, wedging her daughter between her and Andrew. "Drive someplace *away* from the house, please."

He eased on the thumb throttle until they were a good ways from the house before picking up speed. Snow was flying as they bounded over the frozen pasture, headed toward the river. Behind him, Megan wasn't the only one laughing. Obviously Carly had changed her tune. Or rather, the ride had changed it.

When they reached the river, he killed the engine. They all climbed off the machine and removed their helmets.

"That was so much fun." Megan's smile was rivaled only by her mother's.

"Yeah, it was." He smoothed a hand over his hair, his gaze drifting to Carly. "It's been a long time since I've done that."

"Me, too." Leaving her helmet on the machine, Carly shoved her hands into the pockets of her puffy jacket. "I think the last time I did it was with you." She surveyed the river and the mountains just beyond. "And I believe we ended up right about here."

"Can I go exploring?" Megan squinted up at her mother.

"Yes. But stay away from the river."

"Okay." The kid took off down the bank, past the large cottonwood tree he and his brothers used to swing on.

He eyed Carly. "Shall we follow her?"

She smiled then. "Please."

As they walked, his mind flooded with memories. Most of which included Carly. "I guess we used to come down here a lot back in high school."

She watched her daughter scoop up a mound of snow, shape it into a ball and throw it at a tree. “We sure did. I’ve always loved it out here.”

“Really? Why?”

She sent him a frustrated look. “Andrew, you have got to stop being so negative about this place and focus on all the good things the ranch has to offer.” She swept an arm through the air. “Do you not see this? It’s so peaceful here. It’s easy to understand why your parents loved this ranch so much. They had their own little refuge from the world.”

He glanced around. Too many struggles for him to see it that way.

He turned back to her. Through her eyes, though, everything looked better.

“I guess we did do a lot of walking along this path.” Of course, it wasn’t so much about where they were as it was just being with her. He focused on the river. “I was always comfortable sharing things with you. Like I could tell you anything and you’d understand.”

Whap!

“Hey!” He twisted to see Megan grinning at him.

“Gotcha.” She pointed to the spot where her snowball had struck him in the arm.

“Oh, so that’s how you want to play.” He scooped up a wad of snow and packed it into a ball before taking aim at Megan.

“Missed me—”

His second shot was a direct hit.

Next thing he knew, it was every man for himself. Except he was the only man, and Carly and Megan had joined forces against him.

As the snowballs continued to fly, he charged Carly, tackling her into a snowdrift.

Both winded, they stared at one another as their breaths hovered in the chilly air. Holding her in his arms, their faces so close…

"You know, we didn't always just talk while we were out here," he whispered.

For a moment, her eyes searched his, as though they were lost in time. Then the redness in her cheeks deepened. She rolled to her side, and he helped her to her feet.

"We'd better get back to the house," she said, dusting the snow from her pants. "I don't want to leave your father for too long."

Reluctantly he fired up the snowmobile. Him and his big mouth.

When they arrived at the house, his brother Jude was pulling up.

Still wearing his police uniform, he got out of his truck and met them on the deck. "Looks like you guys were out having some fun."

"It was awesome," said Megan.

Jude turned his attention to Carly. "You'll be glad to know that the electricity's back on in town."

"That's excellent news." Smiling, she glanced at her daughter first, then at Andrew. "I'll just check on your father and we'll be on our way."

So much for trying to keep her at the ranch. Now he needed to figure out why she was suddenly so eager to leave.

Chapter Thirteen

Carly was glad to be back home, or at least to Livie's house, instead of under the same roof as Andrew. But by noon Saturday, she couldn't help feeling that the ranch was where she needed to be. Though it had nothing to do with Andrew and everything to do with Clint.

Okay, perhaps a small part of it had to do with Andrew.

She transferred a batch of peanut butter cookies from baking sheet to cooling rack, the sweet aroma beckoning her to sample just one. Maybe two. Or ten.

Resisting, she set the empty baking pan aside and blew out an annoyed breath. In her eagerness to get away from Andrew and the crazy notions his presence seemed to evoke, she'd practically abandoned his father. Sure, Noah and Andrew knew how to give him breathing treatments and would see to it that he took his medicine, but would they monitor him as closely as she did? Would they remember to take his temperature? And what if Andrew needed to work on her kitchen to make up for the time lost to the storm? Without her there to look after Clint, he wouldn't be able to leave.

Megan shuffled into the kitchen from the parlor, eyeing the cookies. "Ooo, can I have one?"

"Help yourself." The more Megan ate, the fewer there were to tempt her.

Her daughter grabbed a treat before dropping into one of the faux leather swivel chairs at the table. She swung her leg back and forth. "I'm bored."

She wasn't the only one.

Grabbing a cookie for herself, Carly rounded the peninsula to join Megan at the table. "What would you like to do?"

Megan broke off a piece of cookie. "Can we go to the ranch? I'm worried about Elsa and Anna."

"You don't think Andrew and Noah can take care of them?"

"Yeah, but it's not the same."

Just like having the brothers care for Clint wasn't the same. "You're right. It's not."

She bit into her cookie, the peanutty taste sending her taste buds into a frenzy. Hard to believe it hadn't even been a week since Clint's pneumonia was diagnosed. Meaning he was far from being out of the woods.

You said you would take care of him.

And even argued against them bringing in someone else to do so. Yet she'd bailed, all because things got a little too cozy with Andrew. If that didn't sound like a coward, Carly wasn't sure what did.

She polished off her cookie and stood, dusting the crumbs from her hands. "Okay, let's go."

Under a crisp blue sky, they headed north on Main Street in her SUV. Seemed the warmer temperatures had brought out all of Ouray today. The sidewalks were bustling with people. With the storm past, everyone was eager to be out and about and, no doubt, ready for spring. Herself included.

Continuing outside of town, Carly found herself second-guessing her impromptu decision. Maybe she should have called first. After all, she'd left them high and dry. What if the Stephens men were upset with her?

Butterflies took wing in her midsection as she pulled into the ranch. This was such a bad idea.

No, leaving so abruptly yesterday was.

Bumping up the long drive, she tightened her grip on the steering wheel. Too late to turn back now.

They had barely come to a stop when Megan grabbed the container of cookies Carly had made, hopped out of the vehicle and started up the deck. Oh, no. Megan was used to following Andrew into the house. What if she walked in without knocking?

Carly shoved her door open and planted her booted feet on the wet gravel. "Megan!"

Her daughter stopped immediately. Looked at her.

She sucked in a calming breath. "Wait for me, please."

A few moments later, the two of them knocked.

When Andrew swung the door open, his expression was somewhere between surprise and relief. Though his smile told her he was glad to see them.

"How's Clint?" She stepped into the mudroom, breathing a little easier.

"Not too good, I'm afraid."

Her breathing all but stopped. This was her fault. If she hadn't run out on them…

"He's refusing his breathing treatments." Exasperation creased Andrew's forehead. "Won't even let me take his temperature."

"That's not good." And the fact that she could hear

the older man wheezing before she was halfway to the family room escalated her concern.

Pushing up the sleeves of her light blue Henley, she knelt beside Clint's recliner. "What's this I hear about you not taking your breathing treatments?" She hated the annoyance in her voice, especially since it was directed more at her than him.

He looked at her with a mischievous grin. "I was just thinking I might oughta do one."

Okay, now she was annoyed with him. Had he been refusing them on purpose?

She pushed to her feet, dug her fists into her hips. "Clint, do you want to get well or not?"

He brought his chair to an upright position. "Now, don't go gettin' yourself all worked up. I said I'd do one."

"Mmm-hmm. And what if I hadn't shown up?"

Despite looking somewhat pale, there was a glint in his eye as he glared at her. "Guess we'll never know."

Guilt kept her quiet and had her stepping aside to ready the nebulizer.

"You need to take your medicine, Mr. Clint, so you can come to the stables and see Elsa and Anna." Her daughter looked very serious as she addressed the older man. "They're getting bigger every day."

"That's 'cause they've got you takin' care of them," he said.

"Speaking of Elsa and Anna—" Andrew smiled down at Megan "—would you like to go see them?"

"Uh-huh." Her head bobbed like crazy with excitement. Then again, those horses were her main reason for wanting to come out here.

"Where's Noah?" Deciding she'd better take Clint's

temp before the breathing treatment, Carly retrieved the thermometer from the side table.

"Checking horses and cattle." Andrew was already on his way into the mudroom with a happy Megan. Carly genuinely appreciated his attentiveness to her daughter. Something Megan had rarely received from her father.

Alone with Clint, Carly pulled the beeping thermometer from his mouth. 98.8. Not too bad. "You were being stubborn again, weren't you?"

"I love my sons dearly, but they don't have your bedside manner."

His words pricked her heart. He wasn't just counting on her. He trusted her.

She shoved the thermometer back into its case, finding it tough to look him in the eye. "I'm sorry for deserting you."

Grabbing the nebulizer mask, she tugged on the elastic band.

Before she could slip it over his head, he reached a hand up to stop her. "Carly, I'd like to ask you a favor."

Lowering her hands, she said, "What's that?"

"I'd like you to help me keep Andrew in Ouray."

Confusion narrowed her gaze. "Keep him in Ouray? For how long?"

"Forever."

Her heart tripped and stuttered. Andrew in Ouray? Forever? What would that mean for her? For them? Staying away from him was challenging enough as it was.

"But Andrew's built a life in Denver," she said. "He's about to close on a new business. Besides, you give me too much credit. What could I possibly do to make Andrew want to stay in Ouray?"

"All Denver has done is steal his joy. When he first

got here, his eyes had lost their spark. But now…he looks better than ever. And you're partly to thank for that." He wagged a finger in her direction. "You, my dear, have far more influence over my son than you think."

Carly begged to differ. If anyone had influence, it was Andrew. Every time she saw him, she felt like a teenager again. He was her first kiss. Her first love.

But he'd chosen work over her. Just like Dennis had done.

"Mind if I think on it for a bit?"

Lips pursed, he sent her a frustrated look. "Don't take too long. We haven't got much time."

Standing again, she slipped the mask over Clint's face. For his sake, she might drop a few hints to Andrew if the opportunity presented itself. For her heart's sake, though, she couldn't help hoping they'd fall on a deaf ear. If Andrew stayed, he'd fight even harder to keep his grandmother's house. Leaving her dreams of expanding the B and B in the dust.

By Tuesday, Dad was doing noticeably better. His color was back, there hadn't been any fever spikes since the weekend, and the coughing and wheezing had subsided considerably. All because of Carly and the care she'd been giving him.

Andrew was envious. He wished he could spend as much time with her as his father had. Because if there was one thing he'd learned since returning to Ouray, it was that life was better with Carly around.

Lately, though, they barely crossed paths. Only when he brought Megan to the ranch after school. Even then, Carly didn't seem to have time to stop and talk like before. Instead, she'd get dinner on the table and she and Megan would be on their way.

Sometimes he couldn't help wondering if she was purposely avoiding him. Ever since the blizzard, things had been different, though he didn't have a clue why.

He wound his truck past the red sandstone formations north of Ouray. In the last few days he'd made great strides in bringing Carly's old home back to life. The mitigation team had completed their work over the weekend, allowing him to get started on the floors.

He frowned. Now that the refinishing process was complete, he'd need to allow a couple of days for the floors to dry. This would be the perfect time for him to get some work done on his grandmother's house. But with Carly and Megan living there, that was out of the question.

Hands on the steering wheel, he eyed the open rangeland with its rapidly dwindling snowpack. He and Carly hadn't even discussed Grandma's place since the fire. But now that things were winding down at Granger House, leaving him only a couple of weeks before the closing on Magnum Homes, he'd need to find a way to bring it up. As a businessman, he could appreciate Carly wanting to expand the B and B. But as the great-grandson of the man who built the house in question, he refused to let it leave the family. Something Carly should understand better than anyone.

Turning in to the ranch with Megan, he hoped that maybe tonight he could convince Carly to stay for dinner. Or that he could at least carve out a little time to talk with her before she left.

"Are you looking forward to seeing your grandparents?" Carly's in-laws had invited Megan to come and visit during spring break next week.

"Uh-huh." She craned her neck, trying to see the corral as they continued past the stable. No doubt looking for the foals. "My cousin, Mia, is going to be there. We always have fun. Who's here?" She pointed to the unfamiliar white SUV parked beside his father's dually.

"I don't know," he said.

He eased the pickup to a stop, surveying the dingy ranch house in front of him and the partially collapsed barn in his rearview mirror. There never had been any shortage of work around this place, but he'd never seen things look this bad, either. He supposed he could help. If he had the time. Which he didn't. At least, not now.

Grabbing his thermos, he exited the truck. He could hardly wait to see what kind of food Carly had waiting for them today. He really did enjoy walking into the house and being greeted with the aromas of fresh baked sweets and dinner in progress.

When he and Megan entered the mudroom, they were met with the sound of laughter. And a voice he didn't recognize.

He sniffed the air. Carly had been baking, all right, but where was the savory smell of tonight's meal?

Disappointment wove through him, even though he knew it was wrong. It wasn't like Carly was their maid. She was taking care of his father out of the goodness of her heart, and he had no right to expect anything more. Yet he did want more. He liked coming home to her. Liked sharing the events of his day with her.

He supposed he'd better get used to it, though. Because once he went back to Denver, he'd have no one.

Inside the family room, Dad sat upright in his recliner, while Carly was on the couch beside the blond-haired woman who'd stopped by Granger House right after the fire. What was her name? Hillary something.

Dad was the first to see them. "There they are." He held his arms out. "How's my favorite nine-year-old?"

Megan giggled, dropped her backpack and gave the old man a hug.

"How was school?" Dad had become quite enamored with Megan over the past week or so. The kid had a way of bringing out the best in his old man.

"I got a hundred on my math test."

"Excellent."

"News like that deserves a brownie." Carly stood, eyeing Megan first, then Andrew, before continuing into the kitchen. "You remember Ms. Hillary, don't you?"

Megan waved. "Hi." Seemingly shy, she remained beside his father.

"Good to see you again, Hillary." Andrew nodded in her direction.

The woman studied him a moment. "Yes. We met the day of the fire, correct?"

"Yes, ma'am."

"Hillary and I were in school together," said Dad.

"Though I was much younger than your father," she was quick to add.

"Three years isn't that much difference." The old man frowned.

Carly returned with a plate of brownies in one hand and a stack of napkins in the other. She offered a treat to Megan first, along with a napkin, then continued around the room. "Hillary brought dinner for you guys."

You guys? As in just him, Dad and Noah?

"Pot roast, smashed potatoes..." Hillary waved a

hand. "Celeste does so much cooking anyway, we're never going to know when that nesting urge hits her."

Carly set the plate on the side table at the end of the couch. "If she's anything like me, she'll be cleaning everything in sight a couple days before going into labor."

Hillary touched a long fingernail to her lips. "Yes, I seem to recall that when I was close to delivering Celeste, too."

"Hillary Ward. A grandmother." His father's smile held a definite air of mischief. "I always thought world domination woulda been more your style."

"That's Hillary Ward-Thompson." The woman pushed to her feet. "And no, darling, not *world.* I prefer corporate domination."

"So how come you're back in Ouray?" Dad looked up at her, one graying brow lifted in amusement.

She tugged on the hem of her crisp white blouse. "According to my doctor, I put too much of my heart into my job and it couldn't keep up. So, considering I have two granddaughters now and another grandchild on the way, I decided there were better ways to spend my time than jet-setting across the globe."

"Woman, you're too young to retire."

"Who said anything about retiring?" Hillary glared at his father. "I'm merely redirecting my focus."

Andrew caught Carly smiling at the pair. Not that he could blame her. Watching the interaction between Hillary and his father was more entertaining than most television shows.

His phone rang in his pocket. He pulled it out to see his attorney's name on the screen. "Excuse me, please." He made his way down the hall to his bedroom. "What's up, Ned?"

"Hey, good news. I just got word that the closing date for Magnum has been moved up."

"Moved up?" A few weeks ago, that would have been great news. But now… "To when?"

"Two weeks from today."

"Two weeks?" He raked a hand through his hair. Granger House would barely be done by then. What about his grandmother's house? That had been his sole purpose in coming back to Ouray in the first place.

"I think the sister is afraid her brother will change his mind."

Change his mind? But they had an agreement.

"That time frame isn't going to be a problem, is it?"

He stared out the window, eyeing the mountains just past the river. "Sorry. My father's been ill. And I've been busy with a project." Not the one he'd initially intended, but one he was coming to wish would never end. "I'll be there, though. Go ahead and email me the details."

A lead weight formed in his stomach as he ended the call. Why did they have to move the closing up? Usually it was the other way around. And for once, he would have preferred it that way. Because for the first time in his life, he actually wanted to be in Ouray.

Chapter Fourteen

Carly wanted to keep her baby here at home.

Watching Megan pack, she tried to douse the ache in her heart with another cup of tea, all the while keeping one eye glued to the window, waiting for the Wagners' arrival. Sure, Megan had gone to visit Dennis's parents before, but never without her. Like it or not, though, her daughter was growing up. And it was important that she maintain a relationship with her father's parents.

Still, the kid didn't have to act so excited about leaving.

If only Carly could go with her. But between the repairs at Granger House, helping with the foals and looking in on Clint, there was no way she could break away.

She huffed out a breath. Sometimes being a grown-up was such a pain. She'd much rather throw herself on the floor and kick and scream until Megan agreed to stay.

"There they are!" Megan practically squealed. She rushed to the bed and tugged her new Hello Kitty suitcase onto the floor. The *thwamp*, *thwamp*, *thwamp* of the wheels as she rolled it across the wooden planks was like a hammer to Carly's heart.

Willing herself to remain calm, she joined her daughter in the parlor as Megan threw open the door.

"Mia's here, too." Both Megan's fists went into the air and she jumped in circles. "Yay!"

Carly peered out the window with the sudden suspicion that having Megan visit was more Mia's idea than her grandparents'. She didn't doubt that the Wagners loved her daughter, but she often got the feeling that Megan was more of an afterthought because she didn't live in Grand Junction like their other grandchildren. Something they'd tried to change for years when Dennis was alive. His parents had played a big role in Dennis's push to move there.

Shaking away the less than pleasant thoughts, Carly set her mug on a coaster atop a side table and moved on to the door.

Mia had rushed ahead of her grandparents, and she and Megan were already hugging on the porch.

Carly pushed the storm door open.

Beverly Wagner waved and gave a half smile as she meandered up the walk. Of course, she never actually looked at Carly. She was too busy scrutinizing Livie's house. Granted, it hadn't been modernized and wasn't in pristine condition, but it was still charming and comfortable. Not to mention convenient. And far better than a hotel room.

Behind Beverly, her husband, Chuck, made eye contact and grinned. "Hello, Carly." He always was the more laid back of the two, able to see the good in everything. Including her.

After a round of hugs and a report on details of the fire, Carly took them next door to Granger House to show them the progress on her new kitchen.

Passing through the front door, she said, "I'm still amazed that they managed to get rid of the smoke smell."

Megan pinched her nose. "It was *disgusting.*"

Chuck smiled and ruffled his granddaughter's hair. "From what I hear, those restoration teams are pretty good."

"And here's your proof." Carly gestured to the sitting area in the parlor. "Not a trace of soot or smoke." Everything there looked virtually the same way it had before. She drew in a relieved breath. "We were blessed that the fire was contained to the kitchen and family room."

"Yes, you were." Chuck came alongside her, wrapping an arm around her shoulders. "And we're thankful that neither you nor Megan was hurt."

Beverly hugged Megan, a genuine smile lighting her typically sober face. "Yes, we are."

Tears pricked the backs of Carly's eyes. Blinking, she led them into the dining room where, again, everything had been restored. The ceiling and walls were soot-free and the antique furniture cleaned. Even the molding around the door, the one that had been charred, looked the way it used to. "I still can't believe this room was untouched by either the fire or the water."

At the opening to the kitchen, she paused. "But this is where we took the worst hit." Excitement bubbled inside as she tugged the protective plastic sheeting to one side, allowing Mia and the Wagners to see in.

"They just installed the cabinets yesterday." She led them into the space. In addition to the cabinets, the freshly painted drywall made everything look so fresh and new, despite the wires that still peeked out of holes where light fixtures, switches and outlets would go. "Andrew covered the floors with this paper so they wouldn't get scratched. But they're a beautiful dark walnut color. Andrew said—"

"Who's Andrew?" Beverly's judgmental gaze narrowed and shifted to Carly.

"My contractor."

"Her *boy*friend." Megan giggled with her cousin, grinning like a goofball, batting her eyelashes.

Perhaps telling her goodbye might be easier than she first thought. "Megan… Andrew and I are friends, but he is *not* my boyfriend."

Megan fisted her hands on her hips, drew her eyebrows downward. "Well, he should be." She looked up at her grandparents. "He's really nice. And he has a ranch."

Carly cringed. While she appreciated Megan's fondness for Andrew, this kind of talk was putting her in a very awkward position.

She turned to her in-laws and forced a smile. "His father has a ranch. Andrew lives in Denver. He's visiting his father." She then glared at Megan, albeit ever so subtly.

Though Beverly didn't say anything, Carly couldn't help noticing the look of disapproval on her face. The silent commentary the woman no doubt had regarding Carly being seen with another man.

By the time they pulled away ten minutes later, Carly wasn't sure if she wanted to cheer or cry. In the end, crying won out. Four whole days without her baby. How would she survive?

The best thing she could do now was redirect her attention. Find something else to concentrate on besides her daughter's absence.

Considering she'd focused on few things besides her daughter in the last nine years, that was going to be tough. The only person she could think of who needed her attention now was Clint. And even he didn't really need her anymore. Still, she'd agreed to take care of him and that's just what she'd do.

And in the evenings, after tending to what little bookkeeping she had, she might even make some headway on Mona's scrapbooks. With Clint's approval, she'd brought all of the boxes back to Livie's earlier this week.

She gathered her things to head to the ranch, yet before she could make it out the door, another round of tears had her reaching for a box of tissues. The doorbell interrupted her pity party, though.

Dabbing her eyes, she drew in two deep breaths and opened the door to find Andrew standing on her front porch.

He opened the storm door. "You miss her already, don't you?"

All she could do was nod as tears streamed down her cheeks once again. Talk about a poor excuse for a grown-up.

Moving inside, Andrew enveloped her in his strong embrace. The smell of fresh air and coffee wrapped around her as he stroked her back, her hair.

She savored his strength. And boy, did he feel good.

"How about this?" He set her away from him.

Still lost in the fog of his embrace, she struggled to focus.

"Tell me one thing that you've been dying to do but couldn't do with Megan."

She hadn't done anything without considering Megan in…ever. She shrugged, forcing her brain to think. "I don't know. Go see a movie at the theater." She looked up at Andrew. "One of *my* choosing."

He stood there staring at her as though she'd lost her mind. Then… "Get your jacket. We're going to the movies."

Carly watched him, recalling the look in her mother-in-law's eye when they discussed Andrew. Going to the movies with him would be almost like a…a date.

And what would be wrong with that?

Clint. "Wait, wait, wait… What about your father? What if he needs help?"

"Sorry, I forgot to tell you. Daniel's back home."

"When did he get in?"

"Last night. Noah and I have filled him in on everything, and since he's eager to spend some time with the old man…" He held out his hand. "This day is all about you."

Andrew couldn't bear to see Carly so sad. When he arrived at his grandmother's house early this afternoon, his intention had been to discuss their joint ownership and what to do with the place. But after seeing the heart-wrenching look on her face, he couldn't bear to broach the topic. All he wanted now was to see Carly smile.

"So, what would you like to see?" Standing in front of the movie theater in Montrose, the bright midday sun shining down on them, he watched Carly as she stared at the marquee. Considering there were only three shows to choose from, it shouldn't take her long to decide. Not like the multiplexes in Denver that showed twenty-plus movies all at the same time.

"Well, they are showing that new romantic comedy with Matthew McConaughey. But I hate to do that to you."

"Do what to me?"

"Make you sit through a rom-com."

"Are you kidding?" He stepped in front of her now. "I happen to be a big Matthew McConaughey fan." Though he would have preferred a nice horror flick. Something good and scary that would have Carly reaching for him.

"No, you're not."

He slapped a hand to his chest and stumbled backward. "Madam, it wounds me that you would question my sincerity."

She looked at him with pretty, tear-free blue eyes. "Okay, fine. Mr. McConaughey it is, then."

They purchased their tickets then headed straight for the snack bar. After all, neither of them had eaten lunch, and the aroma of popcorn was too powerful to resist.

"Would you like butter on that?" The freckle-faced girl on the other side of the counter eyed him first, then Carly.

"Definitely," said Carly. "Oh, and a box of Junior Mints, too, please."

Andrew wrinkled his nose. "You still dump those things in the popcorn like you used to?"

"Of course. How else are you going to get that whole sweet and salty experience?"

Andrew caught the girl's attention. "Make that two popcorns, please."

Carly elbowed him in the ribs. "You didn't used to complain."

"Because back then I had enough money for only one popcorn." Grinning, he reached for his wallet. "Now I can afford my own."

The sun had drifted into the western sky when they left the theater a couple of hours later.

"Okay, I'll admit it," he said as they strolled across the parking lot. "That was a pretty good movie."

"What do you mean, admit? I thought you were a big McConaughey fan?"

He stopped beside the truck. "I am. But not *every* movie can be great."

She laughed, shaking her head. "You're such a goof."

"Perhaps." Leaning toward her, he rested one hand against the truck, effectively trapping her. "But am I a cute goof?"

Her gaze lifted to his. "Maybe."

His eyes drifted to her lips, lingering there for one excruciating moment as he contemplated kissing her. "What's something else having Megan around stops you from doing?"

After a moment, her smile turned mischievous. "Eating dessert first."

While it wasn't exactly the answer he was hoping for, he couldn't help laughing. He straightened and opened her door. "What have you got in mind? Ice cream, cake, pie…? Or maybe something more decadent like a crème brûlée?"

She let go a soft gasp. "I *love* crème brûlée."

That dreamy look on her face was all the encouragement he needed. "One crème brûlée coming up."

He drove them to one of Montrose's finer dining establishments.

"Andrew, I'm not dressed for a place like this."

He looked at her skinny jeans, riding-style boots and long gray shirt. "What are you talking about? You look great."

Since it was still early, they were seated right away, and in a cozy booth, no less. Something that wouldn't have happened in another hour or two. Not on a Saturday evening.

He promptly ordered two crème brûlées, then leaned back against the tufted leather cushion.

"Thank you." Across the table, Carly rested her chin on her hand and stared at him. "I wasn't sure I was going to make it through this day and—" she smiled "—you've turned it into something wonderful."

"You deserve it." He sent her a wink.

Blushing, she unfolded her white linen napkin and placed it in her lap, all the while taking in the river rock fireplace and the rustic wood beams. "So, tell me about your life in Denver. I haven't heard you talk about it much."

"Probably because there's not much to talk about."

Her gaze jerked to his so fast he was surprised she didn't get whiplash. "Oh, come on, Andrew. You owned one of the most successful commercial construction companies in Denver. I'm sure your life is anything but boring."

He lifted a brow. "How do you know Pinnacle Construction was successful?"

"Because your father told me."

"Oh." A minor ding to his pride. He was kind of hoping she'd Googled him or something. Not that there'd be much to find.

The waitress approached. "Two crème brûlées." She set Carly's in front of her before serving his. "Can I get you anything else?"

"Not right now," he said.

Carly was the first to crack through the caramelized sugar, coming up with a spoonful of custard.

"Cheers." She lifted her spoon into the air, then

shoved it into her mouth. Her eyes closed as she savored the dessert.

"Any good?"

"Best I've ever tasted."

"Good." He cracked the hardened shell on his brûlée, knowing he needed to answer her question, to tell her something about himself. But what? "Life in Denver isn't much different than living anywhere else. There's work, church…" He took a bite. "Mmm…"

"What do you do when you're not at work?" Watching him, she scooped another spoonful.

Unfortunately, there wasn't much to his life outside work. He'd rather stay at the office than go home to an empty house. Not that he'd tell her that. "The usual stuff. Watch TV, go to the gym." Man, did he lead a pathetic life or what?

At least here he had his dad or one of his brothers to keep him company. He glanced across the table. Though, given the choice, he'd rather spend his time with Carly and Megan. With them, even normal, everyday stuff was more fun.

He managed to change the subject by bringing up an old classmate, and by the time they finished their dessert, he'd caught up on just about everyone in Ouray, both old and new. And as the lights dimmed, he asked the waitress to bring menus again so they could order dinner.

After their food arrived, he knew it was time for him to share one more thing with her. He could only pray it wouldn't ruin the whole night.

"My lawyer called this week." He cut into his prime rib. "Seems they've moved up the closing date on my new business."

"I guess you're looking forward to it, huh?" Was it his imagination or was there a hint of disappointment in her tone? "Home builder, right?"

"Yes. Custom homes." He stabbed another piece of meat. "I learned about it just before I closed on my old company. The owner passed away unexpectedly and neither of his kids was interested in the business. Seemed like the perfect opportunity." Of course, that was before he came to Ouray. "Don't worry, though. I'll have your kitchen completed and you'll be moved back into Granger House before I leave."

To his relief, she smiled. "I know you will."

"I just hope Dad's back on his feet by then."

"You worry about him, don't you?" She cocked her head, poking at her seafood pasta with her fork.

"It's no secret that I was so wrapped up in my work, I didn't make it back home before my mother died. I don't want to make that mistake again."

Reaching across the table, she laid her hand atop his. "Your mother knew that you loved her, Andrew."

"I know. But I never got to say goodbye. And that will always haunt me." He wanted to kick himself as soon as the words left his mouth. *You're trying to make her smile, not depress her.*

Fortunately, the conversation was on the upswing by the time the waitress delivered their check. It was well after dark when they arrived back in Ouray. He walked Carly to the door of his grandmother's house and escorted her inside.

"Thank you for a wonderful time." Her smile, different from any he'd seen all day, and exactly what he'd set out to achieve, did strange things to his insides. "I can't remember the last time I had so much fun."

"Like I said earlier, you deserve it." Unable to stop himself, he caressed her cheek. "You give so much of yourself to others. But surely we didn't cover everything. So if there's something else you'd like to do before Megan comes home—"

"As a matter of fact, there is." She chewed her bottom lip.

"And what might that be?"

"This." Before he realized what was happening, she pushed up on her toes and kissed him. A kiss that nearly knocked him off his feet.

She started to pull away, but he wrapped his arms around her waist and pulled her closer. Her fingers threaded through the back of his hair as their lips met again. He could stay this way forever.

Because, whether he planned to or not, he had fallen in love with Carly all over again.

Chapter Fifteen

It had been a long time since someone had made Carly feel as special as Andrew had yesterday. He'd catered to her every whim and, at the same time, made her feel like a woman instead of just a mom, caretaker or friend. He'd awakened something in her she'd thought she'd never feel again. Something she was too afraid to name. Because acknowledging it left her open for disappointment. Heartbreak. And yet she'd kissed him.

What *had* she been thinking?

Now here she sat, wedged in a church pew between Andrew and Clint. Every time Andrew shifted the slightest bit, she caught a whiff of fresh air and masculinity that reminded her of that kiss.

As if she needed any reminder. She'd had a hard time thinking about anything else since it happened. Even now, her heart thundered at the memory. Here in church, of all places.

Straightening, she eyed the wooden cross over the pulpit, trying hard to focus on Pastor Dan's sermon. A message based on Isaiah 43. She smoothed a hand over the pages of her open Bible.

"Sometimes we get so bogged down in the past that we forget to open our eyes to the future God has for us," the pastor said.

The future? Something she found very frightening. While her past might not be all that pretty, the future was unknown, and uncertainty was always scary. Especially when it involved the heart. Her gaze momentarily darted to Andrew.

If the future was so frightening, why did she keep thinking about that kiss and contemplating all sorts of what-ifs? Hadn't Andrew told her that he would be going back to Denver once her kitchen was done? That he was about to sign off on another business?

God, I know that anything You have for me is better than I could possibly want for myself. Help me not cling to what I want and be open to Your will.

In the meantime, she would immerse herself in Mona's scrapbooks and do whatever it took to stay away from Andrew.

After the service, the Stephens men congregated on the sidewalk outside the church, beside the towering white fir. Everyone except Matt, that is, who was on call with the sheriff's department.

While Carly wanted simply to whisk right past them, it would be rude for her not to say hello to Daniel, the youngest of the Stephens boys. This was the first she'd seen him since he'd returned from his latest adventure.

She eased beside him. "How was Peru?"

"Awesome." With his medium-length blond hair, blue eyes and sparkling smile, he looked like a young Brad Pitt. "Rafting the Cotahuasi River never gets old. You should try it sometime."

She practically burst out laughing. "Daniel, I haven't

even rafted the Uncompahgre since I was a teenager. And that's in my own backyard."

He chuckled. "Why don't you join us for lunch and I'll show you some photos?"

Lunch? No. She had scrapbooks waiting for her. "I'm sorry. I can't—"

"'Course she's joining us." Clint rolled up the sleeves of his blue plaid button-down shirt.

Her gaze narrowed. "I'm surprised you're even here. You know, you still haven't been cleared by the doctor." Though, looking at him now, one would have a hard time believing he'd been sick. His color was back to normal, he was clean-shaven and, with his salt-and-pepper hair neatly combed, he looked quite handsome.

Lord willing, the doctor would give him the all-clear at his checkup tomorrow. The poor man had given up just about everything he loved to do these past couple of weeks, so she hoped he'd be allowed to return to most, if not all, of his normal activities around the ranch.

"It's only church. It's not like I'm out herdin' cattle." One corner of his mouth lifted then. "But if you're that worried, you'd best come on to the house and help these boys keep an eye on me."

She shook her head. "Don't think I don't know what you're up to, Clint." And even though she really would have loved to join them, the thought of spending another day with Andrew was what worried her most.

"You don't even have to cook," added Noah.

"That's right." The gleam in Andrew's brown eyes sent goose bumps down her spine. "We've got everything taken care of."

"Come on, Carly." Daniel nudged her with his elbow. "It'll be fun."

That's what she was afraid of.

She studied the conifers scattered around the vacant lot across the road, backdropped by Hayden Mountain. Perhaps it wouldn't hurt to go for a little bit. She could look at Daniel's pictures, have some lunch, then tell them she had a prior commitment and needed to leave. They didn't have to know it was the scrapbooks.

"You guys sure drive a hard bargain."

After a quick stop by Livie's to change clothes, she drove to the ranch. She could do this. Having everyone around would naturally deflect her attention away from Andrew.

When she entered the ranch house, her stomach growled at the mixture of smells. She was delighted to learn that they'd prepared elk burgers, homemade french fries, coleslaw and brownies. And they wouldn't let her set foot in the kitchen except to eat. These guys really did have a way of making a woman feel like a queen. Mona would have been proud.

After the meal, while Jude and Andrew cleaned up the kitchen and Clint settled in his recliner, Carly sat at the table with Daniel, poring over the photos on his tablet.

"That looks pretty intense," she said as he turned off the device.

"Most extreme white water in Peru."

"And you think I should try it?" She bumped him with her shoulder. "I think you need your head examined." Laughing, she looked up and saw Andrew leaning against the counter. Evidently they were done with the kitchen.

"Well, guys, I hate to cut this short." She stood and stretched. "But I have some things I need to take care of in town."

Each of them gave her a quick hug, except Andrew, who insisted on walking her out.

"I didn't know you needed to leave so soon," he said as they emerged onto the deck. "I was hoping we could go for a walk."

"I really—"

"Just a short one." His crooked smile made him look like the Andrew she remembered from high school. The one who had been able to talk her into just about anything.

Say no. No, no, no... "Okay."

He started toward the pasture. "Can you believe we're closing in on your completed kitchen?"

"Finally." She tilted her face heavenward, allowing the sun to warm her face. "It feels like it's taking *forever.*" Though it also left her with a lot of mixed emotions. Once her kitchen was done, Andrew would be gone.

"You know what the preacher said this morning about not dwelling on the past?" Andrew took hold of her hand.

"Yes." Ignoring that annoying voice in her head, she entwined her fingers with his.

"Do you ever do that? Dwell on the past."

"More often than I care to admit."

"Me, too." He continued across the winter-weary landscape, looking straight ahead. "But then the verse he referenced went on to say that God was doing something new. And that 'Do you not perceive it?' part almost felt a smack upside my head. Like, 'Don't you get it, buddy? I'm working here.'"

She puffed out a laugh, eyeing the cattle in the distance.

"I'm not sure, Carly, but I think God is doing something new in my life."

"Like what?" She peered up at him, squinting against the sun's glare.

"I don't know." He drew to a stop beside the river, taking in the rushing water before looking at her. "Maybe it's this new business venture. But selling my company—something I never imagined I would do—coming back here and reconnecting with my family." He squeezed her hand and smiled. "Reconnecting with you."

Her heart pounded.

"And this ranch." He let go of her hand and bent to pick up a small rock. "Remember after the blizzard, when we came out here on the snowmobile?"

"Yes."

Tossing the pebble in his hand, he said, "You challenged me to start looking at the good things the ranch had to offer."

"I remember that." She picked up her own stone, rubbed its smooth surface with her thumb. "Though I think it was more of an order than a challenge."

He chuckled, throwing his rock into the water. "In that case, you'll be happy to know that I followed your orders." Hands slung low on his hips, he moved toward her. "Funny thing happened."

"What's that?"

"I'm actually enjoying the ranch, perhaps for the first time in my life."

She couldn't help but grin.

"Being here and talking with my brothers has brought back a lot of memories that have helped me realize that the hardships we endured while I was growing up were what bonded us together as a family and made us stronger. Not the other way around." He moved a step closer. "I know the ranch had nothing to do with my mother's death." He shrugged. "I was just looking for a scapegoat instead of taking responsibility for my actions."

Amid the soothing backdrop of the water, Carly's heart swelled. She'd been praying that God would help Andrew realize the truth. Now she could only pray that he would decide to stay in Ouray. Because despite trying to convince herself otherwise, she wanted him in her life.

Andrew drilled another screw into the hinge leaf for Carly's new pantry door, amazed at how quickly things had progressed.

It was only Tuesday, yet Dad was celebrating a clean bill of health by reclaiming his freedom as a rancher, and Carly's kitchen was nearing completion. Andrew wasn't sure how he felt about either one. Dad couldn't just pick up where he left off. He'd need to ease back into things after being laid up for two weeks. And as for Carly, Andrew would be fine with her project going into perpetuity.

Unfortunately, it didn't look like that was going to happen. The appliances had been delivered and installed yesterday, and thanks to Marianne's help and persistence in following up with their order, the marble countertops were set to be installed tomorrow. All he had left to do then was install the subway tile backsplash and hang the pendant lights over the island. Carly should be able to move back in before the weekend.

And he'd be on his way to Denver.

The thought making his heart ache, he leaned back against the doorjamb. He was in love with Carly again. Perhaps he'd never stopped. All these years and he'd never forgotten her. She was the standard by which all other women were judged. Not that he ever dated that much. Finding someone who even remotely understood him the way Carly did was next to impossible.

But he'd made a commitment to purchase Magnum Homes. Signed a contract. And he was nothing if not a man of his word.

He glanced around the space, pleased with how everything had come together. He and Carly made a good team. Now if they could just figure out what to do about his grandmother's house. Neither had broached the topic in weeks, and he was still clueless about how they were going to find a compromise.

He slid the screwdriver into his tool belt, grinning. He supposed he could marry her. That would keep the house in the family.

Yeah, right. If there's one thing he knew for sure, it was that Carly would never leave Ouray.

Still, if they couldn't come to some sort of agreement on what to do with Grandma's house, owning just half of it did neither one of them any good.

Movement outside the window on the opposite end of the kitchen drew his attention. Carly was just crossing the drive, bringing him lunch. Now that his father had been cleared, there was no reason for her to hang out at the ranch all day. Perhaps this would give them an opportunity to discuss his grandmother's house.

He hurried across the paper-covered floors to meet her at the door. At this point, he no longer wanted her to see the space until it was complete. Which reminded him, he needed to put paper over the windows, too, so she couldn't peek inside.

He swung open the door, quickly closing it behind him. "Why didn't you just text me? I could have come next door."

She sent him a shy smile. “Well, I was hoping to get a peek at any progress.”

“Sorry.” Hands on his hips, he blocked the door. “No more peeking until it’s finished.”

“But—”

He descended a couple of steps, then sat down. “Nice weather we’re having today.” Grinning, he perused the cloudless sky. “Good day for a picnic, don’t you think?” He glanced back at her now. “And since you happen to be carrying a picnic basket…”

She sent him a pleading look. “Not even a little peek?”

“Nope.”

Squaring her shoulders, she narrowed her gaze. “What if I said I’d withhold your lunch?”

He shrugged. “I have protein bars.” Though they held about as much appeal as a brick compared to one of Carly’s homemade meals. Still, he wasn’t about to give in on this one.

“Okay, fine.” She set the basket on the step in front of him with a thud.

“Hey—” leaning forward, he touched her cheek “—just think how exciting it will be to see everything done.”

“I know.” She lifted the basket lid. “But patience isn’t my virtue.” Reaching inside, she pulled out a foil-covered plate and handed it to him. “Hope you don’t mind leftover fried chicken.”

“Are you kidding?” He lifted the foil off the warm plate to discover mashed potatoes, corn and green beans, too. “There’s no such thing as bad fried chicken.”

She pulled out a plate for herself. “I was craving it last night, and since I’m alone, there’s no way I could eat it all.”

"And I get to reap the benefits." He bit into a drumstick. "This is delicious." He took hold of the napkin she offered and wiped his chin. "Seriously, you know you're spoiling me, don't you? I don't know what we're going to do at the ranch now that you're not there helping Dad."

"What can I say? I like to cook and take care of people."

"Well, your husband was a blessed man."

Carly's smile all but evaporated, and her pretty blue eyes clouded over. She set her plate on top of the closed basket, then dropped onto the bottom step.

Only then did he realize what he'd said. He set his plate next to hers and moved beside her. "I'm sorry. I shouldn't have said that. I wasn't trying to open old wounds."

"You didn't." She stared at her clasped hands in her lap. "It's just that I don't think Dennis would have agreed with you."

"What do you mean?"

She drew in a deep breath before looking at him. "My marriage was a sham. Everybody thought Dennis and I were the perfect couple, but we were barely more than friends."

He could see the pain in her eyes and wished that he could make it go away. "Surely it wasn't always that way."

"No." She again looked at her hands as though she was too embarrassed to look at him. "I wouldn't have married him if it had been. But over time, his job took on a higher priority. He worked longer hours, and even when he was home, he was always tethered to his work."

Standing, she started to pace. "One day he announced that he wanted to move to Grand Junction. Said he could make more money there." She sighed. "Perhaps I should have heard him out. Instead, I told him no. We didn't need more money. That wasn't the real reason, though. Inside—" she laid a hand against her chest "—I kept thinking how lonely Megan and I would be in a strange place, not knowing anyone."

She stopped pacing then. "Dennis told me I was being selfish. That the only reason I didn't want to move was because I was afraid of change." Finally she met his gaze. "Then he slammed the door behind him. Two hours later, the police were at my door telling me he was dead."

Andrew's eyes fell closed as he processed her words. He understood just how she felt. He knew all too well what it was like to live with that kind of regret.

"Carly…" Standing, he wrapped his arms around her and pulled her against him, trying to decide who was the bigger jerk. Her husband for not giving his family the respect he should have, or him for bringing up the subject. "I'm so sorry."

She shook her head, tears falling. "I don't know. Maybe Dennis was right. Maybe I am afraid of change."

"Are you kidding?" Andrew set her away from him but still held onto her. "Look at how many changes you've not only faced but also overcome. You're a single mom, a business owner, and what about this fire?" He let go just long enough to gesture to the house. "You're stronger than you think, Carly. And you've tackled everything far better than most people."

"Thank you for saying that."

"I'm not just saying it. I know it."

Peering up at him, she smiled. "You need to eat before your food gets cold."

"Only if you'll join me."

She did, and as she started talking about her most recent phone call with Megan, he realized just how much grace this woman before him demonstrated under pressure. Like the night of the blizzard, when she climbed into a crumbling building to save those foals.

Carly was one in a million, all right. And he couldn't help wondering if she just might be the only one for him.

Chapter Sixteen

First thing Wednesday morning, Carly was busy in Livie's kitchen. Megan was on her way home, so her favorite foods were the order of the day. Peanut butter cookies with the chocolate Kiss in the middle, brownies, Carly's special four-cheese mac and cheese, and, tonight, Salisbury steak. Top that all off with the news that they'd be able to move back into Granger House on Friday and her daughter was going to be ecstatic. This would be a very good Good Friday.

Which reminded her, she needed to make some purchases. A new Easter dress for Megan. A ham. And probably some more replacement items for the kitchen. She'd ordered a lot of stuff online. Things that were now stored in Livie's laundry room. Then again, it had taken her a lifetime to collect all that kitchenware. She just hoped it didn't take that long to replace it.

Maybe they could run to Montrose tomorrow. Nothing better than a little retail therapy to kill time. Besides, Andrew would be too busy putting the finishing touches on things next door to spend a moment with them.

The thought of moving back into Granger House was

a bittersweet one, though. She'd soon be saying goodbye to Andrew. Too soon, as far as she was concerned.

I'd like you to help me keep Andrew in Ouray.

Lately she found herself wanting him to stay, too. If only she knew how to make Clint's—and her—wish come true.

She put the lid on the casserole dish and tucked the mac and cheese in the fridge for either lunch or a side with dinner tonight. She went through the motions of her chores, but Andrew was never far from her mind. No one except her parents had ever encouraged her the way Andrew did. Not even Dennis. Andrew listened to her and was honest with her, not simply placating her with what he thought she wanted to hear.

Like yesterday, when he pointed out all of the changes she'd actually faced and lived to tell about. She'd merely thought of it as overcoming what life threw her way. Perhaps he was right. Perhaps she was stronger than she thought.

With her baking complete, she scanned the functional yet less than appealing seventies-era kitchen. If she were to use this place as an extension of Granger House, the first thing she'd do was paint the dark wooden cabinets a lighter color. Maybe a light gray or white, like in her new kitchen. That would depend on the flooring, though. Given that the house was a hundred years old, she assumed there were hardwoods under this ugly vinyl. If that was the case, she'd have them refinished, perhaps even the same color Andrew used in the kitchen at Granger…

Oh, why was she wasting her time daydreaming? Because unless she could talk Andrew into selling her his half, it was pointless. And until she got the final bill for the repairs to Granger House, she wasn't even sure she could afford it.

She needed to focus on something productive while she waited for Megan.

Like Mona's scrapbooks. She'd already completed Noah's book and was ready to start on Andrew's.

She locked the back door and tilted the blinds so no one could see in before retrieving the stuff from the bedroom. The last thing she'd want was Andrew to come wandering in and spoil the surprise.

After laying out each small stack of photos, she found the handwritten note Mona had penned for her second-born. Did Carly dare look at it? No, not today. It would only make her cry.

She placed it back inside the box and began sorting the photos, putting them in chronological order. What a cute baby he was. And a mischievous-looking young boy. The next group of pictures was of his teen years. That playful gleam in his eyes wasn't nearly as prominent in his ninth grade school picture.

Shuffling to the next image, she smiled. What a handsome cowboy he was, though rather serious. She turned it over to read the note on the back.

> Andrew, age 15. Working the ranch with Noah. My boys worked so hard to be men while their daddy was sick.

Carly flipped the picture back over and stared at the image. That was the summer of the horrible drought. His father had pneumonia then, too, as she recalled. Except it was much worse and included a lengthy stay in the hospital.

She and Andrew were only friends at that point, but close enough for her to know that he and Noah poured all their efforts into helping their parents that year. They'd not only done all of the work at the ranch but also spent the summer building fences for a rancher down the road who had offered to pay them. All in an effort to spare their parents the humiliation of having an adjoining piece of land they'd recently purchased foreclosed on by the bank.

In the end, the boys' hard work wasn't enough, and their parents lost that land anyway. She'd never forget the look on Andrew's face when he came to visit his grandmother shortly thereafter. He was so broken. That was probably when she'd first fallen in love with him.

The doorbell rang, jarring her from her thoughts.

She glanced at the starburst clock on the kitchen wall. Was it really almost noon? If so, then that would be her baby.

She set the stacks of photos in the box and tucked it back in the bedroom before rushing to open the front door to Megan and her grandparents.

"Oh, I'm so glad to see you." She hugged her daughter for all she was worth the moment she stepped inside.

"Mom, you're squishing me."

There was that word again. After five days apart, she would have thought she'd be Mommy once again.

Carly released her. "Guess what?"

"You made cookies? I can smell them."

"Yes, but that's not what I was going to tell you."

"Oh. Okay. What, then?" At least Megan's smile had an anticipatory air to it.

"We get to move back into Granger House on Friday."

The girl's eyes went wide. "Really?"

"Unless Andrew changes his mind."

Megan jumped up and down. "I can't wait to have my room back."

"Any chance we could see the finished product?" Beverly watched her with great expectation.

"I wish you could, but unfortunately, Andrew won't even let me see it. He's got the windows covered and everything. Says he wants to do one of those big reveals like they do on TV."

"He'll let me see it." Megan was too confident.

"Probably not. But you're welcome to try."

Her daughter started for the door.

"After you unpack your suitcase and have some lunch."

"Aw, man." Megan grabbed her suitcase and dragged it down the hall.

Chuck smiled at Carly. "We've heard a lot about this Andrew in recent days."

"Indeed." Beverly looked as though she was accusing her. "Seems Megan is quite taken with him."

"Andrew and I have known each other since we were kids. He's a good friend."

Beverly's brow arched. "A *very* good friend, according to Megan."

Carly loathed the heat she felt rising into her cheeks.

Her mother-in-law stepped closer then and took hold of her hands. "And that's okay."

What?

She jerked her gaze to Beverly's. The woman was smiling. Really smiling. At her, no less.

"Dennis has been gone for five years, Carly. It's time to move on."

Chuck came beside them, laying a hand on each of

their shoulders. "We just want you and Megan to be happy."

A lump formed in Carly's throat. She could hardly believe the words she was hearing. Obviously she had misjudged the woman. Perhaps she should start thinking of her as a friend instead of her mother-in law.

She hugged both Wagners. "I appreciate that. But don't worry." She looked at them now. "I have no plans to head to the altar anytime soon."

Andrew was still in shock. He never would have believed he could have put Carly's kitchen and family room back together in just four weeks. Yet by the grace of God, he'd managed to pull it off.

He was more than pleased with the way things had turned out. He'd even thrown in a few details she wasn't expecting. Now he couldn't wait to see her reaction.

"I didn't think this day would ever come." Carly moved through the front door of Granger House early Friday afternoon, hands clasped against her chest, a big smile on her beautiful face.

"It's so clean." Megan moved into the parlor, sniffing the air. "Smells clean, too."

"I know." Though she'd seen it before, Carly strolled through the space, examining everything from floor to ceiling. "I was skeptical when they said they'd be able to restore stuff to the way it was before the fire." Pausing, she bent over and sniffed one of the antique chairs, then straightened and smiled. "But they did a great job."

"I'm gonna check out my room." Megan ran across the wooden floor, taking a left at the dining room. "It smells good in here, too," she hollered a second later.

Shaking her head, Carly chuckled as she continued

into the dining room, still taking in every nuance. "It's amazing how they were able to freshen everything."

Andrew stopped at the entrance to the kitchen. "Wait until you see what's in here."

Carly's smile had never been bigger. She practically wiggled with excitement as she approached.

"Don't you want to wait for Megan?"

"Megan," she called over her shoulder. "Hurry up so we can see our new kitchen."

"Coming." Her daughter was at her side in no time, both of them looking up at Andrew with those blue eyes filled with anticipation.

"Are you ladies ready to see your new kitchen and family room?"

"Yes," they responded collectively.

"You're sure?"

"Andrew…" Carly ground out the word.

"Okay, okay." Having replaced the old swinging door with a more practical pocket door, he slid it aside, allowing them to enter. "Welcome home."

Just like on those HGTV shows, Carly gasped, her eyes going wide as her hands moved to her mouth.

"Whoa…" Megan moved across the newly refinished floors, turning in circles.

Continuing toward the large island, Carly looked left, right, up and down as if trying to take it all in. "Is this really mine?" She touched the apron-front sink.

"Yep." Watching her, seeing her so happy, filled his heart to overflowing.

Megan climbed onto one of the high-backed stools that sat along the far side of the island. "This is the best kitchen ever." She laid her cheek against the marble, her arms spreading across the expanse as though she were hugging it.

"It's so much brighter." Walking between the island and the stove, Carly smoothed a hand across the marble. Suddenly she stopped and whirled to face him. "Glass knobs? I told you I couldn't afford them."

"I know. But you wanted them." Hands shoved in his pockets, he rocked back on his heels. "My way of saying thank you for all the help you gave us at the ranch."

She opened her mouth slightly, then closed it without saying a word. She didn't need to, though. The tears welling her in eyes said it all.

"What's that?" Megan hopped down from the stool and hurried to the far corner of the room.

"That's your mom's new pantry." He moved beside Carly, gesturing toward her daughter. "Let's check it out."

Megan opened the door and moved inside. "This is so cool."

"I love the door." Carly caressed the frosted glass that read Pantry as they passed. She poked her head inside. "Holy cow." She looked back at him now. "I can't believe all this storage."

"I know. And all we did was utilize a corner that had been wasted space anyway."

Smiling, she said, "How did you get so smart?"

"It's a gift."

Megan squeezed past her mother. "Hey, cool table." She dodged toward his other surprise, positioned near the opening to the family room, beside the wall where the stove had once been.

Placing his hand against the small of Carly's back, he urged her that way.

Her eyes grew bigger with every step. "Is that what I think it is?"

He nodded. "It took forever, but I was able to sand down the old butcher block to use as the tabletop, and Jude turned the legs for me." He looked at Carly now. "He's quite the woodworker. And his specialty is custom millwork. He helped me with some of the window casings that were damaged."

"So that's why you kept telling me to stay away from the shop while you were hanging out at the ranch, waiting for the floors to dry." She fingered the satin finish. "This butcher block was one of the original countertops in Granger House."

"I remembered you saying that. Which is why I couldn't let it go to waste."

She reached for his hand, entwining their fingers. "I can't tell you how much I appreciate this. The table, the knobs, everything. This kitchen exceeds my wildest dreams, Andrew. And I'm glad it was you who made them come true." Pushing up on her toes, she kissed his cheek. "Thank you."

He stared into her blue eyes brimming with gratitude. He longed to take her into his arms and tell her how he felt. That he loved her. But considering Megan was here, he should probably wait.

Instead, he gently cupped Carly's cheek. "I'm glad I was here to do it. However—" He tugged her toward the family room. "There's more to see."

He led them into the cozy space with its warm gray walls, white-slipcovered furniture and natural wood entertainment center that surrounded their new 55-inch flat screen TV.

"This looks like something out of a magazine." Carly continued into the space. "I love the wood accents."

"The TV is huge!" Megan rushed to the opposite side of the room and picked up the remote. "Can I turn it on?"

"Not yet." Carly started back toward the kitchen. "We still have plenty of work to do."

After a little more exploring, they headed back to his grandmother's to gather their things.

He picked up a box from the kitchen counter that contained several shoe boxes. "What's this?"

"Oh!" Carly immediately turned away from the groceries she'd been bagging, hurried toward him and intercepted the box. "It's nothing you'd be interested in."

Then why did she look so sheepish?

"Why don't you take some of the heavier stuff I stored in the laundry room? Like my new pots and pans and that pretty purple stand mixer." Lately it seemed a day hadn't gone by without a deliveryman showing up at his grandmother's door or Carly running to Montrose to pick up replacement items for those she'd lost in the fire. Nothing like giving a woman a reason to shop.

"Purple, huh?" He opened the door to the laundry room off his grandmother's kitchen. "Let me guess. Megan picked it out."

Carly smiled over the box she was still holding. "Yes. I think it'll be a nice pop of color in my new kitchen."

They trudged back and forth between the two houses for the next couple of hours until they'd gotten everything.

"I don't know about you two, but I'm famished." He dropped the final box on the kitchen counter. "What do you ladies say I go grab us some pizza?"

"Pizza?" Who knew it was so easy to get Megan's attention? "Can we?" She deferred to her mother.

Carly glanced around the space that was now brimming with bags and boxes of all kinds. "I don't think I'll be doing any cooking tonight, so go for it."

They ate at her new table, and later, after Megan had gone to bed and he convinced Carly she didn't have to unpack everything tonight, the two of them sat down on her comfy new sofa.

"It all feels so new." She snuggled beside him as he put his arm around her. "Like it's a brand-new house."

"In many ways, it is. New walls, new flooring, new furniture…"

"I love the glass knobs." She peered up at him, her smile making him want to do even more for her. "And you said I was spoiling you."

He chuckled. "You haven't gotten my bill yet."

She playfully swatted him.

"Seriously, though, I'm not going to charge you for any labor."

"Wha—?" She twisted to face him. "That's crazy. Why would you do that?"

"After all you've done for us? Helping with Dad and the foals. You gave up your day-to-day life. I think it's a pretty fair trade."

Brow furrowing, she seemed to ponder his words. "I'm not so sure about that. I mean, how would I have gotten through this craziness without you? The fire, redoing the kitchen… It was all so overwhelming."

He touched her cheek with the back of his hand. "I'm glad God put me in Ouray when He did."

There was that smile again. "Me, too."

Threading his fingers into her curls, he drew her

closer. Breathed in the tropical scent of her shampoo, staring into her eyes for a moment and seeing eternity. The life he wanted. A life he wanted with her. She was the only woman he'd ever loved. The only one he could imagine giving his heart to. And boy, did she have it. Lowering his head, he claimed her lips. Tasted the spiciness of pizza, the sweetness of forever. He didn't know he was capable of loving one person so much.

But he did. And there was only one thing he could do about it.

Talk Carly into coming to Denver with him.

Chapter Seventeen

Carly never imagined there would be so much to do by simply moving back into her own home. But while most of Granger House remained the same, the heart of it, the kitchen and family room, was a complete do-over. Even the simplest things were gone, and it hadn't crossed her mind to add them to her inventory list. Things like a paper towel holder, dishrags and containers to hold flour and sugar. Probably because she'd had those things at Livie's house. Whatever the case, she was looking at either another shopping trip or more boxes arriving at her door.

For now, she'd started a list. Something that was likely to be ongoing as she worked to make her house a home again and an inviting retreat for guests.

Taking a sip of her second cup of tea from the Adventures in Pink Jeep Tours mug Blakely had given her from her tour company, she leaned back in one of the padded bar stools at her delightfully large island and admired her new kitchen. Yet as magnificent as it was, it couldn't dim the memory of Andrew and his kiss. *His* kiss.

Looking back, she sheepishly realized that she was

the one who'd made the first move when they'd kissed before. But not last night. That was a curl-your-toes, make-you-sigh kind of kiss.

The mere memory had her cheeks warming.

Banishing the wayward thoughts from her mind, she focused on today. Since tomorrow was Easter, this was the perfect opportunity to break in her new stove. She'd have to boil some eggs to be colored later, decide on and make the dessert—maybe a fluffy coconut cake—and bake the ham. Even though she still had plenty to get back in order before she could host any B and B guests, she'd invited the Stephens men to join her and Megan for dinner tomorrow. Plus it would give Andrew the opportunity to show them all what he'd been working on this past month.

A few silent moments later, she discovered the best thing about sitting at her new island. From this vantage point, she was able to catch that first glimpse of her sleepy-headed daughter as she shuffled into the kitchen in her pajamas, rubbing her eyes, unaware that anyone was watching her. Like when Megan was a toddler. Only her blankie was missing.

"Good morning, sweetie." She hugged Megan, assisting her as she climbed onto the next stool.

"Morning." She yawned. "What's for breakfast?"

"I don't know. Cereal, may—"

A knock sounded at the back door.

Turning, she saw Andrew on the other side, waving.

"Anybody in the mood for some hot, fresh cinnamon rolls?" he asked as she swung open the door.

She glanced back at Megan. "Guess that answers your question."

Carly pulled three new plates and forks from the dishwasher and set them on the other side of the island as Andrew served up the rolls.

Finished, he licked the icing from his fingers. "There's a great doughnut shop just down the street from my place in Denver. Their doughnuts are so light and fluffy they practically melt in your mouth."

"I like doughnuts." Megan turned to Carly. "Don't you, Mommy?"

"On occasion. I much prefer one of Celeste's cinnamon rolls, though."

After breakfast, while she cleared off the island and counters on either side of the stove so she could start cooking, Andrew brought in the boxes from the garage. Items they'd salvaged from the fire, things like casserole dishes and cast iron skillets, as well as other belongings that had been stored there while the house was being worked on.

"You know, since reworking your kitchen—" he dropped another box on the long counter in front of the window "—I've been thinking about expanding Magnum Custom Homes."

"That's your new company, right?" She filled the large pot with enough water to cover the eggs and set it on the stove.

"Yes." He grinned. "Or will be in a few days, anyway." Approaching the island, he continued. "But what if someone doesn't necessarily want a new home? What if they just want to improve the one they're in?"

Eyeing two glass casseroles that needed to go into the dishwasher, she crossed to get them. "Like remodeling?"

"Sort of. But we're talking luxury homes—" his eyes followed her as she returned to the sink "—so let's call it...reimagining."

"Catchy." She added the items to the dishwasher.

"Right? So what if, in addition to new homes, we offer custom redesigns to help people *reimagine* the home they're in? And we wouldn't limit ourselves to just kitchens and baths. Not when there's so much more out there. Theater rooms and outdoor spaces are hot right now."

She closed the door to the machine, giving him her full attention. "Sounds like a good way to increase business."

"I know it'll take time to get things up to speed and on the path to growth, but I'm used to that. Trying new things is part of the freedom that comes with owning my own business."

"Kind of like when I try a new recipe for the B and B?"

"That's right. If they work, great. If not—" he shrugged "—we move on to the next idea. That's how I was able to grow Pinnacle Construction so quickly. I kept challenging myself to do things better than the other guy." The excitement in his voice had her feeling somewhat dismayed.

Listening to him, she realized how little she really knew about his world outside Ouray. He wasn't some small-town builder. He'd grown a major construction company from the ground up and then sold it for more money than she could imagine.

And hearing him now, she had no doubt he would put every bit as much of himself into this new business. Leaving little time for anything else.

An ache filled her heart. Which was foolish. There were no promises between her and Andrew. No commitment. She knew all along he'd be leaving.

As the day progressed, she tried not to think too much about that aspect of things and simply focused on her house and savoring what time she and Megan had left with him. They all colored Easter eggs, each of them trying to outdo the other two when it came to color and style. She genuinely enjoyed Andrew's company and the way he made her feel as though she could do anything.

Yet the more he talked about Denver and all it had to offer, the more she realized how much she'd come to hope he would stay. But that wasn't going to happen. No matter how badly she and Clint wanted it to.

For the second night in a row, Andrew joined her on the couch in the family room after Megan went to bed. Though for Carly, things didn't feel near as cozy as they had last night.

"You know, I'm going to have to leave Monday to head back to Denver," he said.

She nodded, not wanting to face reality. Why had she allowed herself to believe that maybe this was their second chance?

Taking hold of her hand, he faced her. "These weeks with you have reminded me how good life can be." His dark gaze bore into hers. "I don't want to lose that."

Her heart leaped for joy, excitement spreading through her entire body. This connection between them hadn't been all in her mind. He felt it, too.

He looked at their entwined fingers, his thumb caressing the back of her hand, before he smiled at her. "I'd like you to come to Denver with me. You and Megan."

Just as quickly as her spirits had taken flight, they crashed and burned.

Did he even realize what he was asking? What about Granger House? What about Megan's school? She couldn't just uproot her, take her away from everything she'd ever known.

She thought back to that first and only semester she'd spent in Denver. All those lonely nights in her dorm room while Andrew worked. He said he was saving for their future. What kind of future could they have if they were never together?

None.

I know it'll take time to get things up to speed and on the path to growth, but I'm used to that.

Andrew might be used to devoting himself to his work, but where did that leave her and Megan?

Playing second fiddle, that's where. Just like they had with Dennis. And she'd vowed she would never put herself or her daughter through that again.

Slowly withdrawing her hand from his, she tried hard to keep the tears that threatened from falling. "I'm sorry. I—I can't do that."

He looked confused at first. Then upset. "Can't or won't?"

"Andrew, running your business is your top priority."

"Of course it is. It has to be."

"And I get that. But what about my business? Granger House is important to me."

His gaze searched hers. "But, I—" He shook his head. "Then where does that leave us?"

God, give me strength.

"There is no us." She stood, unable to look at him for fear she'd break down and cry. "We're too different, Andrew. You're driven to succeed. And I refuse to take second place in someone's life ever again."

He was silent for a long time, just sitting there with his forearms resting on his thighs, his head hung low.

She'd hurt him. But what was she supposed to do? He hadn't even said he loved her.

"I guess it's time for me to go, then," he finally said.

She drew in a deep breath as he stood. "I'll walk you out."

They moved silently through the house and out onto the front porch. The night air was unusually warm, but she was chilled nonetheless. Still, there was one more thing they needed to discuss.

"So, what are we going to do about your grandmother's?"

"I told you, I'm not selling, Carly. Not to you or anyone else. However, my offer still stands, if you'd like to reconsider."

"But that would mean giving up my dream of expanding."

He shrugged. "The choice is yours." He stared at her for what seemed like forever. There in those eyes she loved so much, she could see her own pain reflected.

Then, as though resigning himself, his body drooped. He stepped toward her, cupped her right cheek, then kissed the other. "You're the only woman I've ever loved." His words were a whisper on her ear, but they echoed through her heart and mind like an agonizing shout. He did love her. It didn't matter, though. He'd made his decision.

"Goodbye, Carly."

Arms crossed over her chest, she managed to keep her feet riveted to the porch until he pulled out of the drive. Once he was out of sight, she hurried inside, collapsed on her bed and cried until she fell asleep.

The first time Andrew lost Carly, he started Pinnacle Construction and threw himself into his work. When

Mama died, he was too busy living his dream to be there to tell her goodbye. The ache of what he'd done nearly killed him. Instead of pulling back, though, he worked even harder, trying desperately to forget. But it was impossible.

Then Crawford Construction made him an offer. He figured God was trying to tell him something. To slow down. So he came back to Ouray and, for the first time, experienced firsthand all that his life had been missing.

Now here he was again, about to embark on a new business with a busted-up heart throbbing in his chest.

Driving back to the ranch, he swallowed the bitter taste stinging the back of his throat. He'd wanted to argue his case against Carly's protests. Yes, he was driven. Yes, he was a hard worker. But he wasn't her late husband. And if there's one thing he'd learned, it was how important family was to him. He'd never squander that.

Yet he'd heard the pain in her voice, seen it in her eyes, when she talked about her marriage that day over lunch. He could have made her all the promises in the world tonight and she still wouldn't have believed him.

He needed to get away from Ouray. Go back to Denver, close the deal with Magnum, throw himself into his work and forget about love, because it obviously wasn't meant for him.

When he pulled up to the ranch house, there was a white SUV parked beside his father's dually. What would Hillary be doing here this time of night? It was almost ten o'clock.

He heard laughter coming from the kitchen as he entered the mudroom. Following the voices, he spotted his father and Hillary sitting at the kitchen table.

If he was quiet and kept moving, they'd never notice him.

He started through the family room.

"Hello, Andrew," said Hillary.

He cringed.

"Pull up a chair and join us, son." Dad scraped the wooden chair closest to him across the vinyl floor.

The last thing Andrew was in the mood for was conversation. Though he was staring. While he knew there was nothing romantic going on, seeing his father sitting across the table from a woman other than Mama was downright strange.

"I had dinner at Granny's Kitchen tonight," Dad continued, as though he'd read Andrew's mind. "Ran into Hillary, so we decided to come back here for some coffee."

"Thanks, Dad, but I'm going to go pack. I need to leave in the morning."

"In the morning? But it's Easter. We're supposed to have dinner at Carly's." His father stood, his voice holding both surprise and disappointment. "Are you sure this is what you want to do, son?"

"Yes, sir." If only his heart was as certain as his head.

"Did the two of you decide what you're going to do about Livie's house?"

"No. No decision yet." He could only pray Carly would accept his offer, because as long as they both owned that house, they'd be connected. And right now, he wasn't sure he could handle that.

"You like living in Denver?" Hillary peered at him over the rim of her coffee cup.

"Yes, ma'am. I've built one successful business and am about to close on another. Guess you'd say I'm living my dream." At least that's what he used to think. Until Carly came back into his life.

"Or having fun chasing them, anyway." She smiled.

Had he heard her correctly? "I'm sorry. What?"

She stood now, rounded the table. "I was like you. Growing up, I couldn't wait to get out of Ouray. Vowed I'd never come back." Arms crossed, she leaned against the counter. "I wanted to travel the world and be somebody. You know? Successful. And that's exactly what I did."

"Oh. I guess I was under the impression that you lived in Ouray."

"I do. Now. But I should have done it a lot sooner. I was just too hardheaded and stubborn."

"You, stubborn?" His father sent her a curious look.

"Oh, you hush, Clint." She turned her attention back to Andrew. "I had a beautiful home, a nice car, expensive clothes and more money than I could possibly spend. But I was alone. And it was the pits."

Why was she telling him this? He glanced at his father. Or, what had Dad been telling her?

"Well, I'm glad you're here now, Hillary." He pointed toward his father. "This guy needs a good sparring partner."

After bidding them good-night, he went to Daniel's room and closed the door, grateful his brother was nowhere to be found. He didn't feel like talking. Yet as he crawled into the second of the two twin beds, sleep evaded him.

But what about my business? Granger House is important to me.

He understood Carly's commitment. It's one of the things he admired about her. But his hands were tied with Magnum. He was contractually obligated to move forward with the purchase or risk being sued. Leaving him no choice but to go back to Denver. No matter how much he wished he could stay.

He tossed and turned most of the night, thoughts of Carly plaguing his mind. By morning, he knew what he had to do.

He said goodbye to his father then headed into town before the sun topped the Amphitheater, the curved volcanic formation on Ouray's eastern edge. While daylight invaded the sky, Ouray would remain bathed in shadows until the sun topped the mountain almost an hour from now.

Pulling into his grandmother's drive, he couldn't take his eyes off Granger House. From here he could see through Carly's kitchen window. The two pendant lights over the island glowed, telling him she was awake.

He drew in a deep breath as he exited his truck and made his way to her back door. *God, I know this is the right thing to do. Just please help me do it.*

He climbed the few steps and gently knocked on the door.

When it opened a moment later, Carly stood there in her fuzzy robe, mug in hand, her curls going every which way. She was the most beautiful woman he'd ever seen. What he wouldn't have given to wake up to that every morning.

But that wasn't going to happen.

"Andrew." She ran a self-conscious hand through her hair.

"I'm on my way back to Denver. But there's something I need to talk to you about."

"Okay." She moved out of the way, holding the door so he could enter.

He took in the space he'd worked so hard on, hoping to make Carly's dreams come true. And he believed he had. If only he could be a part of those dreams.

"I won't keep you," he said. "I just wanted to let you know that I'm giving you my half of my grandmother's house."

Her blue eyes went wide.

"You can do with it as you please. Renovate it, use it for the B and B or whatever, with the stipulation that if you ever decide you no longer want it, you will give me back my half and let me purchase yours."

"Wow. That's…that's very generous of you. But… why?"

He gazed at her, unable to deny the longing in his heart. "Because I can't think of anyone who would take better care of it."

She smiled now, but not the big, vivacious sort he was used to seeing. This one was more tentative. Sad, even. The kind that made him want to wrap his arms around her and tell her everything would be okay.

"I promise I will. Thank you."

"I'll have my attorney draw up the papers and get them to you as soon as possible."

She nodded, looking as though she wanted to say something more. When she didn't—

"I need to be going." He turned for the door.

"Andrew?"

He turned back, his heart hopeful.

She hesitated a moment. Then— "Drive safely."

He forced a smile, wondering if he'd ever see her again. "I will."

Chapter Eighteen

For the second time in less than twelve hours, Carly watched Andrew pull out of the drive. He was gone. Forever.

She missed him already.

Still, she'd made the right choice, hadn't she? After all, he'd even said that his business was his top priority. Not her, not family. Business. She couldn't live like that again. Watching their relationship dissolve into nothing. Her heart wouldn't be able to take it.

Despite everything, though, he'd given her his half of Livie's house. Making her dream of expanding Granger House Inn possible. So why wasn't she jumping up and down, cheering at the top of her lungs? Wasn't that what she'd wanted all along? Where was the excitement?

Gone with Andrew.

Though he'd never even been a part of the equation, without him, turning Livie's house into an extension of the B and B just didn't feel right.

She downed what remained of her lukewarm tea and set the mug on the island beside the pretty basket containing the colorful eggs they'd decorated. After crying much of the night, she must look like a mess.

She went into her bedroom, knowing she needed to get ready for church. She looked at herself in her bathroom mirror. Puffy, red eyes stared back at her. No wonder Andrew had been so eager to leave.

Turning, she slumped against the vanity. Who was she trying to kid? He left because there was nothing more to say. Their relationship was over. And still he'd given her his half of Livie's house. A move that made her love him all the more.

Tears threatened again, but she blinked them away. Tea. She needed more tea.

Returning to the kitchen, she grabbed another tea bag from the box on the counter, put it in her mug, added some water and put the cup in the microwave. She still couldn't believe she'd forgotten to buy a kettle. Since there was one at Livie's, it had completely slipped her mind. Add that to her ever-growing list of items that needed to be replaced.

Perhaps she should make a run into Montrose tomorrow and see what she could pick up. Hanging out in her new kitchen would only make her think of Andrew. She needed something to distract her. At least for a while.

She glanced at the clock. Almost eight o'clock and still no sign of Megan. She must be worn out from helping them yesterday. Unpacking, moving stuff around in her room.

Mug in hand, Carly moved to the beautiful table Andrew had made her out of the old butcher block. She smoothed her palm over the satiny surface. What a fun surprise this had been. Her gaze shifted to the family room before taking in the kitchen once again. Memories of Andrew seemed to be everywhere she looked.

She eyed the cardboard container of scrapbooks and shoe boxes she'd tucked in one of the four chairs. Whether Andrew was in her life or not, she would still complete them. She'd made a promise to both Clint and Mona.

She placed her cup on the table and picked up the shoe box belonging to Andrew. She knew it was foolish. Why torture herself?

But that wasn't enough to stop her from lifting the lid. There, on top, was the note Mona had written.

Carly picked it up, more curious than ever. What had Mona wanted to say to her second-born son? And though she knew she shouldn't look, Carly desperately wanted to know.

She fingered open the flap on the envelope, pulled out the note card adorned with columbines and read.

My sweet Andrew,
You were always my ambitious one. And so much like your father. You work hard and love even harder. Some think you're a workaholic. Inside, though, you long to be a family man. Or did, anyway. Until your heart was broken.

Carly's hand went to her mouth. Was Mona referring to her? Was she the one who broke Andrew's heart?

Instead of dusting yourself off and moving on, you channeled all of your energy and passion into your business, and it's paid off. But a mother longs to see her children happy. And despite your success, I don't believe you are.

An image of Andrew sprang to her mind. That day six weeks ago when she first saw him at Livie's. He was so intense. Not at all like the man she once knew. Or the man he'd been these past weeks.

Andrew, I pray that you will one day find the strength to let go of the pain of the past and allow yourself to love again. Open your heart to the future God has planned for you. You never know where it may lead.

A tear trailed down Carly's cheek. How could she have been so stupid? Andrew was the kind of man she'd always wanted. Yet she'd let him walk out of her life. Not just once, but twice. All because she was afraid.

Andrew was not Dennis. He'd demonstrated more love and understanding in this past month than she'd experienced in most of her marriage. Andrew went out of his way to show how much he cared for both her and Megan. Like that day he took her to the movies in Montrose and that first night when he taught Megan to play cards.

She tucked Mona's card back into the envelope and set it inside the box, her fingers brushing that photo of Andrew at fifteen. She picked it up. "Oh, Andrew, I do love you."

Enough to leave Ouray and risk a future with him in Denver?

Smiling, she swiped another tear from her face. Mona was right. It was time to let go of the past and see what

God had planned for her future. To do that, though, she had to find Andrew.

But how? It wasn't like she could just call him and say, "I've had a change of heart. Would you mind turning around?" No, she had to prove she loved him and was committed to their relationship, no matter where they lived. That meant she had to go to him.

She hurried into her bedroom, threw on a pair of jeans and a sweater, then gathered a few things and threw them into her tote. Clint would know where she could find him. Where he lived. She and Megan could stop by the ranch on their way out of town.

Finished, she set her bag by the back door and went into Megan's room. "Wake up, baby. We need to—"

Megan's bed was empty.

"Megan!" she hollered as she left her daughter's bedroom, then again as she headed into the family room. Where could she be?

She searched the kitchen, her bedroom, the dining room and the parlor before heading upstairs. "Megan!"

Her sweaty palms skimmed across the banister as panic rose in her gut. She'd heard of children being taken from their beds, never to be seen again.

Finding nothing in the three bedrooms upstairs, she rushed back downstairs and searched Megan's room for any sign of foul play, any hint where her daughter could have gone. The windows were still locked with the blinds closed, and nothing was out of place.

"Megan!"

She went to the front door. It was unlocked and ajar.

Her heart sank into her stomach. She always locked up at night.

Pushing through the storm door, she checked the porch. "Megan?"

The silence reverberated in her ears.

She glanced left, then right. Spotting Livie's house, she darted down the steps. Maybe Megan forgot something and had gone back to retrieve it. She tried the front door. Locked. She rushed to the back. Locked again.

The key. She needed the key.

She hurried across the drive, into the kitchen, grabbed the key and went back to Livie's. Pushed through the back door. "Megan?"

She searched this house, too, her anxiety ratcheting up a notch with every empty room. Her stomach churned, her breaths coming so quickly she was getting light-headed. Where was she?

God, help me.

Pulling her cell phone from her pocket, she dialed 911 and choked back the tears that threatened to consume her.

"Ouray 9—"

"My daughter's missing."

Andrew continued north on Highway 550 on his way back to Denver, staring out over the open range without ever really seeing anything. When he'd arrived in Ouray almost five weeks ago, his plan had been to do the renovations at his grandmother's house as quickly as possible and then move on down the road with the possibility of some rental income. But all that changed when Carly walked in.

Now he wasn't sure if his life would ever be the same. If he'd ever be the same. Because for the first time in his adult life, he wasn't thinking about sales numbers or the next big deal. All he could think about was Carly. What was she doing? Was she already planning what to do with his grandmother's house, or was she sitting there with her cup of tea, missing him, too? And had she tamed those wayward curls?

The thought made him smile.

He was halfway to Montrose when he'd reigned in his emotions enough to call his attorney. So what if it was Easter? Ned would understand. He pressed the button on his steering wheel for the hands-free calling feature.

"Call Ned." The sooner they got the legalities squared away, the sooner Carly could incorporate his grandmother's house into the B and B.

"Hey, buddy." Ned's voice boomed through the speakers.

"I need you to do something for me." He went over what he wanted.

"Sure. Since you're both in agreement, it shouldn't take long at all. So, are you looking forward to getting back to the real world again?"

Strangely, he found life to be more real in Ouray than it had ever been in Denver. Between the fire, the foals, his dad and the blizzard, it had been an eventful few weeks. "I suppose."

"You don't sound very excited."

"Let's just say things in Denver don't hold the same allure as they once did."

"I see. This sudden change of heart wouldn't have anything to do with this Carly person, would it?"

He blew out a breath. "She helped me to see how much of life I've been missing out on."

"Then why are you leaving us?"

Andrew jerked his head toward the backseat, causing his vehicle to swerve.

"Megan?" He overcorrected, veering into the other lane.

A horn sounded from an oncoming car.

"What's going on, Andrew?" Ned asked through the speaker.

Heart pounding, Andrew put on his blinker and eased onto the shoulder. "I'll call you back, Ned." He ended the call and turned around.

"Megan, what are you doing here?" The poor kid was crying. No wonder. He could have killed them both. "Does your mother know where you are?"

"No." Shaking her head, she tearfully climbed over the leather console and into the passenger seat. Only then did he realize she was still wearing her pajamas.

He willed his heart rate to a normal rhythm. "Okay, sweetheart, what gives?"

"You can't leave us." Her bottom lip quivered.

"I don't have a choice, Megan."

"Yes, you do!" she yelled. "We love you and I know you love us, too."

He let go a sigh. Out of the mouths of babes.

Even Megan got it. How come he didn't?

Because until recently, all of his hopes and dreams had been in Denver.

He eyed the child he'd grown to love. Could God have put her here for a reason?

Yeah, to show him what a giant mistake he was making.

"Come here." He took the sobbing girl into his arms, feeling like the biggest jerk in the world. He couldn't have cared for her more if she were his own daughter.

He wanted to watch her grow, to teach her how to drive and protect her from all those dates she was bound to have in a few years.

Most of all, he didn't want to go through life alone anymore. Hillary was right. It was the pits. He wanted to be closer to his father and brothers. And he wanted to be with Carly and Megan. Maybe Colorado's western slope was in need of a good construction/remodeling company.

Whatever the case, he knew in his heart that staying in Ouray was not only the right thing to do but also what God had been trying to tell him the entire time he was there. *Thank You, Lord.*

When Megan had calmed down, he set her away from him. "You're a pretty perceptive kid, you know that?"

"What does that mean?" She sniffed.

Lifting the lid on the console, he pulled out a napkin and handed it to her. "It means that you're right. I do love you. And your mama, too." Except he hadn't told Carly until he'd been walking away. What kind of guy did that?

His cell rang then, his dad's name appearing on the dashboard screen.

He pressed the button on the steering wheel to answer. "What's up, Dad?"

"Jude just called. Megan is missing."

Megan's eyes were wide as she looked up at him.

"I'm on my way to—"

"She's with me, Dad."

"Megan?"

"Yes." He continued to watch a silent, perhaps terrified, Megan. "Tell Carly not to worry. We'll be there shortly to explain."

"I wasn't trying to make Mommy sad," she said as he ended the call. "I just wanted—"

He touched her cheek. "I know. Now buckle up." He waited for the traffic to clear, then made a U-turn and headed back toward Ouray. "We don't want to be late for Easter service."

When they arrived at Carly's, she was out of the house and in the drive with his dad and Jude right behind her before he brought the truck to a stop.

She opened the passenger door and scooped her daughter into her arms. "Baby, you scared me to death. What were you thinking?"

Megan didn't respond. She simply twisted her head to look at him as he rounded the front of the vehicle.

He looked at Carly now. He could tell she'd been crying. Still, she was beautiful. Why had he ever thought he could walk away from her again?

"Would you guys mind taking Megan into the house while I talk to Carly?"

"Not a problem," said his brother, already making his departure.

"Come on, darlin'." The old man held out his hand as Carly set Megan on the ground. A few moments later, the three of them disappeared into the kitchen.

"Thank you for bringing her back." Carly crossed her arms over her chest. "But I don't understand how she ended up with you in the first place."

"She stowed away in my truck."

"What?" Her brow puckered. "Why would she do that?"

"Megan said she overheard us talking last night and then again this morning."

Carly winced, the morning breeze gently tossing those crazy curls of hers.

"Let's just say she thought I needed a little friendly advice."

Carly's mouth twitched, her arms dropping to her sides. "I'm sorry she caused you so much trouble."

He took a step closer. "She wasn't any trouble. At least, not once I got the truck under control again."

"Oh, no." She did smile then.

"Hey, we're both in one piece, and she's home safe and sound."

Carly nodded but wouldn't look at him.

So he forced her to do just that by erasing what little space remained between them and touching a finger to her chin. To his surprise, she didn't pull away.

"I love you, Carly. And I love your daughter, too."

Her body relaxed as though she was relieved. Then she laid a hand to his chest, staring up at him with those blue eyes. "I love you, too. And I'm willing to go to Denver or anywhere else with you, if you still want me to."

Being with her was what he wanted more than anything. But hearing her say those words made him realize how selfish he was even to have asked. She had built a successful business here, and she was an integral part of the community. A community he'd grown to care about a great deal these past few weeks.

Shaking his head ever so slightly, he slid his arms around her waist. "I don't belong in Denver. Ouray is my home, and home is where I need to be."

"What about Magnum Homes?"

"I'm still bound to the purchase. However, I might have to see about getting someone else to run it, because I plan to spend my time here with you."

Lowering his head, he kissed her. This amazing woman who had taught him more about himself than he'd ever known. She was his past, his present and his future.

Still holding her, he looked into the eyes of the woman he loved. "I guess we'd better get ready for church." He stroked her arms. "After all, Easter is a time of renewal and new beginnings."

"A new kitchen, new directions…"

"New life." He smiled, pulling her to him once again. "I guess my parents named the ranch correctly after all. Because I am abundantly blessed, indeed."

Epilogue

Carly couldn't think of any better time than Mother's Day to give the Stephens brothers the scrapbooks their mother had so lovingly planned for them. Mona was an amazing woman who'd raised five wonderful sons, and she deserved to be celebrated.

Of course, the guys didn't know anything about the scrapbooks. They simply thought they were treating Carly to lunch at the ranch because, as Andrew told her, "You're a mom, so it's our turn to celebrate you."

A day at the ranch would be a nice break. Since its reopening, Granger House Inn had enjoyed two fully booked weekends in a row, and she already had bookings all the way into August. By the time Andrew finished the renovations at Livie's house later this summer and they started hosting guests there, this could end up being one of the B and B's best years ever.

With her guests checked out by noon and the kitchen clean, she packaged up some of the leftover lemon cheesecake tarts and fudgy hazelnut cream cookies and headed out to the ranch. She knew the guys would have plenty of good food, but they always appreciated her leftovers. Especially the sweets.

Andrew had picked Megan up earlier from church and brought her back with him. Carly had a suspicion they were working on a surprise of their own. It was Mother's Day, after all.

Turning into the ranch, she noticed a dark gray Jeep pulling in behind her. Another glance in her rearview mirror revealed the driver as the third Stephens boy, Matt.

It had been a while since Carly had a chance to talk with him. She'd seen him in passing around town, but according to Andrew, Matt tended to steer clear of the ranch due to a strained relationship with his father. However, he was here, which meant he'd at least responded to Clint's request.

"Long time, no see," she said when they simultaneously emerged from their vehicles in front of the ranch house.

Matt, who was a couple of years younger than her, smiled as he came toward her. Like Noah, Andrew and Jude, he had the same dark hair and eyes as their father, though she could see a little Mona in him, too. His nose and the shape of his mouth definitely belonged to his mother.

"Sheriff's been working me too hard." He hugged her. "Good to see you, Carly." Releasing her, he nodded in the direction of the new barn. "Looks like Andrew's making some headway."

"Are you kidding? That's been his top priority." In the five weeks since Magnum Homes' owner's son backed out at the closing, deciding he couldn't let go of his father's legacy, Andrew had devoted most of his time to clearing away the old barn and starting the framework on the new. That is, between weekend trips to Denver to empty out his house so he could put it on the market.

"Well, we were long overdue for a new one."

She laid a hand on his shoulder. "I hear you're pretty good with a hammer. I'm sure he'd welcome the help."

He stared down at her. Nodded. "I'll think about it."

"Good." At least he hadn't said no. "Mind helping me carry in some stuff?"

"Not at all."

She opened the back door of her SUV and pointed to the large box that contained all five of the gift-bagged scrapbooks. To ensure there would be no peeking, she'd not only closed the flaps on the box but also sealed it with packing tape.

"This it?" he asked, hoisting the box into his capable arms.

"Yes, sir. Just let me grab these desserts and we'll head inside."

"Sweets, you say? That sounds promising."

She closed the passenger door and started up the steps of the deck. "One of the perks of owning a bed-and-breakfast. I almost always have sweets on hand." As she opened the door to the mudroom, it dawned on her that Matt lived only a couple of blocks from her. "You know, I'm always trying out new recipes. Would you mind if I dropped some samples by your place?"

"Mind? Carly, you're talking to a bachelor. We never turn down food."

She could hear a bustle of activity coming from the kitchen as soon as they stepped inside.

"No. The fork goes on the left and the knife goes on the right." Megan was giving somebody orders.

Matt looked at her over his shoulder. "Where would you like me to put this?"

"Anywhere in the family room is fine."

A lunch of prime rib, twice-baked potatoes and broccoli exceeded anything Carly might have anticipated. Given that they were cattle ranchers, she'd come to expect beef, but prime rib was definitely a special treat. And this one was cooked to perfection.

In addition to the meal, they'd given her a lovely bouquet of flowers and box of truffles from Mouse's. Those two things alone had made her day. But now, as everyone relaxed in the family room—Noah, Andrew and Matt on the couch, Jude and Daniel on the love seat—it was time for Clint and her to make their presentation.

Clint sat on the edge of his recliner, smiling, looking like the healthy rancher she was used to seeing. "You boys might remember how your mama always liked to give you one sentimental Christmas present."

"Like the Bibles with our names engraved on the front," said Noah.

His brothers nodded.

"And those hand-painted signs with our names and the meanings," said Jude.

More nodding.

"Your mother had one more gift planned for you boys." He looked at each of his sons. "Though she never got to finish them." He cleared his throat. "Matter of fact, I'd forgotten all about them until Carly came across the box in Mona's craft room. She agreed to pick up where your mama left off so you could have them."

Carly found herself blinking away tears as she cut through the packing tape with Clint's pocketknife. "Come help me, Megan."

After lifting the flaps, Carly pulled out the red, blue, yellow, green and orange bags one by one, each color a reminder for her of which brother's scrapbook was inside.

She handed her daughter the red one. "Give this to Noah." Then she grabbed the blue one for Andrew and the yellow one for Matt and presented them.

Megan returned for the orange one. "Whose is this?"

"That's Daniel's." She took hold of the green bag. "And this is for you, Jude." She returned to Clint's side. "You can open them now."

Colorful tissue paper flew through the air until each of the brothers had pulled out his scrapbook. When they opened the front covers, the first things they saw were the handwritten notes their mother had penned especially for them.

As she'd expected, tears fell from each man's eyes as they read her final words.

Finally, after a long silence, Noah said, "That's our mama." He sniffed, tucking his note back into the envelope. "Always trying to make us cry." He glanced heavenward. "I hope you're happy, Mama. We're blubbering like babies."

That caused them all to laugh.

Over the next few hours, they shared laughter and memories as each man went through his scrapbook. Carly couldn't remember the last time she'd cried so much.

"Would anyone care for some more cookies?" Still wiping her eyes, she brought the plastic container from the kitchen.

"Oh, no you don't." Andrew intercepted her, taking

the container and passing it off to Noah. "We're not done in here yet."

Not done?

"I have something I'd like to say."

"Oh. Sorry." Heat rose to her cheeks. "Didn't mean to steal your thunder."

He took hold of her hand. "On behalf of my brothers, I want to thank you for completing these scrapbooks for us. It means a lot to us. You mean a lot to us. Especially to me."

Boy, if she thought her cheeks were warm before, the look in Andrew's eyes had them downright flaming.

"Carly, when I'm with you, life makes more sense. You're my best friend and the love of my life." Letting go of her hand, he dropped to one knee and pulled something from his pocket.

Oh, my. He was going to…

Her heart felt as though it might burst with anticipation as he opened the black velvet box and held it out to her.

"Carly Wagner, will you marry me?"

"Um…" She held up a finger. "Hold on one second." She turned toward Megan, who was standing beside Clint. "What do you think, sweetie?"

As if her daughter's smile wasn't enough, she shot Carly two thumbs-up. "Go for it, Mom."

Unable to contain her own smile, Carly looked down at the man before her. The one she loved beyond question and couldn't wait to spend the rest of her life with. "Would you mind repeating the question?"

"You're really going to make me work for this, aren't you?"

"You ain't seen nothin' yet," said Noah.

Everyone laughed.

Again, Andrew looked up at her, his brown eyes alight with love. "Will you please do me the honor of becoming my wife, Carly?"

"Yes!"

He slipped the ring on her finger so quickly she didn't even have a chance to see what it looked like before he took her in his arms and kissed her.

She didn't care, though. She had the rest of her life to do that. With God's help, they had finally put their pasts behind them and allowed Him to open their eyes to the future He had planned for them. A future they would now share together.

And she couldn't think of anything better.

* * * * *

SPECIAL EXCERPT FROM

Read on for a sneak peek at the first heartwarming book in Lee Tobin McClain's Safe Haven series, Low Country Hero*!*

They'd both just turned back to their work when a familiar loud, croaking sound cut the silence.

The twins shrieked and ran from where they'd been playing into the little cabin's yard and slammed into Anna, their faces frightened.

"What was that?" Anna sounded alarmed, too, kneeling to hold and comfort both girls.

"Nothing to be afraid of," Sean said, trying to hold back laughter. "It's just egrets. Type of water bird." He located the source of the sound, then went over to the trio, knelt beside them, and pointed through the trees and growth.

When the girls saw the stately white birds, they gasped.

"They're so pretty!" Anna said.

"Pretty?" Sean chuckled. "Nobody from around here would get excited about an egret, nor think it's especially pretty." But as he watched another one land beside the first, white wings spread wide as it skidded into the shallow water, he realized that there was beauty there. He just hadn't noticed it before.

That was what kids did for you: made you see the world through their fresh, innocent eyes. A fist of longing clutched inside his chest.

The twins were tugging at Anna's shirt now, trying to get her to take them over toward the birds. "You may go look as long as you can see me," she said, "but take careful steps by the water." She took the bolder twin's face in her hands. "The water's not deep, but I still don't want you to wade in. Do you understand?"

Both little girls nodded vigorously.

They ran off and she watched for a few seconds, then turned back to her work with a barely audible sigh.

"Go take a look with them," he urged her. "It's not every day kids see an egret for the first time."

"You're sure?"

"Go on." He watched her run like a kid over to her girls. And then he couldn't resist walking a few steps closer and watching them, shielded by the trees and brush.

The twins were so excited that they weren't remembering to be quiet. "It caught a *fish*!" the one was crowing, pointing at the bird, which, indeed, held a squirming fish in its mouth.

"That one's neck is like an S!" The quieter twin squatted down, rapt.

Anna eased down onto the sandy beach, obviously unworried about her or the girls getting wet or dirty, laughing and talking to them and sharing their excitement.

The sight of it gave him a melancholy twinge. His own mom had been a nature lover. She'd taken him and his brothers fishing, visited a nature reserve a few times, back in Alabama where they'd lived before coming here.

Oh, if things were different, he'd run with this, see where it led…

PHLTMEXP0319